W9-CZJ-348

A Friar's Bloodfeud

MICHAEL JECKS

A Friar's Bloodfeud

headline

First published in Great Britain in 2005
by HEADLINE BOOK PUBLISHING

1

Cataloguing in Publication Data is available from the British Library

ISBN 0 7553 2299 1

Typeset in Times by Avon DataSet Ltd,
Bidford-on-Avon, Warwickshire

Printed and bound in Great Britain by
Clays Ltd, St Ives plc

Headline's policy is to use papers that are natural, renewable and
recyclable products and made from wood grown in sustainable forests.
The logging and manufacturing processes are expected to conform
to the environmental regulations of the country of origin.

HEADLINE BOOK PUBLISHING
A division of Hodder Headline
338 Euston Road
London NW1 3BH

www.headline.co.uk
www.hodderheadline.com

This book is for dear old
Don Morton.
A friend for life to all who knew him.
He's sorely missed.

Cast of Characters

Emma	Jeanne's maid since their youth in Bordeaux, Emma has still not been able to accustom herself to the weather and manners of the English. She sees herself as superior to all pastoral folk, having been raised in a city.

Fishleigh

Sir Odo de Bordeaux	The keen servant of Sir John Sully for many years, Sir Odo is now master of Sir John's manor at Fishleigh, and his jurisdiction extends to the vill of Iddesleigh on the other side of the river. He sees to the land's profit and protects his territory jealously. Sir John Sully is a vassal of Lord Hugh de Courtenay.
Robert Crokers	Under Sir Odo's stewardship, Robert is the bailiff or sergeant, charged with the maintenance of the lands. He oversees the harrowing, planting and cultivation of the crops, as well as harvesting.
Walter	A man-at-arms who serves Sir Odo, Walter is an older man who is used to warfare.

Iddesleigh

Constance	Wife of Hugh, Constance was once a novice at the priory at Belstone, but she had been allowed to leave by the prioress (see *Belladonna at Belstone*). She has a two-year-old child whom she has also named Hugh.
Father Matthew	The local priest, Father Matthew has lived in Iddesleigh for many years and has grown to sympathise with the natural suspicion shown by the locals to all 'foreigners'.

Jankin	Owner of the local inn as well as a farmer, Jankin is an excellent host, and a fount of knowledge about the people in the area too.
David	Known as 'Deadly Dave' for his ability to kill men with boredom, David is a lonely local man.

Monkleigh

Sir Geoffrey Servington	Steward of the Despenser lands, Sir Geoffrey is an older warrior. In his youth he gambled all on tournaments, and lost. After that it was only the support of the Despensers that saved him from ruin.
Ailward	The sergeant of the Monkleigh estates, Ailward is bitter at his sudden fall. His father and grandsire were both squires, and he longs to be recognised as such.
Adam of Rookford	Known as 'Adcock', the new sergeant of the Despenser manor of Monkleigh is keen to make his mark. This job is a great advance for him, and he's excited at the opportunities it offers.
Nicholas le Poter	A man-at-arms, Nicholas is not impressed by Sir Geoffrey and is certain he could do the job more effectively.
Mary	Known as Malkin, Ailward's wife adores her husband.
Isabel	Malkin's mother-in-law, Isabel is used to bereavement, having lost her father to the Irish wars and her husband during the recent civil war between Mortimer and the Despensers.
Pagan	An old servant of Isabel's family, Pagan feels adrift without the two men he had served.

A Map of Iddesleigh
and area
in the early 1300s

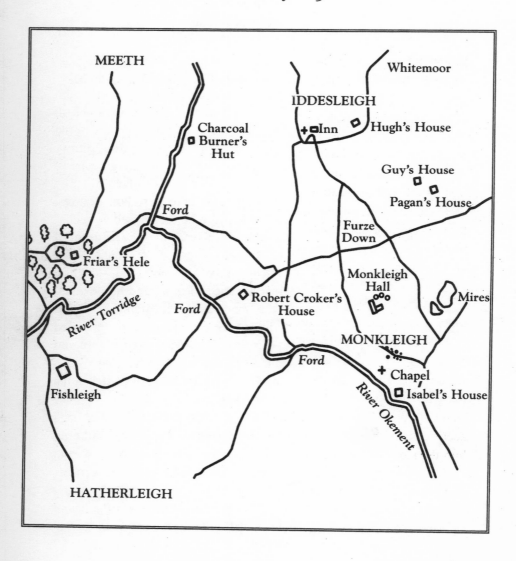

MEETH

Whitemoor

Charcoal
Burner's
Hut

IDDESLEIGH

Inn   Hugh's House

Guy's House

Pagan's House

Ford

Furze
Down

Friar's Hele

Monkleigh
Hall

Mires

River Torridge

Ford

Robert Croker's
House

MONKLEIGH

Ford

Fishleigh

Chapel

Isabel's House

River Okement

HATHERLEIGH

Chapter One

Simon Puttock, bailiff to the Keeper of the port of Dartmouth, sat alone in his chamber listening to the wind howling about the houses. Shivering, he sipped his spiced wine with a feeling of unfocused anxiety, thinking of death.

In part perhaps it was his loneliness. His wife and family were still in Lydford, almost a day's journey across Dartmoor, and he missed them all dreadfully; the weather only served to add to his sense of trepidation and dislocation.

There was a storm blowing in from the south, and every gust made the shutters rattle alarmingly, while rain and hail splattered loudly against them. Indoors the tapestries and hangings rustled and shivered as though being shaken by demons who mocked him from the darker recesses of the room. Outside there was a wild shrieking and thrumming from the rigging of the ships, a sound he would never grow accustomed to. It was too much like insane creatures screaming and gibbering.

Such thoughts would never have occurred to a man such as Sir Baldwin de Furnshill. Simon knew himself to be less worldly than his friend, who often laughed at Simon's nervousness about passing certain places of ill-fame and his cautiousness regarding old wives' tales – Baldwin called them 'superstitious drivel'. 'Only a child could believe such rubbish,' he had once said contemptuously when Simon had told him the story of the Grey Wethers.

The tone of his voice had shown Simon how comprehensively Baldwin rejected such old moor legends, but it was different for him. Baldwin had been bred up in the gentle, soft lands north-east of Crediton; Simon had been born on the moors, and a moorman was always more aware of their history and atmosphere than foreigners. Simon could feel the mood of the moors in his bones. As he grew older, he found that he was ever more attuned to the brooding nature of their spirit.

It was that which tonight made him start and shoot a glance over his shoulder, then round at the blacker corners. There was a sense of foreboding which he couldn't shake off, no matter how hard he tried. He felt sure that it must be something to do with the passing year, the terrible things he had witnessed: the murders in Exeter, Baldwin's own near-death, and the despair of so many people at their bereavement; and he looked forward with hope to a new year that would be happier for all.

If he had realised what was to come, he would have been less keen to see the old year pass by. Yet at the outset that was his only hope: that the events of 1323 would soon fade in his memory and the new year would dawn bright and full of hope.

He was to be disappointed. The year of our Lord 1324 held only more horror and misery. And of all the grim events of those months, it was the first, the loss of his servant Hugh, that was to cause him the most despair.

She whimpered as she heard the man approach. He brought with him a rattling, slow little handcart, laden as before. He didn't need it: she knew as well as he did that she was ruined already. There was nothing more he could do that could increase her terror.

It was a cold room. No matter how hot he made the fire, the warmth failed to reach her. She knew only the damp, the feeling of freezing stone underfoot, the rank smell of rottenness from soggy sacking. It was odd how she felt the chill and moisture, while all the time her nostrils told her that the air was filled with the foul exhalation of flames and heated steel.

A place dedicated to destruction, this. She knew what had happened in such chambers: Christ Jesus, all knew what went on. When the rich and powerful desired something, people were brought here screaming and begging for mercy; later, much later, if they were lucky, they were pulled hence not too badly broken. The still more fortunate were never seen again. Many died while their torturers tried to wring the last sensation of agony from their bodies.

She was not ready for this. She had made prayers to Holy Mother Mary, pleading that she might be saved, but nothing had happened – neither an increase in her courage nor the blessed relief of death to save her from what she knew must be coming.

The man himself had nothing about him to tell what sort of evil lurked within him. Just an ordinary countryman, a little older than most, he stood now beside the little cart piled with its steel tools, the heavier devices collected about the outside like a smith's ranged around his anvil, and looked at her with his unfathomable eyes.

She wondered what colour those eyes would be in daylight. Here they looked simply empty, as though the cell absorbed all colour from him, just as it had sucked away the kindness and compassion. Nothing was left but an enquiring calculation. And she must stand with her arms shackled high over her head, terrified, while he contemplated her like a butcher eyeing a fresh steer.

They wanted her money. All she had in the world was her little manor, and now this murderer was going to take it from her and leave her destitute. She could try to hold back for as long as she might, but in the end he would have it. He would flay her, break all the bones in her limbs, burn her naked flesh. Just as had been done to poor Lady Baret.

He wore a stained and worn linen shirt, and now he drew a smith's apron over his head. It was thick ox-hide, a good shield against fires and burns, and she watched with tense, draining horror as he pulled a long brand from his cart, and set it to lie with its end among the coals.

While it rested there, he eyed her, his face lighted by the orange glow of the fire, making all the creases and wrinkles stand out like the devil's. It gave him the appearance of total evil. Her heart was frozen with fear, and she felt certain that he could sense her dread. And then she became aware of something else. Although it was a dark and gloomy room, she saw a smile break out on his features.

Then he turned away and bent over the fire, and when he faced her again he held the brand pointing towards her.

Lady Lucy of Meeth shrieked as the heat approached her breast, but even as she begged and pleaded for mercy she could see that there was still nothing in his eyes: no lust, no triumph – just a boundless emptiness as though she was nothing, less even than an ant in his path.

Her last thought was, 'This man has no soul' – and then the steel entered her breast and she knew nothing more.

'Perkin! Perkin! Throw it here, here . . . *here*, you son of a goat!'

'Rannulf, *run*!'

'Beorn! Beorn!'

The men slipped and slid in the chill mud, legs already beslobbered, hosen frayed where thorns had ripped, shirts torn where hands had grabbed, and two already bloodied about their faces.

A man was in front of Perkin. He rammed a hand out, catching the fellow above the eye, and thrust him away. Then everyone was converging on him, and he could see the top of one fair head, a darkly bearded face grimacing in determination, a fist, an arm gripped by two hands, a shred of torn shirt . . . and all the while the rushing of blood in his ears, the screeching of men in battle, the slap of bare feet in the freezing mud, the damp splashing of puddles, the panting, the grunting, the groaning . . .

They'd started in the middle of the pasture between the two vills, twelve men and six women from Monkleigh, fourteen men and nine women from Iddesleigh, with a nervous-looking reeve from Monk Oakhampton between them. He looked little more than two and twenty, and his pale hazel eyes flitted from one face to another as he handled the ball. Then, when he felt he could take the tension no longer, he'd reached right down, and then hurled the bladder up as high as he could, immediately bolting from between the two sides.

There had been a moment's silence. All eyes were on the ball, slowing as it rose, spinning gently in the clear, cold air. It was heavy, a pig's bladder stuffed full of dried peas, stitched tightly, slippery to the hand. But as it started to fall, both sides had rushed forward to grab it.

They had strained there in the field as they always did, and when the break came, it was a thoughtless moment on the other side that gave Perkin his chance.

A woman scratched and tore at Beorn, and he grew furious with the pain of the welts she raised on his face. Others would have knocked the vixen down, or retreated before her, but not Beorn. He grasped her arms, then ducked and lifted her over his shoulders. With a hand at the breast of her tunic and the other at her groin, he hefted her high overhead, and then threw her at three of the men from Iddesleigh.

Two of them tried to avoid her. The third, braver or more stupid than they, held out his arms as though he meant to catch her, and took the full weight of her on his breast. The breath gushed from him like water from a broken pipe, and he collapsed, crushed, while she swore and cursed Beorn for fondling her, shrieking her rage as she clambered to her feet.

It was enough. Her words, and the vituperative tone in which they were screamed, made all the other men stop in their tracks and turn to stare at her. Even as Beorn bit his thumb at her, Perkin could see more men and women from Iddesleigh squaring their shoulders and starting to move towards the middle of the field. It was going to end up just as so many other games had.

But as Beorn turned and faced them all, Perkin had seen his opportunity. Martin from Iddesleigh had the ball, and he and two others were pushing forward against two Monkleigh men, Will and Guy. Hearing the woman, they'd turned and become spectators instead of participants, and in that moment Perkin nipped in under their legs, set his hand atop the bladder, and spun it quickly so that it turned from the holder's hands.

Martin turned back to see what had happened in time to meet Guy's fist coming the other way, and he fell back with a curse, blood pouring from his nose. Perkin was already on his knees as Guy and Will set upon their opponents with gusto. They were equally matched, and as their fight raged, and Beorn hurled abuse at the men approaching him, Perkin kept his head low on his shoulders, wrapped a fold of his shirt over the ball to hide it and make it easier to hold, and set off on the path they'd agreed. It took the rest quite some time to realise that he was escaping.

Perkin was fast for all his girth, but as he paused to take stock he saw that the others were gaining on him. The dampness wasn't helping; the ball was slick and difficult to hold when the weather was miserable like this, but he must get the damned thing to the goal, and that quickly. He shot a look heavenwards, grimacing as he saw black clouds coming closer, shivered briefly, and then hared off down the hill again.

It was a matter of honour that they should succeed here where they'd won the prize so often before. If they were to lose, it would be a dreadful reflection on their manhood. After all, it was four years since the men of Monkleigh had lost a game of camp ball to the men of Iddesleigh, and the idea that today their run of success should come to an end was insupportable.

Wouldn't be a surprise, though. There was something about this weather, with the fine drizzle falling like sparks of pure ice, dark clouds overhead, mud everywhere, and sudden scratches from dripping furze and thorns as they pounded on, that took away any confidence.

Someone had told him that this game had started back in the days when giants had lived here. That was why the field of play spread so widely. Other places, so he'd heard, used a single pasture or maybe a couple of meadows, with the goals set up at either end; not here at Iddesleigh, though. Here the men had to battle their way over a mile of desolate land. The game would range from Furze Down to Whitemoor; that meant two hills, two streams, and a vicious climb uphill to finish, no matter which side had control. Starting with the battle for control of the bladder, followed, invariably, by at least one fight, and culminating in a run of at least half a mile, much of it uphill, it was no surprise that by the end both sides, winners and losers, would be equally knackered. If they were horses, they'd be killed out of kindness.

'Perkin! *Perkin!*'

He was startled from his musings by Beorn's shout. The younger man's bare legs were like oak trunks covered in dark moss, and his thick black hair lay lank over his brow, almost covering his dark eyes. Perkin had no idea what Beorn's warning meant, but he took the easiest defence and hurled the ball to him.

'Behind you!'

Perkin feinted quickly right, then shot off to his left. Someone snagged his shirt, and he felt it rip, but then he was free, and he heard a satisfying grunt and muffled oath as his attacker fell. Looking over his shoulder, Perkin saw that it was Oliver, the smith from Iddesleigh, who sat up now, disgruntled, a scowl marring his square features.

Perkin knew him well, and rather liked him when the game wasn't on, but today he was only glad that he'd escaped the man.

He was almost through the stream at the bottom of the gully now, and he started the slow clamber up the other side. Beorn was alongside him, and he grinned at Perkin, hurling the bladder back to him. Perkin caught it with a grunt and gave Beorn a baleful glower. The man had to throw the thing so cursed *hard*! It all but winded him.

This was the line they'd agreed on: it was steeper, and harder to negotiate, than the usual way, but by coming up here to the hill east of the main flatlands, the men from Monkleigh had slipped round the defending line of Iddesleigh, and although they had set off in pursuit Perkin was already comfortably ahead of even the fleetest of foot. He clutched the bladder under his armpit more tightly and gritted his teeth as the rain began to fall more heavily.

Up and up, until his thighs were burning and his lungs felt as though they must surely burst. There were rocks and projecting bushes up here, and he was sure that his ankle would snap if he misplaced his step at any point. And then, blessed relief, he was at the top of the steepest part of the climb, and he could pause, staring back down the hill.

Straggling up towards him were the bulk of his team. Beorn was still nearest, his face bright with sweat and exertion, eyes staring above his beard; behind him were five more men, and Guy and Rannulf were back at the bottom, Rannulf pounding at an Iddesleigh man with his fists while two others looked on. No one would get in Rannulf's way when he was in that sort of mood.

Hefting the pig's bladder in his hands, feeling the weight of all the dried beans inside it, Perkin took a deep breath and began to move towards Whitemoor again. He heard another bellow from Beorn, turned to see what his comrade had seen, and saw a man appear almost in front of him.

Perkin ducked, but he was too late to bolt. A burly arm went about his waist, a shoulder caught his belly, and his breath left him in a woosh of pain. In the twinkling of an eye he was flying through the air and, as though time was standing still for the better appreciation of his predicament, it seemed for an instant that he was suspended as though by a rope.

Not for long, though. Directly ahead of him he could see Ailward, about him a flickering scene: yellow furze flowers, green, red, and then a large, grey rock. At the last moment he flung his arms out and then closed his eyes as the heel of his left hand struck the moorstone, which rasped along the soft underside of his wrist until it smacked into the point of his chin, when he suddenly lost all interest in the game as bright pinpricks of light burst in on his vision.

The bladder was gone, and as he moaned and rolled over, prodding with his tongue at a loosened tooth, he looked up to see his attacker holding the ball. He recognised him now: it was Walter, one of Sir Odo's blasted men-at-arms. Still, he was older, slower. If Ailward was quick, if he could just hold Walter a moment, then Beorn would be there too, and they could win the ball back. But when he stared at Ailward, his teammate was standing steady, unmoving, his legs apart, his eyes anxious.

With a careful swing of his arm, Walter brought the bladder back, and then uncoiled like a snake to send the thing soaring high into the sky, to drop down towards the plain, far beyond the men of Monkleigh's team.

Perkin closed his eyes again. There was nothing more for him to do.

Chapter Two

From the hill at Monkleigh, Isaac watched with his rheumy old eyes narrowed against the weather, mumbling his gums while Humphrey held his cloak about his shoulders, trying as best he could to explain what was happening down on the plain.

'The Monkleigh men are streaming back now. Martin from Iddesleigh has the bladder and is at full pelt. The whole of the Monkleigh team is just behind him, and . . . and Agnes the fuller's daughter is there, she's running at him! Yes, she must capture him . . . she's only feet away now, and— Ach! No, he's slipped round her, a hand in her face, and he's past. Agnes is down . . .'

Isaac had been here for over forty years, so Humphrey had heard, and so far as he could tell, it was a miracle that the man was still alive. No man should have to live in so backward a place as this, not without a significant reward for doing so, in Humphrey's humble opinion. For him, of course, it was different. He was a coadjutor, here to fulfil the offices which were in fact Isaac's responsibility, but were beyond his capability now. At over sixty years of age, by Humphrey's reckoning, the poor old man was deaf in one ear, had a terrible limp from the gout, and was blind at more than twenty paces. Plainly Humphrey could give no credence to anything the senile old man next to him might say; after so many years' passage, it was a blessing that he could remember even his own name. Certainly his estimate of his own age was nothing more than that: a guess.

The game was thrilling, though. For Humphrey, who had seen only one before this, it was exciting to see how the men and women slid and slithered in the mud, their enthusiasm waxing and waning with the fortunes of their sides. He should have liked to have joined them, had he been a little younger, but his post was not that of a mere vill's priest who must throw himself wholeheartedly into every banal activity; rather it was that of a professional adviser and steward of his master's resources. Except that his master's mind was so addled now that Humphrey could scarcely interest the man in any of the issues he raised. It was a wonder that no one else had noticed that Isaac was quite unfitted for his duties until Humphrey arrived, but that was apparently the case.

There were good reasons why no one paid much attention to the decrepitude of the priest. This land was ever filled with enmity. There was the dispute between Sir John Sully's steward, Sir Odo de Bordeaux, and the repellent brute Sir Geoffrey Servington who managed the neighbouring manor, for a start. It made little sense to Humphrey, and he did not care what lay behind the dispute. All he knew was that there was constant bickering between the two parties, and he could play a useful role in the middle, speaking for one side to the other and vice versa, while maintaining Isaac in his post and helping him to keep up the services at the chapel.

The fighting was not only about land, of course. There was the age-old matter of lordships. Sir John Sully was a vassal of Lord Hugh de Courtenay, who had reportedly been close to joining the Lords of the Marches in their dispute with the king and his detested advisers, the Despensers. It was only good fortune and his innate common sense which had held him back. And a fortunate thing, too. Too many others who had not heeded sounder counsel were even now dangling from gibbets and spikes at the gates to all the great cities in the land, and the little manor next to Lord Hugh's, which had been owned by the great general Mortimer before he raised an army against the king was now in the hands of the Despensers. While the Despensers were in the ascendant, Lord Hugh could scarce risk upsetting them, but even so he would not give up parcels of land to them willy-nilly, no matter what they threatened.

And threaten they would. It was their preferred means of acquiring lands and fortune. They had already broken many, even snatching up widows and holding them to ransom or, to their eternal disgrace and dishonour, torturing the poor women until they gave up their children's inheritances. These were evil, dangerous thieves, who could and would attack any man who tried to thwart their ambitions.

While men like the Despensers and their neighbours battled over lands, Humphrey reflected, other men of ambition were left with the potential to take advantage of the situation. There were many about this area with private grudges to settle, and he would not be at all surprised if some of them tried to turn circumstances to their own benefit. Perhaps, in his capacity as coadjutor, he should learn which of the other landowners in the area were seeking to benefit from the disputes.

'Are you enjoying the game, Father?'

Humphrey turned sharply to find Father Matthew from the church at Iddesleigh standing behind him. There was something about the neighbouring priest which Humphrey had never liked – perhaps it was just that he was suspicious of Humphrey's lack of formal documentation. Still, there was little the man could do. Isaac was happy with him, and that was all that mattered.

Isaac muttered, 'It seems very boisterous today. The lads are . . . mmm . . . showing more enthusiasm than they do in church!'

Matthew chuckled. 'It is good to see them letting off steam. And when the pigs are killed, at least this means there's a use for the bladders. Marvellous animal, the pig. Nothing ever goes to waste. I have a brawn cooling even now. The jelly about it is splendid.'

Isaac pulled a face. 'If I tried to eat some I'd be unwell for days. I find only a little . . . mmm . . . gruel is all I can keep down. Still, Humphrey tries to tempt me with little morsels.'

'Does he?' Matthew responded, turning and giving Humphrey his full attention again. Unsettling bastard! To change the subject, Humphrey pointed to a man at the side of the hill.

'Who's he?'

'That grim-faced fellow?' Matthew said, peering through narrowed eyes. 'Oh, he's the man who came here with the woman from Belstone.'

Isaac drew in his breath and shook his head. 'No good. No good can come of that.'

'What?' Humphrey asked. He'd never heard anything about a 'woman from Belstone'.

Matthew answered him. 'She came here some two years ago with this man. He comes and goes, for I think he serves a family in Lydford.'

'She was a nun, and has chosen to deny her vows. She's evil! Evil!' Isaac spat. 'She made her vows, but changed her mind when she grew large with a baby in her belly. They couldn't keep her in a holy convent, so they threw her out to bounce down here to our door. Now she lives in sin with her man.'

'Not quite,' said Matthew more kindly. 'I married them. She was allowed to leave because she had been unfairly coerced into making her vows when she was too young. Her oaths were not valid.'

'That is . . . mmm . . . no excuse!' Isaac expostulated, throwing a hand into the air and almost striking Humphrey.

'It is, Father, it is,' Humphrey said soothingly. 'Just think, if a young child was taken into a life of celibacy without the ability to understand it was a lifetime's commitment. Imagine how he would feel when he grew to maturity and saw his terrible mistake. A fellow who could have been content as a saddlemaker, and a good one at that, for ever chained to a service that made no sense to him.'

'Garbage!'

'Humphrey speaks the truth, I'm afraid,' Matthew said. He did not so much as glance at Humphrey now. Instead he smiled at his old friend. 'The Pope himself has ruled that men and women who took their vows under a certain age should be allowed to retract their oaths and leave without a stain.'

'If they have sworn to God, they should see to their service and the service of the souls under their protection, not worry about escape. Escape! To a place like this!'

Perkin grunted as the others entered the tavern and offered him their sympathy, old friends looking down at him with amusement, some wincing to see his wounds, others laughing at them. Only Rannulf stood and surveyed him without comment for a long period, and then said:

' 'Twas your fault. You lost it for us.'

There was an edge of raw fury in his tone which stirred Perkin. He looked up and nodded. 'I suppose you'd have seen him hiding in the furze there and beaten him?'

'I'd have broken his head for him,' Rannulf gr...
way. You could have run through him.'

Perkin shook his head once and looked away. Th...
activity Rannulf enjoyed, repeatedly insulting a man...
his victim into a fight, and Perkin was having none of it...
your ale. I'm not dickering about the details of the game...

'No. Wouldn't want to tire you now you've lost our winning run for us,' Rannulf sneered. 'You should have got him when you could.'

'Ignore him,' said Beorn.

'I always do,' Perkin muttered. His arm was giving him a great deal of pain, and he would prefer to leave the tavern and go to his bed.

Beorn was one of those men whose hair continued down his neck and over his shoulders. When he went without his shirt during harvest, Perkin had seen how the women would watch him with hungry eyes, staring at his muscled legs, his narrow waist, how his hair travelled down to the crease of his buttocks; but Beorn merely shrugged when he was told. He knew who would be available, and the others didn't interest him. 'Ach, there was nothing you could do,' he said.

Perkin grimaced and turned his head away. 'Rannulf is right, though. I should have guessed someone would be up there. It was obvious they'd have someone who could hold us off. It's what I'd have done.'

'How did they know? We've never gone that way before.'

'So?' cried Perkin bitterly. 'A good general would make sure he anticipated an attack, and that's what they did today. That's why they won. All because of Ailward, too. He shouldn't have been up there. He distracted me.' The man who tackled Perkin was surely there to stop the Monkleigh team – but what Ailward was doing up there was a different matter. He hadn't been with the vill's men at the start of the game. Well, he couldn't have been. No one had outstripped Perkin on the run up the hill. 'Ailward had to have been there before the match started.'

Beorn nodded his agreement. 'He should have stopped Walter. Walter's not one of his men.' There was no need to say more. Walter was one of the Iddesleigh men, a man-at-arms from the Fishleigh estates. Iddesleigh and Fishleigh fellows were as fiercely defensive of their independence as any others. They might be serfs to the lord of the manor of Ash Reigny, but even to him, Sir John Sully, they were a rebellious mob. God's heaven, everyone knew that. The steward and his bailiff had their work cut out to try to keep the peace on his lands. 'Maybe he was just nervous of getting into a fight with the men from up there?'

Very likely, Perkin reasoned: whatever happened, that cunning bastard Ailward would want to retain his authority. If he had been bested by the man-at-arms, a fighter used to defending himself, that authority would have been dented.

Not that it explained why he was there in the first place. He should have been down with the vill's men when the game began.

And then Perkin had a strange feeling. Flashes of colour came back to his mind: the patch of green, then red, before he hit that rock. Odd colours to see up on a moor in winter. They'd all seemed to be about Ailward's feet. And now in his mind a pattern seemed to be forming out of the colours.

Hugh grunted to himself as he finished his bowl of pottage and set the wooden spoon aside. He tore off a slab of bread and chewed it contentedly. Tired, it was true, but at least he was working on things that mattered. There was still the old hedge to be relaid, of course, but apart from that the little holding was in good condition now.

There was a shout, some angry words, and he tilted his head to one side. It was rare to hear men walking about so late; it was close to dark already. Cautiously he rose, and crossed the floor to the door.

His wife, Constance, was quickly at his side. 'What is it?'

'Didn't you hear them?'

'It was just a pair of drunks. Leave them. There's nothing.'

Hugh peered out into the gloom. She was right, surely. What else could it be? He shook his head and wandered back inside. Just as he was about to pull the door shut, he saw a frown on his wife's face. 'Eh?'

'I thought I saw the priest out there with another man . . . but that's daft. He wouldn't be there at this time of night.'

The priest was no concern of his. Hugh peered out again. 'What of it? So long as they're not troubling us.'

'There were some men there earlier,' she said, her pretty face frowning as she remembered. 'The sergeant from Monkleigh, and a man-at-arms from Fishleigh . . .'

'I doubt it,' Hugh said. 'Men from those manors don't get on together.' He pulled the door shut. 'Anyway, whoever is out there,' he said, thrusting the peg into the latch to lock it and dropping the bar into its slots, 'they're welcome to stay there. Me, I'm happy in here by my fire.'

Colours. The wrong colours, the wrong patterns . . .

Even after they'd finished their drinking and the tavern began to empty, that thought still rankled with Perkin. He was among the last to leave, wincing still with the rawness of his inner forearm, his bruised and painful chin, the tooth that seemed to have a red-hot needle at the root, and he stood in the roadway staring northwards towards the field where their opponents had achieved their victory that day, sucking at the tooth as though he could flush out the pain.

The land was flooded with a clear silver light. It was appealing to return home and fall into his bed, cosy under his skins and blankets, but there was something niggling at him as he gazed towards Iddesleigh, and at last he gave a grunt of resignation. The moonlight was an unmistakable hint, so it seemed to him, that God wanted him to go and investigate this. He turned off the roadway and set off down the hill again.

That scene still stuck in his mind, the colours vivid and fresh. At the time he'd given them no thought. The pain and the fear of losing were enough to wipe them from his mind, and he'd stood and walked away from the place where he'd fallen as soon as his legs had stopped wobbling enough for him to get up.

But now he was sure that there was something else up there, and he'd a suspicion that it was the reason for Ailward's presence that day.

The climb was hard, and he felt as though he had aged a good few years in the last half-day. It was one thing to have a fancy about seeing something in the middle of a fight like the one today, and another to make his way up here in the dark when his feet were chilled from the frozen earth, his arm was stinging with each thud of his heart, and his mouth felt as if someone had hit him there with a hammer. Quite another thing, he thought, and he hesitated as he reached a furze bush halfway up the hill, in two minds whether to continue up, or abandon the search and get back to his bed. He glanced over his shoulder longingly, thinking of his palliasse only half a mile away, but then he set his jaw and carried on up the hill.

Breasting the ridge, he easily picked out the place where he had fallen, just as he could easily see where Walter had stood before launching himself at him.

Now he stood where he had been knocked down, staring about him. The rock was there, and there was a flat patch of heather beyond it, but that meant nothing. A deer could have lain here.

A deer which had bled.

Perkin had a strange empty feeling in his throat as he frowned at the ground, reaching down to touch the viscous liquid. It was definitely blood: the tinny odour, sickly and sweet, was clinging to his fingers when he brought them to his nose. It was possible that Walter and Ailward had killed a deer, he knew, but it was unlikely. Much more likely that Ailward had . . . but why should Ailward harm anyone? Perkin had never seen anything to suggest that the sergeant would hurt another man. It was his way to swagger and bully, but surely not to kill for no reason. Perhaps it was something to do with money.

One thing was certain. Ailward had not been up here because of the game. He had been involved in some other activity when the game had approached him.

The moonlight caught something moving about some three feet from the rock, and Perkin saw a fluttering piece of material. He picked it up and looked at it. It wasn't a working man's cloth – this was a fine piece of wool from a rich man's gown. Or a woman's.

He'd seen enough. Walter and Ailward had killed someone up here, perhaps to rob him, or to rape her. Perkin had to return to the vill to call for help.

Turning on his heel, he hurried back to the ridge, and it was only when he was over the brow, taking a direct line to the vill, that he stumbled and fell.

'Pig's *turds*!' he hissed through gritted teeth as his arm stung and flamed. He was surprised it wouldn't light his way, it seemed to burn so hotly, but then his curses were stilled on his tongue as he saw what had tripped him.

The dead body of Ailward lying among the long grasses.

Chapter Three

It was a chill morning in early March when Hugh's family was so brutally torn apart.

Hugh rose, as was his wont, in the hour before light, leaving his woman in their bed, her child snuffling and mewling in his sleep beside her.

He and Constance his wife had lived here for two years now, since they had first met early in 1321, and the birth of her son, young Hugh, had set the cap on their happiness, even though he was not Hugh's child. He was the illegitimate son of a priest, but Hugh cared nothing for that. He adored Constance, and loved her child as if it were his own. An experienced shepherd, Hugh felt he had had more to do with the babe than its real father. When little Hugh was born, he had been there to help; when the infant first turned to suckle, old Hugh had held his head and guided mother and child; when little Hugh was old enough, it was Hugh who first took him outside, Hugh who first made him laugh, Hugh who had introduced him to the mangy dog, Hugh who had cleaned him through the long night when he had an attack of vomiting . . . Hugh adored the lad.

The fire was dead now. Hugh would need to fetch a faggot of wood from the store at the back of the house. He glanced back at the bedding. There was a visible lump where Constance lay, her sweet body clearly outlined under the blankets and skins, the child's smaller figure almost hidden in her shadow.

Outside there was a definite chill in the air. The frost had held off, which was a relief, because Hugh was anxious about some of the plants he'd already set out in the vegetable plot, but with luck they'd survive. It wasn't as cold as some of the mornings he'd woken to when he'd been a lad on the moors.

A lean, dark-haired man with the narrow, sharp features of a ferret, Hugh had been raised in a small farm near Drewsteignton, and his early years had been spent on the hills protecting the sheep. He had loved mornings like this out there. Yes, it was freezing for a man, and when you sat wrapped up in a thick cloak as well as a warm sheepskin jack, you still felt the cold seeping into your marrow. A man could die up there and no one find him for days; men *had* died like that. Hugh could remember one from the next vill, an older shepherd whose huddled figure was found by the boy who'd been sent into the hills with some bread and cheese for him. He'd been stiff as an oak staff when Hugh saw him, frost over his beard and eyebrows, and they'd had to carry him down to the vill like that. There was no point leaving him to thaw on the hill.

It was his time up there on the moors which had shaped the man he had become. For most of his life he had been dour and morose, unbending to the wind and the rain. He was known as one who would protect his flocks from any danger, whether it be men, beasts or the elements. Anyone who grew up on the moors learned self-reliance above all else, and a man who survived the depredations of the wandering gangs of trail bastons, the 'club-men' who robbed and killed with impunity in the last years of King Edward I's reign, was one who was strong in spirit. He could cope with the worst that God could throw.

From the logpile he had a clear view of the moors several leagues south – *his* moors. Usually a line of hulking shapes that loomed on the horizon, today they gleamed in the low sunlight, and he felt a strong affection for them. He loved them as any man loves his homelands.

Hugh stood still, staring, struck with a strange emotion. Not a man prone to sudden fancies, he was aware of an unsettled feeling, as though he might never see this again. A melancholy apprehension swept over him, leaving him with a curious desolation. He was filled with uneasiness, a presentiment of evil, and the worst of it was, he had no idea what lay behind it. It was almost as though the moors were calling to him to leave his home and return to them, but he had no idea why the sight of a winter's chill morning sun on the hill should make him feel so.

He shivered, an uncontrollable spasm that racked his compact frame, and he muttered, 'Someone walking over my grave. That's all.'

Crossing himself against Dewer, the Devil, he bent to his task and began to collect logs and a faggot of old twigs. He cast one last glance at the moors, and surprised himself by realising that he had a poignant longing to see again the rough, scrubby grasses, the heather, furze and rock. Even the black, square keep of the castle at Lydford would be a welcome sight. Not that he could go there just now. His master, Simon Puttock, wasn't there. He was down at Dartmouth, the port all those weary miles away on the southern coast. Perhaps Hugh could return to Simon's house for a little. He was still Simon's servant, after all. He could visit to see that all was well with Simon's household . . .

What was all this about? He wasn't leaving Constance and young Hugh on their own just now. Maybe when the weather warmed and there was a little less to do. He'd wait until then. It was plain daft to think of going at this time of year. He was mazed.

He turned from the view and trudged back towards the house, a small figure, easily missed in the great landscape about him, many miles from any town, his lands enclosed by the woods on the north, west and eastern sides.

Hugh didn't mind. He liked being far away from other people; he had no need of them most of the time. As he shoved the door open and dropped the logs on the hearth, the vague feelings of concern faded.

This was his home. He was safe here.

The way led him along the road from the inn where he had stayed the night, and all Adam of Rookford could think of was the itching.

They must have been fleas. That grotty little tavern was probably alive with the damned things. In all Adam's years, he'd never stayed in a hovel that was more likely to breed them.

He scratched at his neck and shuddered with the cold. Adam, always known as Adcock by his friends, was a man of two and twenty years, slimly built, with a face that would have been pleasing enough if it weren't for the marks of the pox which scarred it. He had regular features, large, wide-set eyes under a broad forehead, a slender nose and rather full lips. His hair was dark, and already receding at the temples, so he knew well enough that before too long he'd look like his old man, Jack, who'd lost almost all his hair by the time he was thirty. Adcock could vaguely remember seeing him with hair when Adcock had been very young, but all his other memories had his father looking more like the vill's priest than a servant in Sir Edward Bouville's household.

Servant he had been, and proud, too. Adcock's father had been with the Bouville family all his life, and the old devil had been justifiably satisfied with his position. He had new clothes each summer and winter, a gallon of ale a day, food, and money when he needed it. When he married Adcock's mother, he was given a small plot not too far from the manor, and he was regularly granted time to go and visit it and see his wife, when his duties allowed. Adcock had only good memories of the old man.

Feeling another itch on his back, he grimaced and swore quietly. He'd not sleep in a cheap place like that ever again. Hopefully he wouldn't have to. Not once he'd taken up his new position.

It was his own fault. If he'd set off when he'd meant to, leaving Oakhampton early in the morning, he'd have reached his new home by evening. As it was, there was the rush to say his farewells, going to see his mother at the last minute and accepting her offer of bread and cheese washed down with some of her best ale – well, he didn't know when he'd see her again; she was getting quite old now, and wouldn't live for ever: God willing, she'd still be alive when he next came this way – and after that he had to go and visit Hilda at the dairy, sneaking up behind her to grab her bubbies as she stood working the butter churn, making her squeak with alarm, silencing her scolding with kisses. It was hard to leave her behind – but they'd agreed she'd best remain until he had saved some money and they could wed.

That was a daunting prospect. Many of his friends had married, but somehow Adcock had never thought of himself as a husband. Yet here he was, ambling along on his pony and already considering how Hilda would look in a small cottage somewhere near the manor. He could install her there and go to visit her regularly, with luck. Perhaps, if the steward was an amiable, understanding sort of man, Adcock could find a place very close. With proximity he could see her more often, perhaps even stay with her each night?

But first, he told himself, he must take charge of his manor. Under the steward, he would be the most powerful man on the demesne.

The steward was Sir Geoffrey Servington, a man whose name inspired respect. He'd been a warrior for many years, and he and Sir Edward had been in all the important battles of the last thirty years. Now he was all but retired, of course, as was Sir Edward himself, although that did not dim his reputation. By all accounts he was a demanding, ruthless taskmaster, determined to squeeze the very last drop from his serfs, but that was what was sometimes needed. When they lived so far from their real lord, some peasants would grow lax and idle. It needed a man with a vigorous manner to keep them under control.

It was daunting to someone like Adcock, though. He only prayed that he might find in Sir Geoffrey a man who was accommodating and reasonable.

He was almost there. Through the trees that grew thickly on either side, he could see smoke and some buildings. They were the first he'd seen since he left that dreadful alehouse in Exbourne that morning. The memory made him scratch again at his neck.

There was not much to see. If he hadn't spotted the buildings, he wouldn't have guessed that this was a thriving little vill. He knew of Monk Oakhampton – the manor was owned by the monks of a great abbey, Glastonbury, and he had heard that it was a very profitable little place. It was no surprise, looking about the area here. There was the ribbon of silver-grey river on his left, promising drink and fishing, and the soil looked darkly rich. From the look of the fields, in which the crops were already creating a fresh lime-coloured carpet, the place was one of those in which farming never failed.

It boded well for the manor he was to join. Close by, surely it would have a similar lushness. Good husbandry and management of the land was all that was needed to make a place like this rich, and he would see to it that the manor where he was to be sergeant would grow in fame for its harvests.

He rode past the small cotts of the Glastonbury estate, and then on for another mile or so, until he came to a clearing in the trees from where he could see his new home.

It was a long, low building, looking a little grubby now where the limewash had faded and started to turn green, with a thickly thatched roof and the aura of wealth. Massy logs lay piled at one end, a makeshift thatch over the top to protect the wood from the worst of the rains. Smoke drifted from beneath the eaves, and there was a bustle about the yard as men darted here and there. Adcock could see that the buildings at the side were where the stables lay, because as he sat on his mount studying the place, he could see horses being brought out by grooms, all saddled and ready to be ridden. Soon a group of men stepped over the threshold and stood eyeing their beasts.

The man in front took Adcock's attention. Even from this distance the fellow clearly had commanding presence, a round-shouldered man with grey hair already turning white. His face was grim, square, and broad as he donned soft leather gloves, and he contemplated Adcock from half-lidded eyes as the newcomer approached the hall. It was a cold, devious look, and when Adcock noticed an archer with a bow at the ready, an arrow nocked on the string, he felt a rush of fear flood his soul. He was suddenly aware that this man was dangerous.

'Who are you?' the commander called as he drew near.

'Adam of Rookford, master,' he answered quickly, feeling himself flush a little under the amused gaze of so many men.

'Oh, aye, the new sergeant,' Sir Geoffrey said. 'You'll be wanting to hasten inside, then, and find some ale after your journey. There's bread and meats. Shout for the servants for anything you need.'

'You are off?' Adcock looked about him for the raches and other hunting dogs, but there were none about other than the odd sheepdog and cattle-herding brute.

'Yes, we go to visit a neighbour or two,' Sir Geoffrey said.

'I thought you were hunting,' Adcock said. He felt the eyes of all the men on him as he reddened and began to stammer. 'I was looking for dogs, but then I realised there weren't any for hunting. Not out here, anyway.'

'You want to see my dogs?' Sir Geoffrey asked, and a strange smile came over his face. 'Perhaps later, eh? For now, you rest until I return.'

He took the reins of the horse brought to him by a shorter, narrow-shouldered youth, and swung himself into the saddle, adjusting his sword until it was more comfortable on his hip, tugging at his glove again, settling himself in his seat. Then he grinned at Adcock, and the new sergeant felt a renewed apprehension.

At his bellowed command, the other men clambered on their horses, and then, when he whirled his arm about his head and set off at a smart canter, the others followed behind him in an untidy, straggling mass.

Hugh was lost in contentment as he carried his tools down to the road where the hedge stood.

It was an old one, this. A good local hedge, with solid moorstone inside to support it, covered with turves. Earth had been piled at the top, and the first farmers would have thrown acorns and berries on to it, or perhaps planted young whips of hawthorn, blackthorn, rose and bramble. Anything that would help to form a prickly, dense mass. And as the years passed, the thin little plants had grown strong and tall, and when they were thick enough the farmers had come back with billhooks and slashers and axes, and had cut half through the inch-thick stems and laid them over, fixing them in place by weaving them between stakes. And the hedge had grown, solid, thick, impenetrable, self-renewing.

All that was long in the past. Hugh had kept his eyes on this one for the last two years, thinking that it was grown too tall and straggly, and he had begun work here a week and a half ago, cutting out all the dead wood, trimming the smaller branches, hammering in new stakes. Now he had to hack at the surviving plants so that he could lay them afresh.

It was all but done. He had only a few more hours' work, and the field could be used again for pasture. That would be a good day. With luck, the ale that Constance had put to brew last week would be ready at the same time and they could celebrate their fresh little success with her best drink.

'God's blessings on you!'

Hugh peered through the hedge to see the priest from the chapel down the road at Monkleigh. 'Father.'

'This hedge is a mess. It must take a lot of effort to keep it clear?'

'Yes,' Hugh said, feeling his former sense of well-being begin to ebb away.

'What is your name?'

'I'm Hugh. Some call me Hugh Drewsteignton or Shepherd,' he responded. He swung the billhook at a stem and sliced three-quarters of the way through the thick wood.

'Well, Hugh Drewsteignton or Shepherd, are you one of the villeins of Sir Odo?'

'No. My master lives at Lydford.'

The priest lifted his eyebrows in surprise. 'Really? What are you doing here, then?'

'My wife lives here.'

'Your wife? Who is that?'

'Constance.' By now Hugh's contentment was all but gone, and he wished that this priest would go too. There were some in the vill who had muttered when he had arrived there with Constance. It was noticeable that one or two had turned away from them when they went to the church door to be married, as though no woman before had ever wedded her man with a swelling belly.

The priest must have heard the tale, because he gave Hugh a very shrewd look. 'I have heard much about her.'

'So?'

'She is a wise woman, so they say. Good with healing potions and salves.'

'Yes. She learned it at Belstone.'

'What did she do there?'

Hugh began to chop at the stems again, concentrating on the work in hand. 'She was busy learning potions and the like, I dare say.'

'Well, you look after her, man. She deserves all the care she can receive.'

Hugh ignored him, and soon the young priest was off again, walking slowly homeward down the Exbourne road, his feet splashing in the puddles and mud. For a moment Hugh wondered what he had meant, but then he shrugged. He had work to do.

*   *   *

Robert Crokers could have saved himself if he had kept his eyes open. The riders would have been clearly visible coming through the trees.

He had lived here only a few short months. Born at his father's house at Lyneham near Yealmpton, he had been sent to Lord de Courtenay's household when he was five, so that he could learn manners and humility, and he had hated it from the first. A great lord's household was never at rest. When it was newly arrived at a manor there was the noise and bustle of unpacking, the fetching and carrying of boxes and chests, and the coming and going of the peasants bringing food for men and beasts; after a few days there would be more uproar as the men set off to hunt morning and afternoon, with raches and harriers snuffling and slobbering about the place, and horses stamping and chomping at their bits . . . and when all was done and the stores were gone, there was the trouble of packing everything up and preparing to leave for the next manor.

When he had heard that this little manor needed a new bailiff he had seen a chance to escape, and Lord de Courtenay's steward had been kind enough to let him. Better that he should be at a quiet manor where he could annoy only a small number of people with his whining and moaning, rather than at Tiverton or Okehampton, where he could upset many more, the older man had said, and then grinned and wished him all good fortune.

This land was good, Robert told himself now. Up here at his house there was plenty of wood, while down at the vill the fields were bursting with health. In many parts of the country people were starving because of the terrible harvests, but here in Devon the populace was a little better provided for. Their diet was geared towards hardier crops, which could bear the dreadful weather. He sometimes thought that the peasants here were like the oats they grew. Both seemed stoical in the face of the elements.

His home was a small building, cob-built under a thatched roof, but it was comfortable and snug even during the worst of the winter's storms. From the door, he could look over a large garden where he hoped his beans and peas would thrive, while beyond the beds was a small area of pasture which rolled down the hill south-west towards the river. The ford was in front of the house, and the lane from it led past his door and on up the hill towards the lands north and east: Iddesleigh and Monk Oakhampton. The way was cut through thick woodland, and few travellers ever passed this way.

Robert was making his way home, a man of middle height, slightly built, with a slender waist and narrow shoulders. He had fine features: his nose was straight, his lips were sensuous, and his brown eyes were intelligent and kindly; and he was as hungry as the peasants on the estate. Food had been plentiful enough through the cold, barren months, but now that winter was drawing to a close and the stocks were low his teeth were aching badly, as usual, and one or two were loose in his jaw as the scurvy started to take hold again. It was the same every year, ever since he'd been a little lad. When the food grew scarce, he began to suffer. If fortune favoured, he would soon recover. He always did when the weather improved.

He was almost at his house when he heard the drumming of hooves in the distance. The sound was loud enough for him to stop and turn, frowning. Horses were making their way down the rough road that led towards the Okement river and the ford that led to the big house over west. Robert had no cause to be anxious, so far as he knew. He was far from the main manor here, but who would dare to attack him on Lord de Courtenay's lands? No one would be so foolish. Still, there was something about the relentless approach that made him turn back and move more quickly towards his door and the promise of safety within.

There was a sudden silence behind him, and he wondered at that. If the riders were heading for Fishleigh they must pass him, surely, and that would mean the noise of hoofbeats would grow . . . unless they had turned off and were even now haring off towards another homestead.

The thought was curiously unreassuring. If there were riders in force around the manor, he wanted to know about them. On a whim, he went to the edge of his garden, peering up the road through the trees. Sounds could play a man false up here. Sometimes he had heard voices which sounded as though they were from only a few yards away, and yet when he had gone to investigate, he had discovered that they were men talking at the far side of the river.

So now he stood frowning, straining his ears to discover where the riders could be. It was only sensible to be wary, especially with neighbours as unpredictable as the men under Geoffrey Servington. When he had first come here, he had been warned that Geoffrey's men were prone to violence. Not long before there had been a scuffle of some sort, and Geoffrey's men had killed Robert's own predecessor.

There was a sharp explosion of noise, and he spun round to find the area before his house filled with horses. He had been too keen to listen out for the riders coming along the track to think that they might approach another way. Somehow these men had ridden through the woods and come at him from the river. He moved aside as their beasts stamped and pawed at the soil, snorting and blowing after their urgent ride.

'You the bailiff here?'

Robert turned to find himself confronted by a thickset figure on a horse. He nodded.

'I am Sir Geoffrey Servington. This land is my lord's, bailiff. So I want you to leave.'

'This is land of Sir John Sully. No one else's,' Robert said, but he was nervous in the face of all these men-at-arms. A black horse backed, stamping angrily, and Robert moaned when he saw it crush his carefully planted bean and pea plants.

Following the direction of his gaze, Geoffrey shouted, 'Get off the garden! After all,' he added, smiling evilly at Robert, 'when we have our own man living here, we won't want him to starve, will we?'

Chapter Four

Hugh brought the axe down one last time, wiped his brow with the back of his hand, and set the axe by the side of his pile of wood. Gazing about him, he grinned as he told himself that he had never been so happy as since he started to live with Constance.

This old tree had collapsed during the year before last, when he'd first come here. Over time the other larger boughs had been cut out, but this one had, for some reason, survived. And then a foul storm had struck and it had collapsed, taking a lot of the old Devon hedge with it.

It was a problem with older parcels of land in this area. The little holding where Hugh and Constance lived was once part of the Priory of Belstone's demesne, but when Constance had been sent here by the prioress it had been empty for some years. The hovel which had stood here had been all but derelict, and when Hugh first saw it his temper had if anything grown more sour.

'Best work on that first,' he had declared, and stood staring at it while Constance gazed at him anxiously. She had been anxious a lot of the time back then, he remembered. About her baby, about her life, whether she had made the right choices, whether she should be here at Iddesleigh at all . . . there were so many concerns for a young woman with no vocation.

What else could a moorman do, though? Hugh knew that a place like this needed a man to look after it, just as a woman needed a man to provide for her. It was all well and good to say to a woman like Constance, 'Woman, there's a place at Iddesleigh. There's a house and some acres. Go and take it. You can live there,' as though that was an end to the matter. But no one who'd ever farmed would think that. No, as Hugh knew, a farm which was left fallow for any length of time would soon be overwhelmed with weeds and brambles, the coppices overrun with small, useless stems, and the house . . . well, it would look as this one had.

Constance was lucky the prioress had given her anything, of course. It was proof of the regard in which she was held by the prioress – but God's ballocks, it was fortunate that Hugh had been here to see to it.

The scowl on his face lightened a moment. Being born on the moors lent a man a suspicious nature, and for a moment Hugh wondered whether that could have been at the heart of the prioress's suggestion that Hugh should travel here with Constance . . . the old woman was certainly crafty enough to see that this servant was already attracted to the former novice. Only it was more than that. Hugh felt the same adoration for Constance that a sheepdog feels for its master. There was no denying it: he loved her. She was . . . well, there weren't words for her.

He'd even given up his master, Simon Puttock, and his family for Constance. Perhaps if he hadn't met her, he'd still be in service with Simon, living with him at Dartmouth. When Master Simon had been given that post – the Abbot Robert's representative in the town with full authority under the Abbey of Tavistock's seal – Hugh had known so many doubts, it had felt as though his heart was being torn in two; but there was no choice as far as he was concerned, not really. He'd seen Constance's new home by then, and although he'd rebuilt the worst of the hovel, there was too much to be done on the land about it for him to leave her alone yet. Simon, who knew him so well, had given him a small purse and wished him Godspeed when they last parted. There was no pointed comment, no demand that he ought to continue to serve his master as he had before, no bitterness: only a wholehearted and generous wish for his happiness.

Hugh could remember that last meeting.

'Hugh, make her happy – and I will pray that God makes you as content with her as I always have been with my darling Meg. Constance is a good woman, and she deserves a man who'll honour her, so look to her, protect her, and you can always send a messenger to me if you are in want. Remember that!'

And with that, Hugh could remember the glistening at his master's eyes. Simon had actually wept at losing Hugh's company. It made

Hugh feel terrible, but there was no choice. Not really. Hugh hefted the axe again and let its weight draw it down into a long branch.

No, Master Simon could always find a new servant. He'd said that he had one already – a lad called Rob – who was efficient and ever cheerful. That was what Master Simon had said: the lad was always cheerful. It was a daft comment. Hugh had always been cheerful enough, God's blood! He normally greeted his master with a respectful duck of the head of a morning. He scowled, remembering: what more could anyone ask?

He swung the axe again, glancing up at the sky. It was darkening in the way that it did in the late winter, deepening to blue overhead with pink in the west. Looking at the remaining trunk, he sniffed, then slung the axe over his shoulder. There would be time enough tomorrow to finish the job, and then it would be a matter of carrying all the logs back to the house. He had a small hurdle which he'd made from the smaller branches, and he reckoned he could lash the logs to that, and hitch it to an ox. The beast would drag the lot back home.

Mulling over his plans for the next day, he wandered slowly through the gathering gloom to the house. Soon he could smell the fire, and he snuffed the air happily. It was good to know that he was nearly home. The mere idea of 'home' was enough to make him smile. When he'd been a youngster he'd had a home, of course, but then he'd become a shepherd, and that lonely life had marked him profoundly.

His path took him over the line of the hill, along the lane westwards, and thence down to the cottage. He stopped once, gazing along the sweep of hills to the south to where, in the distance, he could see his old haunt: Dartmoor, sitting like a brooding animal preparing to pounce on the far horizon, dark and dangerous. Sometimes he liked to think of himself like that: a man of action who rested at present, but only like a moor viper, coiled, alert and ready to attack.

Tonight all he wanted was a quiet evening, and then his bed. The house looked shabby and in need of a fresh coat of limewash and a new roof, but he stood still and smiled at the sight of it. It was all he had ever wanted. A good, solid house, when all was said and done, with space for the animals at the bottom of the slope so that their filth would drain through the hole in the wall, while he and his woman and child slept in the northernmost portion, up the hill. It was a sight to warm an old shepherd's heart.

Sighing happily, he strode into the yard, and had gone six paces when he realised that something was wrong; terribly wrong.

There was a smell of burning pitch, and he had none here at the farm. He could smell the fumes as though they were very close, and it was a few moments before he realised that the odour came from a torch, and that the breeze was behind him.

A warning flashed in his mind, and he began to turn, but he was already too late. There was a shout, a command, he heard a whirling like a nearby flight of geese, and his head was slammed forward as something smashed against his skull.

He could feel sparks strike at his skull, and as his cheek crashed against the dirt of the yard he smelled the stench of burning hair, rank and disgusting. A second blow, then a third, and his head was a mass of pain. There were cries, but they seemed to come from afar, perhaps on the next hill? In front of him he could see the house, and he knew that if he could reach it, all would be well. He would be safe in there. Constance would come to him and make his head better. He knew that.

There was no strength in his arms or legs. It was only a short distance, made hazy by the smoke and the roaring in his ears. He lifted his head, and he heard a man cry out. A boot kicked his temple, and then his chest, and he lay wide-eyed and unblinking, utterly spent.

He could see the open doorway. At the threshold lay his woman. He saw a man drop to his knees in front of her. There was a muted cry, a sound of grief and terror, and he saw the man finish, rise, kick, spit, laugh, draw a dagger, reach down. All was a whirl. Hugh was sure he ought to do something, but his limbs were another man's, not his. There was nothing his mind could do to command his body.

A boot thudded into his flank and he rolled to his belly, hiding from the blows. A foot rested on his back. He heard a shout, a scream, saw the babe, Hugh, held by the legs. Mercifully, his eyes closed, and he heard a roar of laughter, then no more screams from Hugh. A punch in his back, another, and this time he felt an odd sensation. It was as though the punch had gone through his back and scraped a rib.

Hugh could smell smoke, and he felt warmed. He had left the field to come home, and he must have fallen asleep as soon as he got here. The fire was lighted: he could feel the hot breath at his face. It glowed at his eyelids, and he snuggled further down into his bed. It was a lovely bed, soft and yielding, and surely Constance would soon be here with him, her soft body joining with his.

It was a dream. She was a dream to him, and he smiled in what he thought must be his sleep as he felt himself sliding away, as though he was slipping sideways into the darkness of the soil itself as unconsciousness enfolded him.

Friar John was footsore, irritable, and not in the mood for another night out in the cold. He'd already covered too many miles since he'd fallen out with the prior in Exeter, and here he was still wandering about the countryside wondering whether he had made the right decision in leaving Exeter when he had, let alone in coming this way. It had smacked a little of hypocrisy to fly from the city in such a hurry, without taking time to consider.

Still, he had caught his prior in a lie, and one which could lead to others' being harmed, if not killed. No, he hadn't had a choice at the time. It was a shame, though. He'd enjoyed a good reputation there in Exeter. All who met him reckoned that he was the best fund-raiser the Order had seen.

A shod friar, a Dominican, John was one of those who had given up all his worldly wealth . . . not that he had possessed much when he'd first walked to the friary and offered himself. Then he'd been a narrow-shouldered, skinny, rather feeble assistant to a cutler, who had hoped to earn a place as a man of importance in his adopted city of Winchester.

He had had so little good fortune in his life, he thought now. He was the third son of Sir George, a minor knight from the Welsh marches, and knowing he would make a dreadful priest he had early on chosen a life of trade and gone to Winchester. There, when he grew older, he had encountered some of the pitfalls which awaited so many young apprentices in life: a night's debauchery, cross words with his master, an evening frolicking with a maid in a tavern of low reputation, more cross words with his master, and then a blazing row when the maid was discovered in his narrow cot a couple of days later.

Suddenly he was an outcast, adrift in the great city, taking a succession of little jobs that paid him swiftly so that he had something to take and spend in a tavern. The maid disappeared: he had heard that she had later eloped with his master's own son.

During that lonely period he had learned all about the pleasures of life, and almost as speedily discarded them as worthless. Women he could enjoy, ale and wine would delight, but all were sour in the mouth the next morning. Especially the women who demanded money as he tried to leave their chambers. None seemed to remember that they'd wanted him the night before as much as he'd told himself he wanted them. Or, to be more truthful, and John tried always to be truthful, perhaps it was the ale and wine which told him that they seemed to desire him.

Whatever the truth of it, after a year of splendid excess, he had nothing. There was no job, all the women knew he had nothing to give them, and while he had a need for wine in the morning, there was no means to pay for it. And one morning, while resting his back against a merchant's house, hoping for alms, he saw a friar. The man was dressed in a grubby robe like his own, without sandals on his feet, and held only a bowl, which he proffered optimistically whenever he caught someone's eye.

'Good day, master,' he said to John. It was the first kindly greeting John had heard in many a long day. When the friar shuffled off, John found himself trailing in his wake.

It was in the priory that he discovered his true vocation: not to wander about the countryside begging for himself, but to earn alms for the good of all. And he was good, very good. In a city John could bring the money from every man's purse, it seemed, almost with a whistle. In a world in which most friars were educated men, with serious expressions and the look of fellows who should have been rather above this position in life, but were prepared to suffer a little now for their advancement later, like a squire who is first taught how to clear out the stable in the hope that one day he'll understand enough to be a knight.

John, though – *he* was different, and he knew it. Most Dominicans were keen to amass their alms as quickly as possible, then buy some bread and go and preach, find a place to rest the night, and prepare for the next day's begging and preaching. Not John. He had always been a sharp lad, quick with a flattering word, and when he stood by and listened to some of his colleagues preach it made him want to wince. There was no passion, no fire. All they could manage was an injunction to remember the friars (among others) in their prayers, with maybe a hopeful wave of their bowls afterwards.

No good, Christ in Heaven, no! Christ wanted to save souls, and looking amiably foolish with a bowl in your hand might win a hunk of bread and some pottage of an evening, but it wasn't going to maintain a single ecclesiastical establishment. So John had set out to win over richer men without issue: the lonely and sad, the bereaved and desperate, promising them preferential honours in the afterlife, provided that they gave over their wealth to the friary in the here and now.

Of course it had worked. It had been so successful that in Exeter, where he had ended up, he had caused a certain amount of friction between the friary and the cathedral. Still, that was all in his past now. He had left when he saw some of the corruption of the city, and he was well out of it.

It had been shortly after he had joined the priory that he had heard from his mother that his older brothers were both dead, killed in the wars that ran up and down the marches at all times. The Welsh were a froward, cunning foe, and his brothers had been tricked into a narrow valley by the offer of treasure before being slaughtered by Welsh arrows. Ach, the Welsh were ever cowards. They wouldn't stand and fight.

By then, it was too late to tempt him home. His life had the purpose it had lacked before, and he was content. The manor would go to his remaining sibling, a sister. At least the estates would make for a good dowry when she was married.

His reflections were cut short by a pebble. He was wearing boots which a kind donor had given him, but the thin leather was little protection against the ragged stones. The soles of his feet were cracked and throbbing, and every so often he would stub a toe on a lump of moorstone or semi-frozen mud, which would give him a stab of exquisite pain.

It was as he leaned on his old staff with his face twisted, having managed to do this yet again and stemming the tide of curses only with an effort of will, that he saw the light up ahead.

There were many places out here where a man should be cautious, but even the most devil-may-care felon would think twice before harming a friar. In the first place a friar was useful because he might take a man's confession and shrive him; in the second, he had no possessions. There was no point in trying to rob him.

Still, thieves were not the only threat to a man in the darkness. A law-abiding farmer could be as dangerous if he thought that a dark figure in the shadows was possibly a man come to ravish a wife or daughter. Many out in assarts miles from any neighbours would strike first and ask questions later if practicable. John had little desire to court any more grief than he already endured, so he peered ahead, his narrow face screwed into an expression of intense concentration, while his sharp eyes gazed from under his beetling brows. There were no signs of dancing shapes, no screaming or shouting thieves, only a warm glow amidst the trees, and overhead, now he glanced upwards, a thick pall of black smoke. Occasionally a shower of glinting sparks would rise in a rush, only to disappear.

John gripped his staff and started to make his way towards the blaze. The hour was late for a fire in the woods. People tended to douse the flames so that the trees were protected from stray sparks. Even now, when winter had not yet given way to spring, there was still the threat of wholesale conflagration if men were careless, and men were rarely careless.

It was a good half-mile to the fire, and he had plenty of opportunity to survey the area on his way.

He had come from Upcott towards a place he was told was called Whitemoor, in the hope that the tavern at Iddesleigh might offer him a space on the floor for the night. The fire appeared to be close to the vill itself, set away from the path by a short distance, and he approached it slowly and reluctantly, his staff tapping on the ground firmly with every step he took, until he reached the burning buildings and saw the bodies lying all about: chickens, a dog, cats, and then, last of all, the body of a man.

'Sweet Mother of Christ,' he breathed.

Chapter Five

As he stood at the door to his cottage, Pagan could see the men moving about at the big house, and he felt himself slump wearily at the sight.

That house had lots of fond memories for him. It had been the place where he had grown; his father had been the armourer to good Squire William, and when the squire rode to war in Ireland with his lord, Pagan's father had ridden with him. A lord's host needed men who could wield a hammer or an axe. The old man had died there when they reached Kells. There the Scots persuaded the despicable de Lacys to turn their shields and become traitors to Mortimer, their master – Squire William's master. Kells fell and there was a terrible slaughter.

Squire William too died that day, and the family which Pagan had served so long had been thrown into turmoil. It was all very well for William's son, Squire Robert, to be born to a title, but without money a title was worthless. And the family had nothing. Pagan had remained to serve Squire Robert because he could imagine no other function, and all he could do was act as steward to the people he knew so well and hope that their fortunes might change.

As they had – but not in the way he had hoped. With the death of Squire Robert at Bridgnorth, still fighting on the side of his master, Lord Mortimer, there was little the family could do to defend itself. Robert had died in the service of a rebel, and the king's rage at such people knew no bounds. Whole families were punished for their heads' loyal service to their lords; bodies still hung on gibbets even now, years afterwards, and the king's own advisers, the Despensers, saw that they could seize the advantage. They cheated, they stole and they killed to take what they wanted.

That was when the family lost their house. Squire Robert's widow,

Isabel, was forced out by that thief, that deceiver, that disgrace to chivalry, Hugh Despenser. He took everything, leaving them only a hovel in which to live. It was fortunate that Pagan still had his own cottage, for there was hardly space in hers for the squire's widow, her son Ailward and her daughter-in-law, Ailward's wife. Only Sir Odo had tried to help, riding over occasionally from Fishleigh to visit her. Not that Pagan would stay when Sir Odo was there. He knew why Sir Odo wanted to see the widow, and it wouldn't be seemly for Pagan to be there to watch.

Yes, from up here he could see what Despenser's lackeys were up to. Last afternoon they had ridden off to the west, returning only late, after dark, and Pagan knew what they had been doing. Everyone knew. All had heard of the attack on the poor sergeant of Sir Odo's over towards the ford.

Someone must stop them.

Sir Odo was a man who liked routine. Each morning he would rise with the dawn, and call for his horse while he drank weak ale and ate a hunk of bread broken from a good white loaf. By the time he'd finished, the stable boys should have finished preparing his old grey rounsey, and he would walk out to take his early morning ride round his estate.

Today he stood in the doorway and snuffed the air while he pulled on heavy gloves; a middle-aged man of only some five and a half feet tall, he made up for lack of height by his breadth. In his youth he had been a keen wrestler, and he had maintained his bulk over the years: his neck was almost the same diameter as his skull, and his biceps were fully larger than most men's thighs.

His temper was foul today. The grief that had afflicted Lady Isabel on hearing of the loss of her son had naturally affected the manner in which she dealt with everyone else. Sir Odo felt that grief keenly. He was a long-standing friend of Lady Isabel, and to see so noble a lady reduced by the death of her only child was dreadful.

He sniffed and closed his eyes. Seeing a lad of only five or six and twenty die was always sad, but this case was worse than most. Sir Odo had thought that Ailward would shortly be finding his place in the world, that he might recover a little of the family's fortune, but instead he had been struck down by a murderer. Perhaps a killing committed after too many drinks, or a falling out with a stranger, or a local peasant with a grudge against the man who ordered who should work when, and for how much. There were so many men who could have a reason to kill a sergeant.

There was an icy chill in the wind that came from the north and east. It was always easy to tell when snow was threatening, because the wind seemed to come straight at the house, along the line of the Torridge River, and today was no exception. Sir Odo wasn't fooled by the clear sky and bright sunshine. If he was any judge of the weather here, there would be snow before long.

He crossed the yard to his mount and used a block of stone to help himself up. Ever since he'd been stuck in his thigh by a man-at-arms with a polearm, he'd had this weakness. It was all right when he was up in the saddle, because then he seemed able to grip well enough, but the ability to straighten his leg to spring up was almost entirely lost.

It had been a little skirmish, really. Not a real battle at all. A lowly squire, he'd been fighting for Hugh de Courtenay in the last king's wars against the Scottish. They'd reached the Solway Firth, and had laid siege to Caerlaverock Castle at the turn of the century. Now it seemed such a stupid thing, but at the time . . . he had been near the oddly shaped triangular castle when there was a shout that the Scotch murderers were about to make a sally, and he saw the great drawbridge lowered. Immediately, he ran forward with a few others, and reached it as the defenders were starting to make their way from the gatehouse.

Odo felt that old thrill, the excitement of battle, as he sank his blade into a man's throat and saw him thrash for a moment before tumbling down, choking. Four more fell to him during that short action, though there were no more deaths. A small fight, almost negligible. Probably most of the other men there that day had forgotten it, but not Odo.

The men with him kept up a great roaring shout, and with sheer effort they managed to force the enemy back towards the sandstone gatehouse. Odo's opponent stumbled and fell, and suddenly Odo realised that they could push into the castle itself. He slashed at the man's face twice, then turned and roared to the men at the siege camp to join them, and at the same instant felt something slam into his leg. It was a shocking sensation, and the effect was to knock his knee away, so that he collapsed.

After that his battle grew confusing. He had flashes of memory: not because of pain – there was none – but because he was desperate to climb to his feet, to escape before he could be hacked to pieces. A man on the ground would be as likely to be attacked by the men of his own side as his enemy; a fellow on the ground could be preparing to thrust up with a weapon at the unprotected underside of the men battling above him, and there was little opportunity to distinguish friend from foe. Yet he *couldn't* stand. He panicked, overwhelmed with terror as he recognised his danger: he was defenceless here in the mêlée. Trying to crawl away, he was stunned as a crashing blow caught his head, and he felt his skull shake as he fell forward, blood washing over his eyes. He was convinced that he was about to die, and began a prayer begging forgiveness for his sins (which he freely confessed were legion), which was cut short by his passing out.

Later, he awoke to find himself being cleaned by a squire. He was lying on a rich bed, a *real* bed, with soft woollen blankets and marvellous silken hangings.

He coughed, then rasped, 'Have I died?'

'I hope not. He'll have my guts for his laces if you have,' the squire said drily. 'How's your head?'

The squire looked ancient to Odo. He must have been in his forties – couldn't remember his name now – and must have realised how confused Odo was, because he refused to discuss anything with him until he'd rested.

'The best thing after a knock like the one you took is plenty of rest. Have some wine, then sleep.'

'But where am I?'

'You're safe. And being well looked after.'

'My leg,' he remembered. He tried to get up to look at it, but the shooting pain that slashed through his skull at the movement made him want to heave. He sank back on to the sheets.

'You're fine. The leg's still there, although it took a grievous cut. Don't worry, friend. You've made your name today.'

Yes. Of course I have, Odo thought to himself cynically. There must have been thirty or forty men on that drawbridge, and he was sure that he'd heard the gates slam even as he sank down on to his face. 'The castle wasn't won?'

'No. Now go to sleep.'

The next thing he remembered was being dressed in a new tunic, and Hugh de Courtenay and Sir John Sully being there to help him on with his sword. His leg hurt like the devil, but he was all right apart from that. If he turned too quickly, he would feel dizzy, but that would pass, he knew. He'd been thumped about the head often enough when he was a child and learning his fighting techniques, and he recognised this wound as one of those unpleasant ones that would leave him feeling tired and wanting to throw up if he wasn't careful.

Not today, though, he had vowed. Because today he was being taken to see the master of the fourth squadron, the team he had served with. And the youth who was in charge was waiting for him.

Only seventeen he was, but you could tell he was a prince from his courtly disposition. He was polite, handsome, and a strong fighter. Even as Odo stumbled towards him, the future king drew his sword and held it aloft, while trumpets blew and the men all cheered. Odo the squire walked to Prince Edward, but *Sir* Odo left him.

It had been a great day, and although Odo felt much the older man, he had been impressed with Prince Edward's calm and unassuming nature. He and his companions had been bold enough; certainly none of them seemed wary of fighting, or fearful at the clamour of battle.

Which was why Odo clung to that memory. It was good to recall the prince the way he *had* been.

He rode eastwards, and then north, crossing the ford under Crokers's place. He'd heard of the attack there, but there was no sense in approaching it now, just in case Sir Geoffrey had put in a force to guard it. It could be hazardous to go unprotected to a place like that.

Instead, he left the track and took his horse up the hill to the old road, which, muddy, stone-filled, with tall hedges on either side and a thick wood on his right giving glimpses of fields between the trunks, was pleasant enough. It was this land that the Despensers wanted, from what Odo had heard. They wanted to take all the manors owned by John Sully on the east of the river, making their own holdings that much more extensive.

It was always the way: when a man of ambition grew rich, his first inclination was to increase his wealth. Odo couldn't understand it. Hugh Despenser was fabulously rich. Odo had heard men speculate on his worth, and the general view was that he was the richest man in the country after the king himself. A terrible man, avaricious and ruthless. He would take men and torture them for sport, or to make them sign away their inheritances. Not only men, either. It seemed strange that the prince Odo had met all those years before could have grown into a man who tolerated advisers like Despenser.

There were the other rumours, of course. That the king was infatuated with his friend; that his friend had supplanted the queen in the king's affections, that he was the king's lover. It was possible. Odo had no opinion. He did not care particularly.

A twinge of pain in his thigh made him frown, and he massaged his old wound with his fist. It always played up during the winter. Warmer weather was needed, rather than this bleak coldness.

Sir Geoffrey, Despenser's tool, was not difficult to deal with. Not if you knew his mind and understood what he looked for. He was no fool, and he wouldn't risk upsetting people for no reason. No, that wasn't his way. He'd be much more likely to wait until he had his master's instructions, and then he'd obey them to the letter – provided it didn't put him in any danger. And what danger could there be for a man who was in the pay of the king's best friend? None. So if Sir Geoffrey thought he was acting on the advice of his master, he would do anything.

Odo did not need to guess at Despenser's ambition. He and Sir Geoffrey had discussed it often enough in the past. Being neighbours, and having known each other before that for several years, they were realistic about whom they should trust. Yes, both had their loyalties to their masters, but they were in a unique position here, far from their lords. They had a duty to try to get along.

Sir Geoffrey was entirely his master's man. He had joined Earl Despenser's entourage many years before, when the earl was still a lowly knight. Odo for his part was devoted to Sir John Sully. Although the two stewards could have been at loggerheads, they had avoided disputes, and recently had even joined in small ventures together. Sir Geoffrey could trust Sir Odo – he was different from most neighbours, simply by virtue of the fact that he had been knighted personally by the present king on the field of battle. Sir Geoffrey knew that he must be more inclined to assist the Despensers, because they were King Edward's most devoted friends. Helping them meant helping the king. That was what Sir Geoffrey had said to him once, and Sir Odo had not seen fit to deny it. In these troubled times it was safer for a man to keep his own counsel.

Which was why Odo was surprised that Sir Geoffrey was making difficulties about this parcel of land. They had discussed it when Geoffrey took the old manor from Ailward, but Odo thought he had persuaded Geoffrey that this piece was truly Odo's. Ailward's estate had been carved into two, and Odo had only taken a small part. Just enough to protect the ford. That way, hopefully, very few people would be hurt.

Still, if Geoffrey wanted to launch an attack, Odo had no objection. He would relish a little action; he was bored with idly sitting by. It had been a long time since he had known a dispute like this, and he was looking forward to it with an especial excitement. With any luck, once the land was gone and the dispute ended, Sir John would release Odo from Fishleigh, and he could go and rest in his own home.

Isabel was worried about little Malkin. She might be old enough already to be widowed, but she seemed a child to Isabel still. Since Ailward's death, she spent too long just sitting and staring into the distance without speaking for long periods, her expression bereft.

'Mary? Mary?' Isabel sighed. 'Malkin, please . . .'

Mary seemed to come to with reluctance. 'Mother?'

It was what, eighteen months since this young woman had become her daughter-in-law? And until Ailward's death Isabel had only ever seen her as happy, excited and enthusiastic. To see her green eyes grown so cold and empty was torture. Nothing could rouse her. Since she had lost her husband, she had lost all her love for life.

Isabel held her arms wide, and Malkin stood and crossed the floor, walking into her embrace.

It was impossible for Isabel to find the words to explain her own devastation in the face of such tragic despair. For Isabel this was merely the latest in a series of losses. Her life for the last ten years seemed to have been one of continual mourning. Well, she would not sit and wail again, no matter how much she missed her son. She was the daughter of a squire, the wife of another, and mother of a sergeant. She was proud.

Malkin had lost no one before, though, and she wept freely on Isabel's shoulder. The girl felt so frail and soft to the older woman, it surprised her that she had been able to conceive her child. There was no strength to her, not like the women of Isabel's age who were so used to death and trying to survive in the worst of conditions.

'I must seem pathetic!' Malkin murmured. 'I am so sorry, Mother. But I miss him so – and I don't know how I can live without him . . .'

'Child, you know nothing of the world, do you? You are young. Yes, it is right to grieve for your man, but when you are as old as me you will realise that there are always fresh losses. All you can do is weather each storm that comes, and try to protect those who still matter.'

She looked down at Malkin's head approvingly. The chit was soft, but she had adored Isabel's son, and that was enough to endear her to Isabel.

Malkin nodded and sat up, her head averted as though she was ashamed of her outburst. She stood and returned to her stool, picking up her wool and taking a deep, shuddering breath before counting each stitch on her knitting needle.

She was beautiful – there could be no doubt of that. Her blue-black hair was iridescent as a raven's wing, and her face was delightfully shaped: a broad, white brow that curved down to a pointed little chin. With green eyes slanted down at the sides, and full lips, even now in the depths of her misery she was a delight to the eye. It was no surprise that she'd stolen Ailward's heart. More surprising was that she'd been prepared to accept his advances.

Isabel was no fool; nor was she prepared to attribute characteristics even to her own son that were better than he possessed. Ailward was a bullying, covetous fool, who could, maybe, have made a good sergeant given time, but had died first. Not that his foolishness affected Malkin's opinion of him, apparently. She seemed to have genuinely adored him. There had never been any tears about the place while he lived, and she had always been doting. Perhaps it was true, the old idea that love blinded a young wench to her man's true character. If blindness were ever needed, it was in the lover of Isabel's son.

She sighed. Already an old woman at four and fifty, she was lonely, and unlike the widow in front of her had little chance of ever winning another man.

'Sad, Mother?' Malkin asked softly.

It would have been easy to snap at her. What did she have to be sad about? No father, no husband, no son . . . not many even in the last decade had been forced to contend with so much despair. Isabel felt her eyes sting, but she blinked the tears away before they could form. 'No, child. I was just remembering. There's no need for sadness, not when the good Lord is protecting us at all times. My son is gone to a better place.'

'Of course.'

The arrival of the steward prevented further discussion. Isabel held out her mazer for a refill of wine, and she watched as Pagan filled it to the brim.

He was a good old servant, Pagan. It was one of the old Devonshire names. Nowadays all the young men of quality seemed to have the same ones, even in the same family. Isabel knew one in which the oldest boy was called Guy, the following four sons were all called John, and the last two were both William. She knew why it happened – any parent wanted a godparent to be as committed to his offspring as possible, and so named the children after favoured friends. But if a favoured friend became godparent to more than one of the children, it could lead to embarrassing and confusing multiple naming in the family. Isabel was glad that she had only ever had to worry about the one boy. Much easier that way!

Pagan filled Malkin's cup and then set the jug between the two women before leaving the room. He stood at the door, as usual, eyeing both of them, his eyes going about the room: checking the fire was warm enough, that the shutters were pulled shut against the cold evening air, that the dogs were settled out of the way so that they couldn't upset the women. Only when he was satisfied that they were as comfortable as they could be did he quietly draw the heavy curtain over the doorway and retreat to his pantry to clear away the rubbish.

He was one man who could always be relied upon, Isabel thought. There were so many who were unreliable. Men who would steal the rings from a widow's fingers, who would demand money before performing their services, who would eye her with a lascivious tenderness, hoping to receive a better payment in kind for their efforts, or simply pocket a portion of the manor's wealth and fly the place, never to return.

Pagan was not like them. A little younger than Isabel, his family had served Isabel's dead husband's for many years going back into the dim and distant past. The fact that Pagan was still here was a measure of his commitment to them, and a proof of his honour, although he was only a common peasant in truth. At the same time, knights who called themselves *honourable* were stealing manors from defenceless widows like her.

She gazed into the flames, lost in thought.

'Mother? Are you well?'

Malkin's soft voice drew her back to the present. 'Yes! Of course I am,' she snapped without thinking, and then regretted her harshness. 'I am sorry, Malkin. It's just . . .' She waved her hands feebly. 'I don't know how to say it.'

'I know,' Malkin said. Tears appeared in her eyes again. 'I can't think how to face life without my man.'

'That is easy,' Isabel said sternly. 'You survive. I have lost three men now. My father, like my husband's, killed by the Scots in Ireland, Robert himself in that treacherous attack at Bridgnorth, and now my son. My beloved son . . .'

'I loved him so much,' Malkin said.

'I know you did, little sweeting.'

'It seems so hard to imagine that he's gone.'

'The thing to concentrate on for now is my grandson. You have to look after him, child. It is he who matters, who has to be protected. No one else.'

Chapter Six

Sir Baldwin de Furnshill stood in the cool morning air wearing only a thin linen shirt and a fine tunic of flaming crimson, and drew his sword as he faced the rising sun on the grassy slope, tossing the scabbard aside on to the grass and standing still a moment.

He was a tall man, broad and thickset about the shoulders and neck as befitted a warrior used to wearing armour, and his right arm was more heavily muscled than his left from working with heavy weapons. Yet for all his warlike appearance, his face showed a different quality. He lacked the brute arrogance and cruelty of so many modern knights. Instead, he had kindliness in his dark brown eyes – kindliness and a sort of wariness, a man always slightly on guard. A thin beard followed the line of his lower jaw. Once it had been dark, but now, like his hair, it was showing more and more grey. There was more salt than pepper, his wife had said recently, and he could not deny it.

Today he felt unsettled, and it was not merely his wound: it was a curious manor, this, the small estate which had been his wife's first husband's.

It had a lovely outlook, being some miles north of Tavistock but not quite on the moors, with a view of Dartmoor itself. The manor house was a good, solid moorstone building, with sound grey walls, lately whitewashed (Baldwin suspected because the local steward had heard that his mistress's husband was coming to see the place) and thatched well only the previous summer. It stood on a small knoll, as though on its own shallow motte, and all about it at a distance of some sixty yards were woods, with the only bare aspect being to the south, where a man could see almost all the way to Brent Tor on a clear day, so it was said. Sir Baldwin didn't know about that, but he did know that today he needed to try his muscles.

Some three or four months ago he'd been the victim of an attack, and the encounter had nearly killed him. Even now, the wound in his breast was enough to make his chest seize up when he over-exerted himself. The pain was normally a dull ache, but every so often it grew into a flaming agony that seemed to threaten to rip his ribs apart. Last night had been one such occasion.

They had come here to Liddinstone a matter of a month ago. He had promised his wife that they would come to see how the manor was faring, and as soon as he felt able to make the journey from his little estate near Cadbury, a short distance south of Tiverton, they had arranged their affairs, leaving Edgar in charge.

Edgar had been his most loyal servant for more years than either cared to remember. They had met in the hell-hole of Acre in 1291, both arriving in time to witness the city's death at the hands of many thousands of Moors. They had set up a vast siege encampment all about the city walls, and during their time there, Baldwin had found Edgar and saved his life. Subsequently, both had been injured and would have died, had it not been for the generosity of the Poor Fellow Soldiers of Christ and the Temple of Solomon, the Knights Templar, who had rescued them. As a result, as soon as they could, both had given their oaths to serve the Order, and Baldwin became a knight while Edgar became his sergeant. They served together for many years, until the appalling day when the Order was arrested.

Friday 13th October 1307. It was a date that felt as though it had been engraved with a red-hot burin on Baldwin's heart. Each year he felt drawn to toast his comrades on that day, and yet he could not. The idea that he should celebrate their destruction was repellent. No, it was better that he remembered them all on days like today, when the sun was newly risen with the promise of clear weather, like so many of those other days when he and his companions had woken with the dawn.

He held his sword out forwards, his arm straight, elbow and wrist locked, the peacock-blue steel of the blade sitting still in his grip, and he smiled to himself grimly. There were few knights who were as old as he and yet still capable of holding their swords outstretched for any period. He was more than fifty years old now, and although he knew that he could best most men half his age, he had to pick his moments and his opponents.

Yet if there was one thing that the Templars had taught him, it was the benefit of constant practice. A man who trained was a man who could rely on his reflexes, and now Baldwin swung the sword in his wrist, first letting the point drop down then spinning it up on his right, then dropping it and flicking it up on the left of his forearm to form a figure 8. After twenty of those, he threw the sword spinning into the air, and caught it with his left hand, repeating the exercise before tossing it up again and catching it in his right hand once more.

Now he started the serious training. This was basic work, but he had performed these actions almost every morning since his acceptance into his Order. It was only at times of great pain that he had neglected his training, such as late last year, 1323, when the crossbow bolt had laid him low for so long.

He could consider the near-death with equanimity now, although at the time he had been appalled that he could die and leave his wife and daughter without a protector. True, Edgar would be there, and knowing Edgar he would continue to offer his support and what security he could to Baldwin's widow and offspring, but it wasn't the same.

It was a dreadful thought, that his wife should be widowed and left to fend for herself. Of all his nightmares, that was the one which recurred most often and left him distraught, unrefreshed and emotionally drained in the morning.

Jeanne de Liddinstone, as she had been before marrying Baldwin, had been born to a moderately wealthy family, but when they had been murdered she had left to live with family in Bordeaux, only returning when she married Ralph de Liddinstone.

Sadly Ralph proved to be a brute. He took to abusing his wife when she couldn't produce a child for him, and accused her of barrenness. Shortly before Baldwin first met her, Ralph died. A little while later, Baldwin married Jeanne. Now they had a daughter, Richalda.

He lifted the point of the blade so that the tip was in line with his arm, the point up-slanting, and then swivelled his body right, blocking an imaginary hack; with a flick of his wrist he moved the blade to point out to his right, and brought his fist across, the blade trailing, covering a thrust at his head. The sword's point fell and he covered a series of attacks at his legs, always a vulnerable target, especially in this age of staffs and polearms, then began a series of defensive manoeuvres, first to cover his right flank, then his left. At the end of this, he was panting, and there was a fine sheen of sweat over his features, as well as what felt like a small snake of ice on his spine where the perspiration had soaked into his shirt.

The only parts of his body that felt hot were his forearms and his wound.

His breast was so damp, he pulled his shirt away suspiciously and stared down to where the foul, swollen pock mark stood so plainly, thinking for a moment that the damned thing was leaking once more. For the last two months it had seemed fairly well on the way to healing, but before Christmas every time he exercised it had wept a watery, unpleasant liquor, and even some little while after Candlemas it had bled just a little. It was enough to make a man concern himself over his health. Especially now that he had something to lose, Baldwin told himself.

The sun was quite high in the sky now, and Baldwin stood staring ahead. The hills of Dartmoor were licked with a bright orange-pink glow where the sun hit them, while the parts the sun could not reach were blue-grey, with small flecks of what looked like whiteness to show where the frost still lay thickly on the grasses. It was a perfect, marvellous sight to Baldwin, who had spent so many years abroad in hot countries which had no frost to stimulate them.

'My husband? Are you training again?'

Baldwin narrowed his eyes and winced without turning at once. When he faced his wife, it was with an expression of bright cheerfulness. 'My love! I had thought to leave you resting. I didn't intend to wake you. I am sorry.'

'Husband, do you mean you've only just risen?' she asked.

'Of course,' he said with apparent surprise.

'Then you haven't been out here long enough to work up a sweat?'

He recoiled from the questing hand that snaked towards his back, growling. 'Woman, please leave my person. Treat an invalid with a little respect.'

'So much of an invalid that you can stand out here in the frost and the freezing air?'

'I was looking at the view,' he protested.

'With your sword in your hand,' she said with innocent deliberation.

'May I not keep anything secret from your suspicious mind?'

'Husband,' she said sweetly, 'do I hound you for all your secrets? I have no need. You give them up so easily and unintentionally.'

He scowled at her. It was impossible to be angry with her. Jeanne was perfection in his eyes, her round face framed by thick, red-gold tresses, blue eyes like cornflowers on a summer's afternoon, a small, almost tip-tilted nose, a wide mouth with an over-full upper lip which gave her a stubborn look – all in all, he had never seen any woman more beautiful. He growled, 'It is hardly comely for a wife to be so forthright.'

'It is hardly sensible for a wounded man to be testing his scars in the cold like this, especially after sleeping so badly.'

He looked away guiltily. 'It was nothing. I was thirsty.'

'In the middle of the night, and you were forced to leave our bed and fetch water? And couldn't return?'

'I was not tired once I rose, Jeanne,' he said, and then sighed. He picked up the scabbard again, thrust the sword home, and faced her. 'You are right, though. It is this shoulder of mine. The thing hurts whenever I lie still with it, and there seems to be nothing I can do to alleviate it.'

'You should rest it then, husband. Stop this foolish sword-waving in the early morning. Take things more easily; rest more.'

Baldwin nodded. 'Perhaps you are right.'

'Do not patronise me, Baldwin,' she said tartly. 'I won't have it.'

'I am sorry, then.'

'You are still convinced that there will be war?'

Baldwin shot her a look. They had set off on the way back to the house, and her tone was light, but there was an edge to it. 'Yes.'

'I am happy here now,' she said quietly. 'I was not when Ralph was alive. He was so different when he realised that we wouldn't have children. It made him bitter . . . bitter and cruel. You have changed my life for me. There are two men who have been consistently kind to me since I married Ralph: the Abbot of Tavistock, and you. I couldn't bear to lose you, Baldwin. You do realise that, don't you?'

'What brought this on?' he asked with some confusion. 'You will not lose me.'

'If there is a war, I may have to. You may be forced to ride to battle and leave me behind,' she said quietly. 'And when you ride away, you will go to find excitement. I don't begrudge you that, but you won't be thinking of me, will you? Nor of Richalda. You will be thinking of warfare and how to win renown by your prowess. Yet all the time I shall be here ready to mourn my loss . . . well, in truth, I will already be in mourning, because although I shall hope and pray that you will come home, it is possible that I shall never see you again, and that is a very hard thought to accept.'

'Jeanne, I swear to you that Richalda and you will never be far from my mind if it comes to war.' Seeing the doubt in her eyes, he took up his sword, and kissed the cross. 'I swear it, Jeanne! I practise here because I want to ensure that even if there is a war, I am fit enough and experienced enough to return to my home. I do not wish to die because of a moment's thoughtlessness. My training is perhaps all that can save me in a battle.' He looked behind them, back at the moors. When he spoke again, it was in a reflective tone, more gentle. 'You say that I ride for honour and excitement . . . well, it is possible that I could find myself honoured, but it is more likely that I would find myself dead. I have seen war. More men always die through starvation and pestilence than wounds won honourably on the field of battle. I fear that more than anything: a slow, lingering death at the roadside after the host has moved on, alone, without the opportunity to say farewell to you. If I go to war, Jeanne, my thoughts will be with you always . . .'

Jeanne was about to speak when there came an enraged bellow from the house. Jeanne closed her eyes and sighed, and Baldwin cast his eyes heavenwards. 'Is there no possibility of sending her home, Jeanne? Or anywhere else?'

Friar John set his jaw as he made his way rather laboriously up the lane towards the church. He had found a temporary place of refuge last night, a charcoal burner's hut in a coppice west of Iddesleigh, but after the foul discovery at the small holding he thought it might be better to move farther away as soon as he could. Friars were not usually so detested by the populace that they would be attacked, but a prudent man knew when to conceal himself, and a fellow who walked about after nightfall when there were plainly dangerous rogues abroad could soon become a target no matter how innocent.

There were two places on which John had counted in his life: churches and inns. In neither establishment was there anything for him to fear. Today, simply because the church was the nearer of the two, he entered that first, listening with a smile of gratitude to the creaking of the door hinges. To him, unoiled hinges had a sound all their own: the sound of comfort, holding the promise of warmth and dryness. There was a stoup of holy water by the door, and he dipped his fingers in it, closing his eyes and crossing himself fervently.

At times he'd been accused of play-acting. People said that a man who seemed so committed must by nature be more of a charlatan than a genuine man of God, but to that he answered that all must explain themselves before God when the time came. For his part, his conscience was clear. He had devoted his life to God and the spreading of His Gospel, and if men wished to mock, that was for them.

He turned to face the altar and stood a few moments studying the paintings on the walls. All were vivid – if lacking some artistic skill on occasion – and ideally suited to stirring the spirits of a peasant from an out of the way place like this.

That was half the battle. A man must always bear in mind the status and abilities of the folk to whom he was preaching. There was no earthly good in putting forward arguments that had been disputed in Oxford if the audience was a group of shepherds, carters, ploughmen and charcoal-burners. They wouldn't understand the niceties. Now, if John spoke to them, he'd pitch the story at a lower level, curse a bit, give them more of what they heard each day in the tavern. And from that perspective, this little church was ideal. It made the uneducated look at the walls. They couldn't retreat from them.

He knelt and bent his head, praying now for aid. Since finding the man last night, he had much to think through. There was his own mission, which must necessarily be suspended for a little while, and then there was much to learn. Such as, why should a man have been attacked like that in a quiet vill like this? What could have justified such a ferocious assault and murder?

This was a good place. It smelled right, not damp or musty, but earthy, with the tang of incense. A soft, mellow odour that reminded him always of his very first memories of a church.

'Master? May I help you? My name is Father Matthew.'

There was a tall, spare priest behind him, and John turned and smiled, grunting as he levered himself upwards. 'Father, I am glad to see you. I am Brother John, and while wandering these lands I wondered whether you would object to my preaching a little?'

The man's expression hardened. At John's words it looked as though his face was transformed into firm, unyielding *cuir bouilli* – leather boiled until it became almost as hard as metal. Then, just as John was expecting a firm rebuff, the man's features relaxed.

'I am sorry, Brother. The last preacher who came here listened to a man's confession and gave him such a light penance that the fellow went off and committed another crime. Since then, I have been wary of allowing friars to become involved with my flock. But it is silly to think that all friars are the same, just as it would be to say that all flowers are the same colour. Of course you may preach here, and if you wish to make use of my pulpit, you may. I do beg, though, that before offering to hear any confessions from my people you tell me first. There are some here who would be keen to speak to you rather than me. After all, if they talk to me, they will have to face me every day for the rest of their lives. Surely that is a part of their penance, just as much as a series of Pater Nosters.'

'I assure you I could not agree more,' John said. 'In these troubled times, a good priest must see to it that as many of his flock as possible see the errors of their ways. There is so much cruelty and evil in the world.'

'You can have no idea how correct you are,' Matthew said heavily. 'It sometimes seems that the whole world is at war to no purpose.'

'So many petty arguments,' John said. And then he added with truth, 'Feuds and disagreements are rife all over the country. Even in a place so seemingly quiet as this, I suppose?'

'This little vill is the property of one lord, and another craves it. Everywhere is in a ferment. Why, even last night there was an attack on a little holding . . .'

He shook his head, and then glanced behind him at a low doorway that gave into a small storage room. 'Brother, could I offer you some refreshment? I have spent all the morning so far at my glebe, and my hands are frozen even as are my insides. I feel the need for wine. Would you care for some?'

'I should be delighted,' John said enthusiastically.

They went into the storage area, where John sat on a low chest, while Matthew took his rest on a small, rough box which he unceremoniously emptied that he might perch on it up-ended.

'You have much land?'

'Yes, enough. And it is fruitful, God be praised! But the effort at this time of year – breaking up the soil is such cruel work. My hands are not so young as once they were.'

John nodded sympathetically. Matthew's hands were rough, dark-stained by the soil, and each finger had its own callus from the inevitable effort of working his private strips in the vill's fields. One had cracked so badly in the cold that a thin, weeping blood was oozing, but when Matthew saw that John had noticed it, he merely waved his hand and sucked it until the blood stopped flowing.

'Do you have many problems here?' John asked.

'Only the usual: recalcitrant folk who prefer to hold their tongues rather than confess in a mood of penitence, determined never to repeat their mistakes.'

'There would be little work for men of God if all were angels,' John said with a gentle smile.

'True,' Matthew said, but he frowned, peering into his cup as though the wine had turned to vinegar. 'Yet here matters seem to be growing worse.' He was a trusting man, and soon he was telling John all about the attack on the family a short way along the road. 'All dead, and the house burned.'

'You think that it was no common outlaw?'

Matthew shook his head. 'There are too many here who would have been glad to see that family gone.'

'Father? Is there something else troubling you? May I help?'

Matthew sat without speaking for a long time, as though holding a debate with himself about whether or not to speak, but in the end his desire to unburden his soul of his concerns overwhelmed his natural caution. 'There is one thing, my friend. South of here lies a little manor called Monkleigh, where there is a small chapel. For many years past this place has been served, and served well, in God's name, by a holy fellow called Isaac. Isaac is now very old, and I fear his hearing and eyes are failing him. So, some little while ago – it was last summer, I recall – a young priest was sent here to help him. This fellow has been there with Father Isaac for months now.'

'Surely that is good, though?' John asked.

Matthew smiled with his mouth, but his eyes were hard and suspicious when he looked up at John again. 'Aye, it should be. But I have never seen signs that he was truly sent from Exeter, and Isaac told me that he had never complained. And I believe that. He is not the sort of man to ask for help. So since the bishop has not held a visitation here in my memory, how did he come to hear of Isaac's infirmity?'

'Perhaps a friar saw him, or the magnate who lives in the hall decided to ease his load a little?' John hazarded.

'That God-damned scoundrel would rather murder Isaac and steal all he could from the chapel than try to assist an old man. No! The lad Humphrey was not sent here. I know it in my bones. I have seen him in the chapel, and while he is fluent enough in Latin . . . well, he is *too* fluent! You know the sort. He should be at Stapeldon College, rather than in a small chapel in the middle of the waste like this. And he speaks like a friar, too.'

'Ah!' John smiled as understanding broke upon him.

'Yes. I think he must be a runaway. Perhaps even a renegade friar.'

Chapter Seven

Robert Crokers squatted on his haunches at the doorway to his home and stared about him with a feeling of shock.

When he'd been forced away from the place, he'd had to go at once. There was no possibility that they'd allow him to remain. They wanted to make an example of him, that was plain enough: scare everyone into accepting that they had a new lord.

Looking about him now, he could see how well they had succeeded. All the peasants were standing about staring, their faces glum. The house was a burned wreck, the roof collapsed and walls blackened. The pen where he had held his sheep a short way down the hill had been pulled down, and although there were two corpses there, that was all. The others in the flock must have been stolen.

Still worse, for him, was the loss of his bitch. She was ready to whelp soon, a bright little dog who was ideal for the sheep. She never seemed to have to be told much; just a whistle and she'd go and do his bidding, rounding up the flock or directing it through one gate and keeping it together while Robert took them off to new pasture. She had been the best dog he'd ever owned, and he'd hoped that her pups would be as good. They could have been, since they were fathered by a shepherd's dog from the other side of Meeth. And now there was no sign of her. He was more distraught at the idea that she could have been killed than at all the rest of the damage put together.

Behind him, his companion muttered, 'Those murderous . . .'

Robert pulled a face. He felt close to tears to see how all the work he had put into this little holding had been destroyed in a few moments. 'It's not just them, though, is it, Walter?'

'No. It never is.'

Sir Odo was at Robert's right hand, still on his horse, nodding to himself. His face was remarkable for the scars which ranged down the left side, from his temple, over his cheek, and down to the line of his jaw. Many years before, so Robert had heard, Sir Odo had taken a bad fall from a galloping stallion during a hunt, knocked down by a low branch. He had been pulled along, one foot stuck in the stirrup, for many yards along a stony track, and much of the flesh had been torn from that side of his face.

Many thought him a violent, cruel man. Here, where he was the steward of the manor for Sir John de Sully, he was feared and respected in equal measure. Many were terrified of his mere appearance, and children all over the area would be silenced and forced to behave by the threat that, 'If you don't do as I say, I'll ask Sir Odo to visit you!'

To Robert, who worked for him as the manor's bailiff, Sir Odo was a much more genial and kindly man than his reputation would have implied. It was a shock when Robert first met him, because no one had warned him of Sir Odo's looks. Ach, Robert knew that plenty of men would think it good sport to leave a man in an embarrassing position like that, springing upon him the fact of his master's deformity, but Robert had been collected enough when first meeting the steward not to flinch. He simply gave a small bow, then walked to Sir Odo and passed him his papers without speaking.

'They didn't warn you?' Sir Odo grated. His voice was like slabs of stone sliding over each other.

'No one, Sir Odo, no.'

'They never do. Think it's fun to bring men in here who don't know, and then see how they respond, as though someone might one day burst into insane giggling and bolt. Or maybe they think I could leap at someone for his disrespect.' He paused, musing.

'I think there's never any reflection intended on you, sir. Only on the poor fool who enters your hall.'

'Perhaps you're right. I won't have them flogged, then, for their discourtesy . . . not to me, anyway.'

His bantering tone of voice had made Robert realise almost immediately that this man was in reality greatly hurt that some should use his old scars as a means of upsetting new members of the household. It was natural, true, that newcomers should be put in their place by the team which had been there longer, but to make sport of their master's suffering struck him as cruel in the extreme and he decided on the spot that he would never do so himself. Any men he brought here would be forewarned of Sir Odo's wounds.

'You are sure it was that cur's whelp, Sir Geoffrey?' Sir Odo asked now.

'Yes. He and his men were without disguise. They all wore the tunics of their master.'

Sir Odo grunted and turned his eye towards the house again. He sat on his horse like a man who had been born in a saddle, Robert thought, but now the man's head was sunk deep into his shoulders as though he was exhausted by all this talk of their neighbour. 'He didn't think to leave a guard, then?'

'No, Sir Odo. I suppose he knew we'd come in force if we didn't come immediately,' Robert said.

'Of course. And there was no point in coming in the middle of the night. We had to wait for the day . . . So! This is just more needling. He doesn't expect us to give it up without a fight, of course, but he intends to keep on prodding and provoking, and maybe later, he will choose to force us.'

'He couldn't do that!' Robert declared hotly. 'He must know that Sir John Sully has powerful friends.'

Sir Odo glanced at him, and the scarred side of his face seemed to colour a little, as though his angry thoughts were changing his habitual phlegmatic temperament into a fresh, choleric one. 'That prickle is a trouble-maker of the worst kind. He makes no assessment of the risks of his actions, he just takes on any challenge like a bull. If his master told him to lay about him round here with a heavy hand, that's what he would do.'

'You think his master ordered this?' Robert faltered. He had not realised the depths of the mire into which he was falling.

'Do you really think that a man as experienced as Sir Geoffrey would dream of attacking a lord's lands like this without considering the risks? The fact he went ahead shows that he must have been told to, or he had the idea himself and had it sanctioned.'

'Surely a knight wouldn't do something like this,' Robert said and waved a hand about the desolation that was his home. 'Not even if his master told him to.'

Sir Odo looked at him for a long moment. 'That man needs to be told whether or not he should lay a turd in the morning, is what I think. He has a desire to please his master at all times, and no matter who or what stands in the way, he will destroy them if it is his master's choice. And his master is keen to acquire as much as he can.'

'He is a man with a long reach,' Robert said soberly.

'My lords the Earl of Winchester and his son Hugh Despenser are keen to confirm their authority,' Sir Odo said obliquely.

Robert nodded without noticing the knight's quick look. It was only later that he remembered the conversation and understood that Sir Odo wouldn't abuse the Despensers in front of a man he hardly knew. For all he knew, Robert could be a spy for Earl Hugh. 'So what should we do?'

Sir Odo snorted and yanked his mount's head about. 'There's nothing *to* do, apart from warn our master and, through him, Lord de Courtenay. And protect these lands. They are our master's, and no one will steal them from us, not without suffering a great deal of bloodshed!'

Perkin hadn't felt remotely satisfied with the result of the inquest, but what else could be expected? The whole of the local jury had been called to the manor's court, and some smart knight from down Bude way had come up and listened to the evidence, eyeing the body without much enthusiasm while holding a bag of sweet herbs under his nose. The fool looked as if he was staring at a dog's turd, rather than a man who'd been murdered.

Ailward was beginning to smell a bit by then, mind. It wasn't just the coroner who thought the odour was too strong. There was that slightly musty, sweet sickliness to it that spoke of the time the body had been stored since its discovery. To protect it – well, no one ever knew how long it'd take for a coroner to arrive in the middle of winter, and the vill had the responsibility of protecting the corpse from all animals, wild and domestic, on pain of a large fine – they had built a stone wall round it, putting a roof of turves over to save the body from the elements, and there was a man or a boy constantly there to watch over him, day and night, until this Sir Edward de Launcelles turned up.

He seemed less pathetic than some, Perkin reckoned. Stood up there in front of all the jury without looking too embarrassed. Some of them, they looked too young to be wearing the knight's belt and golden spurs. This one at least, for all his apparent smarminess and courtly mannerisms, seemed to have had some experience of life. His face wore two scars which looked like fighting wounds, and he'd lost two fingers from his left hand. Perkin knew that men would often lose fingers there when they were fighting with swords. All too often a man would grab an opponent's blade for an instant while thrusting his own home, and sometimes a finger or two would be severed.

A gust of wind wafted Ailward's scent over the jury and Perkin saw a number blench and gag. It was a bloody foul odour, right enough. He wondered what the other would smell like now. It was a week since Lady Lucy of Meeth had disappeared, and the poor woman must surely be dead herself. Strange that no one had seen her. Her steward had been found on the same day that she had been taken, his body left slumped at the side of the road, his sword out of the scabbard and in his hand as though he had tried to defend her, but unsuccessfully. She was gone, though. No man had seen her since. Perkin was sure she had been taken and killed. There were many who could have desired her for her body, but many more about here would have wanted her lands. They were good and fruitful, bringing in several pounds in cash a year.

Perkin felt sick at the thought, but he could not help but recall that his own master, Sir Geoffrey, had ridden out and attacked Robert Crokers's house on Saturday. Apparently that was because Sir Geoffrey wanted the land for his own master and was prepared to take it at sword's point . . . how much easier to take a woman recently widowed and hold a knife to her throat until she agreed to hand over her properties.

If so, it would be this coroner, perhaps, who came to listen to the evidence. Perkin watched him more closely.

At first he thought Sir Edward de Launcelles appeared to be a fair enough man. 'Where is the First Finder of this body?'

'Here, sir. I am Perkin from Monkleigh.'

'Who can vouch for him?'

As three men from the jury gave their names, Perkin found himself being scrutinised closely. The knight had pale eyes that were the colour of the sky on a grim and rain-filled day: grey with a hint of angry amber. He had very prominent cheekbones, which made him look gaunt, as all the men did after the famine, but his lips were very full and red, as though he was feverish, not pale like those of the men and women who had starved. His chin, too, was pointed, with a cleft in it. The beard was obviously hard to shave in that little gully, and there was a vertical band of black hair in it that looked entirely out of place on such a fastidious-seeming man.

'So you found him?' The corner was curling his lip at the man's body before him.

'I tripped and then I saw the blood.'

So much, there had been. Ailward's head was smashed like an egg, with loose bits and pieces of skull shifting under the ruined scalp. Perkin felt sick just to remember it.

The inquest went much as Perkin had expected, with an amercement for him, more from all the witnesses, and the value of the weapon being guessed at. The coroner's job was to record all the relevant details of a suspicious death, so that when the case was investigated later in court, all the men involved could be called to give their accounts. Amercements were taken as sureties to make certain that all the witnesses turned up at the court.

When the stranger turned up, Perkin wondered who he was. He didn't recognise the man, and he assumed, like the other men there, that the fellow was a passing merchant who had heard about the inquest and decided to go and watch the proceedings. You sometimes got that, when people were staying in an inn: if they heard that there was some form of local dispute or death which could be diverting, they'd go along.

Except this man seemed rather odd. He looked young, well-groomed, and nervous, which was curious in a man who was travelling. Usually the sort of merchant who passed by Iddesleigh and Monkleigh was already stained and worn, especially at this time of year, and they were invariably gregarious, often trying to foist their more rubbishy wares onto unsuspecting villagers. It was hardly surprising, bearing in mind how far they would have travelled already and how much further they must go to reach any decent towns.

The fellow stood quietly at the rear of the witnesses, listening intently, a good-looking man in a newish green tunic with a heavy crimson cloak about him. He carried a solid staff, and at his waist there was a dagger alongside his leather purse and horn.

It was very odd, and Perkin looked away only reluctantly, eyeing the coroner as he pronounced on the case. It was as Perkin had expected: because the vill could not bring forward any suspects who might have killed Ailward, they were to pay the murdrum, the tax levied for planned homicides.

Perkin knew that some believed that he could be the murderer, but for all those who believed he had motive enough there were dozens more who thought it was likely to be Rannulf, or perhaps one of the men from Fishleigh. Fortunately Perkin had good alibis for the afternoon and evening, and in any case he was known for his mild manner. Not enough men in the jury were prepared to accuse him; many others had more reason to wish to kill Ailward. Plenty of others.

But such matters were not the business of the coroner. Perkin listened as the case was wound up, and watched thoughtfully as the clerk started putting his rushes and inks away in his scrip. All Perkin could think of was the detail he had left out.

It was not in his nature to lie. He knew that an oath sworn here in the court was as binding in God's eyes as an oath in church with his hand resting on the gospels. Yet he had felt it might be best not to mention the reason why he had gone up there. He was sure now that Walter and Ailward had been there together. When Perkin stumbled upon them, Walter grabbed the ball to turn all the camp ball players away from Ailward. And the reason was obvious to Perkin now: they were concealing a body.

He had kept it to himself in the coroner's court because he had no proof, and he daren't accuse Walter. What, he should say that Walter and Ailward were carrying another dead body? He'd be laughed out of the court – and then be accused of villeiny-saying, spreading malicious lies about other men. That would cost him at least a huge fine in these litigious times. He hadn't even told Beorn or Guy. Yet he was sure that Walter and Ailward were hiding someone, and he had a suspicion he knew who it was, too. Lady Lucy had been missing for some little while.

Perkin grew aware of the well-dressed stranger sidling towards the knight. As the coroner patted the clerk on the back and made as though to leave, the stranger reached him and spoke urgently. The knight looked him up and down, glanced round the jury and witnesses, and then nodded.

Watching them walk away, Perkin frowned. There was something strange here, he could see, but he wasn't sure what it was. All he knew was that he was delighted he hadn't told the coroner anything of his doubts.

It was only later that afternoon, when he heard of the deaths at the little house at Iddesleigh the day before, that he began to wonder who it was who had arrived to take the coroner away with him.

Late on Tuesday morning Baldwin was aching again when he drew up at the manor at Liddinstone and slowly eased himself from the saddle. He stood a while, slowly swinging his arm, feeling the pain in his upper breast and wincing as the muscles stretched and contracted.

'My love – I was growing worried lest you had fallen,' Jeanne said.

'I did not see you there,' Baldwin said. He passed the reins to the waiting stable boy and only with an effort of will did he avoid reaching up to his shoulder. If he did that, Jeanne would stop him riding and make his life hell.

'I came to watch for you,' she said.

He eyed her suspiciously. There was a lightness to her tone which seemed to belie her words. 'That is all?'

'Of course, husband. The air in the hall is a little stale.'

'I see,' he said, nodding but unconvinced.

'And . . .'

To his secret delight, he saw that she was colouring. If there was something to embarrass her, he would be safe from condemnation for riding too far. 'Yes?'

'Oh . . . nothing.'

And it *was* nothing, Jeanne told herself. Merely the foolish words of a maid who should know better. Nothing more than that.

It was Emma again.

Baldwin had never liked Jeanne's companion, and, to be fair, Jeanne could easily have found a more congenial maid. Yet there was something about Emma's bovine loyalty which comforted her. Emma was stolid and ugly, heavy, slow, dull-witted and moody, and yet she plainly adored Jeanne, and for that reason alone it was hard to conceive of sending her away. Unfortunately, Emma had been very fond of Jeanne's first husband, and no replacement would ever be able to live up to him in her eyes.

This morning, while Baldwin was off riding, Emma had told Jeanne that Sir Baldwin was looking very 'done in', and that Jeanne should demand that he give up all exercise and betake himself to his bed to rest. Emma had very pronounced views on the efficacy of rest for all ills, and she felt certain that Jeanne's husband was in desperate need of it. However, she could not make any comment without comparing Baldwin to Sir Ralph, and this morning she had spoken unfavourably about Baldwin's reluctance to support either of the factions in the country's politics.

Other men were bold and sought to promote the interests of their lords: some the Lord de Courtenay, some the Lords Despenser and the king. 'Because it will come to war, lady, make no mistake!' Emma had declared, jowls wobbling.

It was hard, when Emma was in such a state, not to study her closely. She was short, but with a large frame, and her breast was carried like a weapon, projecting far before her. Her eyes were a soft brown, but Baldwin had once said that they held the bile and spite of a dozen Moors whenever they latched on to him. Jeanne knew what he meant, because Emma's eyes were shrewd and calculating. When she fixed a man with her gaze, he would quail. The jut of her warty chin was enough to make a lion whimper. Jeanne had seen strong market stall holders blench when she fixed them with her sternest look.

When Emma compared Baldwin with her first husband, Jeanne would try to defend him, but in Emma's eyes it was irrelevant what the man said or did. She adored Jeanne, and in the usual way anything that would make Jeanne happy was Emma's delight, but that did not extend to Baldwin.

When Emma and he had first met, she had been entirely unimpressed with his home, his lands and his choice of companions in his hall. Most despised of all, as Jeanne and Baldwin knew only too well, was his mastiff, Uther. Emma detested the old monster, and although even Baldwin could, on occasion, admit that Uther was a little overwhelming at times, he would never admit that in front of Emma, and especially not since Uther had died. If anything, his loyalty to the brute had increased rather than diminished now that Uther was dead.

In like fashion, Emma would not give up her oft-stated opinion that the animal was a vicious monster that should have been killed when still a pup, before he could upset anybody else. The only thing Baldwin had ever done, or rather not done, that had elevated him in her opinion was to decide not to replace Uther when the dog died.

However, his reluctance to speak for either side in the present political climate struck Emma as dishonourable.

'That's what it seems like to me, and I speak as I find. Can't abide people who won't stand by their lords. Look at him! He should declare his loyalties, either to the king or to the Lord de Courtenay. Where's the difficulty in that?'

'Enough, Emma! It is not your place to decide where his duty lies!' Jeanne snapped at last.

'No, my lady, but it'll be his soon enough, when there is a fight down here, on our manor, or perhaps on his own up at Furnshill,' Emma retorted. 'He should state where his allegiance lies, that's all I'm saying. Hoi! You! Where are you going with that?' and she was off after a hapless peasant before Jeanne could reprimand her again.

The worst of it was not Emma's blundering clumsiness in her language, nor the apparent pleasure she took in denigrating Baldwin, a man whom Jeanne was sure Emma had never liked, but more the disloyal feeling in Jeanne's own breast that her husband really should have declared on which side his interests lay. There were so many men for whom life under the present rule was all but intolerable. The

Despensers were notoriously and aggressively acquisitive. They could not see or hear of another man's wealth without attempting to steal it.

No, Jeanne would hate to think that her Baldwin could join the king and the Despensers and fight for them. Only recently the Lord Mortimer had escaped from the Tower in London, and made his way overseas somehow, if the rumours were true. Baldwin had been told by another judge at the Court of Gaol Delivery that Mortimer was in French territory. His liberty had to be a massive concern for the Despensers because they knew Mortimer was the only one of their enemies left with extensive military experience. If he returned to Britain, Baldwin said, he could pose a threat to them, and maybe even the king himself.

'Are you well?' Baldwin asked.

She smiled at his solicitous tone. 'Do not try to change the subject. You know that I was worried about you because if you were to have a fall you might not be found for an age. If you have to go riding, could you not take a man with you?'

'My love, I was only going for a canter around your lands.' Baldwin sighed. 'I have ridden in more dangerous locations, you know.'

'Yes, I know, but a wounded man who falls can die all too easily. You should be resting, husband!'

He groaned. 'I need to be fit, woman! I have to get myself ready again . . .'

'For what? Do you think that if the king was to send his host to Scotland again, he'd order all the oldest knights to join him?'

'I don't think I'm quite his oldest,' Baldwin protested.

'Perhaps not quite,' she agreed.

'I'm good enough for some activities still,' he persisted.

As they had spoken, they had left the stables, and now they stood before the little manor. 'Do not think to get round me like that!' she scolded him.

'If you won't stop your nagging,' he said firmly, stepping forward until her back was against the wall of the manor, 'I shall have to see how I may silence you.'

'You won't stop me by frivolous diversions. I want you to rest more.'

'Don't avert your face, woman,' he growled, mock-aggressively, putting a hand to her throat and turning her face towards him with his thumb.

'Mistress?'

Baldwin stared deeply into his wife's widely innocent eyes. 'I swear I'll murder that . . .'

'We're here, Emma!' Jeanne called happily, slipping under his arm and away. 'What is it?'

Emma looked from one to the other with a scowl of distaste on her face. 'There's a message for the master. Sir Baldwin, I think you should come and see this wretch.'

'Who is it?' Baldwin demanded, furious to have missed an opportunity for dalliance with his wife, but pleased that at least Jeanne could not return to her attack about his resting.

'Sir Baldwin! It's me, sir, Wat. I have an urgent message from Edgar!'

Chapter Eight

Robert Crokers had needed all the Sunday and Monday just to clear the mess from his house. The fire had taken all his belongings with it, and the building was a blackened shell that stank of tar and soot, but with the help of the man whom Sir Odo had brought it was soon cleared out, and the rubbish taken to his little midden.

The worst of the burned rafters had been pulled down, apart from one which wouldn't break apart, and that they had left, assuming that if the weight of three men dangling from it wouldn't move it, neither would some straw thatching. They'd swept and brushed the walls and floor until the stench of burning was all but gone, and meanwhile others had thrown poles up over the roof to create a ridge, to which they nailed long, thin planks. Before long, straw brought from Sir Odo's storehouse had been thrown haphazardly on top, and today two of the men from the vill who were best at thatching came to finish the job, complaining all the while that the men should have waited for them to arrive.

'It'd have been easier if those useless turds had laid the straw more carefully.'

'Ah. If they had more than shit for brains, they'd be dangerous,' his friend commented, chewing a straw.

Still, by the middle of the third day, the Tuesday, the house was almost renewed. There was a roof, and Robert had a palliasse laid out on a low, rough bed. His hearth was soon lighted, and for lunch he was able to set his pot over the fire and make his own pottage from the peas and leaves which Odo's men had left for him.

'Should be all right now,' said Walter. He was a cadaverously thin man, one of Sir Odo's older men-at-arms, who squatted beside the fire and held his gnarled hands to it appreciatively. 'The roof is safe enough.'

'What if they come back, though?' Robert said. 'Here I'm an easy target for them.'

Walter sniffed, his sunburned face the colour of old chestnut. His eyes were almost hidden beneath his thick brows, and he shot a look at Robert, then hawked and spat into the fire. 'They're not after you personally. Just the land. Anyway, I doubt whether they'll be back here for a while.'

'Why? How can you be so sure?'

'They've left a message. They wanted Sir Odo to know they want this land, and they'll gradually try to increase the pressure on him to give it up and leave all the land this side of the river to them.'

'So they could return at any time?' Robert squeaked.

'No. Now they've sent the warning, they'll start to use the courts. This was just to stop anyone arguing and making the lawyers' fees too high. That's all.'

'But Sir Odo can't give up the land – it's not his. What then?'

'They may come back and threaten war, but you should be safe enough. Why'd they hurt you? You're nothing to them. No, if they wanted to do some damage, fine, they'd come here and warn you off, then fire the house. Meanwhile they'd be doing all they could to force Sir Odo, and through him Sir John Sully, off this land. If they could, they'd get the rest of the manor too. They like land.'

'How could an honourable knight behave like that, though?' Robert demanded. 'Surely Sir Geoffrey is a true knight?'

Walter gave him a look in which surprise and contempt were equally mixed. 'Of course he is. And all he's doing is what a true knight should: following his master's bidding.'

Robert nodded. He knew nothing of the ways of fighting men. All he really knew was sheep and sheepdogs.

And now he had neither, he reminded himself as the tears threatened to engulf him again.

When she had first met Wat, Jeanne had been unimpressed by the round-faced boy with the shock of unruly hair and the vacant expression. Although, to be fair, perhaps her opinion of him was coloured slightly by the lad's behaviour on her wedding day, when he drank so much of the strong ale beforehand that as the wedding party left the church door, all guffawed at the fellow who was propped like a sack of swedes at a wagon's wheel. Even as he tried to squint at the crowd, he started to slip down, and only Simon's servant, Hugh, saved him from complete collapse.

Now, though, he had grown into a man with enough good looks to tempt any of the maids in the vill to take a tumble with him in a hayrick, were he to ask them. Jeanne could see her dairy maid loitering at the house's corner, and, seeing how the girl took a deep breath and bent her back slightly as he noticed her, she was sure that it was time to worry about the arrival of an irate parent demanding compensation for the arrival of a fresh bastard in his family. She would have to speak to Baldwin before things got out of hand – but then she noticed that although Wat gave the girl an appreciative leer his expression was serious, even sad, when he looked at his master. There were more important matters on his mind.

Baldwin had not yet cast a glance at Wat, but he too saw the girl, and snapped, 'Wat, take your eyes off her and stop drooling. What are you doing here?'

'Sir Baldwin, it was a messenger came to Edgar, thinking to find you. A lad from Iddesleigh. He'd ridden as soon as the news came, so he said.'

'What news?'

Jeanne could feel her man tense, as though he reckoned that this could be the call to war.

Wat lowered his eyes. 'There's been an attack on a smallholding. Hugh's.'

'You mean Simon's servant?'

'Yes, sir. It sounds like Hugh's dead, and his woman with him. Men rode in at night and fired the place.'

Baldwin was strangely still. Jeanne could feel the energy rushing through his veins, and she tightened her grip on his arm, as though by so doing she could persuade him to remain with her and not to fly off to Iddesleigh.

'Was there any message about who was responsible?' Baldwin asked.

'No, sir. They didn't know.'

'Have they had the coroner?'

'I don't know. They should have.'

'True. So when was this news brought?'

'Last afternoon. Edgar told me to mount and come here as soon as he heard. I had to stop the night at Crediton and came on at first light,' Wat said.

'Good,' Baldwin said. 'And what else did Edgar want you to say?'

'Nothing. Only that he would be packing and leaving for Iddesleigh this morning. He'll meet you there, Sir Baldwin.'

'I see.' He stood deep in thought. 'Wat, you must ride for Lydford and see whether Simon's there at his house. I don't think he will be, but it'll be a good ride for you from here. If he's not there, go to Tavistock to the abbot, and tell him what you've said here. The good abbot will send a messenger on to Simon at Dartmouth, if he's there.'

'Sir.'

'Wait! First take some rest. You must be exhausted. Have some ale and cheese while a horse is prepared, then take a loaf and some meat to pack in your bag. And Wat!' Baldwin reached into his small purse and pulled out a penny. 'Well done for coming here so swiftly.'

While the boy was taken away by the milkmaid to be shown where the pantry was, Baldwin waited for the inevitable argument. When there was no comment, he tentatively cleared his throat. 'I am sorry, my love, but I have to . . .'

'Of course we do.'

He blinked. 'I think I should go alone.'

'With your wounds unhealed? That would be most intelligent, husband. If you fall from your horse between here and Iddesleigh, whom will you expect to find you and bring you home?'

'It is a long road, my sweet.'

'Many are, my love. Which means we should pack. I shall see to it.'

'But . . .'

'You should eat something too, if we're to set off as soon as we can,' Jeanne said firmly, and was gone.

* * *

Humphrey was feeling as though his back was soon to break when he stopped his work and stood slowly, rubbing at the muscles above his buttocks.

There was too much to be done, that was the trouble. Old Isaac had many strips of land in the communal fields, and all had to be tilled. For Humphrey, that meant more work. He had to look after the fields as well as taking the services for Isaac. There could be no leisure for a parish priest. He was another local farmer, just like all the others, and like all the others he must work if he wanted to eat.

Today he was in the strip nearest the road. All the villagers had strips in this great field, and all were widely separated. This was the first of the priest's strips, and his next was way along there, ninety yards or so. Each strip was over an acre, too, so that the amount of land available to each inhabitant of the vill was quite large. Not as fruitful as some places Humphrey had seen, it was true, but it wasn't as desolate as others, either.

When he looked up, there was a man walking along the roadway, a cheerful-looking friar, with a smiling face, flaming red cheeks, and that appearance of *drawnness* which so many friars wore.

They were a scavenging breed, the friars. As Humphrey knew only too well, they were detested by many in the Church, and with good reason. Friars would take the money which parishioners should give to their own church; they offered mild penances when they heard confessions, penances that could do little good to the poor soul who had confessed and whose very leniency must devalue the whole structure of the Church's efforts to prevent sin. In any case, making confession to a wanderer whom a man would never see again was easier, and thus less morally efficacious, than confessing to a priest with whom the penitent tilled the soil, ploughed, drank and ate. There was shame and embarrassment in admitting a sin to a companion, whereas a friar . . . a man could admit anything to one of them and forget it in moments.

Humphrey knew all the arguments against friars. He had heard Isaac rehearse them often enough. Right now he was only glad that Isaac was not here to see the scruffy fellow passing by.

'God grant you peace,' he said when the friar came closer.

'God's blessing on you,' the friar responded.

Now that he was closer, Humphrey could see that he was still less prepossessing than he had originally thought. Humphrey didn't recognise him, which was a relief – that could have been embarrassing . . . As it was, it was annoying to have to stop his work to offer hospitality to someone whom he did not wish to entertain.

'You are far from any main roadway, Brother,' he said.

'Ah, I wander where God wills it,' the friar said. 'I am called John. I had thought to stay in this area and preach a little. Father Matthew thought it would be all right?'

There was a question in his voice which Humphrey could not miss. It was, in truth, a generous question. He had no need to request permission, and this John would have been well within his rights to go wherever he wished, preaching every hour of every day, if he so desired; but there had been friction for some years between Holy Mother Church and the friars, and it was good that this one at least appeared keen to avoid arguments.

Humphrey shrugged a little gracelessly. 'Brother, if you wish to do so I wouldn't stop you, but I am only a coadjutor here. The priest himself is . . . not well.'

The friar's face grew grim. 'It is good to see an assistant helping an older man. Is he very ill?'

'He is. But it is age which ails him. I have heard it said that he has lived here as priest for nearly three and forty years, and from the look of the records in the church, that could be correct.'

'Do you think that my presence could offend him?' the friar asked tentatively. 'I should prefer not to preach where my words could upset a sick man.'

'That is very kind of you, Brother. I think,' Humphry said consideringly, 'that if you preach away from the church here, and not right in front of the alehouse at the top of the road, you will be unlikely to cause him offence.'

'He spends much time there?'

'It is easier for me to leave him in the alehouse than alone in the church while I do the work.' Humphrey shrugged. 'I prefer to know that he is safe. If he were to remain in the church all day, he might fall and harm himself.'

'You are a good man, my friend,' Friar John said. 'And now, if you do not mind, I think I should seek out the tavern – not to preach, but to beg a little bread.'

'Brother, if I had anything with me, I would . . .'

The friar held up his hand. 'Friend, please. I would not impose further upon you. No, I shall go to the tavern. No doubt they earn enough to subsidise a poor wanderer without harming their own pockets! Where is this place?'

Humphrey gave brief directions, and then smiled and nodded as the man carried on his way towards the vill of Monkleigh. He watched until the friar had disappeared round the bend in the road and was hidden by the trees.

'Some wandering preacher?'

Humphrey felt the breath catch in his throat, and he spun on his heel, his heart thundering. 'Pagan! In God's name, man, where did you come from?'

'I was going to the inn to buy a barrel of ale. Why?'

'You half emasculated me, man! Walking up behind a fellow like that . . .'

'What did he want?'

'Permission to preach. Nothing more.'

'You should be wary of such men. No good comes of having those preachers wandering about the place,' Pagan said.

'You don't know what you're talking about.'

'When I was young, they found a friar who'd killed a young boy. He claimed the protection of the Church, of course, but we all knew what he'd done.'

'I hadn't heard of that,' Humphrey said.

'Before your time. If you have a man like that about the place, there's no telling what might happen.'

'It can scarcely be worse than it already is,' Humphrey said. 'Had you not heard about that poor man up east of Iddesleigh, with his wife and child?'

'I'd heard. And there is still Lady Lucy of Meeth. No one knows where she is.'

'So one friar can hardly do much harm,' Humphrey said.

'A friar can always cause more harm,' Pagan said, and he looked at Humphrey with what appeared to be a cold challenge in his eyes that made Humphrey feel quite chilled. 'I would have thought you'd know that.'

Late that night Perkin and Beorn met at Guy's house.

The weather was bitter, and all three were glad of the fire crackling merrily in the hearth. They squatted on their haunches, holding their hands to the flames. Today they had been working on the manor's land, and all were desperate for refreshment.

Guy was married with four children. He had been lucky, and ever since the famine he had waxed wealthy. His strips produced a good crop each year, and so far he had been able to feed all his family without too much difficulty. Last week his wife had brewed a fresh barrel of ale, and the others were here to test its quality. It was commonly agreed that Anne was one of the best alewives in the county, so all three of the men were keenly looking forward to sampling her brew.

Perkin took a long pull from his mug. The house was very crowded, with Guy's wife and children all asleep on the low bed in the corner, while smoke billowed from the central hearth. There was a table, with one low bench running down one side, and a stool for Anne. Apart from that, the living space was filled with the assorted rubbish that houses full of children tended to gather: a rude hobby-horse, dolls made of straw and clothed in scraps, sticks with cross-guards tied in place in imitation of swords, a single small chest with clothes piled on top to save them falling on the damp floor. A vast black cauldron sat nearby, with all the house's plates and wooden spoons protruding from it.

It was small, crowded, and none the worse for that. From here, Perkin knew that his friend could sit and view his wife and children as well as the ox that stood quietly in the far end of the place snuffling at a pile of hay. It was good that a man could contemplate his life.

There was a price to be paid for sitting here and drinking a man's ale. Both the visitors had their knives out and were whittling busily at the bits and pieces of wood Guy had given them. He had need of more spoons for his children, and it was common for men like them to carve as they chatted. There was always a need for a new spoon, a trencher, or a cup, and while the women spun wool their men might as well work too.

'What did you make of the coroner?' Perkin asked Guy.

'A knight. What else?'

Beorn snorted. 'A friend of our master, I reckon.'

'Sir Geoffrey? Why say that?'

'Didn't you see the long streak of piss who wanted to talk to him after the inquest?' Beorn demanded.

Perkin's ears pricked up. 'I saw him, but didn't know him. Who was he?'

'Adam, our new sergeant, although he's always called Adcock, apparently. He went up to the coroner and asked him to go to the big house.'

'You think the master's got an idea about Ailward's death?' Guy asked anxiously.

'The coroner said it was someone else, not us. That's enough for everyone,' Perkin said firmly. 'The master won't want to have a load of accusations flying around here disrupting things. His job is purely to take money from us. He can't do that if we're in gaol.'

Beorn shot him a sidelong look, but said nothing.

Guy frowned, then looked down at the spoon he was carving. 'What of the poor devil up the way?'

They all knew whom he meant. There had been little else discussed in the vill since it had learned of the attack up in Iddesleigh. A whole family wiped out.

Beorn scowled at the fire. 'Who'd have done a thing like that? It looked like a bunch of felons.'

'We know who was out that day, though, don't we?' Perkin said in a low voice, glancing over his shoulder to see that the children and Anne weren't listening.

Guy glared at him. 'I won't have that sort of talk in my house, Perkin.'

'You can try to ignore it if you want, but it's not going to help when Sir Odo comes to defend his own, is it?' Perkin hissed.

'He won't dare,' Beorn said confidently. 'What could he do? Raid and kill a few men from Sir Geoffrey's household? The retribution would be terrible.'

'Sir Odo has the reputation of being a strong, fierce warrior,' Guy said.

'Aye,' Perkin said. 'And I think he'd spit in Sir Geoffrey's eye for a penny. This will leave him sore, you mark my words. You can't attack a peasant in another manor without the lord coming for compensation.'

'If he had proof, you'd be right,' Beorn said, 'but I'd bet a sack of oats that there's no one will own to seeing Sir Geoffrey's men, and that any man who tried to take a matter like this to court would soon find himself out of pocket, and without his lands either.'

'A whole family,' Perkin said, shaking his head. He turned and looked over his shoulder at Guy's sleeping children. The sight was warming, and the idea that a lord could decide to wipe them out was terrifying. 'Why'd he want to hurt them, anyway? They hadn't been here that long.'

'I heard that the woman was a nun who'd left her convent,' Beorn said. 'Good-looking wench.'

'They had a little boy.' Perkin had seen the lad once. He didn't often have need to go so far as Iddesleigh, but he'd once had to walk up past it, and he could vaguely recall a tall, elegant fair woman, with a little boy on her hip.

Guy shook his head. 'What could they have done to deserve an attack like that?'

It was Beorn who sighed and shook his head. 'Whatever it was, it's probably died with them.'

'I saw Pagan earlier today,' Guy said slowly. 'He said that there was a stranger in the area. A friar.'

Perkin glanced up at him. 'So? You don't say a friar could have done that to the family?'

'There are always stories . . . She was good looking.'

'Yes, there are always stories,' Perkin scoffed. 'And there is silliness wherever you look. But that man's family was wiped out in the same evening that Robert Crokers was forced from his home. And you know as well as I do that Sir Geoffrey has looked with interest at all the lands this side of the river. How better to leave a message about his intentions than an attack on a defenceless family?'

Beorn shook his head as he held up his spoon and studied it critically. 'I wonder what did happen to that poor woman from Meeth?'

'I suppose she'll be found someday soon,' Guy said. 'At least she wasn't one of our own born down here.'

Perkin sighed. 'She was a widow. No one to defend her. And her lands must be as attractive as any other to Sir Geoffrey.'

It was no more than the truth. Women were rarely taken and killed here, but it wasn't unknown. To think that a widow like her could be kidnapped and killed was awful, though. Perkin only hoped she had died before she could suffer too much. 'I dare say we'll soon find her, Guy, just as you say.'

Chapter Nine

Sir Geoffrey was in his hall.

This was a good place to live. In his youth, Sir Geoffrey had been an unknown knight in Gascony, and when he had won his spurs he left his home to seek his fortune. Travelling all over Christendom with a lance and the determination to make himself a name, he had won fabulous sums at tournaments, eventually finishing up at a tourney in Fontevrault in Anjou. It was a quiet affair. The French king of the time, Philip IV, felt less strong than he should and wanted to prevent any gatherings of armed men on his lands, and had decided to ban all tournaments from his domain. Of course the County of Anjou was not a part of the royal demesne, but it was felt better not to advertise the tournament too widely at the time. The count didn't want to antagonise the king – but he did wish to celebrate the knighting of his eldest son, so he would have a tournament.

Only a select number of knights were invited to participate, and Geoffrey felt certain that he would be able to make enough money at this last bout to retire. In the year of our Lord 1297, it was time he stopped his idle ramblings about the countryside, and found himself a place he could call his own. Perhaps he could go on pilgrimage with the Teutonic Knights and see what the lands were like in the heathen country they were suppressing? With a good purse earned from this last fight, he could perhaps buy a small castle – or take one, if he could form a small force. Capturing a small town or castle was always a good way to enter the nobility.

So he had gone to the tournament, had wagered heavily on himself, and had lost all his money when he was unhorsed and ransomed by the sniggering Count of Blois. Reptilian man. He'd been lucky: Geoffrey's horse had stumbled on a molehill or something as he went into the gallop, and that little misstep had made the beast slow, turn his head and stamp before Geoffrey could take control, and in that time the count had covered the distance between them. To Geoffrey's horror, he saw the lance almost on him, and before he could move his horse plunged once, and the lance caught him on the breast. His cantle broke, and he was pitched over his mount's rump to land, winded, on his back.

As quickly as he could, he rolled over on to all fours and stood, but even as he did so, a ringing crash on his helm sent him headlong. This time there was no mistake. The count had his sword at Geoffrey's visor, and it was all over: his successes were set at nought.

And yet there had been one good piece of fortune that day. Unknown to him, there had been another knight present at the tourney, a tall, well-formed man: Hugh Despenser. To Geoffrey's relief, Despenser had ransomed him, returned his arms and mount, and offered him a place in his household.

That was long ago, of course. Long before his son grew powerful in the king's favours – and, most guessed, in his arms, too – and long before Hugh Despenser the elder became the Earl of Winchester.

Geoffrey preferred the old Hugh, the man to whom he had been so indebted on that sunny afternoon in Anjou. Immediately, his life had changed, and now he felt it was all for the better. He had been reduced to penury, dependent upon another once more, and all dreams of finding a small town, sacking it and living in the castle were gone, to be replaced by a post as an effective steward in a vill down here in Devon.

First Despenser had taken him with him on the campaign to Flanders with the English king's host. That pointless failure did the king no good, but Geoffrey managed to capture two burgesses and ransom them for a goodly sum, and soon he was a man of some wealth once more.

Many would have thought it odd that one who had aspired to own his own castle should have been content to remain in my Lord Despenser's household. Geoffrey did not care what they thought. He had a warm hall, comfortable clothes, rich tapestries, new tunics every summer and winter, and the life of a minor noble. All without risk. He was happy with that. He had everything he needed from life.

His new sergeant entered, and Geoffrey looked up at him. 'So, Adcock. Are you hungry? I'm about to eat.'

'I think it's a little late to eat now,' Adcock said with a quick look about him.

It was just as though he feared to be attacked in such a den of thieves, Geoffrey thought, and he felt a rush of anger against the man. These were *his* men, and some piss-legged sergeant like this had no right to look down on them. 'Sit here with me. This is the time I learned to eat when I was fighting with the last king, God bless his memory, and what's good for a king can't be bad for a sergeant, can it? Sit here.'

'Thank you,' Adcock said as he took his place on a stool at Geoffrey's side.

He was pale and anxious-looking. Geoffrey knew that since his arrival he had been looking more and more fretful, as though he suddenly realised he was among dangerous men. He looked like a lamb who had woken to find himself in the midst of a wolf-pack. Well, he'd best make the most of his position here. He would be here for a good long time. Lord Despenser had heard of his skills and wanted him here to help Sir Geoffrey, and if Lord Despenser wanted a man, he would have him.

'Boy, you should learn to enjoy yourself more. This solitary life is no good for you. Perhaps we could find you a woman?'

Adcock flinched and looked away. In his mind's eye he saw Hilda bending over her work, her lovely body encased in her old tunic, turning and smiling at him with that tender look in her eye . . . it was enough to make him want to weep. 'I don't want a woman.'

'Aha! So you have one, do you?' Geoffrey said with delight. 'I'm glad to hear it. You should bring her here, then, show her to us, so we can see what she's like. Tell me: is she fair or dark? Long in the leg, or a short-arse? Big breasted or small?'

Adcock felt himself colouring under his questions. It was demeaning to his memory of his woman that this knight should quiz him about her so crudely in front of all the men.

'Answer me! What is she like?' Geoffrey demanded.

'She is my woman. Mine. That's all you need know,' Adcock stated flatly. He would not discuss the woman whom he intended to marry in this manner. She was worth more to him than his post here.

'You won't tell me about her?' Geoffrey growled.

'I do not offer her to you – why should I describe her to you?'

Geoffrey's face blackened for a moment, and he leaned towards Adcock, but then the food was brought into the hall, and he relaxed. Adcock was sure that the older man's hand had strayed to his dagger's hilt, and his heart was pounding uncomfortably with the conviction that he had narrowly escaped death. He tried to sit a little farther away from Geoffrey without moving too ostentatiously.

The food was a loaf of bread, freshly baked that afternoon and broken into hunks. There was a wooden platter of cooked meats, with a pair of roasted pigeons on top, and Geoffrey took one and pulled it apart. He dabbed bread in the bloody gravy on the plate and filled his mouth, glancing at Adcock as he ate. Taking a great slurp of wine, he swallowed, then belched quietly, wiping his mouth on the back of his hand. Realising Adcock was watching, he rubbed his hand on his tunic as though to stop showing himself to be uncouth, before reaching over to pat Adcock on the thigh.

'You'll do, boy. If you can stand up to me in my hall here, you'll hold out against the vill's people too. Well done.'

Adcock took a sip from the mazer of wine before him, his sense of near panic melting away to be replaced by a feeling of . . . what? Acceptance? Perhaps that was it. Geoffrey had stirred him to see how far he could push, and to see what response he would get from Adcock if he threatened violence. Well, he had his answer.

It was a terrible situation, though. Ever since that first day when the men had ridden out from the place, and later Adcock had heard about the attack on the house owned by the neighbouring bailiff, he had understood the kind of manor this was. It was little better than a robber-knight's hideaway. The men here were all strong, sturdy fellows who were good with their fists or weapons, but nothing else. No one in the hall could plant a field or harvest it; all they were good for was intimidating or killing. And Adcock now was one of them. It made him feel appallingly lonely; his dream of bringing his woman here to live with him was gone. He would rather die a bachelor than expose his Hilda to this malevolent household.

At least he had Geoffrey's respect, he thought, shooting a quick look at his master. Geoffrey happened to cast a glance his way at the same time, and, catching Adcock's eye, he gave a quick grin.

Just then a man walked into the hall. 'Sir Geoffrey. There's a messenger here from Sir Odo. He wants to talk to you.'

Sir Geoffrey grinned suddenly, a wolfish baring of his teeth that had little humour in it. He bent his head to his meat and chewed loudly, spitting tiny fragments as he bellowed: 'Show him in.'

Every so often Simon Puttock created a need to visit his abbot in Tavistock.

His new job at Dartmouth as the abbot's representative in the town, checking the customs and collecting all the money due, was hardly onerous on its own, if lonely for a gregarious man, but to have to do it without the support and companionship of his wife was very hard. He missed his Meg every moment of every day while he was there.

Margaret, his wife, was a tall, fair woman, with glowing blond hair that settled about her shoulders like a golden cloud. Her mild manner and calmness in the face of dreadful adversity had always buoyed his spirits, and living away from her for the first time in his married life had been very hard.

But it was unavoidable. She had to remain at Lydford for a little while. Their daughter, Edith, was a woman now, and although Simon would have preferred to have her close to him where he could keep an eye on her, the simple fact was that she wanted to remain in the old stannary town, near to the lad she claimed she wanted to marry.

Marry! She was far too young to think of that sort of commitment. She was only – what? Sixteen nearly? Christ in chains, where had all the years gone? And it was, he had to admit (if only privately), far better that she should be in a place like Lydford, which was secure, quiet, and not filled with drunken, whoring sailors who'd look at a wench and unclothe her in their minds even if their horny fingers didn't try to do so for real.

So as often as possible, Simon would take advantage of the slightest excuse to travel up north from the coast, ostensibly to drop in on the abbot, and then to carry on to see his family. When he could, he would take his time. And he usually could: the new clerk at Dartmouth, Martin, was more than capable of seeing to the job. It did not need Simon's presence to make sure that the money was brought in.

The first two or three times he'd returned, the good abbot had appeared to be amused to see his Keeper coming back, but old Abbot Robert was nothing if not a kindly soul, and he made no comment; he simply smiled easily and suggested that Simon might like to drop in on his wife since he was already more than three-quarters of the way home. It didn't take more than that for Simon to bolt from the room and bellow for his horse.

But not this time. Abbot Robert was for the first time looking his age, and Simon stood in his room with an unpleasant feeling of being tongue-tied. He had never seen his master looking unwell before, and to be confronted with a man who was plainly very old was somehow shocking. It forced Simon to consider what might happen to him, when this generous-hearted individual did eventually die.

'Come, join me near the fire,' the abbot croaked.

He sat swathed in thick rugs at the fireplace, a low table at his side bearing a goblet of strong spiced wine. When he cocked an eyebrow at Simon, he looked again the person whom Simon had grown to love and respect over the years. Abbot Champeaux was much more than merely his master: he was a man whom any would be happy to follow.

The abbot had been master of this abbey for thirty-nine years. When he was elected, Tavistock was in debt, and he had been forced to borrow heavily to keep it afloat. After a lifetime's struggle, he oversaw an expanded demesne, with more churches incorporated, more rights added: the farm of the stannaries on Dartmoor, and the money from Dartmouth too, now he was Keeper. What had been a bankrupt little institution on the boundaries of the moors had become a thriving community, with the valuable asset of the town of Tavistock built up as a profitable venture in its own right.

But the man who had brought about all the expansion was now plainly suffering and Simon had a chill sensation in his bowels. He had known Abbot Robert for many years, and in all that time he'd never seen him with more than a minor cold. A man like him, keen on hunting, on wines, and most of all on ensuring that he left a lasting legacy, had always seemed a force that could not be removed. He was too virile and potent to be deposed, and yet, looking at him now, Simon was struck by the thought that his old master, his old friend, was suddenly frail.

'Abbot?'

'Sit, Simon, sit. I am as you see me – an all but broken reed.'

'But you will recover,' Simon said heartily.

The abbot looked up from red-rimmed eyes. 'Perhaps. But for my money, I'd not put too large a wager on it. It is good, Simon. I don't fear death. I know I can go to God with a clear conscience and my heart rejoices to think that at last I shall have an opportunity to lay down my burden – and I pray I might meet Jesus. It will be good to give up the responsibility for this place, for the abbey and the town.'

Simon had a little business to conduct, but when he hesitantly mentioned it, the abbot waved a hand in an exhausted gesture. 'Simon, save it for the steward. He can help you. For now, tell me, how is your family?'

'My daughter grows ever taller and more beautiful,' Simon said, 'and my little boy, Peterkin, wants to come to Dartmouth as soon as possible to play on the ships. I won't let him. If he ever joined me there, he'd be on to a ship in a moment, and I'd not see him. Knowing him, he'd stay stowed and no one the wiser until he got to a foreign port. He hankers after distant countries and the idea of travel. He's still jealous that I went on pilgrimage last year.'

'So am I,' Abbot Robert said quietly. He coughed painfully, then sipped wine. 'This cold weather is going to take me away, I fear, but I should have liked to see Compostela. It is supposed to be very beautiful.'

He had turned away from Simon, and Simon saw that his gaze was gone to the window that looked out over the river and the bank on the far side. In the past, Simon had stood in this room discussing business, and the abbot had all too often been hard pressed to keep his mind on their discussions, for his attention would fly off to the window whenever there was a flash of russet in the trees that spoke of a deer coming for water. The abbot was an inveterate hunter, and prized his horses and his raches as among his most valued possessions. Now his mournful expression resembled that of one of his mastiffs.

'You will hunt again, Abbot,' Simon said softly.

'No, friend Simon. I fear I shall not,' the abbot sighed. He looked up at Simon and smiled. 'It is as I said, I long to set down my burden. I meant it. You go and see your wife, man. You don't want to be here in a dying man's room. Go and see your family, but come by here on your way back in case there is anything we need to discuss.'

'I shall,' Simon promised. He stood, but only reluctantly. This man had been good to him for so many years that leaving him today was a wrench.

He walked to the door and glanced back. The abbot was slouching in his chair again, his eyes on the fire. To Simon, he looked like someone who was already dead.

Robert Crokers heard the sound from a distance as he stood in the trees.

With no logs, he had to shift each morning to prepare enough timber for his fire, and it was fortunate that this piece of land had not been worked by the coppicers for some little while. He could collect plenty of sticks and thicker twigs to form faggots, and bind them with some old straw twisted to make a twine. He'd need a lot of them: bundles like that burned through in no time compared with a couple of good logs, but when he'd collected a few to be going on with he'd be able to start cutting up some old trunks that had lain on the ground since last winter. They'd not be perfect, not like the logs he had stored in his pile, but they'd do for now, and later he could organise himself to start a new pile.

He was exhausted. Worry about his bitch and what could have happened to her tore at him. She had been his only friend for so long. And then there was the jumpiness that came to a man who had only a few days before been thrown from his land by violence. There was a cloying odour of burnt wood and tar that stuck in his nostrils and prevented easeful rest.

Sir Odo's man Walter was still with him, to be at hand in case of further incursions, and last night their slumbers had been disturbed when the two of them had finally managed to drop off. In the middle of the night there had been a dreadful roaring noise and both men had leaped to their feet, convinced that the attackers had returned.

'Bastards!' the old warrior spat. He grabbed his sword, and was out through the door like a rache seeing a rabbit. Robert fully expected to hear screams and shouts, but he only hesitated a moment before he took up his billhook and ran out.

There was nothing there. Walter stood with his sword in his hand, head lowered as he scowled around him at the woods, but even as Robert arrived behind him he could see that no one had come to attack them.

'Where are they?' Robert asked anxiously.

'Don't know,' Walter said. He stood upright, shoved his sword into the scabbard and thrust his thumbs in his belt. 'Probably in their beds, if they have any sense. Must have been something else we heard. It came from the end, didn't it?'

He led the way round the corner of the house and the two of them could see what had made the noise as soon as they spotted the avalanche of dried mud and straw that had tipped on to the soil.

'I wonder if the rest of the building is safe?' Robert said.

Walter looked at him, then grunted to himself. 'I don't know, but I do know it's warmer in there than out here.'

Recalling that, he could smile again now, but the idea that the house might collapse was a source of fresh fear to Robert. Where the wall had fallen was directly beneath one of the roof supports, and he had the unpleasant feeling that others were probably as unstable. Walter said he'd seen similar damage before, and that it had been cured by putting a plank underneath the roof supports at the top of the walls. Perhaps that would work – but it was a daunting idea, lifting the roof enough to push planks under.

He was still mulling over the easiest way to do it when he heard the low whine. It was a hideous sound, and he felt the hairs on his upper neck start to shiver to attention. He was bent at that moment, reaching down for a longer length of branch, and he stopped what he was doing as the terror of all things with fangs and claws returned to haunt him.

As a little boy he had regularly suffered from mares, and each time it was the same: a wolf, ravening, drooling at the sight of such an easy meal. Even now he thought he could hear the soft padding of paws as it approached him.

With a whimper of fear, he snatched up the branch and whirled.

Only to see his sheepdog, greatly swollen with puppies, stagger towards him and lie down painfully at his feet.

Chapter Ten

Adcock was awake early the next day, and as he prepared himself for an expedition over to the eastern edge of the manor to look at the pastures and assess their quality, he could hear bellowing from inside as Sir Geoffrey readied himself for his ride. It served to make the sergeant's desire to leave the place all the more urgent, hearing that hoarse shouting.

He was still shocked at the way the messenger had appeared yesterday. He'd entered haughtily proud, walking straight down the hall, round the fire, until he stood in front of Sir Geoffrey. All the while Sir Geoffrey sat with a shoulder of mutton in his hands, tearing at it with his small, square teeth until only the bone remained. This he held in his hand and studied. Meanwhile the other men in the hall were laughing and calling the messenger names. At first they had been quiet, but as they grew in belligerence some started to shout obscene suggestions at the man, one even throwing a piece of food at him.

At last Geoffrey had stood and lifted his hand. 'Will you all be silent, please, for our guest?' he cried with mock seriousness. 'This poor fellow has ridden many miles to be with us tonight. He is tired. Would you like some wine, fellow?'

'I am well enough, Sir Geoffrey. I have a message for you from Sir Odo.'

'Oho! Have you!' a man shouted from a bench. Adcock glanced up. It was Nick le Poter again. Always trying to foment trouble, Nick was. He scared Adcock, because he was the sort of man who might kill to settle a dispute, and he was undeniably ambitious. He wanted power for himself here in the manor, and if he ever took over from Sir Geoffrey the whole place would grow even worse, as far as Adcock could see. He only seemed to understand brute force and bullying, nothing else.

Geoffrey leaned slightly to get a clearer view of the man who had called out. He pointed with his chin, and Adcock saw two men from the doorway nod. They walked towards Nick.

'Well, sir? What message does Sir Odo wish me to receive?'

'He sends you his best wishes. He heard that you enjoyed your ride on Saturday, and hopes you enjoyed the hospitality of his manor, but would remind you that it is the custom of visitors and guests to leave a room in the manner in which they found it. He is disturbed that you appear to have broken down the walls, slaughtered cattle and sheep, and threatened the bailiff. He would like you to make restitution. Naturally, he would like an apology too. He will inform Sir John Sully of the offence given to his estates, and will appeal to Lord de Courtenay for support if necessary.'

'He will, will he?' Sir Geoffrey chuckled. Then he glanced to the side.

The man who had shouted abuse was gripped by the two men now, one at each arm. Sir Geoffrey nodded to him. 'Lordings, this fellow was rude to our guest. We can't have that, now can we? How should we punish him?'

Adcock frowned. This was peculiar behaviour even from the little he had seen of Sir Geoffrey. The man, Nick, now held by the two guards, suddenly gave a convulsive heave, and managed to throw off one of them, but in a moment he was grabbed again, and he could only stand mouthing futile imprecations while others gloated and laughed at his predicament.

'What will we do with him?' Sir Geoffrey asked again. 'Well, if no one else will help me, I'll have to think of a suitable punishment myself. You! Fetch me a lash.'

At his command, a fellow from the far table hurried from the room, returning a few moments later with a thin lash. Sir Geoffrey took it and swung it a few times, listening to its sharp hissing. 'I don't want my men being disobedient,' he said lazily, and then walked to the culprit. 'What exactly did you say again?'

Nick said nothing, but only spat on the ground between them. Sir

Geoffrey said not a word, but his face paled with rage. He nodded to the two guards, and the unwilling victim was taken to the top table. While Adcock watched in horror, the man was thrust over the board in front of him, scattering bowls and trenchers, until his bearded face was a scant foot from his own. The guards sprang over the table, still holding his arms, and stood gripping his wrists, pulling his arms outstretched. Sir Geoffrey drew his dagger and ran it up Nick's shirt from his arse to his neck, incidentally snagging the man's back a couple of times, and pulled the shirt from him.

He looked straight at Adcock as he pronounced, 'I will not tolerate disobedience in my manor. Not from any man.' And then he began to whip the fellow's back until it was raw with blood.

Simon had reached his home before the third hour of the morning, and he clattered loudly down the roadway to his house at an easy walk, anticipating his breakfast.

It was always good to ride along the ridge here towards Lydford in good, clear weather. The little town had been a centre of tin-mining for many years, since before the Normans arrived even. The old houses could most of them do with being knocked down and rebuilt, but for Simon there was some charm in the fact that this old outpost seemed to be unchanging. It was a part of the delight of the place.

His house was towards the town's heart, not far from the prison that had been his place of work for so long. He meandered along the road, and then stopped outside the long Devon house that had been his home since he'd been given the job here eight years ago.

Little around here had altered greatly in those eight years. They were lucky indeed that the wars that had so scarred the kingdom had not reached this far west. The fighting had all been on the Welsh March, or farther north at York, Boroughbridge and beyond. There the slaughter had been terrible after the Scottish invasions, so he'd heard.

Here, though, life had continued as it had for decades. His house stood solid and comforting, and beyond it, in the clear morning's air, he could see for miles to the north-west, over sporadic grey wastes of low-lying mist. He swung from his horse and led it round to the back of the house, removing the saddle and bridle himself before slapping the beast on the rump to send him running. Before long the rounsey was pulling at the grasses and chewing contentedly as though he'd never left this place.

Simon left him there and made his way inside. The ceiling was low and he had to stoop as he entered. He met a serving-girl, who gaped to see him. Winking at her he pointed upwards, and she nodded emphatically, so he stepped quietly to the stairs and mounted them as quietly as he might.

In the solar upstairs, he could see that his daughter was still asleep, while his wife was kneeling with her back to him, playing with his young son. Simon stood a moment staring at them, his heart feeling as though it had swollen to twice its normal size. Peterkin was growing so quickly now, Simon felt as though he was missing too much that was important. But there was little to be done about it. He had to work.

'Dadad!'

He saw his wife's startled expression as Peterkin ran past her and into Simon's arms, and then she was with him too, her mouth on his.

'You have a strange idea of a place to meet,' Sir Geoffrey said as he kicked his mount forward. 'This is too much in the open.'

'It was hard to pick somewhere in a hurry, sir,' Sir Odo said calmly.

The two were at the bend in the Torridge river just below Brimblecombe. Neither was in a position to entirely trust the other, and both remained on their horses, speaking low and quiet.

Sir Odo glanced about him as he asked, 'You came alone?'

'Of course! You think I want others to know we discuss things like this?' Sir Geoffrey snapped.

Sir Odo considered him. 'It's as dangerous for me as it is for you, Sir Geoffrey. I can't afford for my master to know that I'm here any more than you can.'

'Then let's stop pissing in the wind and get to business!' Sir Geoffrey retorted.

'Very well. The attacks must stop. It's getting out of control. It's one thing to burn the bailiff from his place, but the killings up at Iddesleigh won't be so easy to cover over.'

'Very funny.'

'What?'

Sir Geoffrey said nothing for a moment. His eyes narrowed, and his face coloured, and then he faced the other knight. 'Is that a joke? If it is, I think it's in poor taste.'

'Those were your men, weren't they? It's the talk of the whole area. The man and his woman and child, so I heard. All murdered, their holding burned, the livestock stolen . . . everyone is saying it was you and your men, that you rode to Iddesleigh immediately after the work you did to Robert's place. Do you mean it wasn't you?'

'What possible interest could I have had in attacking some peasant in his dwelling?' Sir Geoffrey tore his gaze away from Sir Odo, and he stared along the line of the river northwards. 'I assumed it was you and your men.'

'If I was going to retaliate, I'd do it with an assault on one of your manors,' Sir Odo said reasonably. 'I'd hardly attack Iddesleigh, on my own lands, would I?'

'It had occurred to me and my men that you were thinking of blaming us for a second attack. That was why we arranged for a good alibi after we heard about it,' Sir Geoffrey said musingly. 'So if you wanted to make a point of putting the blame on me, it would be a good place for you to attack – somewhere that looks like yours, but which wouldn't upset your master at all.'

'It wasn't me or my men,' Sir Odo said flatly, and now he too was frowning at the view. 'But if it wasn't either of us, who could it have been? Is there a band of outlaws that you're aware of? I've heard nothing.'

'No, nor I. But if there were a small band, they might be keen to avoid upsetting either of us. Perhaps this was merely a short incursion by felons and they took what they could and fled?'

'Perhaps,' Sir Odo said, unconvinced. 'But I should go cautiously for a while. We don't want the balance we hold here to be disturbed. If there is trouble, it will escalate to our lords, and there is no point in that. Your master and mine must baulk at the thought of war over such a tiny piece of land. Provided we continue to niggle at it, they'll be happy. But we don't want actual battle. Besides, it is not in our interests to have the land disputed seriously.'

'Not while it is in our hands and we can profit from it,' Sir Geoffrey agreed. 'We can leave matters as they are for a while. Let the peasants think that we have a truce, and then occasional little attacks to satisfy my master.'

'Good,' Sir Odo said.

He extended his hand. Sir Geoffrey hesitated, and then the pair sealed their pact with a handshake.

Then Sir Odo asked, 'By the way – did you ever learn who it was who killed your sergeant?'

'No. That is still a mystery to us. No doubt we shall learn, though.'

'Have you heard that the widow, young Lucy of Meeth, has disappeared too?' Sir Odo asked keenly.

'No – I'd heard nothing about her. I have enough on my plate just looking to my own affairs without worrying about other people's.'

Sir Odo nodded. 'True enough. Godspeed!' He wheeled his horse about, and set off at a canter southwards.

Sir Geoffrey considered him as he rode out of sight, and then he shook his head and touched his beast with the spur, and set off at a gentle trot. It was a shame he had to destroy Sir Odo. When his master declared that he wanted a new piece of land, it was best to obey him. Those who disobeyed the Despenser tended to have their lives shortened.

When the hammering came at the door, Simon heard the maid going to answer it, and idly ran his hand down his wife's naked flank, then leaned forward and kissed the curve of her waist. 'I could lie here all day just making love to you,' he whispered.

'You have done before now,' she chuckled throatily. She reached out to him and pulled his face to hers, kissing his lips. 'I miss you so much,' she said seriously.

'I miss you too. Hopefully it won't be long. How is Edith?'

'She is in love with him, Simon. She says she won't leave Lydford unless it's as his wife.'

Simon looked away. It was too painful to accept that his daughter was already a woman and ready for marriage. 'She seems so young.'

'I doubt not that I seemed too young to my parents when you wooed me.'

'Perhaps,' he sighed.

She smiled and rolled over on to her back, pulling him on top of her. 'Do you remember how we used to make love all afternoon?'

'Master?'

The shout up the stairs came just as he was preparing to demonstrate that he could indeed recall those not-so-far-off days, and he frowned at his wife as she attempted to suppress her giggling at his frustration. 'Shall I go and send them away, Simon?'

He snapped over his shoulder, 'What is it?'

'A boy has come . . . a messenger, a man from Sir Baldwin, bailiff. It's very important, he says. Urgent.'

Simon kissed Meg a last time, then grunted as he left her body. 'I'll be back in a minute.'

Dressed, he found the messenger warming his hands before his fire.

'Wat?'

'Sir . . . I am so sorry, sir,' Wat burst out. 'It's Hugh. I am sorry, we've heard he's dead, sir.'

'No!'

'Will you go to help Sir Baldwin at Hugh's house?'

Simon did not bother to answer, but hurried up to tell his wife.

Robert Crokers was still weeping as the pups were born.

Someone had tried to kill his poor old bitch and she might never work again. The poor thing was ruined. She had a long cut along her flank, where someone had plainly slashed at her as she ran past, and she must have spent the last few days in terror, not daring to return to her home. God only knew what she had managed to eat, although from the look of her it wasn't much.

As soon as he saw her he picked her up in his arms, buried his face in her neck, and carried her gently back to the house. He laid her by the fire and gave her a little of the meaty soup he had made for himself, watching anxiously as she wolfed it down. She was terribly weak, and her eyes were haunted like a child's who had lost a parent.

Whenever there was a noise she didn't recognise, she started and stared fixedly at the door. When Walter walked in, she was petrified, growling low and rising painfully on her haunches at the sight of the stranger.

'Easy, girl. Easy,' Robert said, stroking her. At the first touch, she flashed her head round, and he saw that she was panting, as though she had run a great distance. Her teeth were ready, and her open mouth enclosed his hand. He didn't move, but spoke to her softly, until at last her rolling eyes were calmed, and she released him. His skin wasn't broken, and he gently scratched her under the chin, where she always liked it. She held his gaze for a long while, and then lay down again, too exhausted to maintain even her fear.

'Poor girl,' he said.

'Found her, then?' Walter said. He had collected more wood and threw it down near the fire. 'Won't last long, from the look of her.'

'She's strong inside,' Robert said.

'She'll need to be!' Walter chuckled, and walked out again.

Robert returned to his faggots later, and brought all the spare wood to the house. He stacked it with Walter's pile over at the far side of the room, then dropped a bundle on to the glowing embers, blowing gently until he had fanned it into flames. He set his bowl over it to heat through, and settled back to wait while the flames warmed his face. As he squatted there, he heard the steps of Walter return, and soon the older man was inside again, throwing another few faggots to join the pile.

'Keep us going for the night, anyway,' he commented.

'Why did you say that before you fetched them?'

'What?'

'I said she was strong inside, and you said she'd have to be.'

Walter looked at him, then stuck a small twig in his mouth and rubbed it over his teeth to clean them. 'Look, I don't know what Sir Odo said to you, but he reckons those bastards'll be back. Won't be immediate, but they'll be back, and next time they'll plan on making sure no one can live here. He's set a boy to watch over us here, and if there's any sign of horses coming that lad will run fast as he can to Sir Odo, day or night, and day or night Sir Odo will come with his men.'

'Why, though? The land isn't worth all that much.'

Walter chuckled aloud. 'Not in terms of peasants or crops, no; but it's good for a lord to tie up his lands, and Sir Geoffrey's lords own most of the land this side of the river. They'll be looking to add more, and that means he wants to clear you and all our men off this part so he can put his own in here.'

'How long?'

Walter looked at him, shrugged and lay down on the ground. He grunted to himself, resting his head on a pillow of rolled-up scraps of cloth, pulled up a blanket, and finally set his old felt hat over his eyes. 'I'd get that bitch well as soon as you can. Won't be all that long. Sir Geoffrey isn't a patient man.'

Soon he was snoring, but not Robert. He could see again the bitter, scornful faces as they trampled his lands, setting their mounts plunging all over his vegetables, tossing torches into his thatch, enjoying the bullying of a man weaker than they were.

It made him furious – and petrified to think that soon they might be back.

Chapter Eleven

On the way to Iddesleigh, Baldwin had to stop to ask for guidance several times. This was not a part of Devon with which he was particularly well acquainted, and although he was fairly sure of the direction, his concern for Hugh, as well as his fear for his wife on the journey, was getting in the way of his planning a decent route.

'How much further is it, Sir Knight? My arse is worn thin with all this plodding along!'

There were many times when he felt he could – or indeed should – have taken a dagger to the foul wench's throat, but he restrained himself with difficulty, and forced himself to speak with patient calmness. 'Emma, I can do nothing to bring us there any more speedily.'

'If you ask me, this is the worst sort of dullness. If the man's dead, so be it. There are people up there to look into it if it truly was a murder,' she said. 'The messenger probably got the wrong idea about it all. He wasn't the brightest coin in the purse.'

'Wat is considerably more intelligent than . . .' Baldwin stopped before the comparison was out. It could only lead to another argument and more embarrassment for Jeanne. In God's name, he *must* make her see how disruptive Emma was. She had to go, somehow. 'Than most,' he finished bitterly.

'So you say. And what of this Hugh himself? Wasn't he the silent fool who used to glare at everyone and everything? A miserable churl if ever I saw one. And only a peasant, when all's said and done. What on earth is the point of coming all this way just to see his body?'

Baldwin turned and said with poisonous sweetness, 'Emma, he was a friend's man, and I esteemed him. That, for me, is enough to spend a little time and some discomfort in seeking his murderer. You were not commanded to join us. If you wish, you may return at once to Liddinstone. I will not stop you.'

'Me? Go back all alone? I could be set upon, and then where would I be?'

Baldwin sighed and faced the road ahead once more.

It had not been his idea to bring the foul bint. She had insisted on joining them as soon as she heard that Jeanne would be leaving with her husband. There was nothing that could give her greater pleasure, Baldwin felt, than ruining someone else's day.

Well, she would not affect his. It was already ruined.

Wat had not been able to give him much in the way of details. All Baldwin knew was that there had been an attack on Hugh's house, and he had been knocked down. From the sound of things, Wat thought that the homestead had been destroyed, and Hugh's family killed, but that seemed unproven so far. They would have to wait until they reached the place before they found out any more.

Iddesleigh. When Hugh had told Simon that he was to live up there, Simon had been glad for his man. It seemed that Iddesleigh was known mainly for its excellent inn, and that the ales and accommodation there were superior to any others on this road. Baldwin felt sure that he had ridden through the place once: he had a vague memory that it lay between Hatherleigh and Winkleigh, that there was a long road that led from Monk Oakhampton, fairly flat and straight, through trees. For the rest, he was sure that the people there had been quite respectful and friendly. He hadn't been there for a murder, he recalled; it was some other little affair farther up at Dolton, but he had stopped at Iddesleigh to rest on his way home. Better, always, to leave a vill where a man had been arrested and tried, and partake of hospitality elsewhere. Men who had seen their comrades, neighbours or brothers attached for the next court were sometimes liable to be poor companions for a meal. Better to seek the next vill, which would almost inevitably have a healthy disrespect for the folk who lived in the barbaric, heathen place all of two miles away.

Yes, he remembered Iddesleigh.

They had set off as soon as they could after Wat had left, but when a man had a wife and child to consider, travelling took longer. Jeanne had carried Richalda in a sling for much of the journey, but it had meant that they must go more slowly than Baldwin would have liked. He daren't hurry with his daughter resting on the horse in front of Jeanne. For now she was snoozing, her pretty head nodding with the horse's movement. Even as he glanced at her, he felt a wave of pride filtering away his anger at Emma. Richalda was so beautiful, so precious . . .

'So how far is it, Sir Knight? My mistress is tired already. We should be seeking an inn for her to rest if it's not nearby,' Emma said.

'Emma! I am perfectly all right. I can manage,' Jeanne declared.

'Certainly you are. It's not an illness!'

'Emma!'

Baldwin felt a sliver of ice penetrate his vitals. Still staring ahead, his eyes widened, and he almost turned and faced his wife, but restrained himself at the last possible moment when he considered the look of triumph that would inevitably appear on Emma's face, were she to realise that he had not any idea that his wife was pregnant again. He swallowed, and spoke. 'It is not far. In fact,' he said, peering up ahead, 'I think that this must be Monk Oakhampton.'

'We aren't going to Monk Oakhampton,' Emma said with slow, poisonous serenity. 'We are going to Iddesleigh, you said.'

'And Iddesleigh is but a mile or two beyond this,' Baldwin said shortly.

The road was as he had recalled it. A series of bends gave the impression of a great distance, but in reality it was a fairly straight path, so far as a Devon roadway could be. Soon the land opened out on their left, and fields appeared, their regular lines delineated by twigs thrust into the ground so that each peasant would know where his strip began and ended. The place looked well-farmed, and the soil had been worked efficiently from what Baldwin could see. It was freshly turned, and, from the odour, manure had recently been spread. Hopefully there would be a good harvest again, he prayed.

The vill, when they clattered in, was a small huddle of houses. There was a group on the road itself, which curved left in front of them, and then right, northwards again. Encircling the houses was a second lane, which led up the hillside, and fronting this was a large longhouse, which was now used half as the farmer's storeroom and byre, but also as an inn. Next to it, on the left as Baldwin looked at the place, was the church, which lay in the right-hand bend in the road. He wondered whether Hugh's body was already in there.

Stopping at the inn, he tied his horse to the rail provided, then reached out his hand to his wife. She took it, and had the grace to look down when she saw the expression in his eyes. He was not cross – good God, how could he be angry with her for falling pregnant? – but he was annoyed that her maid was aware of this marvellous news while he remained ignorant.

'I hope they have some food in there. I'm fairly starved!' Emma said, rubbing her hands together as she sailed past them and in through the wide, low doorway.

'When did you know?' he asked as soon as they were alone, taking their daughter from her. Richalda mumbled sleepily, then set her head on his shoulder.

'I don't really, not yet. But I have a feeling, and I think my monthly time is late,' she confessed. 'I wasn't going to say anything until I was more certain. Are you upset, husband?'

He smiled and gave her his arm. 'My love, if you are right, I shall be the happiest man in Christendom!'

Adcock was settling down to sleep when he heard the muffled noises from outside.

This was a weird place. The men here were all more or less permanently armed, as though they expected a battle at any moment. Yet the land round about seemed ridiculously quiet.

He had mentioned that on the first day, when he had been sent about the manor with a man who the steward had described as a good source of local detail.

'I'm Beorn, sir,' he had said, bending his head respectfully, a large man whose face seemed composed mainly of beard.

'Call me Adcock. I am no better than you,' Adcock said, and he was speaking nothing more than the truth. As he knew full well, a sergeant was only the man set to farm the main activities on the estate. Unlettered, his skill must lie in his ability to persuade people to perform their duties willing or no, so that the manor showed a profit. Any failures or discrepancies were likely to be set to his account.

'Adcock it is, then,' Beorn had said without interest. 'What do you want to see?'

'Let's go and walk the boundaries first. I'll need to know where the holding finishes.'

Beorn had given a slightly twisted smile on hearing that, but he took Adcock all round the place, pointing out the boundary markers on the way, and explaining the small details which a new man wouldn't understand immediately. 'There's the little bog, but see those green reeds farther on? Avoid that, sir. That's the mire. We've been thinking of draining it for an age, but nothing ever comes of it. It's dangerous. When we do clear it, I dare say there'll be some dead oxen, horses and sheep in there, not to mention people.'

'Really?' Adcock asked, staring at the trembling ground with disgust. He'd seen mires often enough before, of course, and he rather thought the first thing to do with a small patch like this was to dig a trench to let the water run away, and fill the hole with good soil afterwards until the land was level, and then something could be made of the ground. He would take advice, and if no one had any objections to advance he would go ahead with the drainage.

Yes, Adcock was untrained in his spelling and reading, but he knew what his job was about. In his last manor he had been the assistant to the sergeant, and together he and his old master had taken the place by the cods and shaken it until every tiny patch of land was fruitful and of value to their lord. Here he would do the same, he decided. The land wasn't different, not really: the soil was good and rich, from the look of the grass; and all the animals thrived, looking sleek and fat, so it was plain to see that there was nourishment in the ground.

'This looks a fine manor, Beorn.'

'Aye, it is.'

'But, tell me,' Adcock said hesitantly. 'The men at the hall all seem to go abroad fully armed the whole time. Is there some fear of attack?'

'It's not fear of someone being attacked!' Beorn burst out with a guffaw, and then he silenced himself and gazed about him with a swift caution. 'You must be careful talking about such things.'

'Why? Tell me what you know.'

'Not for me to say,' Beorn said, and from that moment he was as communicative as any other Devon peasant talking to a stranger.

Pagan had seen to the meal, and afterwards Isabel nodded to him briefly to indicate he could leave the room. He did so, pulling the door closed behind him and breathing in the cool air of the early evening before making his way homewards. It was a goodly walk, up to the north-east of the old hall, and he peered at it jealously as was his wont.

In the past he would have slept in the house with the two women, but Lady Isabel preferred that he returned to his home at nights now. It was since Ailward's death, he recalled, as though she didn't trust him any more . . . or perhaps because she wondered whether he might learn something?

That was daft, though. What could she think he might . . .

Pagan stopped and slowly turned to look back towards the house where Isabel and Malkin lived. Isabel had grown rather short with the younger woman recently. If she suspected that Malkin could have killed her own husband, could Isabel think to protect her daughter-in-law and grandchild by keeping all knowledge of that petit treason from her own steward? She'd not want anyone to hear of it, certainly.

It was hard to imagine Malkin could have committed such an act, though. Even today she had been very weepy. It was growing to be her usual condition. One of the maids had told him that Malkin slept very poorly. There was the sound of weeping into the early hours every night.

'It'll drive me to despair, it will,' the maid had said.

Pagan had little sympathy with such feelings. So far as he was concerned, the servants all owed their service to the family. It was wrong to speak of tears late into the night – and yet he daren't speak harshly to the girl in case she stopped telling him how the women were. It mattered to him.

Certainly Malkin was very sad since the death of Ailward. Lady Isabel was different – she mourned her son, but she remembered her husband with more affection. She missed him dreadfully, as a woman should. Losing him had meant losing her companion. Naturally she didn't feel the same about Ailward. He was not formed from the same mould.

Not at all the same mould, as Pagan knew only too well. Which was probably why Lady Isabel felt it better that he should not be in the house now that the two men were dead. Having Pagan there once more could prove too much of a temptation to the old strumpet.

It was all very disorientating to a newcomer, but Adcock had done the best he could. He had ordered that the little bog should be emptied, showing the peasants how they might dig a trench to release the moisture from it. Later, he felt sure, the second bog could be drained too, but better to start with one and see how it went. After that, he went to study the middens, check the fields, see how the animals fared in their winter stables, and begin to take a hold of the place.

It was not easy, the more so because he was sure that there were a hundred different secrets about the manor.

For one thing, as he had noticed from the first day, it was a remarkably heavily manned place. Usually a house this size would have one knight, and then would depend on a number of servants and peasants, armed with billhooks and daggers, to protect it. The idea that anyone could need the three and twenty fellows who lived here was laughable.

Then there was the curious way in which the manor was kept. Visitors were not encouraged, and when strangers appeared all the men in the place kept quiet. Sir Geoffrey would talk, but the rest would stand silent and surly, eyeing the newcomers with grave distrust. Even provisions brought from the vill were left at the door and taken in when the household rose. Late, normally. There was a deal of singing and gambling of an evening, and little by way of religious observance. In fact Adcock had been surprised by the lack of any Christian sentiment among the men in the hall. Oh, he knew that often the priest in a vill would give men leave to go to their fields of a Sunday morning before Mass, provided that they attended church later, because it was often impossible for a peasant to find time to harvest his own crops after he had performed his statutory labour for his master otherwise, but to learn that of all the household only four men would go to church on a Sunday came as a shock.

And finally there was the attack on his neighbour's sergeant.

It was wrong; to set upon a neighbour in his own house on his own land struck at the heart of all Adcock believed. To him it seemed clear that it was a matter of simple blackmail – if you don't pay me, I'll come and burn your house again. And it was that which persuaded him of the sort of manor into which he had arrived.

If he was to be sergeant in a manor that was little better than a den of thieves and rogues, at least he would do his own duty well, though. Which was why he was pleased to see that the bog was draining nicely. Hopefully before long it would be empty and he could show how more land could be cleared for use.

But now, as he rolled over in his bed, he could hear more muttered orders and a clanking of metal. There was a rattle as steel was dropped, and a hissed curse against the offender, and then he heard clattering hooves and the noise of men mounting and riding off.

And at that sound, he closed his eyes tight shut and prayed that, whomsoever they were seeking, they might miss him.

Chapter Twelve

Baldwin woke to find the morning overcast and grim. He rose quietly, leaving his wife in the small bed, and pulled a linen shirt over his nakedness as protection against the cold.

The inn was a pleasing house, with one large communal room for travellers, and this smaller chamber up some stairs to keep it farther away from the damp floor. It had the disadvantage that smoke from the fire would rise into it, but there was the huge advantage, so far as Baldwin was concerned, that there was no space for Emma. She had slept downstairs with the others in the communal room.

Downstairs, Baldwin asked a maid for some fresh water to drink, because when he had lived as a warrior monk he had chosen a frugal life. The expression on her face told him that this was forlorn hope, though, and he sighed and reluctantly asked for a weak ale – and a word with her master.

The owner was soon with him: a smiling, friendly man with the large build of a Devon farmer and a round, cheerful face. 'Just back from the pasture,' he commented, wiping his hands on his towel. 'It's thirsty work, too. How can I serve you, master?'

Baldwin motioned towards his barrel. 'Would you join me in a drink?'

'I'd be glad to.'

'Your name?'

'Jankin, sir. From Exbourne. I took over this place when my wife's father died, and have lived here ever since. It's a good vill.'

'I am known as Sir Baldwin, I am Keeper of the King's Peace, and I have been called here because of the murders.'

Jankin's face grew blank. 'It was a terrible thing, sir. All of them dead like that. But what makes you say it was murder?'

'It was what I was told – that the family was murdered.'

'I don't know where that came from, sir,' Jankin said. 'Here everyone said it was an accident.'

There was a stolid certainty about his tone, but Baldwin saw something else in his eyes: a blankness, as though there was more to the story.

'When did it happen?' Baldwin asked, toying with a coin.

'There's no need for that, sir. You're paying here already. Put your money away. Let's see. I think it was about five days ago now. He used to live only a short way up from here, just round the corner of the hill, maybe a quarter-mile off. Him and his wife and their boy. Lovely family, they were . . .' Jankin's expression altered subtly. 'Well, the woman and the little boy were. The man, Hugh, he was a little more – reserved, you might say.'

Baldwin smiled. 'You mean he was a taciturn old devil?'

'You could put it like that,' Jankin agreed happily. 'God forbid that I should speak ill of a dead man,' he added, hastily making a rudimentary sign of the cross. 'Still, he was an old-fashioned moorman as far as I could see. A fair man, good with his hands, and if he gave his word he'd stick to it.'

'Has the coroner been to hold his inquest?'

Jankin studied his ale. 'A coroner did come up here.'

'That's not quite what I asked.'

'He did come and hold an inquest.'

There was a reservation there as well, Baldwin noticed, but rather than make an enemy of the man he changed the subject. 'Who found them?'

Jankin shook his head. 'That's the terrible thing, master. They were killed one day, but no one realised until the next morning. A passing labourer came and raised the alarm, but by then it was too late to help any of them. All were dead.'

'So this fire happened in the middle of the night?'

'I suppose so. A dreadful accident.'

'Unless it was an attack from a fighting force. And it must have been quite a force to subdue Hugh,' Baldwin mused. 'If I knew him, he wouldn't succumb to any man easily – most especially if the attacker threatened his woman.'

'I think you're right there,' Jankin agreed. 'You knew him, then?'

'Yes,' Baldwin said absently.

'But nobody heard men passing by here? Did they come from the other direction?'

'Master, it was agreed that it was an accident. A tallow taper, perhaps, which fell on their floor rushes. I doubt we'll ever know precisely,' Jankin said, and looked down again.

'If there had been an attack, you would have heard men passing by?' Baldwin pressed.

Jankin pulled a doubtful grimace. 'We had a lot of men in here that day, for it was a little celebration. It was the feast of St Matthias the Apostle, and because we have a fellow in the vill who was named for the saint, we always have a party here. The folk here like to celebrate, and it ended late.'

'So if there had been a party of men . . .?'

'No one would have heard. Not if it was a squadron of the king's knights with all their squires and archers.'

'You say it ended late?'

'Well after the sun was down – but at this time of year there's so little daylight, almost everything is done in darkness, isn't it?'

'Especially murder,' Baldwin muttered.

'I am afraid so. There's nothing a murderer likes so much as darkness to cover his deeds.'

'Why should someone attack and kill Hugh, though? He was scarcely a powerful, dangerous man, was he?'

'No,' Jankin admitted. 'Perhaps that was why it was thought to be an accident.'

'Could you imagine men at arms attacking him?'

Jankin was perplexed, and again Baldwin saw he avoided his eye. 'I have thought about that myself.'

'Do you think someone could have desired his woman and she rejected his advances?'

'If a man did that, he'd have carried her off like . . .'

'Yes?'

Jankin gazed back at him. 'I do not want trouble, master. You are a rich and strong man, with men to guard you, I dare say. Me? I'm a farmer who scrapes a living, and I have some money come in from running this place. My wife brews a few gallons of ale a week and I sell it for ready cash. We don't make a huge profit, but we stagger on. I don't want to be murdered for talking too much.'

'Friend Jankin, you are helping me to understand what has been happening here, and I swear to you now that if any man comes to threaten you, he will have to answer to me directly. I will have men set here to guard you if need be. However, for now, anything you tell me I shall keep entirely to myself until I can assess how you can be protected.'

'Master, that's no security! How long could you have a force remain here to look after me and my wife? Five days? Six? A fortnight? What of the wealthy men who live here and would like to destroy me as they'd squash a fly that sat on their bread at mealtime? They'll still be here in a year, in five years, and they can take their time with me.'

'If they are so well known to you, they'll be known to others too,' Baldwin said reasonably. 'Any man could tell me of them. Now you said that they'd have carried Constance off, as they did someone else. Who?'

'There was a young woman at Meeth,' Jankin said. He began slowly, his reluctance only gradually overcome by his natural hatred of injustice. 'Lady Lucy, she was. A pretty little thing.'

'You say she "was". Is she dead, then?'

'She may be. About two weeks ago, just before we had the local ball games, she went missing. She'd been out to Hatherleigh, I believe, to market, but at some point on her return she was taken. Her servant, a man called Peter, was murdered and left by the roadside. The coroner went and saw him ten days ago, but apart from imposing the usual fines on everyone, there was nothing to be done.'

'Was there no sign of the woman at all?'

'Nothing. She simply disappeared.'

'Husband? Father? Who went to seek for her?'

'She's a widow, and the manor was her husband's. Her father is dead, I think, but he lived north somewhere, a long ways off. On the marches, I think. There was no one here to protect her. Only her servants, and, as I say, the man with her was killed.'

'And what is the opinion of the people here in the vill?'

Jankin looked up at him with a set jaw. He paused, looking deep into Baldwin's eyes as though gauging whether he could trust this tall, dark-haired man. Then his eyes dropped away to his hands, and he toyed with a splinter of wood.

'You really want to know what I think, sir?' he said in a low voice. 'I think it was the Despensers' man. He took her.'

Adcock had seen this man in the distance, but never from close to before.

'I'm Pagan,' he said when Adcock asked, and spat into the road.

'Where do you live?'

'Is that a joke?'

Adcock was startled by the man's ferocious response. 'Friend, I know very little about this place still. I know few people and . . .'

'Then you should know that I am the steward to Lady Isabel, who was lady of this manor until your master evicted her, stealing her estates, her home and her life. Now she has nothing.'

'Her husband?'

'Was killed in the last wars, God remember him, and because he was honourable and stayed true to his lord, your lord saw to it that his widow lost all.'

Adcock looked away. The older man's eyes were unwavering, and in them there was only bile and hatred. It made Adcock feel worse than insignificant to be treated in this way. 'Well, I am sorry to hear that. I had no hand in it, though. I'm just the steward here.'

'Aye. And you know who you replace? Her son. It was her son who died, so don't think that you'll win her favour if you tell her you're the man sent to fill his boots!'

'Sweet Jesus!' Adcock murmured to himself as he walked away. 'Save me from old servants like him! I only wanted to be friendly.'

But wanting to make friends was difficult. The peasants did not trust him. All looked on him as a spy in Sir Geoffrey's pay, and none would drink with him or talk for long, except about matters that affected the manor. As he continued on his way, when he glanced over his shoulder, he saw the man Pagan in the distance, still staring at him with those narrow, malevolent eyes as though accusing him of stealing another man's position. It was hardly fair to suspect Adcock of plotting to take his predecessor's place when Ailward had died days before Adcock had been called here, in God's name!

He was almost at the bog, swamped with feelings of melancholy, when he saw the rider in the distance.

Whoever it was, the man was riding fast, and Adcock peered with interest at the approaching figure, forgetting his own woes for a moment.

The fellow rode hard, like a man with a terrible mission, but when he saw Adcock standing by the roadside he made for him and reined in hard, making his rounsey skip and slither on the icy surface.

'Friend, I am seeking Iddesleigh – can you tell me where I may find it?'

'Of course – keep on this road, and you'll soon be there. It can only be a mile or two distant. You are looking for a friend?'

'I am looking for my servant's killer! Someone has murdered him, so I've heard!' Simon spat. 'You know of the murder?'

'You were the master of Ailward?' Adcock said. 'I am here in his place, and . . .'

'Who? No, I'm here because of Hugh. Hugh Shepherd or Hugh Drewsteignton, he may have been called. Someone has told me that he was killed along with his woman and child.'

Adcock felt a sharp pain in his breast. 'When was this?' he gasped.

'I don't know! You say the vill is up there?'

'Yes, just stay on the road and you'll soon be there.'

'My thanks. Godspeed!'

Adcock stood staring after him as the man shouted at his mount, spurring it to a gallop again, and with sparks flying from the shoes the beast leaped away like a bullet from a sling.

There was a dreadful sense of conviction in his breast. He remembered the coroner's visit three days ago, and Sir Geoffrey's insistence that Adcock should invite the man to lunch at the hall before going on. There had been mention then of deaths at Iddesleigh, but Adcock knew no one up there and had paid little attention as they spoke of a family murdered in the next village. It had meant nothing to him at the time.

But now he had seen the pain that those deaths had caused. A man, his woman and his child, all dead. And who could have committed such a crime?

Adcock knew too well which band of men in this area was most likely to carry out an attack of that kind.

Friar John, too, was fully aware that there were dangerous men in the area.

He sat and poked at his fire, feeling curiously disconsolate. He had come here hoping to find some sort of sanctuary for a little while, and instead here he was, hiding in a rude shelter, a more than half-ruined cottage, with a man who had been near to death for the last few days.

The fellow lay on a thin blanket, his eyes wide and staring. His face was fixed into a glower of such malevolence that several times when John caught a glimpse of it, he had been tempted to cross himself: the man looked so much like a demon. Even now, as the flickering flames caught his features, John had to shudder. There was something in his eyes that spoke of a mind driven to lunacy, and as the light caught them, the reflection almost looked as though the fire was in his soul. It made John think that the poor fellow was already living in a hell of his own, and the idea was fearfully compelling.

He knew little enough about him. When he picked him up from the ruins of the house, the man had been unable to speak. He'd merely sat, his head in his hands, rocking slowly back and forth and moaning to himself. John had pulled him away from the wreckage of the building, uttering kind, soft words to calm him, and then settling him on the ground with a few blankets he'd found hanging from a branch. The woman must have washed them and left them hanging to dry. And all the while the flames began to take hold in the house.

'Wait there, I'll fetch help.'

'No! No! No one else!'

'Man, you need a room to sleep in and some help. I can't do much for you. I don't have the knowledge.'

'No one. I must keep away, somewhere safe . . . can't go to vill. Must stay away . . .' His voice trailed away while he stared about him with wide, anxious eyes. 'They killed her, my Constance! Raped her and killed her! Where's my boy? Where's Hugh . . .'

John shook his head. Inside the doorway he had seen the child tossed into a corner. 'Let me fetch the watch. There must be someone even in . . .'

'No. No one.'

'Man, that's foolish. I have to fetch a priest, maybe, or a leech. You aren't well. I'm sure you need a bleeding.'

That was when the injured man had reached up and grabbed his robe with a fist that shook as though the fellow had the ague. 'No one! They'll kill me too!'

'Who will? Who did this?'

But the man had used his grip on John's robe to pull himself up, and he had no energy, seemingly, to speak further. Instead all his will and energy was devoted to hobbling along on John's arm towards the lane, where he stooped and picked up a billhook and an axe. He thrust both into his broad leather belt, then stumbled and all but collapsed. John helped him up.

There had been few times in his life when he had seen a man so badly in need of aid. From his crabbed gait it was clear that he was in pain from a number of wounds, although mercifully there appeared to be little blood. What there was seemed to be on his back, but the man wouldn't allow John to look at it. 'Later. Got to get away from here.'

His right leg was giving him trouble, but he still half hopped, half staggered along, clinging on to John with the desperation of a man, so John thought at the time, who was petrified with fear for his life. That was the only reason why John had helped him, really, and why he'd agreed not to call for the hue and cry or the local bailiff. He reasoned that if the man was so shocked and scared, it would be cruel to force him to go to speak to the law officers. Better, perhaps, to take him somewhere where he might recover himself. John himself could speak to the officers later, when this man was settled.

'Can't stay Iddesleigh.'

It wasn't a statement that invited debate. John could understand why, of course. If the man thought that his attackers were from that vill, he'd be unlikely to trust to folks there to look after him. 'What of Monkleigh?'

'No! Can't . . . can't stay near here. I've got to get away.'

'Man, you are not going to travel far with that leg,' John said reasonably.

'Hugh.'

'What?'

'My name: it's Hugh.' The man turned and looked at him, and although it wasn't quite madness, there was a terrible purpose in his eyes now which shone through them even here in the darkness. 'I'll travel as far as I need, Friar.'

'I don't blame you. I'd want to run away too, but . . .'

Hugh turned and gave him a stare from feverish, maddened eyes. 'I'm not running away. I need to get better so I can find them.'

Chapter Thirteen

Pagan walked into the chapel and knelt at the altar. It was chill in there, and the tiled floor was uncomfortable, but he was used to it. He'd been coming here to pray all his life, and he tried to do so every day, although he treated the Sunday Mass with a special reverence.

He had never understood the way of so many people today. They all hurried from one place to another and paid little attention to their souls. Even Sundays, which should have been days of rest, were treated with . . . flexibility. The priest himself, old Isaac, had often told them that God wouldn't mind them hurrying to fetch in the harvest before church, provided they all listened to the service and didn't doze.

So many of them seemed to think that the chapel was a quiet refuge from nagging wives or the troubles of the manor, where they could forget all their worries for a little while. It shouldn't be like that. God expected more from his people, surely.

Pagan himself liked to pray for the men he had known. There were so many who had died in the famine eight years ago, and then there were the masters he had loved. He liked to pray for them all.

It was while his rosary was slipping through his fingers and he was saying some words for poor Ailward that he heard the door rattling. He finished his prayers and made the sign of the cross. As soon as he stood, the old priest chuckled drily.

'So, you young reprobate. You've been misbehaving again, have you?'

'No, Father. But I like to come and pray. You know that.'

'Pagan, you pray more than most others in here. It is good to see you. When I think of the godless, murderous sons of whores at Monkleigh, I could burst with anger. Your penitence is an example.'

'Thank you, Father.'

'I will be dead soon. You know that?'

'You have many years . . .'

'No, I'll soon be dead. And when I am, the lad will be in charge.'

'Your coadjutor?'

'Humphrey.' The rheumy old eyes took in Pagan for a moment. 'The lad will need help; protection. You help him. He will think he's not good enough. God knows, he might even try to run away. Stop him. Keep him here. He has a good heart, I am sure of it. He may even come to realise it himself, given time.'

Pagan frowned at him with confusion. 'What do you mean? He's a priest, isn't he? Why would he run away from his people?'

'Because not all men are what they seem, Pagan. Sometimes a man may be in a job which he's not supposed to have. But he'll make a good priest. Don't worry about that. You just look after him. I won't be able to for much longer.'

On the second day, the Monday, when Hugh was less stiff and more able to make the distance, John woke him at dusk and the pair of them crossed the river to the woods at the other side, and up the lane to a ruined cottage John knew of: a shod friar and the man he'd rescued. Sitting in the ruins of an old house, with a fire that was smoking more than John liked, at least the two of them were warm enough.

Hugh was in a dreadful state. He was pale and in much pain. His face was twisted with it, and with his terrible desire for vengeance on the men who had destroyed his life. He wanted them to die. All the time he slept, his hands gripped his weapons, and his features moved alarmingly as he ground his teeth, whispered sweet words as though to his wife, and then shrieked with horror and rage . . . Still, the wound in his back appeared not to be serious, which was a relief. It was only shallow, a blow struck by a man standing above him, thrusting down. His blade had caught a rib and glanced off it, saving Hugh's life. It took away a flap of skin, but that was all. There was some weeping now, but no pus.

John wiped his face with his eyes closed. It was impossible to rest just now with Hugh requiring all his attention during the day, and then crying out and weeping at night. John could not take his ease, and it was impossible to ask anyone else to come to help him. Hugh had begged him to send a messenger to his master's friend at some place called Furnshill, and it was sheer good fortune that he had found a stableboy from Exbourne who was leading a horse back to his inn after a guest had borrowed it. John had promised him a reward once he had delivered the message. The fact that he was not from Iddesleigh or Monkleigh was a reassurance. Someone from the locality might have gone straight to the men who had tried to kill Hugh.

It was hard to concentrate now, though. So much despair, so much fear. And John knew the same terrors. He could understand how desolate Hugh must feel, having lost his family. After all, a friar gave up his own relatives when he joined the convent. John himself only had the one member of his family left now, and it was years since he'd seen her. In fact he was quite scared at the thought of ever meeting her again. She'd probably give him hell for his behaviour in the past. Always convinced of being right, she was a hard woman to argue with. Still, her husband was a good man, and perhaps he would have worn off some of the rougher parts of her nature. Who could tell? She might even be a mother.

He shook his head and smiled. It would be good to see her again.

Then he opened his tired eyes again as Hugh burst into sobs of grief. No, he must stay here a little longer, to make sure that this poor injured man was safe. This was no time to go gallivanting across the country to find a sister he hadn't seen in nearly twenty years.

Nicholas le Poter felt as though his back was on fire. The slightest movement made each scab pull at his flesh; it was like having burning pitch tipped over him.

It could have been worse. In his anger, Sir Geoffrey could have done more if he'd wanted: had his nose clipped, or his ears cut off for offering insult to a man there to parlay. Not that it was much comfort knowing that. The son of a whore had done enough damage as it was. It would soon come to the younger Despenser's ears that Sir Geoffrey had been meting out unjust punishments to those whom he trusted.

Not that Sir Geoffrey knew that Lord Despenser had put Nick here to watch the steward's behaviour. Lord Despenser was no fool, and he wasn't going to trust even an old man who'd spent years in his father's service like Sir Geoffrey without having someone else there who could keep an eye on things.

At first it'd seemed the place was well run and effective enough. The peasants certainly seemed to have their lands well in hand, and it was easy enough to see that they were completely docile under Sir Geoffrey's control, but there was a weakness to his authority, so Nick thought. He'd wanted to laugh when he saw how Sir Geoffrey tried to negotiate boundaries with Sir Odo. That was ridiculous! The men who ran the estates for the Despenser need not ask for favours or make offers. They could demand what they wanted.

It was sensible to take the land east of the river from Sir Odo. Odo couldn't keep it if they demanded it, and scaring the fool of a bailiff from the place was the first stage in grabbing it. Next would be to get the lands farther up, all the way to Iddesleigh and beyond, if possible, so the Despenser territory would be more or less self-supporting in manpower. If they had the Meeth lands as well as Iddesleigh and Monkleigh, they would be able to begin to threaten Lord Hugh de Courtenay.

Of course, if the lands expanded, clearly Lord Despenser would need a man with more brains than this burned-out old fool in charge. Lord Despenser would want someone younger, more ambitious – and ruthless. Someone like Nick.

Nick grimaced and shifted himself uncomfortably. His back felt dreadful. Still, he hoped that he would soon be in a position to offer Lord Despenser additional territory and influence, and when he did, Sir Geoffrey would be out of his post, and Nick would have it. He'd make certain of that.

But there was something strange about all this. Nick had heard something about the old lands when he was last talking to Ailward, on the day Ailward died. It was something he'd been trying to find out about, because it could explain the negotiations which Sir Geoffrey kept holding with Sir Odo – and why Sir Odo still held lands east of the river.

The two of them had stolen the Despenser's lands.

* * *

Simon reached Iddesleigh a few minutes after leaving Adcock, and as soon as he arrived at the inn he flung himself from his horse, shouting for an ostler, and marched up the steps to the great oaken door.

'Where's the master here?' he bellowed as he walked in.

'He is here, Simon,' Baldwin said mildly, standing and crossing the floor. 'And I have to tell you how sorry I was to hear about Hugh.'

Simon could say nothing for a few moments. He took Baldwin's hand and held his gaze for a moment, and then cleared his throat gruffly, turning away, 'So was I. It came as a great shock. Why should he expect danger here? In a quiet rural vill like Iddesleigh?'

He had wandered to the table where Jankin still sat. Jankin looked up at him and half shrugged his shoulders. He had seen plenty of distraught men: men who had lost their wives, men who had lost their sons or their daughters. It was one of his jobs as the innkeeper to try to offer some solace where he could, and he did so now.

'Master, you've travelled far. Sit, let me fetch you some ale, and then some food to break your fast. I will tell you all I know about your servant.'

Baldwin briefly told Simon all that he had heard already, and when Jankin had bellowed through the door at the back to his wife for some food, and had returned with an immense jug of ale and another cup for Simon to sit with the travellers, both Simon and Baldwin looked at him.

'Master Jankin, you have been very frank and helpful. Now I would ask for any more information you can give us. You said that the Despensers' man had taken the Lady Lucy. What did you mean? Why should he?'

'The Despensers have a manor just south of us here, Monkleigh,' Jankin said. He sipped thoughtfully at his ale. 'Good brew, this one . . . Wish I could get it right more often . . . Well, their man is called Sir Geoffrey Servington. He's a large bully of a man with the manners of an ox. Maybe fifty years old, maybe a little fewer. Strong, harsh, confident.'

'You describe half the knights in the king's host,' Baldwin pointed out.

'True. Well, he has been here as steward to the Despenser manor for these last seven years, and I dare say he is efficient enough. But he's like so many men of power, can't possess it without using it. He bullies where he may, trying to win stores and victuals for free wherever he can.'

'It is the way of strong men,' Baldwin agreed. He didn't approve of such behaviour, but he knew it was hard to stamp out.

'Except things are getting worse here, since his master has grown so . . . so . . .'

Baldwin eyed him cautiously. The innkeeper was uncomfortable. 'Master keeper, let me put your mind at ease. I am a Keeper of the King's Peace and my interest is purely to find the murderer of my friend's servant. I care nothing for the loyalties of individuals, and to be honest, I doubt even Despenser or the king himself cares about the opinions of an innkeeper in the depths of Devon. Anything said here will be kept between us.'

He reached into his tunic's neck and withdrew his small wooden crucifix. Over the years he had worn it close to his skin every day. It had travelled with him when he first sailed for the Holy Land and the disaster that was Acre; he had borne it in the islands when he had finally made good his pledge and joined the Knights Templar; and he wore it and wept when he saw his friends die in the flames of an intolerable fire, a fire which had been lighted by bigotry and deceit.

'I, Sir Baldwin de Furnshill, Keeper of the King's Peace, swear that I shall not divulge your name to any man in connection with what we discuss and I will not give away any information about powerful men to anyone at all, neither your friend nor your enemy. I swear this on the Gospels and by my faith that I shall die and rise to Heaven.'

Simon took hold of it. 'I also swear this. I, Simon Puttock, Bailiff to the Abbot of Tavistock, will not give away your name or your help to me in finding the murderer of my companion and servant and his family. And I swear also that I shall find his murderer and see him pay for his offences.'

Jankin sat back and eyed them both. 'I think we ought to have another ale,' he said, and grinned.

'Right,' he continued when they had all emptied their cups. He set the three cups in a triangle. 'Sir Geoffrey lies here to the east, far

down south of us. He is Despenser's man through and through, but
he's not averse to a little money on the side. Just here, west of him, and
reaching northwards up to here, is Sir John Sully's land. He's not in
the pay of Despenser, he's a loyal vassal of Lord Hugh de Courtenay.
Sir John doesn't live here, though. He spends most of his time over at
his other estates, especially Ash Reigny, where he's lord of the manor.
So all the affairs of his place here are in the hands of Sir Odo de
Bordeaux. Sir Odo lives *here* at the manor house of Fishleigh. His
estates are extensive, and cover all this.' He waved a hand airily.

Simon looked at the cups. 'And the two of them are at daggers
drawn?'

'Yes. Lord Hugh de Courtenay is not a natural ally of my Lord
Despenser, so I think, and that means that Sir Geoffrey has his master's
agreement to harry and upset all the affairs of Lord de Courtenay's
estates.'

'And Hugh's lands were on the de Courtenay estates?' Simon
frowned.

Baldwin nodded. 'The good Prioress of Belstone let Hugh and
Constance have use of it, but she had only rented it from Lord de
Courtenay, and didn't own it.' He turned to Jankin again. 'So you
believe that Sir Geoffrey could have launched an attack on Sir Odo's
lands? Why? Just to irritate?'

'I don't know. I shouldn't be surprised. If he intended to try to force
Sir Odo to give up some of the lands nearer the Despenser estates . . .?'

Baldwin nodded. 'I have heard of such tactics before. Sometimes a
man who is enormously powerful can decide to take over his neighbour's meagre belongings. But one attack on a man doesn't necessarily
mean that he's intent on invasion and theft.'

'No, but when there have been other attacks, it starts to look
suspicious,' Jankin said. 'There was one on Sir Odo's sergeant the
same day as the attack on your man, Bailiff. A force of rough men-at-
arms turned up there, so I've heard, and threatened him until he left
his land. A sergeant, forced off his own land! All his animals were
rounded up and killed or driven off, while his garden was flattened.
He has nothing now, except what he can claim from his master.'

'And you mentioned Lady Lucy, too,' Baldwin reminded him gently.

Jankin shook his head and stared at his cup. 'She's from Meeth, over west, north of Odo's manor. A nice little estate there, she has. It was hers with her husband, but now she's gone missing, like I said. Everyone here believes it's Sir Geoffrey again.'

'Why?' Simon demanded.

'Look, sir,' Jankin said, rearranging the cups once more into a triangular pattern. 'If Sir Geoffrey take us here, at Iddesleigh, then he has a nice stretch of land all the way up from Exbourne, down this way, up to Dolton. It's a good spread, and it'd give him a bit of a power base down here in Devon.'

'Why would he need it?' Baldwin asked, but then he guessed at the truth before Jankin could speak. 'To pressurise Lord Hugh!'

'I think so, yes. If he can take a few parcels of land, make his own controls increase, then he can start to threaten Lord de Courtenay. There are so many murmurings, masters,' Jankin added, leaning forward, his voice dropping. 'We may be out of the way here, but we hear mutters and rumours nevertheless. Everyone is talking about the Despensers and how cruel they are.'

'It is one thing to threaten a sergeant from his land, another to talk of capturing a lady and holding her, surely,' Simon said.

Baldwin was aware of feeling cool, and he glanced at the fire, thinking it must have died, but it was was burning brightly. He felt a sudden anxiety. If there should be war again, it would be a harsh affair. There were too many bad memories already, and a civil war would mean families split against themselves, brothers fighting each other, perhaps even sons fighting their fathers. If it came to war, it would be the worst he had seen. 'It has been done, Simon,' he said heavily.

'By whom?'

'The Despenser.' Baldwin's head tilted and he toyed with his cup, then refilled it and drank it off in one gulp. The strong ale hit his stomach like burning oil. It only served to increase his discomfort. 'They took a lady and tortured her only a short while ago. A knight's widow. Stephen Baret was killed at Boroughbridge, I have heard, while fighting against the Despensers' men. A little later his wife, Madam Baret, was taken by Despenser and tortured to make her sign away her lands to him. I have heard this, and that the young woman was so badly maltreated that she lost her mind completely. She is a lunatic now.'

'Sweet Jesus!' Simon breathed.

Jankin nodded. 'That's what I'd heard too. When I heard that Lady Lucy was gone, I wondered whether it could be the same. And then I thought about her lands,' he added, and moved the great earthenware jug until it formed a square, resting above the Sir Odo cup and left of the Iddesleigh one. 'Because she has more than these other three estates all put together, you see. If a man wanted to carve out a nice part of Devon for himself, he could do worse than take over her land with the others. Especially if he owned Iddesleigh too, because then he could just swallow up the whole of the Fishleigh manor entire. And he'd have a goodly portion of land to set against even a man like Lord Hugh de Courtenay.'

Chapter Fourteen

When John rose and left the room to fetch some water, Hugh was glad to see him go.

Shepherd, farmer, moorman and more recently servant, Hugh had lived with the companionship of others, but he was essentially self-reliant. He had friends, and he valued them, but right now he knew that they were all far away. His master was many miles to the south; his friend Edgar, the servant of Sir Baldwin de Furnshill, was miles east at the manor near Cadbury. He might be on his way, but he had responsibilities; Hugh was alone here.

Men had taken it into their heads to attack him, and had killed the only woman who had ever looked at him. He wouldn't weep. He couldn't. But the sight of her was in his mind, her smell seemed to be in his nose, and if he closed his eyes he could almost feel her body. Everything that he was, everything that he loved and wanted, had been taken from him. Perhaps by rogue felons, just a wandering gang of outlaws who had spotted his house and seen an easy target for their malice. They approached it, raped his woman, killed her, and thought that they'd killed him too.

Except he knew that was ballocks. It made no sense. If there was a gang of outlaws in the area, he'd have heard. You couldn't hide a murderous group of men so easily, not in a place like this. And Hugh knew that the men of Monkleigh were keen on taking hold of Iddesleigh. It had been a subject of conversation for a long while. Everybody in Iddesleigh knew it.

And Hugh was an outsider, as Constance was too. He could be attacked without upsetting the lord of the manor of Iddesleigh. He was a safe target.

It was easy to kill Constance and force Hugh from their land. Very easy, he thought, and hurled his axe at a log. It struck and rolled over and over, the blade embedded in the wood.

Perkin was out at the bog and digging when Adcock arrived, and he groaned inwardly to see the new sergeant. He looked over at the other men working with him. Beorn was quick to see the point of his gaze, shot a glance over his shoulder, and set to with more enthusiasm than before, although one lad seemed only to find amusement in Adcock's appearance. He stood and peered at him. 'That the new sergeant, Perkin? Dun't look much.'

'Just dig, 'Tin.. He's here to see whether we're working, and you setting your arm on your shovel and looking at the view ain't likely to impress him much, is it?'

'I just wondered what he was like.'

Perkin grunted. If Martin wanted to get into trouble, that was his lookout, not Perkin's. Perkin had no authority to order him about.

He didn't want to be here at the bog, and he wasn't happy about his position in the manor. Ever since finding Ailward's body, he had been more and more unsettled. Men had disputes, yes, and once in a while someone might be struck down, but it was rarely anything so disgraceful as a murderous attack. Far more common that a man would get roaring drunk and try to swing a fist, only to have his head clubbed by a comrade who was keen to keep the peace.

Ailward had been murdered, though. There was blood all over him from the smashed skull, and Perkin reckoned that although the coroner had registered the stab wound on the naked body as they rolled it about in front of him, so that the jury could see it and agree with his findings, it was the ruin of his head that killed him. The stab came later, to make sure of him. Perkin had an idea that a man like *that* suspicious son of a Barnstaple whore wouldn't have let anyone attack him from in front. Only someone behind him could kill him, so his attacker had perhaps beaten him with a club, or perhaps a rock?

Perkin stood up suddenly, scowling ferociously as he considered this new possibility.

'You are doing well,' Adcock commented. He had drawn level with Perkin as the peasant had mused on the murder, and now he stood at his side and peered down into the channel cut from the stream towards the roadway and the bog beyond. 'With luck it will not take long now.'

'No, master,' Perkin muttered.

Adcock glanced at him. 'Perkin, I don't . . . I am not here as a lord or something, to make your life harsh. All I want is to make this estate work well for all of us. And then we'll have a good surplus, I hope, and no one will go hungry.'

'Good.'

'But you don't trust me?'

'It's not that. I'm just thinking of that inquest. It seemed odd that the coroner should be asked to come back here.'

Adcock reddened. 'I think it was just coincidence.'

'What was?'

'That the coroner was another knight of our master, Lord Despenser.'

Perkin was watching his face, and as Adcock spoke he realised what the man was implying. The Despensers were taking an interest in the murder of their sergeant, which was natural, but perhaps it meant the findings weren't entirely unbiased. And then there was the other matter . . .

'Did the coroner go to the other murders?' he asked casually.

'I believe he did,' Adcock said, as calmly. 'But I do not think he had much time to spend there.'

'That would be no surprise – he was here for an age, eating and drinking with Sir Geoffrey,' Perkin guessed.

Adcock was suddenly nervous. This peasant was too knowing for his comfort. He hated his own suspicions: that the coroner had been called here to leave Ailward's death open, that he'd been bribed not to rock Sir Geoffrey's boat. Adcock had heard Sir Geoffrey and the coroner talk quietly about Iddesleigh and the murdered family up there, and later, as the coroner was leaving, Adcock saw a little purse pass between them. It could only mean that Sir Geoffrey wanted the murders covered up, and that he was paying to protect his own men – or himself.

It was a foul reflection. To live in a manor where he suspected his own master of murders was appalling. As it was, he daren't even think of bringing his woman within miles of the place in case she was raped.

He nodded harshly, staring back at the bog. It would not be long before the workers had cut the channel far enough. And then they would see the water gushing from the mire to the stream and away. Better to concentrate on that, on his work, than on his new position and the fears that were drowning his senses.

There were other tasks for him, though. He had seen that a pasture farther up the hill needed to have its hedge renewed. Perhaps he should attend to that. He'd leave this unsettling churl, and get on with his other duties.

Perkin watched him go, and then turned back to his work. 'Come on, you lazy sodomites! What, looking for a sheep to shag, 'Tin? No? Then dig, boy, dig!'

Jeanne could feel Simon's pain as soon as she saw him. 'Oh, Simon, I am so sorry!'

Baldwin had insisted on fetching his wife as soon as Jankin's wife brought out their food, and now Jeanne and the two men sat at the table with a platter filled with pig's liver, bacon, kidneys, and a loaf. Jankin did not believe in guests going hungry when they could leave his inn replete.

For Jeanne the table would have appeared daunting at the best of times, but today, seeing Simon so distraught, she found it was impossible to do justice to such a spread. She put her hand on his with sympathy.

It was plain that Simon was feeling his loss. His eyes were sunken and red-rimmed; his usually hale features were pale and he had acquired a curious habit of rubbing his thumbs against his fingers, as though both hands were raw from handling his reins. He'd bitten his nails to the quick, too, and she saw that two fingers were bleeding from over-enthusiastic nibbling.

'Yes, well. He was a good friend as well as a loyal servant,' Simon said after a moment. He half-heartedly speared a kidney and some liver.

Jeanne tried to keep him company with two thick rashers of bacon, and watched with horror mingled with respect as her husband filled his own trencher. It was a strange sight, to see Simon eating little, while her husband heaped his plate. Jeanne excused herself from eating too much by trying to feed the little girl in her lap.

'Did he mention that he'd made any enemies here?' Baldwin asked after some moments of chewing.

'He didn't say so. If he'd given such offence that a man decided to kill him and slaughter his wife and child too, I'm sure he would have told me. It's not the sort of thing I'd expect, though. And if he had offended someone so deeply, I'm sure he would have realised the danger. He would have made sure he was safe, or at least he'd have made sure that his wife was. Hugh was no fool when it came to fighting.'

'I remember,' Jeanne said. She had seen him in fights. In Tavistock he'd knocked a man down before she had even realised the fellow was a threat.

'He was astute enough,' Baldwin agreed. 'But the cleverest man can fail to see into another man's heart, can't he?'

'If that's the case, we'll likely never know what happened, then,' Simon snapped. 'I can only tell you what he said to me, and that was that this was a pleasant, unspoiled place with no fighting. He didn't look as though he thought he was in any danger at all, any of the times I've seen him. And now he's dead.'

'The innkeeper doesn't seem to think he was disliked at all. He behaved like an old moorman, and kept himself to himself,' Baldwin mused, unaffected by his friend's temper. 'Perhaps someone else could tell us more? The local priest should be a good man to ask.'

'Yes, let's go there. Are you ready?' Simon asked. His own plate was all but untouched as he pushed the stool from the table.

'No, Simon. And I would like to see you eat that before we go anywhere,' Baldwin said mildly, and when he saw the expression on his friend's face he continued, 'if we find Hugh's killer, Simon, I want you fit and ready to help catch him, or *kill* him. Hugh wouldn't be glad to know he'd been the cause of Meg's being widowed just because you came here to avenge him and weren't prepared.'

Simon looked furious and leaned forward a moment as though to utter a fierce denial, but then he looked down at his hands and shook his head slightly. 'Hugh was a friend for many years. I will find the man who killed him, and I will see him hang, but you're right. I won't kill myself.' He poured another cup of ale and sipped, then upended it. 'To Hugh!' he declared.

Baldwin and Jeanne both drank to Hugh as well, and as they held their cups aloft Baldwin met Simon's gaze and gave a sympathetic grin. And as they stared at each other over the table top, there came a grumbling roar from behind Baldwin, and he felt the flesh on his back creep as the hated voice rasped out: 'Ah, good. Food! Thought it must be time by now. Mind you eat up, lady, we don't want you starving now you're eating for two, eh? Give me that platter. Ah, the kidneys are rare. That's how I like them, so they still taste strong. What? What? What are you staring at? Give me a cup of that ale. It's not as good as our manor's, I expect, but I am a bit thirsty.'

And Emma sat on the bench beside Baldwin, who watched in horror as the juices dribbled down her chin from her open mouth.

Father Matthew grunted to himself as he lifted himself from squatting before the altar, and turned to leave the church just as he heard the footsteps outside.

Two men and a woman walked in, all taking water and crossing themselves. Matthew didn't recognise any of them, but it was clear enough from their clothing and behaviour that they were not peasants. He immediately ranked them as merchants or traders on their way through the vill, before he saw the marks of chivalry on the older of the two men. This fellow with the trim beard that followed the line of his jaw was obviously a knight. His thick neck spoke of the years of training with a steel helmet on his head; the right shoulder was clearly more powerful than the left, as you'd expect in a swordsman. Not only that, either. It was also there in his eyes, which were stern and authoritative. He was not a man who would be easy to lie to: those eyes looked very intelligent.

'Father?'

'Yes?'

It was the second man who spoke, the one with the red, sad eyes, who looked as though he had recently been bereaved.

'We are here because of the murder of the man Hugh with his wife and child. He was my servant. I want to learn what I may of this affair.'

'My son,' Matthew sighed. He looked over his shoulder at the altar and closed his eyes. 'Come, sit yourselves here. Be at ease.'

There were no seats in the nave, but he led them to a low projection in the inner wall at the rear of the church, where they could perch a little more comfortably. Matthew himself waved away the knight's offer of a space. 'No, good knight, I've been kneeling for some while in prayer. It may be good for a young man to pray for many hours, but I have calluses on calluses at knee and ankle now. I think I would do myself more good by standing for a little while.'

They introduced themselves, and Matthew looked from one to another, his gaze resting shrewdly on Baldwin after a few moments. 'So, a bailiff who has lost his servant, and a keeper who wishes to help his friend? You must have valued this servant very highly, Bailiff.'

'I did. Can you tell us anything about his death? Did he have any enemies?'

'I have to confess, I do not know of any,' Matthew said. 'There are some petty disputes in the vill, but nothing that would bear upon your man. No, if he died as a result of a dispute, I should think that it was by accident. Two men fought, and he stood in their path.'

'Perhaps Fishleigh and Monkleigh?' Baldwin interjected.

'You have heard much,' Matthew said more flatly. He did not wish to discuss the politics between those two manors with strangers.

'We have heard a little. We have much more to learn,' Baldwin said. 'And you haven't answered.'

'It is possible, but I know nothing about such matters. They are the realm of powerful people, not me.'

'Who owns the living here?' Simon asked. 'Is this the advowson of one or other manor?'

Matthew bridled. 'You mean to suggest that I would conceal a murder just to keep my seat here? Sir, you malign me!'

'He did not mean to, Father,' Jeanne said. 'However, you can see how distraught we are. Is there no help you can give us?'

'If you wish to learn more about the two manors, perhaps you should ask old Isaac down at Monkleigh chapel. He knows much more about the history than I do. I've not been here all that long, in truth.'

'What of his body? Is he buried?' Simon asked.

'I am sorry . . . no. We found the remains of his wife and the little boy, too. He was lying in the corner of the room, so wasn't quite so badly burned, but the man . . . his body must have been entirely consumed by the fire.'

Baldwin cocked his head. 'Entirely? In a small house fire?'

'It was hardly a "small" fire, Sir Knight. It destroyed the place. It's possible that there are more bones inside, but I think it unlikely that they'll be found.'

'What of the others?' Simon asked.

'As soon as the coroner had completed his inquest, they were buried in my cemetery. Would you like me to show them to you?'

Simon and Baldwin exchanged a glance. Simon said, 'Yes, please, Father. I would like to say goodbye to them. They came here seeking peace, and they deserve a kindly word if nothing else.'

Chapter Fifteen

Emma sat back and eyed the wooden trenchers as the others walked out, then hurriedly took the choicest leftover scraps and set them on her own, soaking up the juices with a hunk of bread.

This was a foul little place. There was really nowhere as attractive as Bordeaux, where she and Jeanne had spent so many happy years when they were young. The climate, the wines, the markets . . . and here all there was was mud, dirt, smelly and uncouth peasants who hardly knew how to address a lady, and rain. Always rain. It was a revolting place to live.

Of course she had agreed to come here as soon as her charge was chosen by Sir Ralph. He was a good man. Always respectful, polite, sensible. Well, until he began to blame Lady Jeanne for their lack of children. Then he changed a lot. But that was only to be expected. He was a knight, and he wanted an heir. What was a marriage if God didn't bless the union? The whole point of marriage was children.

On hearing a little sniff, she looked down at the bundle of clothing beside her. Richalda was asleep, but she kicked even when dead to the world, and now her little feet began pounding at Emma's thigh. The woman glanced about her narrowly, and then put a hand down and started to stroke the mite's head.

Sir Baldwin was all right, really. Not so bad as a master. His manor was dreadful, with a poky little hall, a piddling solar and pathetic lands about it, but for all that he had advanced, with Jeanne's help, and he was a fairly successful officer. Not that Emma would ever admit to his face that he had any skills or qualities that she could admire. She preferred to keep her distance from a master. Always.

It would have been good to have children of her own, but that wasn't going to happen. Not now. No, better that she concentrated on

Jeanne's. This one and the one to follow. Who could tell? There may be more later.

Baldwin was a lot better than some she knew of. Some women lived in constant fear of their masters. And she had known a bad experience, too . . .

It was more than ten years ago now, when it had happened. He was Jeanne's uncle, the man who had taken the girl in when she was orphaned. He had chosen Emma as a maid for her, and took a close interest in both girls. At the time Emma had thought his concern was purely that of an uncle who sought to ensure that his niece was well cared for, looking to Emma's behaviour and training to ensure that Jeanne grew to be a courteous and elegant young lady, a credit to him and the household.

But it wasn't just that. Emma realised only afterwards that she was not the first. She wouldn't be the last, in all probability, either. The maid who looked after his wife was treated the same way, and if anyone were to complain, well, the street was just beyond the door, and a maid could as easily be on one side of the door as the other. Emma knew she wouldn't last ten minutes on the streets. So she assiduously saw to Jeanne's every need so that Jeanne need never complain about her, and accepted that each night she might be visited by the lecherous old bastard.

Escape to England, this wet, cold, cheerless part of the realm, was still escape. She detested almost every aspect of the place – but she wouldn't seriously want to swap it for Bordeaux, not for all the wine they exported!

Perkin stood back as Beorn jumped down into the trench. They had driven a channel all the way up to within two spade spits of the bog, and now they needed only a little more work to be able to see the water drain.

'Go on, you old woman,' he called to Beorn, and the peasant showed his teeth in a smile, then started to drive his shovel into the boundary of the bog. Perkin watched with amusement.

The first shovelful hurtled through the air and narrowly missed Perkin, landing with a damp slap only a foot away from him. 'Hey!'

The second would have hit him in the midriff, had he not leaped backwards. 'You mad bugger!'

Beorn grinned again, and took two more spadesful, and then climbed from the channel quickly as a filthy-looking black-brown tide began to breach the remaining wall. It swirled, mud slid aside, and suddenly there was a dark stream trickling through a narrow fissure of soil. Soon the trickle had washed the fissure into a breach that bubbled with the draining water.

'Tin was up at the front, peering down into the bog. It was a strange sight, he thought. Usually it would be a soggy mass of matted rushes and grass that looked like a continuation of the pastureland all about, but now, as the level sank, the top of the bog was gradually starting to lower itself.

There were spots, he saw, where the rushes or grasses remained in place as the water seeped away. As Perkin called a boy and told him to go and find the sergeant and fetch him here to tell them what to do next, 'Tin stepped forward cautiously, testing the firmer clumps with his foot. The surface gave, like mud, but was held together with the mat of vegetation. Soon the water was low enough for the full extent of the bog to be seen as it dropped below the level of the surrounding pasture. Beorn was in the ditch again, shovelling out the excess mud before it could block the channel and stop the water flowing away, and 'Tin watched him flinging black mud towards a cursing and laughing Perkin, who rolled balls of mud and hurled them back.

'Tin grinned at the sight, and turned for a last look at the bog's level. It was slowly falling around him, but in the middle it seemed to be dropping much faster, as though in there it was more like a pool of water, and not a bog at all. Things were sticking up from there, and 'Tin peered more closely, repelled and fascinated simultaneously. People had said that there'd be dead animals, even a few men, probably, because this bog had been here for as long as anyone could remember, and he wondered what a man who had died many years before might look like. There was a brown twig lying in a grassy hillock, and he grinned as he imagined it might be a hand, twisted and broken, and cast aside as though this was merely a midden.

Nah! There was hardly likely to be anything here. If anything, some

long-dead cow's carcass or a sheep that had wandered this way before
'Tin was born. Nothing more recent than them. Wouldn't be a man,
he told himself sadly. No one had been missing for so many years that
the chances of finding a human body down there were remote. It was
a shame, because he'd never had a chance to go to witness a hanging.
In the old days, hangings used to happen here on the manor, apparently.
Then executions were made a bit less arbitrary, and instead of being
able to hang anyone he wanted, a lord of the manor had to have the
coroner there, make sure everything was legal and stuff . . .

'Tin was annoyed that he'd missed out on those old days. Men were
braver then, not like the present lot. If they'd had a little courage,
they'd have been off to the wars rather than hanging about the vill
here. He would. He wanted to join a host and fight; he'd be good at
that. Except his mother would go completely potty if he told her . . .

Then he frowned and blinked. As the waters receded, they left a lump
in the filth at the bottom of the rank pool. He could see the shape amidst
the mud, and where he had seen the twig in the little clump of grasses he
now saw that a thin, frail stick-like wrist connected it to a thicker one, as
though they were forearm and upper arm leading to a shoulder . . .

'Perkin! *Perkin!*'

There was nothing to show that this was the grave of two people who
had been loved. It was a small, almost square hole in the ground, with
soil heaped over it and a few heavy stones piled on top to stop animals
from rooting about and digging up the bones. A spare wooden cross
had been made from a couple of lathes lashed together, and this was
thrust in at the head.

'There was no money to pay for the funeral or the mourners,' the
priest said sorrowfully. 'I used some of my own funds to do the best I
could for them. Of course they'd only been here a year or so, so there
was hardly anyone here who really knew them.'

'Two years,' Baldwin corrected him coldly.

Simon heard his voice, but could say nothing. In his breast there
was only a great emptiness, and as he stood staring at the bare little
cross he felt it welling up and rising to his throat, threatening to choke
him. He daren't trust his voice. Instead he made a pretence of clearing

his throat, but the action was belied by his having to wipe his eyes.

He had scarcely known this woman. When he first met her, she had been a fearful novice in need of help, and it was to Hugh's credit that he had given it. Hugh had taken her away from the convent where she had been so unhappy and brought her here, and had protected and served her to the best of his ability. Monosyllabic, morose, taciturn Hugh had given up everything for this woman, and now, because Hugh was dead, this pathetic grave was all that would ever be erected in memory of Constance. Simon felt another sob start to grip him. It washed over him like a shiver of utter coldness, as though the whole of the winter was condensed upon his shoulders and spine, and he shuddered with the bone-aching misery of it all.

He had lost Hugh, and Hugh had had life, woman and child stolen from him. In the midst of his intense wretchedness, Simon felt a rising surge of something else: rage.

If Constance had been unknown to him, perhaps Simon wouldn't have been so moved to fury, but the sight of her grave, and the knowledge of what had been done to her and his man, swamped his sense of justice with the desire for vengeance.

He spoke quietly. 'Have a carpenter put up a proper cross. One with jointed timbers and their names carved on it.'

'If you are sure,' Matthew said. 'Be assured, though, she had all the benefits of a Christian burial, and I prayed with the mourners all night before burying her.'

'I am grateful. And let me know how much the mourners cost, and I'll pay for them.'

'There is no need . . .'

'I want to,' Simon snapped harshly, eyes blazing as he spun round to confront the priest.

'The other man has already paid. The man-at-arms.'

She had only once known a man's love. That was something she still found painful to recall, the memory was so poignant. When she had been at Jeanne's uncle's house for some while, she had met a boy delivering meats to the kitchens, and she had stopped whatever it was she was doing.

He was slim, but with broad shoulders and thick thighs. His hands were elegant, with long fingers, and they weren't yet calloused from work. But it was the face that attracted her. Long, with a slightly pointed chin, it bore a faint beard of reddish-gold, and a tousled mop of fair hair that begged to be stroked and patted into a neater shape. His eyes were laughing blue, and his mouth looked as if it was made to kiss a girl. He was perfect to her.

She and he had managed to meet every so often. Back in those days, of course, Emma had been slimmer, but very full-busted, and she liked to think that she was pretty enough in her own way. Not that many would have argued. Men often pinched her buttocks, like women prodding and poking at slabs of meat on the counters at the market; and there was the behaviour of her master to prove her allure.

When she left Bordeaux to come here, she had lost him. Perhaps he was the only man who could have made her happy for life. Yet at the time she had no thought for that. She was leaving to start a new life in England – a life with her mistress, but without Jeanne's uncle. That in itself had been enough to make her happy . . . and when she'd told poor Ralph, he had been devastated. Now she could see why, but at the time she was irritated, thinking that he should be glad for her, for this wonderful opportunity.

His face when she left him that last time was desolate. She was sure now that he must have gone home and wept for a week to see her go.

Heaving a sigh, she shook her head. There had been other men in her life. There were plenty of them in any household, and she'd made her use of them when she'd wanted to, but not since Ralph had she known the all-devouring love that a woman needed. That was something she would never know again.

And a good thing, too! A woman had better things to do than go mooning about after men. There was no point in all that flirting and circling, like a dog and a bitch sniffing each other. No, better that she should be beyond such diversions. She was an old maid now, nearly thirty years old. It was best that she should forget any thoughts of love.

Which was why it was so annoying that her thoughts kept bending towards men.

* * *

'What other man?' Baldwin managed after a few moments.

'The man-at-arms. Haven't you seen him?' Matthew said.

'No, we have only been here a short while. Was he from one of the local manors?' It seemed quite possible that the murder was the result of some dispute between local lords. After all, from all Baldwin knew of Hugh, he would be perfectly capable of giving insult to a rich and powerful man – intentionally or not. Burning down a house with the man and his family inside was not the act of a peasant with a grudge, it was more brutal than that. More the behaviour of a minor war-lord who was bent on removing an annoyance. But that must mean that Hugh was in the way of someone. Why? What possible obstruction could Hugh be, other than the fact that he was an obstreperous, froward, stubborn churl to deal with at the best of times?

Although it was no excuse for his murder, it may be that Hugh's manner and demeanour could hold a clue to the crime, and Baldwin stored that thought for later.

'It is quite possible,' Matthew said with a certain cooling of his manner. 'Again, I think you should speak to Isaac at the chapel in Monkleigh. He would know the men-at-arms that way better than I do.'

'There are many down there?' Baldwin asked.

'They don't show their faces in daylight if they can help it. They live in the manor all higgledy-piggledy, and only seem to come out at night. As though they are nervous of being seen.'

Baldwin nodded, and now he thought he had a possible group of suspects. He had no doubt that a man-at-arms who was less than entirely honourable could find Hugh's mulish behaviour to be intolerable. If he had insulted a man from the manor, that man might well decide to repay the insult.

He would visit this chapel and learn what he could.

Perkin winced and wiped at his face with his upper sleeve. The smell here was appalling, and he was reluctant to reach down and pick her up, but someone would have to. Beorn was standing at the other side of the body, and now the two of them reached underneath the corpse's torso and lifted her from the shallow, muddy grave. They were up to their groins in the thick mud still, but it was a relief that the worst of the filth seemed to have drained away. Perkin had the black mess up to his breast from falling into a deeper pool, but Beorn had managed to avoid the worst of it.

'It's her, isn't it?' Beorn said quietly.

'Looks like it,' Perkin responded shortly.

They both knew her by sight. Lady Lucy had passed through their vill often enough. She had been a slight woman, attractive, with a snub nose and long fair hair that somehow had always escaped from her coif or wimple when she was out. Perkin could remember the way that she had smiled as she snared a stray tress and tried to tuck it back neatly. Somehow she always ended up with more loose than before, but she'd always grin at her failures, as though it didn't matter anyway.

That was before her old man died, of course. After that, she had grown a great deal more reserved, and her rides tended not to encompass the Monkleigh roads, as though she knew she was in too much danger there.

As she had been. Someone had taken her and broken her limbs, and then killed her. This was no accidental falling into a bog and drowning – not unless she had bound the rocks to her waist herself. She had a great blackened wound in her chest.

Adcock was already waiting at the edge of the bog, and Perkin and Beorn carried her to dry land and set her down as gently as they could.

'The poor woman!' Adcock said in a hushed voice. 'Does anyone recognise her?'

'Lady Lucy of Meeth,' Perkin said, and although his voice was cold, he knew that Adcock had to be innocent of this killing. He only arrived here after she had disappeared.

'She was in there?'

Perkin forbore to answer.

'She must have been murdered and thrown in,' Adcock said.

'She was resting near the middle of the bog. Someone knew this place and chose to carry her there and drop her in,' Beorn said.

'He was a brave man, then,' Adcock guessed. 'Most would fear to enter a bog – especially carrying a heavy burden like her.'

'There were ways to cross it which were safe,' Perkin said shortly. 'Many of us knew them.'

'What is all this?'

The familiar bellow startled the men. There was a slow clopping of hooves as Sir Geoffrey rode up to join them, and sat on his horse staring down at the body.

'Sweet Jesus! What is this?'

Adcock began, 'The men say it is Lady Lucy of . . .'

'I can see who it is, man! What in God's name is she doing here?'

'She was murdered, Sir Geoffrey,' Perkin stated, bending his head respectfully.

'How can you tell that?'

Perkin could scarcely keep the contempt from his tone even though this was his master. 'She has had all her limbs broken, sir. Then someone stabbed her, tied rocks to her, and threw her into the mire here.'

'Probably a raping, then,' Adcock said. 'She must have been a pretty little thing.'

'Rape?' Perkin repeated.

'Yes, rape. Quite right,' Sir Geoffrey said. 'Who pulled her out of there, though? The coroner will have something to say about that.'

'We couldn't leave her in there, Sir Geoffrey,' Perkin said.

Sir Geoffrey looked down at him. 'And who found her there?'

Martin stepped forward nervously. 'Sir, I saw her first. It was as the water fell away from round her.'

'And who ordered that the mire be drained?' Sir Geoffrey demanded, but his eyes were already on Adcock.

'I did, sir. It's my job to make the land as profitable as I can, and there's little enough money in bogs.'

'You may think you were doing the best for the manor,' Sir Geoffrey said sarcastically, 'but I hardly think that forcing us to call the coroner and incurring a fine for murder is very helpful. Perhaps . . . we could simply throw her back in.'

'It's drained now,' Perkin reminded him coldly.

'There is still the second bog,' Sir Geoffrey mused.

'No, sir. We must send for the coroner,' Perkin said bluntly. 'He must come and examine the poor woman. She has been murdered at the least.'

' "At the least"? What else has happened to her,' Sir Geoffrey scoffed.

In answer Perkin took her hand and moved it. 'Her arms are broken, and look at her hands! The nails were pulled from this one. Do you think she did this all to herself?'

Chapter Sixteen

When Simon first saw it, he thought that the house on which Hugh had lavished so much attention might have been empty for years: the walls had crumbled, and the roof was entirely burned away, showing blackened timbers thrusting upwards like the ribs of an enormous animal. There was nothing to indicate that this had until recently been the home of a contented little family.

When Baldwin, Jeanne and he reached it, all of them spattered with mud from the track, they were struck by the sense of sadness that lay about the place. Someone had already started to remove stones from the walls, and bits and pieces of wood from the little fence Hugh had built to protect his vegetables had been taken. It was natural enough that local people would come and liberate useful items, but it only made Simon feel an increased anger, as though they were deliberately eradicating any memory of his servant.

Baldwin was peering at the track beyond the property, and now he walked a short way up it, his eyes fixed on the muddy path.

Jeanne knew how his mind worked in situations like this, and left him to his careful perusal of the land, instead going to Simon and putting her hand on his shoulder.

'I am so sorry, Simon. I don't know what Baldwin would do without Edgar. I can imagine it must be terrible after knowing a man so well for so long.'

'I just wish I'd been here to protect him . . . he looked after me so well for so many years . . .'

'He would have known you'd have been here to protect him if you could have been,' Jeanne pointed out. 'He was loyal to you because he knew you loved and respected him in turn.'

'It wasn't enough to save him, though,' Simon said bitterly.

Baldwin joined them. 'There have been a few horses here, but not for a long time. More recently there have been several men on foot, mostly passing up and down the lane. I would guess some six or seven in total. Wait!'

He had seen some marks in the mud, and now he darted from the lane up into the wide garden of the house. At one point he stopped and slowly walked towards the house, his eyes fixed to marks in the soil. That done, he shook his head, and walked along to the fence. At a point where some stakes had been taken, he studied the ground carefully, then wandered back towards the lane, but once there he shook his head.

'This is impossible. I can see perhaps as many as eight feet, but of course they may have come here when the fire was seen – to try to help douse the flames or save the people inside. Some were definitely here afterwards. One man's feet certainly led up to that fence. He stole bits and pieces from it. Some of the prints are undoubtedly those of the men who took the rocks and wood from the house.'

'I suppose someone will have had the bressemer already,' Simon said.

'A good lintel is hardly likely to have been left behind,' Baldwin agreed. 'Do you mind if I have a look inside, Simon? I want to see if there's anything to learn.'

'Just don't step on his bones if they're there,' Simon said. He gave a humourless half-chuckle. 'It sounds like a joke, doesn't it? It's hard to imagine that he was burned away completely.'

'Yes,' said Baldwin shortly. 'It is.'

Simon turned away as Baldwin set off towards the door. Baldwin knew that his friend was squeamish about dead bodies generally, but today he was surprised – he would have expected Simon to show more interest in the scene of Hugh's death. And then he recalled that the first time he had met Simon had been during investigations into fires and murders near Baldwin's home. Simon had often said how he had found it hard to eat pork afterwards, because the odour was so similar to that of scorched human flesh. The idea of finding part of Hugh's body would be naturally revolting – perhaps 'horrific' would describe it better.

Baldwin had more experience of death and the destruction which men could wreak on each other. He had a belief that any murderer left clues about his motives and his personality at the scene, and he hoped that there would be something here for a man with a naturally enquiring mind to learn. Outside all was a mess of mud and footprints, but perhaps inside there would be less disturbance.

In his life he had seen many men who had been killed by burning, and there was much about this story which he found frankly incredible. He had witnessed Jacques de Molay being burned at the stake, and he recalled how many of the people of Paris had swum the Seine to reach the spot where Jacques had died in order to collect fragments of his bones. They were saved afterwards as relics. That thought was uppermost in his mind as he stood in the doorway gazing at the devastation inside.

Many feet had been in here, stirring the fine ashes that lay all over. From the threshold he could see the main chamber of the building, although there was a second, smaller room on the right which could be entered through a narrow, doorless archway. That led to what had once been the storerooms, Baldwin guessed, the buttery and pantry. This main room would have been Hugh's living area.

Looking about him, Baldwin could see a larger patch of slightly different-coloured ash lying in the middle of the room. That, he thought, must be where the hearth had been. From there he began to make out certain details about the place. There were a couple of thicker charred timbers, which looked as though they could have been the legs of a solid bedframe. To the side, right in the angle of the wall, there was an area that was significantly scuffed, and there, he guessed, was where the child had been found. Jankin had said that he was found lying in a corner, and the disturbed area looked about the right size for a little boy. It made Baldwin feel inexpressibly sad to think that the child might have crawled there, away from the noise and terror of attacking men. Perhaps the lad had seen Hugh die, and his mother fall. Being a realist, and remembering the woman's soft beauty, Baldwin had to wonder whether the lad had also witnessed her rape. It was more than likely.

The ashes appeared uniform over the floor, and Baldwin crouched down to view them from a lower angle to see if there was anywhere a lump which could have been a body, but there was nothing. The only thing he did notice was that the ash appeared to have worn in a channel from this doorway to the room at the back of the house. It led close to the wall, all the way round the room until it reached the archway.

A man walking might make such a little gutter in the surface, Baldwin thought to himself. Footprints wouldn't last in this soft, feathery ash. A faint gust of wind would remove definition from all edges unless the ash grew damp, and this was still very dry. Slowly he rose to his full height. Taking a grip on his sword's hilt, he pulled it a short distance from its sheath as he started to follow the trail. No, he could see no footprints, but the ash was so light it blew about his ankles even as he walked. Any prints would have been blown over and concealed in moments. Baldwin stepped slowly towards the open doorway. Inside the chamber it was darker, but suddenly Baldwin saw that there was a flickering. Someone had lit a fire in there. Even as he realised that, Baldwin could smell meat cooking. He set his jaw, drew his sword fully from his sheath, and was about to spring inside when he was stopped by a voice.

'Sir Baldwin, please don't prick me with that. Steel's no good for my digestion.'

Humphrey closed the door behind him as he heard the men approaching. He froze a moment, thinking that someone was coming to fetch him, but he told himself not to be so stupid. No one could have seen what lay inside the chapel. He glanced over his shoulder and scowled at the party. 'What is it?'

Perkin was not of a mind to be spoken to so churlishly, not after his morning. 'There's a dead woman at the manor. We want a priest to speak the words over her.'

Sweet Jesus! It had been a long time since Humphrey had spoken the *viaticum* over the dead. He hesitated and licked his lips. 'Who is it? I didn't know there were any women unwell?'

'There aren't,' Perkin said gruffly. 'It's Lady Lucy, the woman who disappeared a little while ago at Meeth. She was found this morning. Someone killed her and threw her into our bog.'

'Good God!' Humphrey said and crossed himself. He shot a look at the chapel. 'Um – very well. I shall come, but keep quiet out here. Father Isaac is asleep.'

Perkin shrugged. 'He's an old man. He deserves a little rest. We'll keep silent, don't worry.'

Humphrey hurried back inside, fetched his purse with the bottle of holy water, glanced at the altar and crossed himself hurriedly, then joined the men outside. By the time they were all walking up the lane towards Monkleigh, his mind was working quickly. 'If she was on your lands, did no one see her?'

Perkin could hear the false casualness in his voice. 'It's none of us, if that's what you think, Father. I had nothing to do with it, and I don't think any of my friends in the vill did either. She was . . .' He paused, seeking the right words, but could find no subtle phrase to hide the truth. 'She was tortured before she died. Someone broke her bones and hurt her before he killed her.'

'Who would do a thing like that!' Horrified, Humphrey stopped in the lane to stare at him. 'You have been listening to stories put about for children!' But no one replied, and Humphrey felt a hollowness in his throat as the import of their silence struck home.

All had heard of the brutality of Sir Geoffrey's master. The Despensers were ruthless in pursuit of their ambitions. Everyone knew the tales of people run down on the roads when they were recalcitrant; the king's brother, Thomas of Brotherton, had been coerced into renting lands cheaply to Despenser, and later he had to give them over entirely; even the king's niece, Elizabeth, Lady Damory, had been forced to surrender the lordship of Usk, despite being Despenser's sister-in-law. Lady Damory herself had been left with almost nothing of the vast inheritance she should have been able to enjoy.

Humphrey was silent as they walked up the lane towards the field which had been drained, but now it was the silence of dawning horror.

It had seemed such a simple plot at first. He'd arrived at Hatherleigh a penniless outlaw, constantly on the run, and at first he hadn't noticed the shambling old man behind him. When he turned and spotted the clerical robe he had wanted to bolt. It was only when he saw that the priest was almost blind, and very obviously in pain, that he had slowed and considered his options.

The trouble was, for a renegade like Humphrey, it was very difficult to survive. What openings were there for a man like him – the life of a thief and draw-latch? Spending the whole of his life from here on fearing the steps behind him, wondering whether it would be an officer hoping to catch him? Or should he find a nice quiet location where he could hide for a while, unconsidered, unnoticeable, gathering his resources until he could run again, take a ship abroad, make a new life somewhere else?

But for him it would be difficult to find somewhere to hide. There were no easy places of concealment, and in any case he had no money. Everything he had once possessed was still with the men who had taken it from him.

This priest was clearly ancient. He shuffled along the street like a beggar himself, stumbling into people, peering at them with eyes that were almost blind, apologising for his clumsiness. Humphrey began to follow him, watching him closely, because already a faint glimmering of an idea was forming at the back of his mind.

Isaac soon wandered off the main thoroughfare, and seemed content to wait by a cart in an alley nearby. Humphrey took his post in a darkened doorway. He peered at the old man, wondering how old he was, a speculative frown wrinkling his brow as he sucked his bottom lip. Yes, this man could well be his escape from this miserable existence. He looked at Isaac and saw a bed, food, a fire . . . Isaac was a refuge of sorts.

A youngish man arrived, short, stout, with mousy hair and a cast in one eye, belching happily. 'Sorry, Father.'

'It was a sound to be proud of, my son. The ale house?'

'Yes. It was good in there. No dancing, though.'

'Good. Dancing is a terrible thing. It's the devil's way of tempting youths and maids into sin, you know.'

'Yes, Father,' the man said. He was plainly unbothered by the warning. This was one of the old-fashioned priests, then, opposed to singing and dancing at any time, one of those men who would baulk at the thought of a maid and a man indulging their natural desires. So be it. Humphrey could act his part.

The cart moved off, lumbering slowly, and Humphrey let it go a way before he set off in pursuit . . . little realising how far he would have to walk. Yet it had been worth it. He trailed along after the cart until it left the town, and then he was fortunate enough to see the carter wave to a watchman at the edge of the market. He hurried to the watchman and said, 'Excuse me, friend, but that cart, was that the miller?'

'Him? No, he's Guy from Monkleigh. There's a mill there, but he's not the miller.'

'And the priest with him? He is also from Monkleigh?'

'Yes. Poor old sod. He is from the chapel out there, but he's as blind as a bat; deaf too. Can't keep that job for long.'

'Thank you.'

And that was that. A few days later, he walked into the chapel, freshly tonsured, clad in his old garb, and with a happy smiling visage to present to the world. When the old priest appeared in the doorway, Humphrey carefully checked behind him to see that he was alone, and presented his parchment. 'Here I am, Father.'

While the milky eyes peered at the letters, then rose again to Humphrey's confident, smiling face, Humphrey could scarcely keep his joy from bubbling over. At last he was safe.

Since that glorious day, some seven months ago, he had been here, and he had performed a useful service. Isaac was incapable of fulfilling his priestly functions, let alone looking after his fields. Everything was left to Humphrey, and it was lucky that he had the training for it. He took the services, married many youngsters, blessed the living, baptised the newborn, and in every way conformed to the locals' perception of a good priest. He pandered to Isaac's views on all aspects of life, stopping dancing and music in the little chapel's yard, loudly condemning those who gambled with dice in the nave during his Mass, and living up to the tiresome old bigot's expectations in every way he could. The fact of Isaac's deafness and his blindness were merely bonuses. They made it all but impossible for Isaac to realise what Humphrey was up to.

Yes, for seven months he'd been safe and secure in his life here, and now, suddenly, this had to happen. He was involved in dangerous politics, if his imagination was not leading him astray, and could soon find himself accused of murder if he couldn't find a way out of it.

The body lay beside the almost empty bog, which now held only a shallow layer of filthy mud, water pooling on it in some places. There was a foul exhalation, as though many animals had died and were rotting there. Humphrey cleared his throat, then swallowed. 'Have, er, have you summoned the coroner?'

Perkin was still looking down at the woman. 'Yes. He should be here before long, if he has any sense.'

'Why do you say that?'

'He's a knight from our Lord Despenser's household. He will wish to come and ensure that there's no embarrassment for his lord, no doubt.'

'The poor child,' Humphrey said as he squatted beside the body. She had plainly been in a lot of pain before she died. Her arm was broken, and her nails had been ripped out. Then he saw her face.

Humphrey had seen death in many forms in his life – who hadn't? – yet this woman's passing was remarkably poignant. To think that someone could have tortured her and flung her into the bog without the opportunity of a shriving was appalling. The man must have been a monster. He closed his eyes, clenched his hands together and began praying for her, muttering the *viaticum* and finishing with a Pater Noster for good measure.

'Who could have done this?' he demanded as he rose, his task over. His eyes flew angrily over the others. 'Well? She didn't fly here, and it would have taken some effort to throw her into the mire. Someone must have had help to do that, surely.'

'None of us here,' Perkin said. He sighed and looked up into Humphrey's eyes. 'Who do you think did it?'

That was not a question Humphrey intended to answer. They all knew who it must be: the steward of the manor, Sir Geoffrey. His master must have ordered the death of the woman who wouldn't give up her lands, and Sir Geoffrey had captured her, then assassinated her and hidden her body here in the mire, thinking it would remain concealed for ever. Not alone, though. No one man could have carried her out to the middle of the bog and dropped her in. She might have been light, but with those stones tied to her to make her sink, she would be too much of a weight for one man wading up to his belly in the foul mire.

'Who would dare walk into a bog?' he wondered. 'He must have been mad.'

'There was a way. Men who lived here knew the path,' Perkin said.

Humphrey shivered. The thought of wandering over this repellent mud, always expecting to be swallowed up . . . whoever it was, he must have been filthy afterwards, too.

Afterwards Humphrey was glad to return to the chapel, where he opened the door quietly and relocked it from the inside before crossing the floor to the small chamber on the southern side where the two men had lived their quiet lives.

He was still there, of course, sitting up in his chair; he hadn't moved. The open, dull, white eyes still stared up at the ceiling, his jaw still hung slackly, the hands still dangled, and Humphrey returned to his previous occupation, sitting on the floor and staring at him, wondering what on earth he could do now. With his mentor and protector gone, there was far less security for him here. At any time he could be discovered. But where else could he go? That was the thought that exercised him as he squatted there on the floor.

Where could he go?

Baldwin thrust his sword home again with a feeling of bemusement. 'Edgar? What in God's good name are you doing here?'

'Sir Baldwin,' Edgar said, bowing to him and walking past him out of the chamber. 'I knew you would be here soon, so I came on ahead.'

'Why?' Baldwin growled. 'You ought to be at the manor.'

'Hugh was a friend, sir. I was not of a mood to leave his death unavenged if by my presence I could help him.'

'You knew I would be here with Simon, didn't you?'

Edgar smiled in that lazy way he had. On occasion it could be utterly infuriating, but at other times, like today, it simply served to remind Baldwin why he had been so glad to retain Edgar as his steward after they had left the Knights Templar. The lean, dark man was confident and assured in all things, and now he was surveying Baldwin as though assessing his strength. 'How is your breast, sir?'

'Don't change the . . .'

'Until you are mended, I should be with you when you could be in danger.'

'You are arrogant, Edgar, but it is a delight to see you.' Baldwin chuckled. 'It's a lot better than it was, but I don't think I'd be good in a fight just now.'

'We are too old for new wounds,' Edgar said.

'What were you doing in there?'

'I arrived here yesterday and saw how the place had already been robbed, so I thought I should remain here in case anyone else tried to get inside. A couple of men did yesterday. I spoke to them and no one's been back since then.'

'Have you learned anything?' Baldwin asked as they made their way from the house and out into the fresher air.

'Little – except that Hugh isn't in there.'

'As I thought,' Baldwin agreed.

Simon and Jeanne heard their words, and Jeanne gaped, although Simon merely gave a tight smile to Edgar in welcome, and then looked to Baldwin to explain.

'It is plain that Hugh wasn't burned to death in there – or if he was, his body was removed afterwards.'

Jeanne looked from her husband to Edgar. 'How can you be so sure?'

Baldwin said, 'My dear, if you want to burn a living man, it takes at least two cartloads of faggots. Even then you'd have plenty of larger bones remaining, like the skull or the hips. Think how long it takes for a beef rib to burn in a fire, then think about all the bones in a man's body. That house burned hot, I dare say, but not hot enough to entirely eradicate Hugh. He was skinny, but there was enough of him for a vestige to remain.'

'But what, then? You think someone stole his body away from here?'

'Yes,' Baldwin said. 'That is exactly what I think.'

But he would say no more as he led the way back along the track to the inn.

Chapter Seventeen

Sir Geoffrey was in a foul mood when Adcock entered his hall just before noon. 'Have you enjoyed your splashing in the mud, boy?'

Adcock bridled. 'I was doing my duty, Sir Geoffrey.'

'Your *duty* could get you into trouble. Your *duty* could get your head taken off your shoulders,' Sir Geoffrey rasped.

Adcock paled as he heard men behind him moving closer. He glanced round and saw that they were the same men he had seen holding the hapless Nick. In his belly a snake of fear began to squirm, and he felt a queasiness in his breast. 'All I did was order the bog to be drained. It seemed the best thing to do at the time.'

'And now we're going to have to explain a dead wench's body on our land, boy, aren't we?' Sir Geoffrey said snidely. 'And that might mean a lot of trouble for our master. He won't be pleased, Sergeant. No, he'll likely be very unhappy, and when he's unhappy, he *takes it out on mother-swyving churls with no ballocks like you*!'

He had approached to a matter of a few inches from Adcock, and now his spittle flew in Adcock's face as he shouted.

'You *pathetic piece of turd*! You're *useless*! What is the point of you? You eat our food and drink our ale, but all you do is bring bad luck on us! What made you go to that bog?'

'I just saw it. Beorn told me there was a bog there, and I wanted to see it, so I could decide whether to clear it or not,' Adcock said. He was badly scared now, alone in the hall with no one else around to see what could happen. Men had died in similar rooms with stewards of the Despensers, he knew.

'You don't decide to clear any other mires without telling me first, yes?' Sir Geoffrey said more coolly.

'Yes, of course.'

'Why did you want to clear that particular bog?'

'I said: I just wanted to drain it to start to bring that piece of land into use.'

'And I said: why that particular bog? Did someone suggest it to you?'

Adcock raised a hand in a gesture of submission.

At once it was grabbed by the man on his left. His right hand was taken by the other, and as he looked wildly from one to the other Sir Geoffrey's fist struck him under the ribcage with the force of a galloping mare.

His vision went black, and he found he couldn't breathe. Doubled up with pain and the desperate need to suck air into his lungs, he retched drily; his vision clearing, he felt a slight tremor in his stomach, and he gulped in a small breath of air. It almost made him sick. Then he collapsed again, his chin falling on his breast, while the two men held his arms up, so that they were almost as painful as the blow to his belly.

'I'll ask you again, churl. What made you go to that mire?'

'I didn't know anything, Sir Geoffrey. I was only trying to serve my master.'

'Why that place? Why today?'

'There was no reason!'

This time, Sir Geoffrey resorted to kicking him in the groin, and Adcock's vision blacked again. He felt his arms released, and he collapsed on his face among the filthy rushes, gagging, curled into a ball of pain like a hedgehog hiding its soft underbelly from attack. His arms were about his stomach to protect it, and he threw up over the floor, a weakly green bile-filled vomit that stung his throat and his nostrils.

'A last time, boy! Who suggested that place?'

'Beorn . . . he took me to it . . . didn't say to drain it . . . was my idea . . .' Adcock choked.

'Entirely your idea?' Sir Geoffrey snarled. His boot came back, ready to kick again.

'No! Not again!' Adcock pleaded. 'It was Nicholas le Poter. He suggested emptying it . . . he said you'd be pleased to have more land to farm. It was him, not me!'

'You don't *fucking* do anything here without my permission, *boy*, because if you do once more, I'll have *you* shoved in the bog with stones to hold you down, and you'll never be seen again,' Sir Geoffrey hissed in his ear, and then the three men left Adcock alone. Soon afterwards he heard the shouts and rattling of hooves as they rode away.

He couldn't rise for some minutes. A servant came in, and seeing Adcock wriggling on the ground he called for help, and tried to help Adcock up, but Adcock had been manhandled enough already that day. He shook his helper's hand away and rolled on to his knees before slowly pushing himself up. His ballocks were a pool of pain so intense, he wondered that he could live. Even when he stood, there was a sensation as though both were twice their usual size and hanging behind him, pulling his belly out of his body. It was so agonising, he could only stand leaning against a table and weep for a long time. Without support, he could do nothing.

'Master, can I get you anything?' the servant asked sympathetically.

It was tempting to demand a horse, and then to throw his few belongings together and ride from here, just whip the beast and let it take him anywhere away from this hideous manor, but he knew he couldn't. He was not a free man: he had taken the Despensers' salt, and he was a part of the household now.

He left the hall and walked to where he had his palliasse in the chamber where the men slept.

On the way, he couldn't help but weep hot tears of despair. He was sure that, like Ailward, he would die here. And it would perhaps not be very long before it happened.

Jankin saw them return with a sense of genuine pleasure. 'Lordings, please, let me fetch you some ale or wine. And this gentleman is a companion of yours? Well met, friend. It is most pleasant to see you.'

In all honesty, although having a knight staying with him was no strain, this new fellow had a dangerous look to him. He was one of those, so Jankin thought, who would smile happily while slipping a knife in a man's belly. Not the sort of traveller to insult. He'd have to speak to his wife and the servants and make sure that these folks were well served. No need to cause offence – especially when it was likely to result in someone's getting hurt.

There was another reason to welcome them back, of course.

'Er – madam, your maid was distressed that you had left her here alone.'

'Ah. Where is she?'

'At present, I think she's in my buttery with a pot man. She was very thirsty.'

'Thirsty? Do you mean she's drunk?'

'Scarcely,' Jankin replied honestly. He had never seen a wench with a more alarming capacity for alcohol.

'And she has my daughter with her? Bring them to me,' Jeanne commanded with an iciness in her manner.

'You have Emma with you?' Edgar asked.

Baldwin answered. 'Yes. Jeanne thought it best to bring someone in case my wound should be exacerbated by the journey here. She believed that having so potent a protection against outlaws would be sensible.'

'I doubt many outlaws would risk life or limb by attacking her,' Edgar agreed equably.

Jeanne listened with half an ear. She was alarmed by the thought that Emma could get herself too happily ensconced in a buttery with barrels of ale. The woman was here to help her and look after Richalda, not to drink herself stupid when left alone for a few moments.

'Mistress, I was bereft when you left without me!'

'You could have easily walked from the door, I believe,' Jeanne said with poisonous sweetness. 'Or did you take a wrong turn and end up in the buttery instead?'

'I was asked to go there to help clear up some mess, and while we were there we thought to make sure that the casks were all right. I didn't drink the place dry, if that's what you mean!'

'That is good. Now be silent, please.'

'Mistress . . . but, Bailiff, I am sorry to hear about your man. He wasn't the best servant, I know, but it is always difficult to lose someone you've known . . .'

Jeanne hissed, 'I said silent!'

'Oh, very well. I don't have to speak.'

'Good,' Baldwin said pointedly. 'Master Jankin, could you please fetch me a little wine with water?'

Malkin was exhausted already, and it wasn't even lunchtime yet. She felt so *weak*, so *feeble*. She was a pitiful creature, quite useless. Look at Isabel, in comparison. She was a real woman: strong, resolute, unbending in adversity, cunning and quick to take advantage no matter what. She wouldn't sit and mope like Malkin, she'd get off her rump and start planning for her future.

But what future was there, really? Malkin wasn't going to fool herself. She could perhaps survive for a little while, but without a husband she was merely fodder for the appetite of strong men. If any of them wanted her, they could force her to accept their advances, once a decent period of mourning had passed.

To be fair, the idea was not repellent, if the man concerned had some money. The main thought uppermost in her mind was that she needed security for herself and her child. Ailward's child. And there lay the problem, of course. How many men would be prepared to take on a woman who already had a babe of her own? There were few enough who'd be happy to take on the upkeep of another man's boy.

She had loved him so much, her Ailward. Since his death, she felt as though a part of her had withered. A soft, kind, happy piece of her soul had been cut from her, and it left a hole. It was impossible to keep her mind on one thought, impossible to plan or look to the future.

Ailward had been so close, so he had said, to making their fortune. He wasn't above making a little money on the side, of course. He had a lot to live up to, with his father and grandsire both being such honourable men, and if he was ever going to work his way up to renew the fortunes of the family he would have to fight every step of the way. From a knight's son to penury was a sharp fall, and he had felt the humiliation deeply. Her Ailward had been devoted to making the family wealthy again.

She had no idea how he had intended to do that. If she was honest with herself, she didn't want to know. He had sometimes a sort of focus, a concentration, that excluded her, and on occasion she had felt that he wouldn't be entirely averse to gaining money by means that weren't completely legal. 'Sometimes,' he'd said, not long before his death, 'a man has to prove his brutality in order to be a good, loving father to his family.'

He had worn such a serious expression, and his words were uttered so firmly, that she had felt quite anxious at the time, but then she had lightened the atmosphere, laughing at him, throwing a soft cushion at him and making him apologise for being too solemn and stern-looking, and he had chuckled. Now she recalled his expression, she realised his gaiety had been just a little bit forced, as though he had wanted to explain something to her, something awful, and her change of mood had prevented him from telling her.

She packed up a basket of food, shaking her head at the memory. It was all too painful still. Especially that dreadful day when the men had arrived here to tell her that her man was dead. Murdered. And now there was the appalling sense that he was going to go unavenged. Nobody cared enough about him to bother to find his murderer.

Pagan stood at the door, and seeing her carrying the basket outside he pulled the door wide, not looking at her as he waited for her to leave. For her part, she had no wish to meet his eyes. She left the house and walked along the lane, pulling her cloak tight about her against the dreadful cold. The sight of Pagan only seemed to increase the chill of the air.

He had been different since her husband's death. She felt that he had been more attentive than before, and in the midst of her greatest despair, while she bemoaned her loss and Isabel tried to conceal her growing contempt for such a display, it was Pagan who seemed to appreciate and understand her grief.

If she were a man, she would be out there finding out who had done it. Pagan should be doing the same. The man who had killed Ailward was still there, in the vill somewhere. Perhaps he was even in the homestead here. Or was it Sir Geoffrey, as she feared? The steward could have desired to remove the man he had ousted. Ailward was a potent threat while he lived.

But Pagan should be able to do something. He was a strong enough fellow. Yet just now, when the man should have been helping all the more, Isabel had turfed him unceremoniously from the house. Perhaps that was so that he could speak to the neighbours and learn what had really happened – but Pagan, although a good steward and servant, was not the sort of man to inspire confidences from the other men of the vill. They had learned to respect him, some, perhaps, to fear him over the years. But few would want to socialise with him, and fewer still would accuse other men of murdering his mistress's son.

She continued down the track until she reached the side lane that led to the chapel. Here, she pushed the gate wide and crossed the cemetery, reaching out to open the door. To her surprise it was barred. She knocked and called out for Isaac, then Humphrey, but there was no reply, and eventually, shrugging, she set the basket down, and set off to make her way homewards.

Inside the chapel, Humphrey sat with his head in his hands, trying to shut out the noise of Malkin's knocking. Then, with a gradual clearing of his brow, he realised what he must do.

With a new purpose, he stood and lifted Isaac's corpse from the chair. If it had been discovered here before all this other trouble, Humphrey would have been fine, but what with Ailward dead and the family up at Iddesleigh being killed, and now Lady Lucy too, there were too many bodies. One more would be suspicious, and it was always easy for people to look on a foreigner as the most likely suspect. He had seen that before, when he'd run away.

The convent had been a good place to live, but not once old Peter grew interested in him. Before that he had been able to live and study happily enough . . . but afterwards there was no peace.

It came to the crunch when Peter was serving food one day. It sounded pathetic now, but at the time . . . Peter would insist on serving the younger men under his care, and Humphrey was one of them. Every meal, without fail, Humphrey saw all the others getting more food than he did, and the anger boiled up and up until his rage knew no bounds. And then one day they were in the garden and Peter snidely commented about Humphrey's ability to kill off any plant worth growing, and Humphrey couldn't help himself. He was holding a heavy shovel, and as Peter turned away, he . . . he just slashed with it.

There was a strange, crisp, wet sound, and Peter crumpled into a heap. His left arm windmilled once, and then his left leg began to kick and thrash, but only for a few moments, and then he was still.

He could see the body even now. The man with a slice through his skull as though Humphrey had swung an axe at him, and an obscene flap of flesh and bone, the blood shining bright and viscous to mark the injury.

There was no doubt that he would be held responsible as soon as the tragedy was discovered. It was his fault. He was a murderer, in God's name! The truth was so appalling, he stood there a while simply staring at the body, unable to appreciate the depth of his crime. And then he had allowed the spade to drop from his fingers and slowly turned as though in a trance to head to the main gate. He walked through it and just kept on walking. He had walked ever since, until he reached this little rural backwater.

And now, with this second body, he must move on again. There was no time to waste, either. At least this time he would have belongings to take with him. Few enough, but there were a few. He must pack.

Chapter Eighteen

Jankin had just finished serving the small party when a sudden burst of noise announced some more customers, led by the sturdy figure of David atte Moor.

As a landlord, Jankin knew that he must try always to be friendly and accommodating. He had lived in the area all his life, and by and large there were very few men with whom he couldn't get on, but there were some . . . and David was one of them.

His voice was pitched always to irritate Jankin's ear: it was a kind of braying noise, which always made Jankin think of donkeys. Which was why one nickname for David was 'David the Donkey'. Then again, on most evenings, when David had drunk his first ale, he would get maudlin drunk, and woe betide any man who was within earshot then, because they would invariably receive a full and detailed summary of his life so far, how unfair it was that his father died when he did, leaving David with such terrible death fines to pay that he almost lost all his farm as a result, that he suffered more than anyone during the famine, and that women never understood him (whereas Jankin knew damned well that they understood him only too well). It was this ability to talk a man to near-suicide that had led to Jankin's other name for him, which was 'Deadly Dave'. Few names he had invented over the years had seemed quite so suitable as that one, somehow.

David was broad-shouldered, pot-bellied, and had a long but chubby face that wore a constant look of blank incomprehension. Today he was leading Oliver and Denis, and all were talking so quickly that a man might have thought them already drunk, except that they all took one look at the party of strangers and went silent in a moment, eyeing them as suspiciously as only a Devon man could.

Jankin took his place at the barrel of ale, a jug at the ready, and waited, his eyebrows raised enquiringly. The three joined him at the bar, but as usual it was Deadly who monopolised the conversation. Oliver tried to speak a couple of times, but it was a pointless exercise.

'You should have seen the lad's face,' Deadly started.

'Well, he always had a nervous . . .' Oliver began.

'He had that. Now, though, the poor fellow's broken. I've seen boys like him before, when they've had a shock. Never any good. One boy was never any good again. Remember Rance? Laurence Millerson, from over towards Hatherleigh? He saw something scared him, swore it ruined him. Couldn't stay in his house after that.'

'Rance saw a mare, he said. A ghost, and he . . .'

'That was what he said at the time, but he wasn't sure. Anyway, if it were a ghost, that'd be one thing, but seeing a body covered in filth and all, just exposed like that. Terrible. If Rance had seen that, I dare say he'd have fallen dead on the spot.'

'Well 'Tin didn't, he just . . .'

'Yeah, just you wait, though. He's all right just at the minute, but he'll soon be unwell. You mark my words, he'll be faint and sickly for a day, then he'll start to fade. Always happens.'

Jankin glanced at Oliver. 'What's happened?'

Oliver opened his mouth and spoke in a hurry. 'It's young Martin down the way. He found a dead body. Reckons it's Lady Lucy, from . . .'

'Meeth. You know she went missing a while ago? Well, poor chit, looks like she didn't go far,' Deadly said, shaking his head.

He seemed to be aware always when someone else was about to speak, and leaped in with his slightly raised voice, deadening all conversation. This was no exception. As Jankin saw Oliver take a breath as though to speak again, Deadly moved slightly so that he blocked Jankin's view of the other man entirely. 'And you know the worst? Not just where they found her, but what those bastards had done to her. You'd hardly credit that even that mad group of unchivalrous murderers and serf-whippers would do something like that, would you?'

Jankin shouldn't have done it, but he had had enough of Deadly in his inn over a number of years. He frowned a little, turning his head to one side as though slightly hard of hearing, and peered at Deadly enquiringly. 'Keep on,' he said, moving away a short distance to refill the jug.

Seeing him walk away, Deadly did what he always did. He spoke louder to dominate the conversation and prevent anyone else from providing the gossip when he could himself impart it.

'It's obvious, isn't it? Those mad fools at Monkleigh captured her to steal her lands. She was tortured, Jankin. Tortured to death, if the truth be known, and her a poor widow, too. It's shameful that a man who calls himself knight could behave like that. Shameful!'

Jankin fitted a scandalised expression to his face. 'Now who do you mean? Not Sir Geoffrey?'

'Who else, Jankin? I swear this, if that poor girl hadn't been discovered, her lands would have been taken by Sir Geoffrey and absorbed into his manor within the week. Perhaps now she's been found, maybe, just maybe, her unfortunate soul will receive justice, eh? Not that it's very likely. The poor chit had no family to speak of, did she? There's no one to ensure a fair result even if Sir Geoffrey were to be uncovered as her murderer.'

Jankin could see Deadly's expression subtly alter as the rest of the room went silent. Suddenly Deadly appeared to realise how loudly he had spoken, and Jankin felt a little ashamed at the way he had led him on, but if he hadn't, he knew that Deadly would have been unable to keep his mouth shut anyway. There was no point crying over a fool who put himself in harm's way.

There was a long moment's hush, as though the walls of the inn were themselves waiting for the blast of condemnation that must surely follow such an atrocious allegation from a man of so lowly a class, and then the silence was broken by the drawn-out rasp of a stool's feet against the packed earth of the floor.

'My friend, I would be very grateful if you could join my friends and me.'

'I don't think I can, master. My apologies, but I have to . . . um . . .'

But looking into the serious dark eyes of the knight, Deadly suddenly found that he could defer his departure. And would do so.

* * *

Friar John heard about the dead girl at almost the same time as Baldwin.

He had been walking up towards Meeth, breathing in the cool air and feeling that although the last few days had been traumatic, at least he had done all he reasonably could after finding that burning hovel.

The land was so delightful here. He remembered it clearly, and the low, unwarming wintry sun was of a mood to light everything with a contrasting golden hue, while the shadows were longer and darker than at any other time of year.

It was cold, yes, and his fingers felt as though they were close to freezing entirely as he walked up the slope. They had turned blue, and he thought that if he were to clench his fists too swiftly they all must shatter and fall off. The wind made his robe feel as insubstantial as a linen shirt, and he could feel his breast's flesh contract, his nipples so cold that it almost felt as if they were suffering from the opposite mortification: being gripped by red-hot pincers. Strange how freezing weather could make a man's body react so agonisingly.

Still he had experienced worse. He was only glad that he had a pair of boots to wear, for if he had to rely solely on his old sandals, he didn't like to think what would have happened to his toes by now.

To reach Meeth from the shelter where he had left Hugh he had to climb a hill, and then traverse its edge, the river on his right. From here he could see the small town clearly. A good, pleasant little place with the spire of the church rising prominently over it. There, over on the far side, was the hall he'd heard of. Broad, clean, with yellow-gold thatch and a number of outbuildings, it was a picture of calmness and comfort. The sort of place a man might go to when he was determined to rest from the world: quite idyllic.

He stopped. It called to him, but he wasn't ready. He wanted to go down there, but something told him he shouldn't yet. There was a dragging weight at his feet that prevented his continuing. It had been so long . . . No, he would go elsewhere.

Returning the way he had come, he gazed about him. When he saw Fishleigh, he paused, and then made his way towards it, crossing the little wooden bridge and wandering up to the hall.

Fishleigh was a good-sized manor, and John stood puffing for a moment at the bottom of the little hill on which it stood. A wide house, it looked well cared for, with a fresh coat of limewash, although the thatch had been patched so often that it would need to be replaced in the summer. However, it didn't look as though it had suffered over the years. God Himself knew how long it was since John had been down here, and in that time he had travelled so widely, it was a miracle he still had any feet. It would be interesting some day to sit down and consider how many shoes' soles he had worn out in his wandering: how many oxen's hides he'd caused to be used just to protect his feet.

He continued up the hill, leaning more and more on his staff as he went. The trouble was, friars tended to be on their feet so much. His were enormously painful: his heels were split and cracked, like wood beaten too often. And heavens, but they hurt.

The place was as he remembered it. In fact, the years might not have passed at all, so little changed did it appear. The only difference was, there was more of an armed presence noticeable, but that was the norm nowadays. He saw men-at-arms wherever he went.

It was dreadful to admit it, but the whole country was enfolded in fear. The king's appalling treatment of his enemies after Boroughbridge had left the kingdom in a state of terror, feeling as though it was waiting, tensely, for the next page to be turned in this chronicle of fear.

The path up to the door of the manor was quite steep, and now John could see that the approach was further controlled by a high wall about the front of the house itself. It gave an aura of preparedness, as though the house was sitting and waiting for a force to arrive. Even the actions of the men about the place bore it out. There were several serfs working in the garden immediately in front of the hall, and they all stopped their digging and raking to stand staring at him as he approached.

John was worried about the man he had left in the ruined cottage, but he knew that there was little he could do. He'd promised the fellow that he wouldn't divulge his whereabouts, and he'd rather tear out his own tongue than forswear that oath. But there was a need for food for them both, and perhaps a little wine or ale, so he must beg something without betraying the existence of his charge.

The great door did not have an alms bowl, but in a manor like this, so far from the nearest town, that was no surprise. In a town, each merchant would put out a bowl containing at least a tenth part of every meal, so that beggars and the homeless could count on something to eat. Here, though, there were few itinerant people. Spare food from the master's table would be allocated to the poorest of the parish, or more likely sent straight down to the pigs. There was no waste in an efficient manor like this one.

'Friar?'

It was a short, round-faced man with a paunch like a lord and a grin like a conman. He stood a short way from John and apparently gave him a close inspection.

'My friend, I am desperate. I have come all this way, and have been without food or drink since yesterday. If you have anything to spare, I would be very grateful. Perhaps I could preach to your master and his men for my food?'

'Friar, I'm the master here. I'm Sir Odo, and I am very happy to offer you my hospitality – but no preaching, thank you. I'll wish you Godspeed, but I'd be happier if you didn't slow the idle sons of the devil in their work!'

'Of course. I understand. Perhaps I should come back on Sunday,' John said.

'You'd be most welcome. The men go to Hatherleigh for their preachings. Will you be there?'

'Perhaps. I am walking all over. If I am still in the neighbourhood, I shall make my way there,' John said with a smile.

'Be careful, Brother. This area is not so safe as once it was,' the man said, suddenly serious. 'I'm afraid that it's growing more dangerous every day. Less than a week ago a family was wiped out, and my own bailiff was attacked and driven from his home.'

'It is a terrible thing when a man decides to turn to evil,' John said sententiously. He made the sign of the cross over his breast. 'I have heard that there have been attacks about here. Poor serfs have enough to contend with without seeing their comrades and neighbours killed.'

'It's not only them, Brother,' Sir Odo said confidentially. 'My neighbour here has been murdered too. The body of Lady Lucy from

Meeth has been discovered on Sir Geoffrey Servington's estates at Monkleigh.' He sighed. 'I'm afraid fear runs through every heart in this county.'

John could only agree. He himself was feeling as though his own heart must stop from sadness. He had so looked forward to seeing her again – and now his sister was dead.

Chapter Nineteen

Led to the little group sitting at the table, David felt as though he was being taken to stand before the justices of gaol delivery. There was the same sombre atmosphere about them, the same steady, grim faces staring at him, the sense of violence being held on a tight rein, but only for a little while. These men and women looked on him with undisguised suspicion, even though he knew he'd done nothing. Not that it would help to know you were innocent, as he told himself morosely, if you were dangling from a rope.

The man who'd come to fetch him was the grimmest David had ever seen. He was tall and good looking, with a well-trimmed beard that looked out of place – beards were so rare today. His eyes were so dark that in this room they looked plain black. When he caught sight of those eyes, David felt as though every secret he had ever concealed was laid bare. It would be impossible to gull this knight . . . and he pulled his gaze away from the other's as soon as he could, just to avoid being snared by it. But in so doing, he found himself fixed by the unblinking stare of the taller of the two men sitting at the table, a grey-eyed individual with an expression that teetered between rage and devastation.

Thankfully, there were two women at the table, too. One was nursing a child, and did not look up, but the other met his gaze with a still more truculent expression than the men. It was a relief to look away from her and see that the second man at the table was smiling. His open, contented appearance gave David a moment's comfort, until he saw that behind the cheery exterior there was a cold determination. He would be the fastest of any of them to pull a sword and sweep a man's head from his shoulders, David reckoned, and he felt as though the ale he'd just drunk had turned to acid in his stomach.

'You are called David?'

That was the first one again. He hadn't seated himself again, and David felt intimidated. He shuffled his feet and stared at the ground as he nodded. This was turning out to be one of the worst days of his life.

'I am Sir Baldwin de Furnshill, Keeper of the King's Peace. This is my friend, Simon Puttock, Bailiff to the Abbot of Tavistock. We heard you talk of a body being found, and you mentioned that a man in the near vicinity might be guilty of killing this girl. Is this so?'

'Master, I don't . . .'

'Yes or no?'

David lifted his eyes unhappily and met Baldwin's grim expression. He nodded. 'It could be . . .'

'Were you making up the crimes of which this man was guilty?'

David didn't know what to say. If he were to repeat the accusations, he would almost certainly die before long, because the steward of the Despensers was always eager to repay any man who dared to blacken his name. If Davie retracted his words or denied them, news that he had uttered them would get out, and he'd still be hunted down by Sir Geoffrey, more than likely, to be made an example of, and these rich strangers wouldn't be about the place to protect him.

'He doesn't seem to have much conversation, Sir Baldwin,' the smiling man said. 'Shall I take him outside and ask him again in private for you? I'm sure I could help his memory.'

'No, Edgar,' Baldwin said thoughtfully. 'I don't think that'll be necessary. Will it, David?'

'Master, I don't know what to say!' David burst out.

This was worse than he could have imagined. Now he was being threatened by this determined-looking brute, as though he was some mere scruffy felon picked up in the street. He wasn't like that. He was a good man! If he'd had more luck in his life, he could have been a bailiff, or even the vill's reeve. It didn't take a huge brain to do that, and he could keep tally of the grain harvested each year, he could maintain the peace on the demesne if necessary, and make sure that all the peasants performed their obligations to the lord on their days.

But no, he hadn't been fortunate enough to achieve even that. He'd never been elected at the annual court which allocated responsibilities to the men in the vill, even though he had tried to make them understand he was quite capable. There was a clique of men who ran everything here, and he never got asked to help because they didn't like his face or his manner or something. He didn't understand why.

All he ever wanted was to be popular. That was why he got straight to the heart of any gathering, so that he could not only join in, but also let people see what sort of man he was, so that they would *like* him. He had learned early on in life that to remain shy and nervous would only lead to loneliness. Better by far to go to others and chat to them as an equal.

'Well?' Baldwin asked again.

He mumbled, 'Um, all I know is that the lady was found, sir, and there's been enough men wondering how she might have got there.'

'Where exactly?'

That was the empty-eyed man. He looked as though he'd died, but no one had told him yet. David threw him a quick look, but it was only when the large woman nearby spoke that he realised he must respond. She had a rough, harsh voice.

'Answer him, you fool. Do you think we all want to sit here watching you squirm for no reason? We all heard you, so it's too late to regret saying villainous things about him, lord or not!'

He cast her a poisonous glance, but there was no denying the truth of her words. The ugly bitch had warts on her warts, and her foul face was lowered like an enraged boar's, while her massive bosom rose and fell alarmingly. It attracted his unwilling and fearful attention, no matter how much he tried to look away.

'Well? Or do you want my man here to take you outside and give you an incentive to talk?' the knight said.

'She was found in the bog on Sir Geoffrey's lands, like I said,' he said at last, defiantly holding his head a little higher.

'And there is already gossip about who might have killed her?' Baldwin pressed him.

'Of course there is,' David said, more quietly though, and glancing over his shoulder to see who else might be listening. 'Who wouldn't believe it of a man who worked for the Despensers? We know of them even here.'

'You will take us to where this body was found,' Baldwin stated.

David's mouth fell open. 'Me? But what will they do to me when they see that I've brought you to them?'

Baldwin eyed him with distaste. 'You have a duty to take me and the bailiff to the scene of the crime, man, and you will do so. If there is danger for you in this, there is far more danger in not doing so, because then a dangerous murderer will remain at large in this area. So you should take us to the scene, no matter who the killer was, so that we can find him.'

'And in the meantime,' Edgar said, leaning forward, 'what do you know about the family just over the way there?'

'What, the foreigner and his woman?' David asked, genuinely surprised. 'What of them?'

'You know that they were killed and their house burned down?' Baldwin asked.

David glanced over his shoulder again, but Jankin, the only man within earshot, seemed to have developed a fascination with a bit of dirt on a drinking horn, and was spitting on it and rubbing it against his sleeve. David unwillingly turned back to the knight. 'The coroner decided that they'd had an accident.'

'An accident? It was rather an uncommon one, surely?' Baldwin retorted.

'That was what the coroner said, not me,' David said reasonably.

Baldwin looked past him to the innkeeper. 'Jankin – is this true?'

'Yes. The coroner happened to be here because of the murder of another man, Ailward, the sergeant up at Sir Geoffrey's manor.'

'This same Sir Geoffrey who David says . . .'

'I didn't actually say he did anything!'

'Very well, the same man on whose land the latest body has been found? This Ailward was his man?'

'Yes. So the coroner was here for Ailward, and since he was in the area, he came here to view those bodies too.'

'What did he find?' Baldwin demanded.

'That the hearth fire hadn't been banked and the house caught light.'

'Is that what you thought?' Simon burst out. 'Where is the man's body?'

'If I believed it, do you think I'd have been so open with you?' Jankin said calmly.

Baldwin nodded. 'So why have you been so frank?'

'Because . . .' Jankin looked away, out through the unshuttered window at the rolling grassland and trees in front of his inn. When he began to speak again, his voice was quiet and reflective. 'Perhaps because I could see that you cared, and I thought others should care too. The coroner didn't – he didn't give a damn about them. He knew what answers he wanted, and he made sure he got them. All the while, Sir Geoffrey's men were waiting nearby, watching and listening to all that was said. It wasn't *right*, sir. That's what I reckoned.'

Baldwin nodded slowly. 'You are right, good keeper. You are right. But we shall make this right none the less. I shall see to it.'

Walter was leaning against a tree when he heard the sound of hooves.

It made his heart flutter, and he felt a sharp pain in his breast for a moment or two, while the sweat broke out on his forehead. He knew too well what hooves could mean. The picture of the woman's dead face sprang into his mind, and he felt the bile rise in his throat, just as it had during the camp ball game when they had heard the men running towards them.

Even when the hoofbeats passed away, his anxiety remained. Ridiculous that the mere sound of hooves could have such an impact on him.

Christ's pain, but that day had been terrifying. They'd thought they'd be safe up there. Ailward had said that no one would run out that way – everyone would be down at the main field. They always went that way. And then there had been the sudden roar from all those down on the plain and Walter saw the fixed, straining face of Perkin rushing up the hill towards him.

It was the work of a moment to spring on him, knock him down, and hurl the ball away. With all the other men behind him, it was impossible to try to do anything else. Ailward hid the dead woman, Walter threw the ball and shoved Perkin back down the hill after it.

Then, when the men were all out of the way, they'd lifted the body again and carried on their way. They had to get rid of her before they did anything else. If they were found with her, they would be hanged for certain.

No one would protect them.

They had ridden up the road so quickly beforehand that Baldwin was pleased to have an opportunity to see how the land lay round about. He had not taken any notice on the way here.

The vill of Iddesleigh lay on the side of a low hill, the land dropping away gently to the south. From the road it was impossible to see much, for on the right was a stand of trees which obscured the whole view, while on the left there were fields for a short way, and then another section of woods. There was plenty of sound timber here, Baldwin reflected. It was good land, with plenty of space for cattle and sheep, pasture and arable. Perfect for a lord who wanted to make his holding pay its way.

Jeanne and Emma had stayed at the inn. There was little point in their coming with the men to view this young woman's body. Better that they should remain safe, in case this knight Geoffrey should grow angry at the appearance of a Keeper of the King's Peace. It would not be the first time that a man had taken offence at Baldwin's arrival.

'How far to this place?' Baldwin asked David.

He trudged on disconsolately. 'I don't know. It takes me a short while to get there. It's only over there. Maybe a mile or so more.'

Baldwin smiled thinly at his tone. He could all too easily understand the man's disgruntled mood: David had gone to the inn for a quiet drink, hoping to impart a little gossip to his companions, and had instead been caught up in this investigation. There was every probability that it would lead to great trouble in the future. Still, his irritation was nothing to Baldwin's concern at Simon's appearance. The bailiff looked quite exhausted. It was one thing for Baldwin to wince every so often as he flexed his muscles and felt that terrible pain in his breast again, but quite a different matter to see Simon so wearied and upset by the loss of his man.

It made Baldwin wonder how he would cope were he to lose Edgar.

Edgar had been such an intimate part of his life for the last thirty years or more, it was hard to imagine how he could survive without the man. Edgar was not merely some servant who remained with Baldwin from reasons of loyalty; he had shared the key moments of Baldwin's career. Edgar had been there at Acre with him, had joined the Templars with him, and then had remained with him when the Order was betrayed and dissolved. If Edgar were to be murdered, Baldwin would feel the same as a man who lost a brother, or a son.

That was clearly how Simon felt too. He had lost a close companion whom he had trusted for many years, and he felt the guilt of not having been there when Hugh needed him. If Hugh had indeed been killed. Now he thought about it, Baldwin wasn't sure why it was that he had been so convinced that Hugh must have been murdered. Perhaps it was simply some confusion: wasn't it possible that Wat passed on a message that Hugh was *dead*, and Baldwin had assumed he'd meant *murdered*? Or maybe Wat himself had made the error; on being told Hugh was dead had made the natural assumption, for Wat, that there must have been something unnatural about the death.

Yet men did die daily from accidents. There had been the prints of many men outside Hugh's burned-out house, but they could have been trying to help . . . or gawping at the smouldering remains. There were always a lot of people who would go to stare at another man's misfortune. They'd drink ale while watching a poor soul hang; they'd travel miles for a good execution, especially if it was a noble who was to be killed. An accident like this was meat and drink to most peasants. They'd all seen death, and this one was the death of a man who was a 'foreigner' and therefore not of any great social importance – it wasn't as if he was related to anyone at all. He was dispensable. Easily forgotten. Irrelevant.

That word made Baldwin's back stiffen. The thought that a man – even a miserable, whining, froward son of a cur like Hugh, and God knew how often Baldwin had cursed him under his breath – could be thought of as *irrelevant* was a disgrace. There were some, he knew, who believed that it was worthwhile hanging any number of men to make an example, but Baldwin was not one of them. Only the guilty should be condemned, he thought. The innocent should always be protected. If the innocent were forced to suffer, there was no justice. Justice existed to protect all: the strong, the weak, the innocent and the poor. There was no point in justice if it provided for only the strong and the wealthy.

Which made him look more sympathetically on David. The man was tedious, and Baldwin had taken a dislike to his sullen manner at the inn, but now he felt guilty at his initial reaction. 'David, where do you live?'

'Back up there.' He pointed to their left, eastwards. 'I've a small cottage up there.'

'It's good land.'

'We grow enough to live.'

That was the proof of a plot of ground, Baldwin knew. It had to provide. That was how a man measured his space: could he live there. Nothing else mattered. 'On the day that the family was killed, did you hear anything or see anyone?'

'Nothing. It was Saturday night. I was up at home.'

'Was there anyone with you?' Simon asked sharply.

'Why should there be?' Davie whined. 'I'm not married.'

'So no one can vouch for you?'

David looked at Simon, and then a smile spread over his face. 'Yes! Pagan was there. He lives a short way from my house, and he was there that night.'

'Pagan?' Baldwin enquired.

'He's the steward to Lady Isabel – the woman who used to own all the lands about here, from here down to Monk Oakhampton and the river.'

'Where does she live?'

'Down there now. Since Sir Geoffrey took her hall,' David said.

'And where is the hall?'

'There it is. Up on the hillside there.'

There was a strange feeling about this place, Jeanne thought. She sipped wine as she sat at the table rocking Richalda in her lap, listening as Emma slurped.

It was very sad to think that Hugh and his woman were dead. She had liked Hugh a great deal, and she knew full well that it was rare for a man like him to find a companion. Sometimes a shepherd or peasant farmer would meet a woman and marry, but a man like Hugh?

'I never liked him,' Emma said. 'He was uncouth.'

'You should remember that you are talking of a dead man, Emma,' Jeanne said sharply.

'There is no point in hypocrisy,' Emma said, and burped.

Jeanne recalled that her maid had already been in the buttery for some while. 'Are you drunk?'

'Me?' Emma exclaimed horrified. 'I hope I can hold my drink, my lady.'

'Then do so. Hugh was a kind man, and he was honourable. That is all that matters.'

Emma sniffed. 'He still took a nun from her convent.'

'That is nonsense!' Jeanne said hotly. 'He only helped a poor woman when she had already left her convent because she should never have been there in the first place.'

'So you say. I believe that a woman who has become a Bride of Christ should not resign her position. She chose her path and renounced it when it suited her.'

'She was not there legally, Emma. She was taken in there when she was too young to choose,' Jeanne said with a cold anger. This kind of small-mindedness was no more than she should have expected from her maid, she knew. Emma was a strangely cold, unkind woman, but she was a habit now as much as a companion. 'If you cannot keep a civil tongue in your head, then best it isn't exercised.'

'It's not my fault if the chit betrayed her God and her vocation,' Emma grunted. 'But if you prefer me to keep my thoughts to myself, I'm sure I don't mind.'

Jeanne snorted and turned from her. Emma's unforgiving, almost brutal nature sometimes made her so angry, she could have happily told her to return to Bordeaux. But then she had to remember that Emma herself had given up everything for Jeanne, her home in the city with all its beautiful cloths and decorations on display, and come here to this miserable, cold, wet land where the nearest thing to civilisation was the monthly visit to Tavistock. Emma had decided views on Tavistock.

Just for once Jeanne wished that Emma could have shown a little compassion. Sitting here, she saw that Matthew the priest had entered the inn and now stood at the bar with a quart jug in his hand. He turned as Jeanne glimpsed him, and she was sure that he was surreptitiously trying to watch her from the corner of his eye.

Somehow Jeanne felt deeply unsettled by the sight of him. She was certain that he had overheard at least a part of her conversation with Emma, and something about the set of his shoulders made her think that he was not impressed with what he had heard.

Chapter Twenty

David grew more disconsolate as they approached the channel of thick, brackish water that trailed down from the drained pool.

There was a small group of men hanging about the place. Baldwin noticed one in particular, a brute of a man, rather like a bear, who reminded him of someone. It was a little while before he realised that the man was very like the hunter and tracker, Black, whom he had used so often in his early days as keeper in Crediton. There were the same strong features in his face, the same thick dark hair, the same strength in the shoulders – and then there were the differences.

Black would never have looked away as though already cowed. He'd always meet a man's eye, no matter what the station of the man concerned. There was something about the hunter that made him confident in the presence of anyone. That couldn't be said for any of the fellows here. There was a consistency in their nervousness in the presence of strangers that seemed wrong. It was almost as though they were petrified of any man in authority.

Baldwin snorted and dropped from his mount. 'You! Come here.'

The large man glowered, but obeyed. 'Sir?'

'I am Sir Baldwin de Furnshill, Keeper of the King's Peace. I have heard that there's a dead woman here. Where is the body?'

'Sir Geoffrey has taken it, sir.'

Baldwin was still for a moment as he digested this. 'Where has he taken it?'

'Back to the manor, I expect. He wants to have an inquest as soon as possible, I think.'

'Interesting,' Baldwin commented. 'He wants an inquest, so he removes the evidence first.' He could feel the anger beginning to boil within him. This was intolerable! Everyone knew that a dead body should remain where it was until the coroner had been to view it. That was the king's law. He made to return to the saddle, but Simon shook his head and slipped from his own mount.

'Who are you?' he asked. 'What's your name?'

'I am called Beorn.'

'A good name. I'm Simon Puttock. Show us where she was found.'

Beorn led them to the brackish pool, what was left of it. 'She was there.'

'How?' Simon asked 'On her belly or her back?'

'Back. Her hand stuck up, as if she was waving to tell us she was there. It was terrible. Poor young Martin found her.'

'Is he here? Can he tell us more?' Baldwin asked eagerly.

'No, sir. He threw up three times, and now he's back at home. I saw her there, though, and helped bring her to the land, so I can tell you all you want to know.'

'You know who she was?'

'Lady Lucy of Meeth, yes.'

'And she was a widow?'

'Her husband died a while back in battle, yes. She's been making the best of things ever since, so I've heard.'

'She disappeared a while ago?' Simon asked. 'That was what we heard in Iddesleigh.'

'Yes. She went to Hatherleigh market, and on her way back we reckoned she was attacked.'

Simon shook his head. 'She was alone?'

'No. She always had a servant with her, usually a swordsman. That day it was her steward. He was found by the side of the road later. There was no sign of her, though.'

'Was she the sort of lady who would trust a stranger?' Simon asked.

'No woman is that trusting, is she? No, she was taken against her will. She must have seen her man die, and then she was taken away. And later killed.'

'Do you think she'd died a long time ago?' Baldwin said.

'No. You know how a body can be when it's been stored under water? She was foul-looking because the skin of her hands and feet was loose and ready to fall away, but for all that she was well preserved.'

'It is scarce surprising,' Baldwin observed, looking about him and blowing in his hands. 'It is so cold, any body would survive well.' He gazed about him at the land again. 'This is a curious place. It is far enough from the house. Where is the nearest homestead?'

'Probably my own, sir, over there beyond those trees to the east,' Beorn said.

'And you saw nothing, heard nothing recently which could have been a man bringing her here?'

Beorn's dark features rose to Baldwin's. 'If I'd heard someone bringing her here, I'd have told you by now.'

Simon burst out, 'What about when you found the body, though? Would you have sought out a king's man to catch the killer if we hadn't appeared here?'

Beorn met his stare calmly. 'Of course not. If I was to go to any man it would be to him, Sir Geoffrey. This is his land.'

Baldwin smiled drily. 'And no point going to a murderer to tell him about one of his victims, is there?'

Sir Geoffrey supervised the carrying of the body to his hall. The peasants had gone to Beorn's house, which was nearest, and fetched his front door to use as a stretcher. Sir Geoffrey had them take her through the door at the rear of his hall and deposit her in his solar. He stood at the back of the little chamber as the men gently set her down and glanced at each other with that embarrassment which men have in the presence of death when the dead bore no relation to them. When Sir Geoffrey gave an irritable gesture with his hand, they all trooped out.

'You poor fool,' he whispered thoughtfully, looking down at her. 'You couldn't do what was safe, could you?'

It was sad. He left her there and went into his hall, pouring himself a large mazer of wine and moodily throwing himself down into his chair. The discovery of her body boded badly for him and the manor.

A man walked past the door and peered inside. Seeing Sir Geoffrey seated there, he hurriedly removed himself, and the knight felt a slight grim satisfaction that at least his reputation was intact. None of the men would dare to infringe his privacy.

Not yet.

But there were signs that his grip on the place was starting to dissolve.

Whenever a man grew to power, there were always others who desired his position. Here Sir Geoffrey had a number of men who were vying for his post. Some, like Edmund Topcliff, were content to wait until Sir Geoffrey was already gone before trying to grab the stewardship; Nick le Poter was less patient. If he had an opportunity, he would pull a dagger at Sir Geoffrey's back some day, and try to take the place by force. That was the true reason why Sir Geoffrey had punished him the other day. The damned eunuch was as much use as ale without malt – he wanted power here, and would do anything to undermine Sir Geoffrey to win it. Well, Sir Geoffrey wasn't going to let him take his seat.

They were such cretins! *Idiots* the lot of them. It never seemed to occur to them that a man like Sir Geoffrey, who had fought in a hundred battles and skirmishes, who had controlled men all his adult life, would understand their plans. He had seen through Nick's little attempt to remove Sir Geoffrey's closest sergeants almost before the fool had cooked up the scheme. And what was the point? Maybe he'd succeeded in killing Ailward, but Sir Geoffrey had simply replaced him with someone who was nothing to do with Nick's camp.

And Nick was certainly a snide little man. Clearly determined to advance himself, Sir Geoffrey thought. He'd happily see the estate ruined for his own profit. If it was down to him, he'd have captured Lady Lucy and tortured her an age ago, determined to rob her of all her property and inheritance. All the men knew how the Despensers had treated Madam Baret. Sir Geoffrey had been forced to explain to them all that Lady Lucy was a useful buffer for now, and if they were to attack her it would provoke Sir Odo. He would have the approval of all, including Sir John Sully and Lord de Courtenay, if he was to espouse the chivalric excuse of protecting a defenceless widow who'd been attacked by an unscrupulous man in the pay of Despenser.

No, Sir Geoffrey believed that to harm her could only serve the interests of his master's enemies, and sought to persuade his men that they should leave her alone.

Nick wouldn't have had the gumption to do that. Just as he hadn't the intellect to see how necessary it was that they should maintain the attacks on the de Courtenay estates, but meanwhile continue holding discussions with Sir Odo. Odo was no fool, and he'd know that it was a means of holding him at bay, but while they kept up the pretence of discussions, neither side could entirely satisfactorily claim to having a reason for a fight. And Sir Geoffrey could bide his time until he was ready to launch an attack on Sir Odo. Meanwhile, Odo's men were demoralised and irritated, seeing the regular attacks by Geoffrey's men going unpunished. Sir Geoffrey had heard that three or four of Odo's men had left the hall recently, disgusted by what they saw as the pusillanimity of their master.

Poor Odo. Sir Geoffrey knew too many men just like him. He imagined he was still living in the times when a man could get by through life knowing who was a master by birth. He was older, too old perhaps for this modern age. Today the men who were reaching the heights of the government were the men who were younger, thrusting, more energetic, more determined. You didn't get to a position of power and stay there just because you were the king's cousin or even because you were noble by birth; now you had to work to show the king that you'd pursue his interests, no matter what. Piers Gaveston had been an unknown when the king elevated him to control of Cornwall and Ireland; Hugh Despenser was an impoverished knight when he took the king's fancy and now he ruled the realm with little if any interference from the king himself. And so it was all down the line. Those who wanted power and were astute and ruthless enough to try to seize it were the ones in authority now.

Those were the watchwords of the day: ruthless and astute. Sir Odo was neither. He'd been here too long, growing old among these peasants. He'd lost his edge.

Hearing the door open, a shout and a scuffle of feet from the yard behind the hall, Sir Geoffrey turned his head to listen, and soon heard the regular thrumming of cantering horses: several of them. It didn't sound like a massive force; not like Sir Odo coming with a host to repay the manor for the damage done to that bailiff's hovel, and he relaxed. If there were so few horses, his men could defend the place without difficulty.

He had to protect his manor, because that was the only way to defend his own position. And he must expand the territory, so that his master could be sure that his own authority was growing to match his importance in the country.

'Sir Geoffrey?'

'What is it?'

'Some men . . . one says he's Keeper of the King's Peace. He wants to look at the woman found up there.'

'Tell him to . . .' Sir Geoffrey bit back the rest of his words when he saw three men in the doorway.

They were not an immense force, but something in the way that one stood by the door on the balls of his feet, smiling coldly, while the other two approached him at a distance from each other, like men who were prepared for a fight, made him reassess their threat. These were men who could use their weapons.

'Who are you?' he asked coldly. 'Why do you threaten me in my own hall?'

'I am Sir Baldwin de Furnshill. You may have heard of me. I am Keeper of the King's Peace. This is my companion and friend, Simon Puttock.'

'In that case you are welcome,' Sir Geoffrey said. It was always best to show courtesy to a king's officer. 'Do you want some wine? I have some here.'

'We want to view the dead body before the coroner arrives. The coroner has been called?'

'Yes. I have asked him to visit us.'

'He seems to have been here a lot just recently.'

'We have been unfortunate.'

'Yes. A murder and a fire before this present murder. Is is most unfortunate, as you say,' Baldwin said. 'It was lucky that the coroner was on hand to investigate both.'

Sir Geoffrey frowned. 'Ailward, my man, was murdered; but the other, that was a mere accident. The coroner told me so.'

'This coroner, his name was?' Baldwin enquired.

'Sir Edward de Launcelles. Do you know him?'

'There are not so many coroners in Devon and Cornwall that one could remain unknown to me. Yes, I know him. He is a vassal of Hugh Despenser, isn't he?'

'I believe so, yes.'

'As are you, of course,' Baldwin said. He remained standing very still for a moment. 'Now, where is this body?'

Hugh stood when he heard the footsteps outside. He could do so now without a need for his staff, and he listened intently as the steps approached. They were like the friar's, but Hugh, with a shepherd's ear for detail, could tell that they were not as confident as they had been earlier.

'It's me, don't worry,' John said as he entered and saw Hugh's staff in his hands. John carried a small parcel wrapped in linen. 'They were very good to us,' he continued. 'Eggs, some bread and a small portion of sausage. They were more generous than many. Um.' He carefully placed the package on the ground at the side of their hearth and stood staring down at it. He was at a loss to know what to do.

The shock of hearing of Lucy's death had seemed to dislocate his world. He was the same man; he still had his responsibility to Hugh, and he wanted to do all he could to help this stranger with his loss, to aid him in his recovery if possible; and yet all he wanted to do just at this moment was run to seek out her body and weep over it. He had already lost his home since his argument with the prior – now he had learned that the last member of his family was also dead. There was no one but him. He was the last of his line.

'You seem quiet,' Hugh commented.

He watched the friar as John knelt and opened his parcel. To his eye the friar had grown suddenly distant. Before this, John had been talkative and cheerful, as though determined to lift Hugh's spirits by any means available, but now he was quieter, like a man who'd realised he should be more cautious.

'It's nothing to do with you,' the friar said. He remained looking down at the food. 'Well, I suppose that's not strictly true. It is something to do with you. I have heard of another death today. A young lady.'

'And the sergeant of Monkleigh was killed,' Hugh grunted as he let himself slip down to the floor. 'Ach, my leg hurts still!'

'We could soon have it looked at,' John said. 'There must be someone about here who has skills with medicines.'

'No. I'll not go about in full view until I'm well enough,' Hugh declared sourly, staring at the little fire with a lowering expression.

He wouldn't. Not until he had recovered enough to know that he could kill the men who were responsible for his Constance's murder.

Never before had Hugh felt such a consuming rage. It was a ferocious, burning fire in his breast, and it made him feel as though the fact of his desire – no, his *lust* – for revenge alone was fuelling him. Nothing mattered to him apart from that. He had to find the men who'd killed his woman.

Friar John turned to glance at him. 'Are you well, friend?'

'I'm fine,' Hugh muttered. In his mind's eye he could see the figure stooping over Constance again. He was sure that she'd been raped, too. No man would have minded doing that to a woman with her looks. She'd been so beautiful . . . Hugh could feel a choking sensation in his breast, and moved his thoughts on to other subjects. He couldn't submit to the all-encompassing horror of her death and the emptiness of his own existence without her.

Being alone was a fact of life to a moorman, of course. He'd been used to his own company for much of his youth, and the idea of a woman of his own had been a very distant dream when he wandered the moors above the River Teign. His thoughts had been geared to a place of his own, perhaps his own small flock, and maybe some years later, when he'd saved enough money, he could think of negotiating for a woman's hand. Not for love, though. Mainly so that he'd have help to work his land. That was the way of things.

After he met Constance, everything changed. He wasn't a farmer – that dream had faded when he first began to work for Simon Puttock and realised he could be happy as a servant to a kindly, sensible man. Margaret was a good mistress, too, and their children had been as good as his own, he'd thought. And then he met Constance and learned that the respect and affection of a woman of his own was more attractive even than the stability he'd enjoyed with Simon and Margaret.

When she gave birth to her child, it had capped his pleasure. The lad wasn't his, but he didn't care. The father was long gone, and Hugh would be all the boy would know. Little Hugh had been a happy, smiling boy, always into everything as soon as he could walk. He'd only been up and about for two weeks when Hugh saw him toddle uncertainly into the pool at the side of the house. If Hugh hadn't been there that day, little Hugh wouldn't have lived beyond it.

The idea that the child could have been killed was a weight on Hugh's heart as he sat and stared at the fire's flames. If only he'd been nearer . . . yet he had not been far away. Surely he should have heard her screams.

'Master Hugh? Please, eat some of this sausage. It'll do you good.'

'I don't want it to do me good!' Hugh snapped, but then took the proffered food with an ungracious snort. He didn't want the stuff, but he did want to be fit and healthy again so he could find the killers. 'Did you learn anything about the attack on my house?'

The friar shot him a look, then sighed. 'I did ask at the vill over the way there, but they knew little about it. All they said was that there'd been a fire.'

'What about the coroner?' Hugh pressed eagerly. He had known several coroners from his work with his master and Sir Baldwin. 'Who was it?'

'A man called Edward de Launcelles, apparently,' John said with a sigh. 'It's not a name I have heard before, but he was already here for the inquest into the death of some other man.'

'Must have been Ailward,' Hugh guessed. 'He was found just before all this.' He shot a look at the friar. 'Didn't he look at my place?'

'Yes,' John admitted heavily. 'Apparently he took it to be an accident. They all think you're dead – you were burned to death in the house, they say.'

Hugh gaped with dismay. 'They say I died? That it was an accident? How can they say that? It was murder! There were men there, they killed my Constance, and left me on my face in the dirt! Why would they say I died with her?'

'Perhaps, my friend, because they knew how devoted you were to her,' John said gently. 'No man could have missed that.'

'The coroner should have realised I was alive,' Hugh said, uncomforted by his tone. 'Why'd he think I was dead?'

'He must have been in a hurry and confused. You know how often the coroners are changed. All they do is keep records so that the justices know how much tax to impose when a man or woman dies. They don't concern themselves with details,' John said, hungrily watching as Hugh slowly devoured the sausage. It was Friday, and John was fasting as always. He would eat no meat today.

'It's not right,' Hugh muttered, and then the grief passed through his soul like a wave of ice, freezing, jagged, cruel, and his head fell on his breast as he wept for his woman, her son, and the life he had loved so dearly. 'It's not . . . it's *not*!'

'My friend, life rarely is,' John said sadly, and he turned away as Hugh sobbed, for he did not want Hugh to see the tears in his own eyes.

Chapter Twenty-One

Robert Crokers felt good that morning. He had slept better, and as his bitch lay patiently waiting he knelt nearby, watching.

'Poor old girl,' he whispered.

'You mooning after your bitch again?' Walter called.

He was not a sentimental man, this Walter. So far as Robert could make out, he'd been a wandering man-at-arms for some while, and only fairly recently had come into the de Courtenay fold. It was a surprise to Robert, because he knew that Lord de Courtenay and his vassal Sir John Sully were both reluctant to take on mercenary fellows. Far better that they should have men who were long-term servants, those who owed allegiance from their oaths rather than selling it for a few coins. Nobody liked a mercenary.

'She's always been a good bitch,' Robert explained as he left her in her corner and walked over to join Walter.

'So she should be. If a dog don't work, it has to be made to. If it can't, has to be killed. That's how dogs are,' Walter said unsympathetically.

'You don't like their company?'

Walter pulled a face. 'I've been bitten too often to trust the damned things. No, give me a good rache and I'm happy. An animal that'll hunt for the pot, that's a useful thing – but a sheepdog? What good's that to me? All they ever do is snap at your heels or worse. I had one go for my cods once. Damn near got them, too. Had a great bite out of my tunic, and I had to kick it to get it to let go. Damned thing.'

Robert wondered idly what Walter could have been doing when the dog took such exception, but it wasn't the sort of question a man could put to a mercenary. It was all too likely that he'd hear something he'd really prefer not to know. 'How long do you think it'll be before they come back?'

Walter shrugged and glanced out through the doorway. 'If they feel sure of their ground, it'll be a long time. If they're nervous, they may try to come sooner. Doesn't matter which. They won't want to kill us. We're not important to them, and there's no point killing those who aren't a danger.'

'If we're unimportant, surely that makes it easier to kill us?'

Walter looked at him pityingly. 'If we were at war, our lives wouldn't be worth a penny, but as it is, with us over here and no real threat to anyone, they'll just chase us off the land, and by the time we're gone word'll have reached Sir Odo and twenty or thirty men will be here to take the place back again.'

'So how will it end?' Robert asked. 'From what you say, we'll be harried away, then come back, time after time. Where can it end?'

'It'll end when the Lord Despenser comes and forces his case,' Walter said with another shrug.

'But if Lord de Courtenay comes and defends the place . . .'

This time Walter's glance held more contempt than pity. 'You think so? Say de Courtenay comes here – what of it? Oh, he's been here in Devon for many years, and he owns much land, I've no doubt, but he's never been a close friend of the king's, has he? He's no relation either. So if he comes and tells my Lord Despenser to leave the place, who's going to have to go in the end?'

'Lord de Courtenay has more men here, though,' Robert said confidently.

'And there are many who'd prefer to stay on the side of the king and his personal friend and companion, too. And that means my Lord Despenser. If Despenser decides he wants this land, mark this, friend, there is no one who'll be able to keep it away from him. And if it comes to that, you and I'll be irrelevant. We're only pawns.'

'Sweet Christ!'

'So I wouldn't worry so much about that hound of yours. Rather, I'd be looking to sharpening any knives or swords that I had about the place. And then thinking about getting the dog ready to fight again. She isn't much use lying on her flank all day, is she?'

Robert looked out through the door at the small trampled area of garden. 'How long? How long before it's over and I know whether this is to remain my home or is going to be stolen from me?'

Walter snorted and hawked, spitting into the angle of the wall. 'I'd reckon we'll know in about the next month or so. If Despenser decides he wants this, he'll make it plain.'

'What would you do then?'

Walter hunched his shoulders as he considered. He'd been here only a year and a half or so, and by Christ it had been good. In the past he'd served in the king's host, even travelling to the king's lands in France for a while, but in a life of fighting he'd never found such . . . such ease of spirit as he'd found here. That was it, yes. Ease of spirit. In other places he'd fought and been scared, and sometimes his companions and he had won and they'd taken much booty; at others they'd been thrashed and they'd lost everything. There was always the chance of being ruined at any time.

Here, though, he'd learned that there could be benefits to peace. He hadn't had to take up weapons against men who were bigger than him, or fight with a band of fellows who were likely to desert him just when the battle grew harshest. Instead he'd discovered that the lands about here were conducive to relaxation. There was little work that truly had to be done today.

'I'd stay with Sir Odo for as long as I could, I reckon,' he said at last. 'That's it. He's been good to me. I – I like him. I can respect him. I think I'd stay with him even if he lost everything.'

'You'd be that loyal?'

Walter stirred himself, irritated by the questioning. 'Why? Do you think that I'm just a mediocre felon because I don't have a master? I am a free man, not tied to some land. I am as loyal as any man deserves. Sir Odo saved me when I needed help. I'll repay that. What'll you do? If the Despensers decide to take this manor, they'll still need a bailiff here, so you may well find yourself wanted anyway.'

'But I'm Lord de Courtenay's man.'

'You can protest all you want, but you'd best think about that if you want a home to live in. If Despenser chooses, Lord de Courtenay won't have any household to be loyal to. Look at Earl Thomas, the king's own cousin. He's been executed like a felon. Then there's King

Edward's favourite general, Lord Mortimer. He's under threat of execution if he's ever found again. Those two were loyal to their king too. How long do you think de Courtenay can survive if Despenser takes against him the way he took against those other two?'

Baldwin eyed this knight with the same cold, dispassionate interest with which he studied any other man he suspected of murder.

Sir Geoffrey was a confident, square-jawed man with the manner of a natural bully. Baldwin had known many like him, although usually there was one clear flaw in their character. A bully would usually give himself away with bluster and arrogance. Not so this knight. He hadn't threatened or sworn at the sudden interruption of his privacy. Perhaps it was because he was intelligent too, that he offered wine and allowed them to remain in his hall without calling for guards to remove them as he could have. After all, even the Despenser's men had to be wary of insulting the king's own officials . . . in public, at least.

There was more, though, Baldwin reckoned. This man was no fool, and he wanted to know what the Keeper knew. He wanted to trade information, perhaps, or was it only that he wanted to win Baldwin over, if that was at all possible?

'Come with me,' Sir Geoffrey said, tilting his head slightly to one side and giving a self-deprecating grin and shrug, like a peasant who'd been caught out in a little ruse.

That manner of his made Baldwin wonder whether the man was actually as intelligent as he had initially suspected. If he had thought to conceal a crime he himself had perpetrated, surely the worst thing he could have done would have been to bring the body here. To attempt to hide her in his own hall would immediately have the effect of adding to any suspicions about him.

But Sir Geoffrey had no foolish delusions that he might be free of suspicion, of course, Baldwin told himself. Sir Geoffrey was an astute man. If he had been involved in this woman's murder, he would have made sure already that his men were briefed to give him an alibi; if another man had killed her, surely he would want to make sure that the killer was speedily discovered.

She lay on a door on the floor of the solar. Her body had spent some time in the water, Baldwin reckoned: although he was no expert in bodies retrieved from mires, the flesh of her hands appeared almost like gloves, and looked as though it would pull away at a touch. Simon, he realised, had walked straight in and now stared down at her at Baldwin's side.

Thinking again of how Simon had kept back from the ruins of Hugh's house, Baldwin was surprised. Simon could usually be relied upon to remain at the rear of any investigation like this, but today he was right beside Baldwin, and Baldwin wondered why, until he saw Simon's face. The bailiff had wondered whether there could have been any error, and whether this could have been Hugh's wife. That it was not was not in doubt. This lady was dark-haired, with probably a dark complexion in life; Constance had been very fair of skin and hair. Simon took one look at her and subsided, moving behind Baldwin, his head hanging.

'Who has identified her?' Baldwin demanded of the knight.

Sir Geoffrey shrugged. 'I have men here who know her well enough. I can find others, if you wish. There's a local priest who knew her. If you don't trust our word, you will believe a priest, I suppose?'

Baldwin turned and gave him a long stare. The man was insufferably confident now that the men were all in here looking at the body, but whether it was the confidence of the innocent, or the bluster of a guilty man, Baldwin could not tell. 'Which priest?'

'Humphrey or Isaac down nearer the river. Anyone will tell you where you can find them.'

'Why did you remove the body to this room? You know the law. She should have remained where she was found.'

'How often would a coroner demand that a drowned man be left in the river where he was found? Don't be ridiculous. She was in a pool of water. It would be stupid to leave her there. And in any case, this poor child was a neighbour almost. I could not let her remain there. I fear that if the law demands that an innocent young woman like this should be left in the wet grave in which she was discovered, the law deserves to be ignored.'

'You did not intend to see whether you could hide her?'

Sir Geoffrey grinned more widely. 'Sir, is she hidden? How many

men did I tell to keep silent about finding her? None! I merely sought
to protect the body of a dead neighbour from being consumed by wild
beasts, because no matter how much I tried to have her person guarded,
in this weather my peasants would have left her alone while they went
to find more adequate clothing, or sticks for a fire, or a hovel in which
to shelter from the rain, and in the meantime she would have been
eaten.'

'When was she last seen?' Baldwin asked.

'Oh, I don't know. You need to ask her household.'

'I shall. She came from Meeth?'

'Yes. She was Lady Lucy of Meeth. Husband died in the war against
the king, so she had no one to protect her.'

His gaze had gone to her as though regretfully, Baldwin thought,
but that should be the natural reaction of any man who learned of a
poor widow who was taken and killed.

Baldwin subjected the corpse to a close examination, speaking all
the while. 'Edgar, see this? Her left arm is broken – above and below
her elbow. And the right is broken below the elbow. Both legs have
been broken too. There is a great wound under her left breast.
Someone stabbed her, but not with an ordinary weapon. It is grossly
opened . . . a terrible wound. The poor child. This looks like torture,
followed by a stabbing. At least her death was swift enough. Would
you have any idea when she could have been put in that mire, Sir
Geoffrey?'

The steward shook his head decisively. 'Of course not. She was
probably thrown there by someone passing by. It's an easy place to
reach from the road, as you saw today, I expect. Anyone could have
flung her in and ridden on to Monk Oakhampton or Exbourne. There
is nothing to make me suppose that she was put there by someone
from my household.'

'Yet she was tortured. Somebody must have had reason to do that to
her.'

'Someone who might, for instance, have desired her?'

Baldwin smiled without humour. 'You think so? A man who craved
her body so much that he was willing to destroy it in order to prevent
another having it? Or someone who wanted to make her a compliant

bed-mate? How many women have you known who would willingly sleep with a man who had tortured them?'

'What else could it be?'

'Oh, I am sure we can come up with some suggestions to cover the facts,' Baldwin said mildly. 'But I think that there is little more to be learned from this poor child's broken body. You have sent for the coroner, you say?'

'Yes.'

'And he is a knight who owns his loyalty to Lord Despenser. As you do. That will make matters much more convenient.'

'That is the second time you have mentioned that we both owe allegiance to the same man,' Sir Geoffrey commented. His eyes looked lazily at Baldwin, the lids falling until he seemed close to dozing. 'Does that mean that you have some comments you wish to make about my master?'

'Not at all. He is not here,' Baldwin smiled.

'Then, perhaps, you have something to say about me?'

'No. I am simply intrigued that so much should be happening here, and by the coroner's assumption of an accident up at Iddesleigh. That was a very convenient decision, was it not?'

'Iddesleigh?'

'The coroner suggested that the house fire was an accident. I think it was a murder. Men went there and murdered a woman and child.'

'I heard of that. Yes, a man and his wife and child died, so I heard.'

'Certainly the woman and child are dead.'

Baldwin was aware of Simon throwing him a look, but Baldwin refused to return it. He was watching the knight in front of him very carefully to see whether his words had affected him.

Sir Geoffrey eyed him doubtfully, but Baldwin did not see any guilt, only a little surprise. 'Well, if you have questions for the coroner, you will be able to ask him before long.'

Baldwin looked back at the body on the rude stretcher. 'I think I may do that.'

'Do,' Sir Geoffrey said.

Glancing up at him, Baldwin thought he had a little of the stillness of a snake preparing to strike. Rather than provoke him further, he would have left the room, but Sir Geoffrey was blocking his path.

'There is one thing you should consider, Sir Baldwin,' he said quietly. 'Bear this in mind. If I was going to murder, I would not be foolish enough to hide the body on my lands just when I was going to expose that very area to the gaze of all my villeins. If I killed, I would leave the woman's body somewhere else. Perhaps on a neighbour's lands, if I sought to do him a foul turn.'

'You have many enemies?'

Sir Geoffrey showed his teeth. It could have been a smile, but it could equally have been a snarl. 'What do *you* think?'

Chapter Twenty-Two

'What are you talking about?' Simon demanded as soon as they had remounted and ridden away from the hall. 'You said in there that Constance and young Hugh were both dead, but you implied . . .'

Baldwin brought his horse nearer Simon's. 'Simon, Edgar and I have seen men burned at the stake. You've seen bodies brought out from burned-out cottages, too. A man doesn't simply burn away.'

Edgar nodded. 'A man takes cartloads of wood to be completely immolated, Simon.'

'But what else could have . . ?'

'If Hugh was hurt, he would find a place to hide until he was well, wouldn't he?' Baldwin said. 'And then he would return to exact vengeance.'

'He could have escaped that place only to die alone somewhere else,' Simon said with a gasp. His grief was rising again. It felt like panic. The idea that his man could have been injured, and had run off like a stabbed hog to die in a lonely, miserable, cold place far from anyone he loved, was more than Simon could bear. He closed his eyes and didn't quite catch Baldwin's next comment. 'What?'

'Wake up, Simon!' Baldwin snapped. 'This is the first chance we've had to discuss this. We've had people with us up until now. I wasn't going to talk to you about it at Hugh's ruins, but I am sure that Hugh did not die there. The question is, did he die at all, or was he free to escape?'

Edgar shrugged. 'Obviously he was free.'

'What are you saying?' Simon protested. 'How could you think that he would choose life when his woman was dead? He couldn't have lived.'

'Clearly he did,' Edgar said flatly. 'He sent a messenger to me.'

Simon's jaw dropped. 'He . . . how do you know this?'

'The messenger was from a friar who met him somewhere round here. He told me that the friar was agitated, but that he had been told to pass on the message. If Hugh is in the hands of a friar, I should think he would be well enough.'

Baldwin nodded. 'I did not even think of that. I simply assumed that the messenger came from the vill.'

'My first thought was, who there could have known where I was,' Edgar said. 'There were some who could have known where Simon was, but not me, I thought. That was why I asked.'

'And it was a good thing you did,' Baldwin said. 'So let us assume that he is alive and recuperating. That means we have an urgent task.'

'Why assume that?' Simon said, reluctant to accept this leap of faith. 'He may have died.'

'If he had, I think the friar would have told someone,' Baldwin said. 'A friar need not fear the local politics. No, I think the fact that they are still silent and apparently hidden means that they are both alive. So we have the job of finding the killer before Hugh tries to.'

'I would have no difficulty with Hugh finding the murderer and killing him,' Simon said, and spat into the road. 'He deserves whatever Hugh does to him.'

'I agree,' Baldwin said, but now there was an unusual note in his voice, a tone Simon had only rarely heard before. Baldwin swung his arm and winced at the pain in his shoulder. 'But we have to remember that Hugh has been known to get things wrong before, Simon. I don't want to have to protect him after he's killed the wrong man.'

Humphrey was happy that he'd done all he could now, and he was about to pack his meagre belongings when the heavy pounding at the chapel door made him stiffen and wait, considering what he could do.

The only thought in his mind had been of escape, and he was almost ready to leave. He'd done it before, and he was more than ready to slip off again. It wasn't the best weather for it, of course, but at least he could depart at night and find a new post somewhere, anywhere, and begin again. There was no point in hanging around here any longer. He was convinced of that. If he did, he might be hanged.

'Who is it?'

'Father, it is the Keeper of the King's Peace, Sir Baldwin Furnshill. I understand you saw the body of a young woman on Sir Geoffrey's land today. May we speak to you?'

Humphrey closed his eyes and swore to himself. God was playing games with him now. So near to escape, yet he was in danger again. He stared at the altar and the plain cross accusingly, his lips pursed in anger. 'Oh, very well,' he said, and slipped the bolt open, stepping into the chill daylight.

The men before him were alarming. The Keeper, of course, was worrying enough. Any man whose job involved tracking down and arresting felons was not the sort of person Humphrey wanted to be involved with, not with his past. Still, he managed to smile coolly and eye the three with what he hoped looked like calm disinterest. 'You wanted to speak to me about the young woman?'

'Yes. What can you tell us about her?'

'I did not know her, if that is what you mean. She was the widow of a knight at Meeth, I understand. That was what Perkin told me, anyway.'

'Perkin?'

'One of the peasants. He was the man who found Ailward after the football.'

Baldwin nodded. 'You mean the sergeant who died?'

'Yes. He was killed up on the moor near Iddesleigh. I reckoned it was because of the camp ball. Perkin was running up to the goal when he saw Ailward. It was because Ailward appeared there in his way that a man from Fishleigh was able to knock Perkin down and take the ball, and it was because of that tackle that Monkleigh lost the game. Not many forgave Perkin that loss. And I doubt he forgave Ailward for distracting him.'

Simon listened with rising anger. This was all nonsense. The man was talking about some game of camp ball, while he wanted to learn about his man. He pushed his way forward. 'What of the . . .'

'Simon, please wait,' Baldwin said. He glanced at his friend and gave him a sympathetic smile. 'We have to try to get to the bottom of all these stories before we can hope to learn what became of Hugh. There must be a connection between them all.'

'Hugh?' Humphrey repeated, looking from one to another. 'Who's he?'

'He was the servant of my friend here,' Baldwin said. 'And his wife and child were killed up beyond Iddesleigh a few days ago.'

'Oh, the man who died in the fire,' Humphrey acknowledged.

'You agreed with that conclusion?' Baldwin said.

'The coroner said it was an accident, didn't he?' Humphrey said.

'I believe so,' Baldwin said without emphasis. Then he added, 'A coincidence that the coroner was here for Ailward's death just when this man and his family were killed too.'

'And now another woman's dead too,' Simon snapped. 'What is happening here, priest?'

Humphrey licked his lips and glanced from Simon to Baldwin. He was in two minds, but there seemed little point in trying to conceal anything from them. It wasn't as if the matters had anything to do with him – and he would soon be gone anyway.

'Everyone thinks she was killed by Sir Geoffrey. He and his men are vassals of Despenser, and you know *his* reputation. Lady Lucy had land and could perhaps be bullied into giving it up, while your man was one of several who were beaten up and told to go.'

'He wasn't "told" anything,' Simon spat. 'He was slaughtered with his family.'

'It was meant as a message, I think,' Humphrey explained. 'Others have been used in the same way. There is a man called Robert Crokers over the way there, who is sergeant to Sir Odo of Fishleigh. He had his home burned too. That was the same day as your man.'

'A message . . .' Simon mused, his eyes narrowing as a thought came to him.

Baldwin peered with keen interest. 'You are sure? He was attacked the very same day?'

'Yes. A party of men went to Robert's house in the late afternoon. It was the very day that Adcock arrived to replace Ailward. They rode off as Adcock got there, and forced Robert out before setting light to his house. Your man died later that night, so far as I can tell.'

'Why attack my man?' Simon asked. 'What would be in it for this man Geoffrey?'

'He wants more lands for his master, I suppose. The more he has, the better it reflects upon him, and the more authority he has himself.'

Baldwin and Edgar exchanged a glance. 'That makes some sense,' Baldwin said slowly. 'But we have heard this from many others in the area since we arrived. Is there no one else who could have a desire to take lands? Or is it possible that someone could have wanted to attack Hugh and his family with a view to making everyone *think* that it was Sir Geoffrey who was responsible? There are too many possibilities.'

'I don't know. All I can say is, it fairly shook me to my sandals to see that poor woman in the bog up there – and the knight was remarkably keen to get her out of sight. I've never seen a woman like that . . . soaked in black water . . . poor woman!'

'What of the dead sergeant, this Ailward? What can you tell us about him?' Baldwin enquired.

'He was a hard taskmaster, but a bailiff has to be, doesn't he? Sergeant or bailiff, it's all the same thing. They are there to make the land pay for the lord. The vill has to have enough food to live on, but all the rest is for the lord, and sometimes it's hard. Ailward was a brawny fellow, fast with his fists or his staff, but to his credit, I think he was a kindly soul to those who actually had little. He talked hard, and sounded a cruel fellow, but if a peasant needed money, he would lend it. His wife adored him.'

'How long had he been sergeant?' Baldwin asked. He could sense that Simon's ire was rising once more, but he shot his friend a look that made Simon half turn away.

'Since before I came here. Some while as a bachelor, more recently as a husband. I understand his family used to be wealthy, but then they fell into . . .'

'Yes?'

'Well – disgrace. The war two years ago. When the king won, there was nothing left for Ailward. That is what I have heard.'

'Another family ruined,' Simon said bitterly.

'Where do they live?' Baldwin asked.

*   *   *

As the waves of nausea rolled through him, starting from the pit of his belly and rumbling upwards, Adcock rolled out of his cot and fell on to the floor on all fours, retching.

The pain was exquisite; quite unlike anything he had experienced before. He felt as though his ballocks were going to explode. This was no simple, geographically isolated ache, it was all-encompassing, from his knees to his breast. It felt as though he was one whole mass of bruises from his chest to his thighs. Walking was impossible. Sitting on a horse with this tenderness was unimaginable. All he could do was crouch, choking with the fabulous anguish that brightened and flared from his groin. His head fell to the floor, for his entire soul was dragged down to his ballocks, and nothing else mattered.

'You still lazing about?'

Adcock didn't hear him the first time. He was entirely concentrated on his wounds, and it was only when Nick le Poter gave him an ungentle push with his boot that Adcock collapsed, weeping with the torture of it, his eyes still firmly closed. He opened them when the waves had subsided a little, and looked up to see his fresh tormentor.

'So, you've learned what our mad master is like, have you?'

Nick was still unable to pull a jacket or shirt over the lacerations on his back, and he must continually move his muscles to ease the itching as the bloody scabs tightened and the scars formed. At least the worst of the actual searing sensation was gone now. One day of grief, and it was more or less all right. He'd suffered worse.

Adcock whispered. 'I think I'd guessed already.'

'He's off his head. You upset him, did you?'

'All I did was do my job. There was a mire out on the Exbourne road. You know the one? I had it drained, that was all, but in the bottom there was a dead woman.'

'What?'

'Someone from Meeth – Lady Lucy? She was only young, but she'd been tortured. Even I could see that, and I know nothing about death. She had great welts on her where someone had burned her, I think.' He winced.

Nick saw his expression, his mind racing. 'And we both know who could do that to someone, don't we?'

* * *

Jeanne accepted the wine from Jankin with a graceful inclination of her head. Emma was starting to get dozy, she could see. The maid was looking about her belligerently, like an old hen who had mislaid her corn and thought one of the cockerels in the run might have stolen it. Soon, like a hen, she appeared to forget all about them, and instead sank back on her stool, resting her back on the wall behind her and grumbling to herself.

The trouble which Jeanne had so often tried to explain to her was that, when complaining about a hostelry, it was usually best to wait until she had left the place. Emma was notable for many things, but the subtlety and moderation of her voice were not among her attributes. It was as Deadly Dave reappeared, apparently glad to have escaped from Jeanne's husband from the glare he threw her as he stood in the doorway, that Emma began to make her feelings known.

'Look at this place. Little better than a sty.'

'Emma, keep your voice down.'

'Why? No one would hear me here. Anyway, I doubt any of them would want to dispute it. Look at the state of the place! And the men here. Look at them. As ungodly a mob as I've ever seen. Only that one's moderately clean. I can see why Sir Baldwin chose him as a guide. I can tell you, mistress, I'll be glad to be back home at Liddinstone.'

'Moderate your tone,' Jeanne commanded urgently.

'We're only here to look after Sir Baldwin, after all. And he's gone off on his own already. What's the point of our being here?'

Jeanne clenched her jaw and, as Richalda mumbled in her sleep in her lap, took a moment to force her voice to calm. At last she said, 'Emma, Sir Baldwin is safe because he has his servant Edgar and his friend Simon with him. I need not fear his falling from his mount into a ditch while there are two strong men at his side. However, he needed us on the way here. And he needs us to be here when he returns, not lynched because . . .' she lowered her voice to a malevolent hiss, 'because you insult all the people of this good vill. *You will be silent!*'

'Harrumph! Don't see what you're so upset about. It's not like the little family up the road were close to you, is it? That scruffy tatterdemalion Hugh was ever a foolish little man, you used to say.'

'Perhaps I did on occasion,' Jeanne said with spirit, 'but I never took pleasure in denigrating him like you, and I would prefer not to hear any more insulting words about him now the poor man is dead.'

Emma snorted and gazed about her once more, her small eyes seeking fresh amusement. 'Shame about his wife. Her being a nun and all.'

Jeanne winced. She could almost hear the necks creaking as all the men in the room turned to stare at the two women. 'Emma, be silent!'

'Why? She was a nun. Don't you remember? Hugh met her at Belstone, and she . . .'

Jeanne leaned forward and removed her cup of wine. 'You have had enough.'

'But I haven't finished it!'

'I think you have!'

Emma sank back and sulkily cast an eye about the room again. 'Look at this place! What do you want?'

This was addressed to a boy who, intrigued by the conversation which all had heard, was leaning round to peer at Emma from between two older lads.

'You stick to your drink and leave two ladies alone,' Emma said haughtily.

'Was it true?' called a man from the bar near Jankin. 'Was she really a nun?'

Jeanne glared at Emma, but failed to catch her maid's attention.

'Yes. Of course she was. Poor chit, she won't have a chance to confess her sins now, will she?'

'Shouldn't have buried her, should you, Matthew?' said another man. 'If she were a runaway, she shouldn't be put into the churchyard, should she?'

'Specially if she had a bastard!' another called. 'She had a boy, didn't she? If she was a bride of Christ, that lad was a bastard. Stands to reason.'

Matthew cast a look at Jeanne in which several emotions were mingled, and Jeanne held her chin up with a supercilious look in her eye. She would not have Hugh's wife's memory impugned. 'Yes?'

'May I speak with you a moment, my lady?' he asked, slipping from the bar and crossing towards the door.

Jeanne remained seated for a moment or two, before nodding and standing, gently shifting Richalda to her shoulder. When Emma moved to join her, she hurriedly held out her hand and shook her head. 'You wait there,' she commanded sternly. 'And this time keep silent, as I said. I don't want any more trouble!'

Emma glanced about her with a slightly curled lip.

'Not much chance of me causing trouble in here, is there?'

Hugh left the house for a moment, wondering how well his leg was healing. To his surprise, it held up well as he crossed the ground outside, and he felt a sudden burst of confidence. He would be able to use it, and that meant he could seek to avenge Constance. It was all he wanted.

She had been so good for him. He'd learned the delights of family life, the joys of a home filled with the sounds of a child at play. Resting before his fire, his exhaustion seeping away, the glowing flames warming his face after the chill of the wintry wind, he had known real happiness. It was a strange sensation, one he had never fully experienced before.

The worst of it all was this feeling of guilt. If only he had returned to the house earlier and not dallied at the hedge, perhaps he could have saved her, protected her from the attackers. He could have done – he *should* have done; he should have been there for his woman.

He could feel the hot tears of frustration and rage prickling again. The idea that she died alone, crying for help while . . .

But he was not so far away that he could have missed her screams, surely? She had a good voice, and when she scolded her son Hugh could usually hear her from up in the field. Yet that day he had heard nothing. She must have called for him, though, because she must have known that no one would go to her rescue if she didn't. Constance was no fool. She must have realised that Hugh could have heard her if she had cried out. He wasn't that far away. She knew that.

Surely, though, he must have heard her screaming.

Suddenly Hugh tottered. He had to reach out an arm and support himself against the wall. As his legs weakened and he slowly sank to the ground, he felt the sobbing start again deep in his breast.

If he hadn't heard her, it was because she had not called for him. And she hadn't called for him because she didn't want to have him there to witness her shame. Or, worse, because she didn't want him to be hurt. She had kept quiet as the men took her and killed her, accepting her fate while her man worked so near. She had died quietly so that he wouldn't himself be hurt.

He covered his face and tried to keep the sound of his heartfelt weeping as quiet as possible.

John found him there later, his arms outstretched against the wall like a man on the cross, his eyes cast up to heaven; a man who sought for help in his despair.

Chapter Twenty-Three

Jeanne was quite prepared for a fight. There was no priest alive who could scare her. She knew too many good men of God to be fearful of a fellow like this, a lowly vill's vicar. If Matthew had been bright enough to have any prospects of enhancement, he wouldn't be here in this little parish. He'd be in Exeter with the bishop, or studying in a university.

He stood waiting outside, and when Jeanne saw him he glanced at the inn, then beckoned her to follow him.

To her surprise he did not walk to his church, over to the right. Instead, he led her down the left-hand track to the roadway, and then further eastwards, along the path towards Hugh's burned-out house. When he reached it, he stood with his hands tucked in the sleeves of his robe against the chill.

'Father?' Jeanne prompted.

'When I came here, I was only very young,' Matthew said inconsequentially. He was gazing about him at the place, almost as though he had forgotten that Jeanne was there with him. 'At the time this was the home of the manor's cowherd. He was a good, bluff man, old Sandy. Named for his hair, he was. Quite a yellow-golden colour it was, although by the time I came here it looked as though the colour had been washed out. He was an old man. His wife had died a long time before, although I can't remember why now. Sandy did tell me, but whether it was a fever or an accident, I can't tell. There have been so many deaths since I first came here.'

He looked back at the building. It was a sad sight. Once it had been a thriving place, with the cowherder coming home at the end of his day to see all his children running towards him, his wife perhaps in the doorway, wiping her hands after her day's work: looking after the children, cleaning them, washing soiled clothing, cooking . . . and he would be exhausted after working in his fields or seeing to his master's herd with his oldest boy. It was a life Matthew could understand. His own father had been a cattleherd.

'Do you think that the house will be rebuilt?' Jeanne asked, seeing the direction of his gaze.

He sighed. 'I hope so. It's dreadful to see a home broken down like this. Shocking somehow to think that it could be so easily destroyed.'

'Surely someone will see the walls and put up a new roof. There are not that many spare plots with good walls.'

'I shall see whether I can persuade Sir John Sully to restore it.'

Jeanne frowned. 'Wasn't all this land owned by the prioress of Belstone?' The prioress had given this little holding to Constance, she recalled.

'It was, but over time much land has been sold to support the priory in its trials. The priory has little money, and must shift for itself most of the time. I've heard that this holding was sold off some eighteen months ago. The prioress retains rights to the church and to some of the land, but mostly Sir John Sully is responsible now. I shall have to tell the prioress what has happened, though. The poor woman. She had been a nun, you know.'

Jeanne smiled sadly. 'Please tell the good prioress that Constance is dead. But be in no doubt, the prioress knew of her and released Constance herself. She had been made to swear her oath before she was old enough. And when she fell in love, her prioress was kind enough to remind her that her vows were not valid. It was the prioress who gave her this land, and when Hugh joined her she was no nun.'

Matthew searched her face with a narrow-eyed intensity, but at last he drew a huge sigh of relief and gave a small smile. 'That, my lady, is a great weight from my mind. I dislike the idea of punishing the dead, and in all honesty I didn't think that the child could have been so sinful as to have renounced life in a priory. She seemed too good and kind to me. I had feared when I overheard your maid that I had married a woman who was already betrothed to Christ, and the idea terrified me. If you are sure that . . .'

'Write to the prioress. She will be pleased to confirm that I am right.'

'That, then, is one problem out of the way.'

She glanced at his face. 'You still seem perturbed, Father. Is there anything I can help you with?'

'No, I think not.'

'Are you worried that you might have to explain to the men of the vill about her?'

'I shall have to explain to them that she was no nun. That will please many of them.'

'But something is yet worrying you?'

He smiled wearily. 'There is always something to worry a man when he has several hundred souls to protect. But yes, if you will have it, there is one thing: I am perturbed that poor Constance could have been killed because a man desired her.'

'And who could that have been?'

'There are many men in the vill, but I do not think it was a man from here.'

'You think that they are all uniquely good?' Jeanne asked with a raised eyebrow.

He grinned at that. 'No. I have my share of cowards, bullies and evil ones. But I find it hard to believe that any of them would dare to risk Hugh's revenge, and still fewer would dare to risk their souls by murdering both of them and their child.'

Jeanne saw no reason to advise him that the child was not Hugh's. It would unnecessarily complicate matters. 'So who?'

'There is one man . . .'

He stopped and stared at the ground at his feet, uncomfortable. Then he looked up again and met her gaze resolutely. 'I was worried about a runaway here because I feared that this woman could be the second in the vicinity.'

'There is another?' Jeanne gaped.

'I believe so. The coadjutor at the chapel at Monkleigh.'

'I don't understand – you mean that he is about to run away?'

He showed his teeth again. 'No. I mean that he already has. I think he was a friar, and now he's arrived to take advantage of a rather foolish old man, Isaac the priest.'

'What has alerted your suspicions?'

He shrugged. 'Little things at first. When he arrived, his hands were clean and not horny. They had never seen hard labour. He was clearly a man who had spent his time in a cloister or scriptorium rather than a field. Yet he told me that he had run his own parish church with his own glebe. That was plainly untrue, for he knew nothing of farming. The vill's men had to help him with everything. I was concerned when I heard that and other rumours, concerned enough to contact a friend at Exeter. He deals with diocesan matters, and I asked him what he could tell me about this Humphrey.'

'What did he tell you?'

'That as far as he knew there was no coadjutor sent to help Isaac. No one at Exeter had any knowledge of a younger priest being sent here to help, but of course the bishop could have acted alone in this.'

'So he might be a felon?' Jeanne said.

'Perhaps, but if he is, he is a felon with an unusually good grasp of Latin and the Church's rites. I thought to test him, so when I was passing I dropped in to witness a service he was conducting, and he was word-perfect so far as I could tell . . . it is some years since I was taught myself, and it is possible that a little of my own service is not so correct as I could wish, but I comfort myself with the thought that I do try hard to be a good priest. I think that is all most of us can aspire to: being good enough. If I can direct some of my parishioners away from the paths of folly or evil, I have done my job.

'But so far as I can tell, Humphrey is a trained churchman, although he is not the vill's coadjutor as people had thought. Which leaves me with the interesting question of who he is and why he is there.'

'Have you arrived at an answer?'

'I am afraid not. I can only assume that he left his abbey, priory or church under a cloud of some sort; but what does that matter? If he is a good priest to the men of his parish, surely that is sufficient?'

'Perhaps. What does your heart tell you?'

He looked up at the sky. 'In God's name, I do not know. He seems a sound parish priest, but he may have a good reason for showing that face. What if he is concealing another aspect in order to gain an advantage? I am very concerned that there might be some ulterior motive here. That is why I was going to write to the bishop to ask him whether he sent this man. But Isaac stopped me. He said Humphrey was *his* concern, not mine.

'And in the meantime?'

'In the meantime I am trying to watch him. And I do so. But while the two vills are at daggers drawn, it is hard.'

Sir Geoffrey was in a cold rage as he walked along the hall and out to the rear. The second building was constructed at right angles to the main part of the house, a long, low block with narrow windows set high in the walls and one doorway in the middle.

It was the way he'd demanded it. When he'd first come here at Earl Hugh Despenser's request, the accommodation had been simple and old fashioned. All the servants and men-at-arms lived in the main hall with him. He had the solar and all the privacy that implied, but meals would be taken in the hall, just as with any other old lord.

Not Sir Geoffrey, though.

One of the first lessons he had learned in his journeys was that money was becoming more important than a man's oath of service. In the past a man would kneel before his lord and put his hands together. His lord would put his own hands about the vassal's, and the two would swear their vows; one to serve and honour, the other to reward with food, drink and clothing, as well as as much booty and money as he needed.

But in the last few years that whole structure of service owed and repaid had begun to fall apart. Sir Geoffrey had seen it first some little while ago when he started to see the mercenary gangs forming. Then it hadn't seemed a threat, and yet Sir Geoffrey had wondered about them – he wasn't sure how he'd react if someone offered him a large treasure of money instead of an honourable life of service to his lord. No, he wasn't at all sure.

So when he was sent here as steward to this little manor, with the clear instruction that he should build it up to help form a barrier against Lord de Courtenay's ambitions, he had insisted that there must be a separate building to house the mercenaries. The men weren't there for the benefit of Sir Geoffrey or Lord Despenser, they were there solely for their own profit, and couldn't be trusted.

Most of the men were out of the place at this hour. He knew that. There was only one man who would still be there, and that was the man he had thrashed. Sir Geoffrey threw the door wide and stormed in. To the left was the main stable area, but on the right was the accommodation for the servants and men-at-arms who had been hired by Sir Geoffrey.

It was a noisome room, this. The odour of piss and sour ale filled the place, along with the reek of filthy clothing. Small beds had been set out on either side against the walls. These were not mere palliasses spread over the floor, but well-built cots with rope springs and thick mattresses. No expense had been spared when the carpenter had come here, because the men had insisted that they should have decent beds and bedding. Just one more sign of the greed of their kind, Sir Geoffrey thought.

As he peered about him in the gloom, Sir Geoffrey saw that one of the beds still had a figure lying upon it. He strode to it and stared down at the snoring shape.

Lying on his belly, his back bared, Nicholas le Poter was breathing stertorously through his wide mouth. The reason for his snoring was plain enough. At the side of his bed a large jug of ale had toppled over, the remaining drink spreading over the rushes on the floor. Sir Geoffrey looked down at it, then back at the sleeping man.

Le Poter was useless to Sir Geoffrey. He had come with good recommendations from another knight in Despenser's service, but all he had done so far was foment trouble. There was no doubt in Sir Geoffrey's mind that this man wanted his position, but he wasn't ready to give it up yet. He had wanted to remove le Poter for some time because of the fool's machinations, and now he felt as though he had little option. The murder of the Meeth widow, and the fact that her body had been found here on the demesne, meant that Sir Geoffrey's position was badly undermined. And it was Nick le Poter who'd suggested that the mire be drained. That, to him, meant that le Poter might well have killed her and dumped her body there to throw suspicion on Sir Geoffrey and ruin his reputation. If Sir Geoffrey could be removed from the manor, who knows? Perhaps Nick le Poter could take over his job.

He kicked the mattress. Hard. There was a squeak of protest from the bed itself, but the carpenter had known his job, and it survived, although it moved several inches over the packed earth of the floor, nudging into the wall.

'Wake up, you dog's *shit*!'

'Wha . . .?'

'I said, wake up! You've no reason to be asleep, have you?'

'What's the matter? You feel you left too much skin on my back?'

'Yes, I do,' Sir Geoffrey snarled. 'And I have a need for more than just your flesh, man! Do you know what happened today?'

'So the men found a little body in the bog. What of it?'

'I don't think I like your voice, le Poter. I think you seem to know all about this woman's death.'

'What I don't know, I can guess,' le Poter spat. He raised himself on all fours and made as though to clamber from the bed and on to his feet.

Sir Geoffrey didn't hesitate. He swung his boot and caught le Poter in the belly. The breath left the man's body in a single gasp, and le Poter arched, and then crumpled. He collapsed on his side among the rushes, and stalks pricked at his scabs like fine daggers. He moved to escape the agony, but only succeeded in driving some straws deeper into his tormented flesh. He moaned with the pain, unable even to gather breath enough to scream.

'You know *nothing*! You are insignificant, Poter. If I wanted, I could kill you here and now.'

'It doesn't matter – the Lord Despenser will soon learn what you've been doing!'

Sir Geoffrey hesitated. 'What?'

'Stealing a part of his manor, sharing the profits with Sir Odo. That's what you've done, isn't it? Creating a nest which you and he are feathering!'

'I don't know what you're . . .'

'Then you're more thick than I thought, *old man*!' Nick spat. 'That land where Robert Crokers is bailiff, that was all part of Ailward's manor when you came here. You didn't know that? Sweet Jesus, and I thought you were clever, once!'

A boot thumped into his flank once more, and he hiccuped with the pain. Straw stabbed his back and he tried to scream, but before he could the boot returned and caught his belly. The breath exploded from him like water from a fountain, and he choked, gasping for air.

Then he felt the nick as a sharp blade drew blood from his throat. A little rasp and then, oh, such a smooth cut, just like a razor sticking in a cheek. He could feel the marvellous edge slip into his flesh, and he suddenly stiffened, convinced that his master was about to slit his throat for him. He could hear Sir Geoffrey's rough breathing like a lover's lustful panting, could feel the warmth where the breath brushed his cheek.

'That's enough for me! You don't belong here, le Poter. I think you should go away, and quickly. You won't get far, though, because the hue and cry will soon find you. I'll see to that. You run off, fellow, and see how far you can get. I'll have the men after you as soon as they're back from their work, and I don't think they'll be happy to think that you could have done that to her and brought disgrace on all of us. No, they won't like that one bit. If I were you, I'd hurry to get away.'

Abruptly the knife was whipped away, and suddenly he was released. He fell back on to the rushes, the stems a fresh torture, and could do nothing for a long while but sob.

Chapter Twenty-Four

'This is all a waste of time!' Simon muttered viciously. 'What's the point? We know who was responsible ultimately, and that's Despenser.'

'Who would be as guilty as the murderer here,' Baldwin agreed. 'However, we don't know who it was who gave the order to murder Hugh that night, just as we don't know who it was who actually rode out to his house.'

'We know that bastard knight has the men to do all he wants, and that he craved the land for his master,' Simon said. 'He invaded Hugh's farm to scare all the other locals into supporting him. He doesn't care about the folks under his command, he just enjoys power. And perhaps some other things, too. Did you mark his manner when we were in his solar?'

'He was restrained,' Baldwin said.

'Restrained, my arse! He was angry that we'd entered his hall, but he was humble in the face of the girl's body,' Simon spat. 'That child was beautiful in life, I'd guess, and this is a quiet, dull, empty sort of place. Not like Exeter where a man can find a woman any time of the day. No, a fellow like Sir Geoffrey would learn to desire a woman, then grow more and more frustrated if she didn't reciprocate his feelings. And how could a youngster like her reciprocate his feelings? She was little more than a child.'

Baldwin shot Simon a look. 'You feel strongly about that young woman.'

'Why in God's name shouldn't I? How could a man gaze on her pretty face and not wonder what she would look like in life, how she might smile at a sally, how she might sigh and lie back at the sight of her lover, or how she would scream to see the weapons of torture brought nearer and nearer . . .'

'Simon, she was a widow, and now she is dead. It is our duty to learn who murdered her. No more than that.'

'A lot more than that, Baldwin. She is dead, and the same man killed her who killed Hugh and Constance and the boy!' Simon shouted. He flung an arm back up the track towards Sir Geoffrey's hall. 'That so-called chivalrous knight in there did for her. You heard the priest – Humphrey said that all in the area know Geoffrey is guilty. He led the attack on the man at the other farm . . .'

'Robert Crokers,' Baldwin muttered.

'Yes, and then he took his men up to Hugh's place, and did . . . that.'

'What of the woman?'

'Probably took her some while before.'

'But where would he have kept her while he subjected her to torture? There would have to be a place somewhere near here where he felt he could do that to her with impunity.'

'In the hall itself, I expect,' Simon grunted. His anger had drained from him, leaving him morose and dejected. If Hugh's killer was a knight like Sir Geoffrey, then there was little chance that Simon could ever bring him to justice. Yet Simon burned with the desire for revenge. He would avenge his servant . . . his friend.

'His hall?' Baldwin said. He glanced about him as though seeing nothing. 'In his hall with all his servants? I doubt whether his men-at-arms would care too much, from what I have seen of them, but I doubt whether it would be possible for him to conceal the torture of a young woman. No, if he had brought her here, I think that many of his servants, all those who had been born in this area and knew her and her family, would have reported his crimes to others. It would be impossible for him to keep such an act secret.'

'Even when his crimes are known and discussed widely, the local people dare do nothing against him,' Simon growled.

'That may well be true,' Baldwin said.

'Perhaps there was a small house nearby?' Simon muttered. 'He owns half this vill.'

They were approaching the little cluster of buildings that Humphrey had indicated included the home of the dead man Ailward, and Baldwin glanced about him with interest. He was aware of Edgar moving forward to trot at his side, as always aware of potential threats before Baldwin had noticed them. Realising Edgar had seen something, Baldwin peered more closely and saw the figures in among the trees. They looked like men who were hiding from the little force, but scared people could try to defend themselves. It only took one arrow, as Baldwin knew too well, to end a life. His own had nearly been cut short by one late last year.

'Come,' he said. 'Let's find Master Ailward's widow.'

It took him some time to come to. The water on his face brought him round again, but only to a slow, painful wakening, and then suddenly he felt the stabbing at his back, and Nicholas le Poter gave a low groan and threw himself over on to all fours, choking and coughing.

'I had to wake you up! Nick, you have to go!' Adcock whispered.

'I can't move! My back is too bad.'

'You *have* to. You can't stay here. It's too dangerous. You heard what he said. If you stay here, you'll be killed.'

Gradually Nicholas felt his strength returning. He couldn't move quickly, not with his back the way it was, but he could at least clamber to his feet. Pushing with his fists, he forced himself upwards, and grabbed Adcock's arm, pulling himself up to the sergeant's shoulder.

'You heard him?'

'I couldn't miss his words,' Adcock said. 'Go! He'll set his hounds on you else.'

'He wouldn't dare.'

'He will have you killed, man! You have to run. I don't care what he thinks, but all the locals will blame anyone from this hall for her murder, and if you fit the picture, you'll be executed for it.'

'I can't!'

Nicholas shook himself away from Adcock. He didn't trust the sergeant entirely. The lad was too new to the place. There were others he could turn to . . .

There was no one. Nicholas curled his lip at the realisation that he was alone here. The men he might have trusted in a battle, the men who were his comrades, would reject him now. They weren't fools.

They'd look to their own interests, and that would mean aligning themselves with Sir Geoffrey.

He was still considering when he heard a shout. Running to the window, he put his hands on the inner edge of the frame and stared out. There, up at the line of the trees, he saw a man from the hall. He was laughing, and as another man shouted to demand what he'd seen, he reached down and picked up a rabbit by the hind legs.

The sight made Nicholas grin, because a slingshot that killed a rabbit was proof of a good aim, but then his amusement faded. The man up there had been a drinking companion for some months, but now he wondered whether, if there was a good price on his head, say a mark or two, that man, Stephen, would think twice about putting his sling into action against Nicholas. There was no need to consider the thought for long. Stephen would put a bullet into his head as quickly and as easily as he had the rabbit's.

It was a thought which plagued him as he rolled his spare belongings into a parcel and hurried from the hall. As the light faded, and what warmth the sun had brought quickly dissipated, he stood wondering where he could go and what he could do. It was scary, this feeling of confusion. He hadn't had it before. Usually he knew exactly what to do and when. Only hours before he had been a powerful man, sure of his place in the world . . . and now? Now he was nothing more than a wandering vagabond, at best. At worst, he was a target at which any man might loose an arrow. He was entirely alone. There was no bed, no home, no fire nor friend. He had nothing, absolutely nothing. All was lost. And the worst of it was, he hadn't *done* anything.

Not that it would help him. Many a man hadn't done anything, yet still ended on the gallows tree. As would he, if he remained in this area. There must be a place somewhere for him to go.

Then he remembered Sir Geoffrey's expression as he ordered Nicholas to be held so that he might flay the flesh from his back; his expression this afternoon as he said he would hunt Nicholas down. There was no possibility of mercy from Sir Geoffrey.

And then he felt a bolt of revelation. It was Sir Geoffrey who had done it! Sir Geoffrey had taken the woman and tortured her and killed her. No one else in the hall would dare to do that. Only the master. And now he was blaming Nicholas for the crime he himself had committed!

Well, Nicholas wouldn't wait to be chased. He wouldn't be another man's quarry. No, there was one place where he would be safe – he'd go there now. And from there he'd declare his innocence and Sir Geoffrey's guilt to the whole world.

Perhaps this was how he could take over the vill. If Sir Geoffrey was shown to be a molester and murderer of women, it might assist Nick's own ambition.

'Speak to me about it,' Friar John said gently.

He had helped Hugh back inside their rough shelter, and now Hugh sat cross-legged on the floor, his back to a wall. The fire which John had lit glimmered and reflected from Hugh's face, and changed his appearance from moment to moment: sometimes he looked like an avenging angel, or devil, while at others he was more like a man composed of complete despair. John wasn't sure which emotion would set the seal on Hugh's life, but he felt certain that one or other of them would become Hugh's driving passion. Revenge or desolation and hopelessness. There was no middle way for him.

'I can't think why she'd have not called to me,' Hugh said. 'She'd have known I'd have got to her, and I could have maybe saved her.'

'Friend, perhaps she was sure that you could achieve nothing. It was her greatest gift to you, setting her own life as nothing.'

'She couldn't have,' Hugh said. 'Not thinking they'd kill her boy. She must have realised that little Hugh would die too, and she'd never have left him to suffer without doing something.'

John closed his eyes and considered. 'My friend, some people find extraordinary strength in the most dire circumstances. Perhaps she knew that her boy was already dead, and she knew she must also die, but sought to protect you? Or even maybe she thought her son was safe? She thought she might save both of you.'

Hugh tried to recall exactly what had happened that night. The memory was so *indistinct*. He clenched a fist with frustration, desperate to call to mind a tunic, a face, a shock of hair . . . he had seen so little, though. There was scarcely anything before he was knocked to the ground. 'Who could do that to her?'

'It is not her alone, I fear,' John said hesitantly. 'There is another, a Lady Lucy from Meeth, who was also captured. I heard today that she too is dead.'

'I know of her,' Hugh admitted. 'Heard that she'd gone missing. Nothing more than that.'

The friar shook his head slowly. It seemed dreadful to think that his own Lucy could be dead and unremarked in a place like this. 'Is there anyone in the vill, or in a neighbouring parish, who had a grudge against you or your lady?'

'None!' Hugh said emphatically. He was monosyllabic at the best of times, but now the use of words was a torture to him. He had the same thoughts running through his mind: she had saved him; she had died without calling for his help. He began pounding his fist into the ground, heedless of the pain.

'There is no one whom you could have upset?'

'Me? No.'

'Then what of her? Could she have unwittingly angered someone?'

'No. I can't believe that. She was always kind.'

'Perhaps it was a misplaced love for her, then?'

'There were too many men there,' Hugh said with a firm shake of his head.

'Perhaps the land, then? Could another have desired the land itself?'

'The land?' Hugh scowled at the fire, and John was reminded of a picture he had once seen of Satan eyeing a new soul.

'I have heard of attempts to push one man or another from his land if it is worthwhile, so that another can steal it and enrich himself,' John said.

'But why kill her and leave me alive?' Hugh demanded.

'Perhaps they thought you were dead?' John said with a shrug. 'Or they didn't want to kill you, only her?'

'Why?' Hugh rasped.

John remained silent for a long moment as he reflected on his own words. It would be a curious thing if someone had intended to kill the woman and leave her husband alive to avenge her. Why should anyone do that, leaving himself open to being attacked? 'No, that is nonsense. No one would do that,' he said at last, shaking his head. 'Come, Hugh. You should rest again.'

'How can I rest, knowing that the men who killed her are still alive and walking about?' Hugh said. He glanced at his fist. It had been bleeding for some while, and he gazed at it with surprise. He had felt nothing.

Adcock was relieved that he had at last persuaded Nick to save himself, but now he sat back on his palliasse and considered his own position. If only he could do the same as Nick and run. If he were to do so, however, Sir Geoffrey could demand his return.

But there was no need for him to sit back here and wait for Sir Geoffrey to come back and bully the nearest man, now that Nick was gone. Adcock stood and pulled a shirt on, wincing as the movements made his belly surge and the pain from his cods rose up almost to his throat, so he thought. It was so intense he wanted to be sick, and he had to physically swallow back the bile before he could walk to the door.

From here he had a view of the yard behind the hall. Opposite were the stables, with the top of the yard open, giving on to the open land behind. There were some scattered buildings, the kitchen, a brew-house, storerooms, but apart from them the way was open to the east, and that was the way Adcock went now, rather than risk meeting Sir Geoffrey at the front of the house.

The walk was easy enough usually, but today, with his ballocks so painful and swollen, each step was a trial. Adcock walked up the shallow incline towards the top of the hill, and there he stopped, staring about him. To the south, he could see Beorn and Perkin at the mire still, while north and east all was clear. He continued east, eyes on the ground, walking slowly and carefully.

'Not enough work to do?'

Sweet Jesus! Adcock thought. The last man I wished to see.

Pagan stood by a tree on the path that led north. Seeing Adcock's face, his expression tightened. 'Are you all right, boy?'

'I am fine,' Adcock gasped, and threw a look over his shoulder.

Pagan rarely felt guilt. It was not his habit to wonder whether his actions were reasonable or not, but seeing this lad in such pain made him regret his words the last time they had met. 'Come here, lad. Sit.'

Adcock was in no position to argue. There was a tree trunk at the path's side, and he willingly sat on it, while Pagan unstoppered a small wineskin.

'Drink some of this.'

He watched while Adcock drank and nodded, a little colour returning to his cheeks. 'That's better.'

'Aye, well, what's happened to you? Was it Sir Geoffrey?'

'Yes,' Adcock admitted, and then told Pagan all about the body in the mire and Nicholas's escape.

'You did well to leave the place. He can be the devil when he's angry,' Pagan said. 'I've seen that before now.'

'But what can I do?' Adcock said.

'Keep your head down and get on with things as you see fit. There's nothing else for you,' Pagan said. 'And hope for better times.'

Chapter Twenty-Five

Sir Edward de Launcelles was still at the inn at Roborough when the flustered cattleman's boy arrived late in the afternoon. He remained seated near the fire, his great fur-lined cloak pulled about him as he watched the lad rush into the warm room, and felt only a comforting certainty that at last his miserable exile here was soon to be ended.

The trouble that he was being put to! Christ's teeth, if he'd realised how much time and energy would be taken up by the job, he'd never have agreed to being installed as coroner. There were any number of other jobs, in God's name, and most of them didn't require a gentleman to survey the noisome remains of long-dead peasants, who'd have smelled rank enough in life, without the added stink of three or four weeks of lying in the open. It was worst, of course, in the summer months, when bodies would become flyblown in no time. There had been one last year which had been reasonably well protected against the depredations of wild animals, but was in an even worse state as a consequence, perhaps. When they tried to pull the body over to view any injuries, the rotten carcass had fallen apart and a swarm of insects of all kinds had risen from it. It had been like watching demons leaving a possessed soul, his clerk had said at the time, recoiling in horror, crossing and recrossing himself against the sight.

That clerk had soon left his service.

This was no job for a man like Sir Edward either, though. Better by far that he should have waited until something else came up. There were so many gifts in the grant of his lord, now that Hugh Despenser was the king's first adviser. So many manors were being appropriated by the Despensers that Earl Hugh was always looking for loyal and reliable men to run them for him. Perhaps Sir Edward could get one now?

'Over here, boy!' he called.

The post had seemed attractive at first, because an assiduous coroner could always find some infraction of the law and thereby impose a few additional fines, some of which could be pocketed. But when the communities were as poor as these Devon vills, it made all the effort of riding out, viewing repellent corpses, and questioning the jury, seem wasteful of his time. Better by far to have a quiet, pleasant manor – one like Sir Geoffrey's.

The old devil was comfortable there. A goodly force of men-at-arms with him, pleasant estates to manage, and the occasional bit of banditry when life grew dull . . . it couldn't be much better. If Sir Geoffrey was ever to leave, Sir Edward would be pleased to take over Monkleigh.

'Sir? Are you the coroner?'

Sir Edward hitched his cloak up over his shoulder, where it had fallen away. 'What do you want, boy?' As if he didn't know.

'Sir, there's been a body found. A lady, sir, murdered.'

'A lady?' Sir Edward shot out, and sat up in his seat.

That wasn't at all what he'd been expecting.

Humphrey hurried along the track, his pack heavy over his shoulder. There was every hope that he might escape without being seen, and the idea of getting away from these cursed vills was entirely appealing. Without thinking, he had taken the obvious route from the chapel, sticking to the main roadway which was so much easier to pass along than the others – but it did mean he was more likely to be discovered by chance as he hurried up towards Iddesleigh.

He stopped and stared about him. He was on the long, flat plain that led up to Iddesleigh itself, and he could see the vill up ahead nestling on the side of the hill, the great white bulk of the inn, the grey moorstone church over to the left. They sat on the side of the little mound, and the road went down into a valley after curling round them both.

But almost in front of the church there was a second road that dropped down to the river, he recalled. He could see it now. If he could just reach that and take the way to the ford, cross the river and head towards Meeth

– but there was no safety there either. Men all about the place would be seeking the murderer of Lady Lucy. He knew that well enough.

He could weep. This whole matter was so *unfair*. All through his life he'd tried to be good and decent, to live by God's laws, and to serve his people in the way that God would have liked, and now here he was, a renegade, no home to go to, his only refuge gone, and his living with it. All because a man had once bullied him, and now someone else had died.

At least he knew of a small place where he might be able to hide for a little while, he told himself, and he took a good long look about him again. From behind him he could hear the noise of many horses, the baying of hounds and shouting men.

It was enough to decide him. Throwing his pack over the low hedge on his left, he scrambled after it, ignoring the cuts and scratches from blackthorn, rose and bramble. In the pasture he gripped his pack again, then ran quickly over the grass to the far side of the meadow where the lane led down towards the river.

It had been a long day, and Simon was growing more and more fretful as he jogged along on his horse between the houses of the little estate.

Everything seemed to be passing by him in a whirl. The news that Hugh, Constance and little Hugh were dead had come like an unexpected lance-thrust in his breast. It had unseated his reason, disabled his power of thought, addled his mind . . . all he could do was visualise his old companion glowering ferociously in an argument, or recall the man on all fours pretending to be a horse for Edith. Hugh had been such a miserable sodomite in so many ways – and yet he was still a loyal companion. Simon had missed him when they had separated, Hugh to come up here, Simon to take up his new post in Dartmouth, but he'd never imagined . . .

Since reaching this vill matters had not improved. There were too many men who could have had a hand in his death, and there appeared to be no motive unless it was the simple one of land theft, intimidating Hugh's neighbours into the bargain. It was the way Lord Despenser worked; in all likelihood it was the way his vassal Sir Geoffrey worked as well.

He set his teeth at that thought: he could not attack a man like Sir Geoffrey. It would take a much more powerful, wealthier individual to do that. Even if he found the money, attacking the knight might make him an enemy he couldn't afford. Simon didn't want to leave his wife a widow. Meg deserved better than that. So did his daughter.

But Hugh deserved better than to be forgotten and left unavenged.

And now there was this new thunderbolt: Baldwin and Edgar were both convinced that Hugh was still alive. Simon didn't know how he should feel about that. Clearly he would be delighted if his man wasn't dead – but that was not assured. Hugh could have been grievously wounded and perhaps even now lay at death's door, or had passed through it. It only required a small wound to kill a man. And if he was alive, what then? Should Simon help him to prosecute his wife's killer, again at risk to his own family? Or should he try to prevent Hugh's attempt at revenge in order to protect Hugh himself? Simon was also aware of a nagging jealousy that his man had sought to get a message to Baldwin rather than Simon himself, but he knew that Hugh couldn't have known he was going to be at his home just then. Hugh would have sought the aid of Edgar first because he was nearest, and would pass the word to Baldwin with all possible speed. With a Keeper of the King's Peace on his way, Hugh could rest more comfortably, and he would have known that Baldwin would before anything else have sent a messenger to fetch Simon himself.

Yet he still felt that small prick of jealousy as they rode into the little farmstead.

Edgar had stopped to confirm which house was Ailward's widow's, and they had been directed towards a long, low house that stood above most of the others, with a good-sized yard before it. There were chickens and a pig rootling about, but they scattered before the hooves of the horses. Beyond a low rickety fence lay a garden area, with plenty of winter greens, and then the house.

Smoke issued from a little vent in the thatch, but it could have emanated from any number of gaps. The thatch was ancient, from the look of it, dark and rotten, and to Simon's dull eye it looked close to collapse. They'd have to put up new thatch this year.

It was the sort of job that Hugh would have relished. He'd have complained, of course – he always did. It was his birthright to moan and whinge about every task he was asked to do. There was no job so quick and easy that his truculent nature wouldn't demand that he should grumble until Simon had grown bored with his voice. Usually the whining tones would continue until long after the task had been completed.

A smile came to his face. Simon remembered one day back at Sandford when Hugh had helped to build a new door. He had still been bitterly bemoaning the way that Simon took his skills for granted when night had fallen, and Simon could hear him at his bench, sleepily declaring that he wouldn't do such menial work for no appreciation ever again.

There were so many memories of his man. All the times when they had been scared or anxious, like the occasion when there had been a gang of desperate men armed with knives and sticks during the famine, or later, when there had been the felons on the moors. Simon could remember so clearly how Hugh had scowled at the ground when Meg had told him how he had protected Jeanne and her during the fair at Tavistock. Then he had protected Simon's daughter Edith, too, when she had been at the tournament at Okehampton. Simon had never quite got to the bottom of that, but he knew that Hugh had done something from something Baldwin had said, and from the absolute refusal to discuss the matter on Hugh's part. And Hugh had been a good, strong companion when Simon had lost his first son, and had helped Simon wrap the little body ready for burial.

Oddly enough it was rather like losing his son, this feeling of grim, grasping sadness that tore at his throat whenever he thought of his old friend. There was the same incapacity to think clearly about anything, the same urge to rage at the unfairness of it.

A young woman with her black hair loose in the cool air, clad in a long blue dress and a heavy fur-trimmed cloak of crimson, and carrying a small basket, appeared from behind the house. She appeared almost unaware of the men on their horses, and walked with firm footsteps from one point to another, peering under boards, at the vegetables in the middle of the garden, along the bottom of hedges, and inside the flat bed of an old two-wheel cart. On her face was a fixed frown of concentration, but Simon was certain that in her green eyes there was enough grief to swamp even his own.

Baldwin glanced at the others, then spurred his mount onwards. 'Madam, I seek the widow of Ailward.'

She gave a sharp intake of breath, almost dropping her basket. 'Lordings! I . . . who are you?'

'I am Sir Baldwin de Furnshill, Keeper of the King's Peace; this is my friend, Bailiff Simon Puttock, and my servant Edgar. We are . . .'

'My Lord Despenser has heard of Ailward's death?' she gasped hopefully. 'He seeks to avenge my husband's murder?'

'Malkin, sweet, be still!'

Baldwin looked over to the door and saw an elderly woman standing there listening. 'Lady? You are this woman's mother?'

'In the law, yes. She married my son,' Isabel said. She stepped forward. 'I am Madam Isabel of Monkleigh.'

The ride to Iddesleigh was usually pleasant. Sir Edward had come this way several times, for when he had to view a body it was always best to visit another Despenser manor where he could count on good victuals and a decent bed for the night. In any manor where the Despenser's writ held sway Sir Edward was assured of a good welcome and the best of everything the manor had to offer. Such was the case at Monkleigh, he had recently learned.

Up here, heading towards Sir Geoffrey's hall from the north, he would pass for a short while along a broad expanse of heathland, a plateau from where he could see for some miles. Then, sinking down among some trees, he began to descend to the river, clattering through the ford, then climbing and passing round the higher part of the hill on which Iddesleigh was perched.

A good vill, this. He liked the stolid, well-maintained properties, the neat and trim little yards and gardens, the good fields and pastures which lay in front. All was ordered and gratifying to a methodical eye like his, but today he was seething, and he scarcely glanced about him as he followed the old track past the inn, taking the right hand turn to Monkleigh.

'When was this woman found?' he asked again.

The messenger spat and repeated the story of the draining, the gradual appearance of the hand, then the rest of her body.

'It is fortunate that I was still there for you to find me,' Sir Edward said. 'I can view her and hold my inquest without delay.'

'Very lucky.'

'There had been a death. A carter's boy fell from his horse and was trampled,' Sir Edward said, a faint hint of defensiveness creeping into his voice.

'Yes. Is he buried?'

'Yes.'

This was *ridiculous*! It was one thing to pressurise a man like Odo from the lands he was supposed to maintain in order to provide Lord Despenser with an additional parcel he had not expected, but Sir Edward had not offered to be associated with the unchivalrous murder of a woman. 'Did you mention that she was a widow?'

'Lady Lucy of Meeth. Her husband was killed in the battles two years ago.'

That was all the confirmation Sir Edward needed. So the cunning devil had sought another means of enriching himself, copying his own lord by capturing a woman and trying to force her to hand over the key to her lands and properties. That was not part of the plan when Sir Geoffrey had invited Sir Edward to participate in his little deception. Then the idea had been only to take over some of the de Courtenay lands. His men would fight, probably, but not too fiercely because the gibbets still held the grisly remains of some of the knights and barons who'd been declared traitors after taking part in the rebellion two years ago. With those eloquent reminders of what could happen to a man who stood against Despenser, there were all too few who would take the risk of incurring his enmity. Even a lord like de Courtenay would hesitate before throwing himself into an attack on Despenser lands. Even if provoked.

But this was potentially stupid. If this woman had a brother, a cousin, an uncle, who would be prepared to defend her memory and take back the lands which would now pass to him, Sir Geoffrey could soon find himself challenged personally. A man so appallingly wronged would have few scruples about making the torture and murder of his relative a cause for feud.

Unless, of course, Sir Geoffrey had already assessed the risks and learned that there was no other man involved. That this woman's lands would be unclaimed once she was removed. Then it would be easy to see why Sir Geoffrey might throw caution to the winds and attempt the theft.

Sir Edward's respect for Sir Geoffrey's daring and craftiness grew with every step on the way to the manor.

Chapter Twenty-Six

Isabel sat on her stool, and the three men were waved towards the table. As in so many peasants' homes, there were only stools for the master and mistress, which meant that when Ailward had come home from his work he must have found himself perching on the edge of the table, because Baldwin was somehow convinced that no matter how strong the man had been he would have been hard pushed to it to gainsay the formidable woman who was his mother.

She was clad in grey wool, a heavy cloth that sagged shapelessly above her belt. In her youth she must have been a handsome enough woman, though. Baldwin could see through the years to when the high cheekbones and steady, firm brown eyes would have been attractive. Her lips would have been less thin and grey, too, more full and rosy, while her hair, now entirely grey, would have formed a thick brown mane. Her hands were callused now, but the fingers were long and elegant, and Baldwin was sure that she would have been an enticing catch for her man.

'We are both poor widows now, you see,' Isabel said quietly as the men chose places to rest. Simon crossed his arms and leaned next to Baldwin at the table, while Edgar took up a languid pose at the doorway, ankles crossed and thumbs stuck in his belt. As always, his face wore an accommodating smile, but Simon knew that his eyes were cold. A killer's eyes.

'When did your husband die, madam?' Baldwin asked. He had often found that early on in an inquest it was better to have people talk about any matter rather than leave periods of silence. Then, when they were used to speaking, he could suddenly allow gaps to return; invariably the questioned person would speak hurriedly to fill them. In this way he often gained his most valuable information.

'He was a brave man. A squire. But the mad Scots saw to him in Ireland when they invaded the king's lands there.'

'He was killed in Ireland?'

'While the traitor Bruce was harrying our men in Scotland, he sent his brother to Ireland to attack the king's servants there. My father-in-law, Squire William Monkleigh, said farewell as soon as the call went up for men to join the king's host. We never had any doubts that he'd be back soon enough. But he was slain at Kells.'

Baldwin nodded. 'That was a fearful battle, so I have heard.'

'As have I,' she said slowly, nodding to herself as old women may. 'And my husband was also slain. Squire Robert. He was a fierce-hearted man too, and he likewise was killed in his lord's service.'

Baldwin nodded and shot a look over his shoulder at Edgar, then at Simon. His face was serious. 'He was also a squire?'

'Yes. But he was poorer. When his father died, much of his wealth was with him, as is natural. We lost his horses, armour, and much treasure. My husband and I struggled, and we intended to make up for the losses, but it was hard. Very hard. And then he too died.'

'How?'

'At Bridgnorth,' she said coldly, looking away.

Baldwin could see the tear form in the corner of her eye, and followed its path as it moved slowly, as though reluctantly, down her cheek. It found a crease in her skin and followed it to her jaw, where she irritably wiped it away. 'So your husband and his father were vassals to Lord Mortimer?'

'He was our liege. When he asked my men to go to him, they obeyed.'

Which explained a lot. Baldwin nodded. 'My lady, I am sorry to hear of your losses. Your men were honourable to their commander.'

'My family is poor now, but we had our pride. My men never lost that, and no one can take it from me.'

'But then your son too was found dead?'

'It was wrong!' she declared hotly. 'How could they murder him like that and hope to escape justice? They weren't content with taking my husband, now they have killed my son too! I damn the Despenser family! I damn them to hell for eternity! Thank God some men here still have some honour. Sir Odo will protect us.'

'You know him?'

'Sir Odo has lived there at Fishleigh for many years now. He was there before Ailward was born, and he'll still be there long after the brutal rabble in Monkleigh are all gone,' she asserted.

'He has said he will help?' Baldwin pressed her.

'He visits me here, to make sure we are all right. We need all the compassion we can be given in this sad time!'

As she bowed her head to her hands in grief, Baldwin's attention returned to the other widow.

She had set aside the little basket of the eggs she had been seeking when they arrived, and now sat with her eyes downcast as her mother-in-law spoke. She looked the kind of young woman who had never been able to speak in the expectation of anyone's listening, Baldwin thought.

'Who do you think could have been responsible for his death?'

It was the older woman who answered for her. 'Sir Geoffrey, of course. Who else could it have been?'

'Why?' Simon demanded. 'You told us that Ailward's father was a vassal to Roger Mortimer, but Ailward was steward to Sir Geoffrey. Why should Sir Geoffrey want to harm him?'

'You know what has happened to Mortimer in the last few years! First insulted, then forced to go to war against his king, and all because of the Despenser. And now the bodies of Despenser's enemies hang all over the kingdom like common felons. Despenser has no hesitation in killing those whom he sees as his natural enemies, and any friend of his enemy is his enemy also.'

'My husband's fate was sealed as soon as Lord Mortimer ran from the king's gaol,' Malkin said softly.

Simon glanced at her while Baldwin continued to question the older woman. This woman Malkin was very attractive, and it made her grief all the more sad to witness. It made Simon realise that his own sense of being overwhelmed by the loss of Hugh was perhaps out of proportion to his loss. Yes, Hugh had been a close companion, and a good, loyal, and usually truthful friend. This woman, though, had lost her husband. From now on she would be alone in the world unless she could win herself a new man. Her grief was the mature heartache of a wife whose life must soon change.

'Is this your property?' he asked quietly.

Malkin glanced at Isabel, who was now denouncing Despenser and all his henchmen with no restraint and less subtlety, as if she wondered whether she ought to speak without asking Isabel first. 'No. It is owned by Sir Geoffrey and the manor.'

'What will happen to you if he throws you from the land?'

She shrugged. 'We shall leave.'

'If your father-in-law and his father were both squires, then surely they had their own demesnes?'

'When he died in Ireland, Isabel's father-in-law lost much; her husband scraped together enough to arm himself by mortgaging his lands, and when he died too, all those who had debts owing from him came to demand their money.'

'With him dead, surely the debts were unenforceable?'

She met his gaze. 'A man who has died while serving a rebel who's holding his banner against the king's has few friends to fight even unfair actions. Especially when the Despenser decides to take over the debts.'

'How so?'

'He sent this Sir Geoffrey, and as soon as he arrived he told us that the king had made over all our lands to Despenser. They were forfeit and added to the Despenser's holdings.'

'So – you mean that the whole of the Monkleigh estate was yours originally?'

'Yes. And they forced us from our home and made my husband work for them as a menial, their bailiff. They couldn't even recognise him as a steward. They had to make him suffer for his father's actions.'

'I had no idea of this.'

'You know the grossest insult? They have blackened the name of the vill with their depredations. Raiding other tenants' holdings nearby in an attempt to force people from their own lands so that Sir Geoffrey can steal it for himself, and more: he has taken to hiring many felons in the hall. Most of them stay hidden behind his walls because he cannot allow them to be seen in public in case they are denounced and arrested for the common thieves and cut-purses that they are.'

'They are surely there in the hall for all to see,' Simon said lightly.

'You think so? He has some five and twenty men there, I think. How many do you see when you visit them? If you are lucky, you may see one man-at-arms and his sergeant, but all the others who are about the manor in daylight are his villeins. There are none of his draw-latches, rapists or murderers in evidence while the sun shines. They only come out at night, like mares!' She had paled, and as she spoke she clutched at the neck of her tunic with a fist clenched in anger and dread.

It took Nicholas le Poter some little while to realise that the place was empty, and as soon as he did, he stood and gazed about him with panic setting in.

This little chapel was surely the only safe place for him. He had to find a place of sanctuary where even Sir Geoffrey's men would be fearful of entering. Then he could wait until the coroner arrived and gave him protection to escape. That was all he needed, a place to wait, but if there was no priest here, if Humphrey was gone, there was nowhere for him to stay! He thought even now that he could catch something at the edge of his hearing, as though there was a mass of hounds being collected, and he remembered what Sir Geoffrey had said – that he could run now, but his men would be along to hunt him.

He'd seen enough hunts. There'd been a villein who'd been accused of stealing from the hall, taking a wooden spoon. The man had denied it, but Sir Geoffrey hadn't believed him and they'd let him run, setting off shortly afterwards with the hounds. The body had been dragged back, its heels bound to Sir Geoffrey's saddle, and when the man's widow had seen it, she'd fainted dead away. Someone had said she'd died a week or so later from the horror of seeing her man's body flayed of all the flesh on his buttocks and back where he'd been dragged over the stones. Nicholas wasn't sure that he'd been dead at the start of that return journey, although he had been pricked by two boar-lances already, but he was certainly dead by the end of it.

The chapel was silent and as cold as only an empty building can be.

He'd shouted as he first bolted up to the altar, gripping the cloth anxiously as he stared about him wildly.

He had two choices: remain and be caught and killed, or flee again and find another, safer refuge. Where, though? There was nowhere else . . . unless he managed to get to Iddesleigh. There the church would offer greater protection than this little chapel. Here, without the priest in charge, he could be dragged out without trouble; even if Isaac and Humphrey had been here, it would have been touch and go whether the pair of them could have defended him against Sir Geoffrey's men . . . but if he could reach Iddesleigh, he'd be safe enough. The way would be hard, and he'd have to hurry, but he could make it.

In the distance he was almost certain he could hear the squeaking of harnesses and the baying of hounds. It decided him. He let go the altar cloth and fled through the door and out to the road, and then, staring wildly and fearfully up at the hall, he set off at as swift a pace as he could manage towards the little vill that stood out so prominently on the hill ahead, without noticing that he had left his pack behind.

While Nicholas bolted, Humphrey was already almost at his chosen resting place. He followed the roadway down the hillside towards the river, and at the bottom, where the river cut through in its shallow, rocky path, he splashed through the water with a grimace against the freezing cold.

Over the river the hillside was fairly thickly wooded, and with the sun already very low in the western sky, he knew a faint trepidation and a chill that felt as though his bones were sensing the cold before his flesh. It was a superstitious sensation, not a rational one, he told himself. There was no point in fearing ghosts and creatures of the night, not when he was more likely to suffer from the worst of what men could do. And their worst would be extremely unpleasant.

He wanted to get into a place where he could rest for the night and sleep. There was a path which led off through some trees towards a small assart, and, spotting it, he sighed with relief. He'd thought he'd missed it. Picking up his feet more quickly, he scurried up the track towards the little place he recalled from several months ago.

When he was last here, he had been exploring, partly to understand the lie of the land in this little parish, but also because he knew that it was possible that one day he would need to know how best to escape the vill. He'd stumbled upon this little deserted assart by pure chance, and at the time he'd instantly thought that it could be a useful location to bear in mind, should he ever need a quiet, secure place of concealment.

It stood in a tiny clearing, he remembered. An old, slightly tumble-down cott with the thatch holed and rotten, it wouldn't provide any shelter from the rain or much from the wind, but for a one-night stay, it had the benefit of being off the beaten track and safe from investigation.

When he caught sight of it, he heaved a sigh of relief and stood a moment. There was an atmosphere of homeliness about it that tore at his memories, making him feel sad that he had lost his own home so many years ago. It was ruined, though. Worse than he remembered from when he'd last been here. The roof was almost all gone, and the door which had stood here had rotted away, and fragments of the planks that had constituted it lay haphazardly all about.

Hearing a crack behind him, he recalled what he was doing here, and darted into the clearing, then headed straight for the door. There was another crackle of broken twigs behind him in among the trees, and Humphrey felt the blood course more urgently through his veins. There was someone there! He must have been followed. For a moment he stood, irresolute, staring wildly over his shoulder at the thick boles of the trees, now smothered in their own twilight. Then he shot forward to the doorway, entered, and sprang back to stand with his back to the wall, panting heavily. 'God's blood,' he muttered.

Now, his scalp crawling, he realised what had made the place appear so pleasingly homely: the odour of wood smoke. Now he could see that there was a good little fire of dry wood burning in a makeshift fireplace ringed about with small rocks in the middle of the room, and he felt his fear return to flood him. Slowly, cautiously, he leaned over to peer through the doorway.

And he shrieked as he caught sight of a mad, glowering face only inches from his own. Then he felt the crunch of a cudgel at the back of his head, and he forgot his panic as he slumped headlong into a vast pool of blackness.

* * *

Baldwin had heard their last exchange and he looked at Malkin now, asking, 'Do you think Sir Geoffrey could have been personally responsible for your husband's death, or was that an act by one of his men, then?'

'I am certain it was him. He could have paid one of his men to thrust the knife home, but it was his order that led to my Ailward being killed.'

A man had entered now, a tall man with greying hair. He stood in the doorway scowling suspiciously at the men talking to the two women. 'Who are you?'

'Pagan, don't worry. These men are here to learn what happened to the master,' Malkin said.

'We know what happened to him,' the man spat. 'He was killed so he couldn't claim his lands back.'

Baldwin pricked up his ears. 'Was there a chance that he might?'

Malkin drew a deep breath. 'I had lodged a complaint at the king's bench to demand my own lands be returned to me. Part of the manor was my own dower, and I wanted it back. And Ailward had never stood against the king. He had always remained a loyal vassal. Yet he was being punished for what his father had done. That was wrong – and I think that the king must have realised it before long and offered to return to us all of our lands. Sir Geoffrey knew that. So he had Ailward killed.'

'It is a serious allegation to make against a man who is so strong,' Baldwin commented.

'You think I don't know that!' she hissed, and she met Baldwin's look with eyes that seemed to blaze with a sudden green fire. 'I have lost my husband and my lands, my servants . . . my future. All gone – and you tell me I make serious allegations because I want justice against the man who was responsible?'

'If he had your husband killed, you should be careful. He may try to do the same to you,' Baldwin murmured.

'If he tries, he'll find we're not so easy to kill!' Pagan declared. He stood with his arms crossed and jaw jutting defiantly. 'Any man tries to break in here, he'll find more than just two widows . . .'

Isabel held up her hand and spoke gently. 'Pagan, that is enough. There's no need for more rancour here. Besides, you don't sleep here overnight. That could be . . . indecorous.'

'You don't have a man to sleep here with you?' Baldwin asked.

'We are in a strong enough group of buildings. If any tried to break in here we would be able to protect ourselves,' Isabel said. 'And Sir Odo has promised support if we need it. All we need do is send for help, and he and his men would be here.'

'It may be safer to let Pagan stay here,' Baldwin said.

'It would not be right to have a man sleeping in our household. We are two widows. There are plenty of others here to protect us.'

Baldwin nodded, unconvinced. Turning to Pagan, he said, 'You were servant to Ailward?'

'I was servant to his father, then to him. I made my vow to serve his father and I haven't faltered. I'll protect their memory just as I did their bodies when they lived, and now both are dead I'll protect their women as well as their honour.'

Baldwin watched Isabel as she smiled at Pagan. He guessed that there was a closeness between them, and it was no surprise. How often had he heard people in Crediton talking in hushed, shocked tones about widows who had married their stewards? Time beyond count. And yet he found it a little surprising in this case. Isabel did not look the sort who would be inclined to mix with a man like Pagan. She was too haughty by nature.

He nodded. 'That is good, Pagan. If someone were to come here to attack and rape or kill your mistresses you would naturally be right to protect them. Now, is there anything any of you can tell me about the death of Ailward? Anything you have remembered since the coroner came?'

Pagan looked from Malkin to Isabel and back. 'There is nothing I can think of. Ailward was found lying up on the hill leading towards Whitemoor. It was near to the stream, I think. Up at the top of a little rise.'

'I do not know this area well. Is there someone who could take me there?' Baldwin asked.

'Such as the man who found him,' Edgar suggested.

Baldwin nodded. 'Yes, that would be best,' he agreed.

'That's easy enough. You need Perkin from Monkleigh. He's one of the men who used to be ours,' Pagan declared. 'If you tell him I said he should take you up there, he'll do it.'

Baldwin smiled thinly. 'I think I can make sure he does. What does he look like?'

While Pagan described him, Simon stood and stretched his legs. It was good to think that they'd soon be leaving this sad little hovel to return to the inn. He wanted to get away from this house and the feeling of cloying misery that hung about it. After losing Hugh, he had enough sorrow already, and he didn't need to share in other people's.

Outside the light was fading quickly, he saw, and he found himself wondering how well this place really could be protected against an attack. If a force of men were to ride through the vill and assault the house, they must succeed speedily. It took little time to hurl flaming torches on to a roof and set the whole ablaze, after all. Sir Geoffrey seemed a ruthless enough man. No doubt he would destroy this place with the women inside it in a moment if he thought that they were a threat to him. Just as, maybe, he had killed Hugh.

Hugh had lived on a patch of ground that was not on Sir Geoffrey's manor, but was contiguous with it. If a man was to try to expand his holdings, stealing a plot like Hugh's might make sense. Especially since Hugh was without a defender. Others about Iddesleigh were no doubt villeins, peasants who owed labour to their master in return for his protection: but Hugh was a free man. He had no one to defend him.

It seemed curious to him that the women were keen to have Pagan sleep away from their house. It would be more sensible to have their most loyal man sleeping in the hall with them. Yet it wasn't distrust, surely, because they were happy for him to remain with them during the day. Their fear for their reputation could end with their being captured.

'One thing,' he asked on a whim. 'You mentioned, Madam Malkin, that part of the manor was your dower. Where was that?'

'It was the land nearer the river north and west of here. My husband's family owned Monkleigh and the lands east of it, but mine owned the river and the banks for a mile or so. The fishing alone was worth a fortune. We used to harvest the salmon each year. Now we have nothing.'

Baldwin frowned. 'But surely that is the land which is now disputed by Sir Geoffrey and Sir Odo?'

'Yes. I think Sir Geoffrey has sold our lands to Sir Odo – and I gave no permission for that!'

Chapter Twenty-Seven

At that moment, Sir Geoffrey was feeling very little like a threat to anyone. He sat on his horse and bellowed while the grooms and hounds milled madly in the yard behind the hall. There was an insolence about the villeins today, a sulkiness that was not normal.

'You! Get the men ready, damn their souls!' he roared at Adcock. Then he struck with his lash at a hound which had approached too close to his mare's legs. 'Get back, you devil!'

Adcock eyed the men unhappily and, catching sight of his master's expression again, hurriedly limped over to join them. 'Come on, you heard Sir Geoffrey. He wants us all to help find Nick.'

He felt sick to think of the poor man out there in the wilds and the cold, stumbling onwards through the gathering gloom, knowing that at any moment he might be spotted by Sir Geoffrey's men. It was a dreadful thought: being hunted like a wild animal, the full complement of Sir Geoffrey's foul companions riding after him, shrieking and whooping in glee as they saw their quarry, while all the time Nicholas le Poter's terror increased and he forced himself to run, run, run . . .

Beorn answered. 'We don't want any part of this.'

'You refuse to join a legal posse? You can be punished for that. You know it, don't you? Come on, you're all grown men. All you have to do is show willing.'

'Willing? And willingly help chase a man to death?' Perkin said. 'If he's guilty, then it's as likely as not that your master is involved, sergeant.'

Adcock shot a nervous glance over his shoulder. 'Don't speak so loud,' he pleaded. 'You don't know what he's capable of!' God, but his ballocks still ached so much! He couldn't bear the thought of another beating.

'We've seen enough, of him and his men,' Rannulf declared. His legs were apart, and his arms crossed, but he looked ready for a fight. From all Adcock had heard, he usually was.

'If you don't go and help him, all that'll happen is the man will be caught anyway and probably he'll die. There's nothing much we can do to stop that. But if you stay here, he'll make life for all of you hell. You know he can. He'll impose new fines, take most of your crops, stop your women marrying who they want to . . . there's no end to his power. You know that. Make a stand if you want, but think of how it'll hurt your womenfolk.'

Perkin stepped closer. 'You know that Sir Geoffrey is saying that le Poter killed Lady Lucy? Why'd he do that?'

'Just to rape her, I suppose.'

'Which is why she was tortured? Whereas if it was Sir Geoffrey, he could end up with her lands and manor, couldn't he? Which do you think is more likely?'

Adcock desperately sought for the words that would allay this man's suspicions without declaring his own doubts, but none came to him. He saw Perkin give a grim nod.

'You think the same, don't you? Why should we go and seek to punish someone for Sir Geoffrey's crimes, just to help deflect any blame from Sir Geoffrey? He's no lord of ours.'

'You won't come?' Adcock asked desperately. He hated to think how his master would react if all these men refused.

It was Beorn who snorted long and loud. He hawked and spat out a gobbet of phlegm. 'Damn Sir Geoffrey, and damn Nicholas le Poter. They're two of a kind. I suppose if we're all there, we can decide whether to protect le Poter if we want. We can't do a thing if we leave him to Sir Geoffrey's mercy.'

Perkin grunted, and Rannulf scratched at his ear. One or two other men shuffled and refused to meet Adcock's eye. It was that more than anything that told him they'd go with Sir Geoffrey's posse. They knew what sort of retribution Sir Geoffrey could demand from those who thwarted his will.

Adcock went back to his little horse and climbed on to it unhappily, sinking down very gently and carefully. He had his dad's old sword swinging heavily at his hip, and a coil of rope was tied to his saddle, with which, he guessed, they might bind the man while he still breathed, and bring him back to the hall. It left him feeling most uncomfortable.

As the hounds were released, he set off towards the rear of Sir Geoffrey's party. The sun was low in the sky, but at least up here with so few hills to the west, there was still enough light to see by.

A few of the hounds had gone off to follow the trails of badgers or rabbits, and had to be whipped into line. Sir Geoffrey had given an old bloodstained shirt of Nicholas's to the master of the hounds, and the man had thrown it to all of them before setting off. Now there was a conviction in their voices as they gave vent to their excitement, and the men were soon clattering down the lane from the hall, over the roadway, and southwards towards the little chapel.

'He's gone to claim sanctuary,' Perkin guessed from Adcock's side.

Adcock couldn't disagree. 'But what'll Sir Geoffrey do if he's inside?'

'He doesn't care about the niceties, our master. I expect he'll send us in to haul Nicholas out.'

Adcock shivered. He couldn't do that. It was not just cruel and unfair to drag a man from sanctuary, it was blasphemy. He couldn't break the sanctity of the altar just to satisfy Sir Geoffrey's bidding.

He looked up at Sir Geoffrey's back. It exuded confidence, and Adcock knew that the steward would break any man who stood in his path. A picture of Nicholas's back flashed into his mind. The flesh ripped apart, the blood oozing thickly . . .

Edgar rode along easily. Their path took them east to the main road from Exbourne to Iddesleigh, and he was looking forward to a pot of ale when he reached the inn again. The thought of a good, hot fire was appealing, especially when associated with a bowl of pottage and maybe some rabbit or pork to go with it. He jogged along contentedly enough.

The setting sun painted the sky with pinks and purples, and he reflected how much his wife would have enjoyed the scene. Petronilla was always looking for beauty: she saw it in flowers, in water, in bird feathers, and here she'd have found it in the sky. It took little to make her happy. So long as he was behaving, anyway!

It was a sobering reflection that while he was here still, happy with his wife, poor Hugh's family was gone. Edgar was at bottom a pragmatic man, and he knew that if someone tried to rape and kill his wife, they'd have to kill Edgar first. The idea of living knowing that someone had done that to her was so appalling that he could feel a shiver of revulsion travel down his spine at the mere thought. It would be unbearable.

He wanted to know who had done this to Hugh's family so that he could look them in the eye and try to understand what sort of man could perform such a foul act. Oh, he had seen plenty of felons in his time, and all too often they were dim, gormless men who saw an opportunity and took it. That explained only too many sudden attacks and killings. But that wasn't what had happened at Hugh's place. There it hadn't been a sudden, random assault. It had been premeditated, as far as Edgar could see.

There had been a party at the inn, which had concealed the attack – but everyone in the vills about here could have known about the party at the inn that night. There was nothing secret about it.

Simon and Baldwin were silent as they rode and Edgar did not see any reason to break the peace. They ambled along, the twilight darkening the country about them, hearing the screeching of a blackbird as they disturbed her from her perch, the sudden clatter of a pigeon overhead, the distant mournful call of a fox. There were so many noises. Even the wind seemed loud as it whistled in his ears.

And then he heard the other noises. With ears that had been attuned for almost all his adult life to the sound of potential danger, he heard a squeaking of leather, the high-pitched jingling of metalwork, and then, as he turned his head and frowned in concentration, the cries of men and the baying of hounds.

'Sir Baldwin! Listen!'

Sir Geoffrey was annoyed with the delay. Trying to gather all the villeins together had taken an age, and then the miserable curs had tried to avoid their duty. They wouldn't get away with that sort of shirking, not while he was master of the manor. No, they'd damned well learn to obey.

Nicholas le Poter was a fool. He might have thought he could evict Sir Geoffrey, but it was the last mistake he'd make. When this posse caught up with him, he'd be pulled apart. Literally.

'Sir Geoffrey? There are men ahead.'

He swore quietly under his breath. Round the curve in the road, he suddenly saw three men on horseback. They stopped at sight of his little force, and one horse reared as the hounds reached them.

'Sir Baldwin!' he bellowed. 'I am glad to see you, sir. I am chasing the man who killed Lady Lucy. Have you seen him going this way?'

Baldwin and Edgar exchanged a look. Simon was glowering down at a hound that kept darting under his mount, making the rounsey skittish.

It was Baldwin who responded. 'We've seen no one on this road.'

Sir Geoffrey swore under his breath again. This was not turning out as he had planned. Surely the hounds weren't mistaken . . .

'Sir Geoffrey, they're going down towards the chapel,' his huntsman suddenly called.

'After them! He's trying to reach sanctuary!' Sir Geoffrey shouted and set spurs to his horse.

He was aware of his posse springing into the chase behind him. Yes, as he passed by the angry-looking bailiff, whose beast was dancing like a tamed bear, he saw the main part of the pack turning off the road and taking the little lane that went down the hill to the chapel. That was where the fool had gone, thinking he'd be safe down there. Well, he was mistaken. Sir Geoffrey felt his lips pull into a snarl of satisfaction as he urged his horse down the incline towards the chapel.

It was quiet. The dogs were at the door, sniffing and protesting, although two or three had trotted off towards the fields nearby. He ignored them, but bellowed at the top of his voice. 'Nicholas le Poter – come out and surrender or I shall have you pulled out.'

'You will not!'

Sir Geoffrey turned to see the calm face of the Keeper at his side. 'Sir Baldwin, this is a matter for my manor. It's none of your concern.'

Baldwin was quiet for a moment. He glanced about Sir Geoffrey at the men with him. There were some few, he thought, who looked like ordinary peasants from the vill, but others . . . others were different. He recalled the widow's words about men who would keep to the hall in daylight and only appear at night, and he told himself that the careers of some of these fellows would bear little scrutiny. He had not seen so many dangerous-looking characters together in many a year.

'I think you are wrong,' he said at last. 'If there is a man in there who has committed murder, it is very much my concern. It is my duty to seek felons and murderers. And it is not your place to command a man to leave a place of sanctuary, either.'

'It is not sanctuary. It's a chapel, and it has never been declared sanctuary to my knowledge.'

'Perhaps not. Nevertheless, it is a holy chapel and you will not desecrate it by entering with armed men and pulling a defenceless man from within.'

'I can do what I like on my estates,' Sir Geoffrey declared more quietly, his voice dropping.

'Not while I am here, Sir Geoffrey,' Baldwin said calmly.

'Out of my way!' Sir Geoffrey grated and reached for his sword's hilt.

As he did so, he heard a swift rasp of steel from his right. Glancing down, he found himself staring at a naked blade held by Baldwin's man.

'You dare draw steel against me?' he growled.

'Against any who threaten my master, yes,' Edgar said happily.

'You will regret this!'

'I doubt it,' Baldwin said coolly. 'Now, please, do you wait here while I go inside. Edgar, you stay with him.'

Jeanne was still at the inn, although she would have been happier to leave and go for a walk. Richalda had fallen asleep, and Jeanne had set her down on a bench nearby. From experience she knew that Richalda could sleep through a charge of cavalry. The noise in this bar would be nothing to her.

The racket was growing, too. First Emma declared that she needed more wine, then that she needed food, that she was starving, that her head ached; all of which were interspersed with comments on the local population, the quality of the staff, especially Jankin, and the general lack of amenities.

In the end, from sheer embarrassment, Jeanne left her to it. She slipped out of the inn and stood outside just as the sun was fading. As the door closed she distinctly heard her maid demanding a quart of wine, and 'None of that pissy water you call wine round here. I want a good dark red. Quickly, man!'

Jeanne closed her eyes in shame. If there was ever a time when she could have cheerfully discarded her maid, it was now. Even when she had first been introduced to Baldwin, she had not been quite so appallingly rude. Not that Jeanne could remember, anyway. Admittedly the woman was atrocious in any company, but her behaviour today had been even worse than usual.

At a burst of raucous laughter, Jeanne shuddered, convinced that someone was gaining revenge for some of Emma's foul comments, and she walked quickly away from the inn. The church was a short walk away, and she felt the need for a little spiritual comfort just now. She was almost at the small gate which barred the entrance to the vill's pigs and dogs when she heard panting and rapid footfalls. Turning swiftly and frowning into the gloom, she saw a figure lurching up the lane.

Jeanne was a lady of quality, and the thought that a man could be approaching her at this time of night in a distressed state was hardly pleasing, but she was only too aware of the responsibilities laid on a Christian who found a fellow being in a state of need. She was tempted to go to the inn's door and pull him inside to the warm, but something in his manner told her that it would be pointless. He came past the inn with his gaze fixed and staring, almost lunatic from the look of him. Jeanne shivered to see how his face was so set, like a man who was already wounded to death, but retained just enough energy in his legs to carry on. In fact, she thought he looked like a man who must keep moving, as though he must die as soon as he stopped.

He came closer, and Jeanne hurriedly made her way to the church. She had entered the yard at the eastern point, and she walked round to the southern door and opened it. Behind her she could hear the desperate rasping breath of the man.

The priest was already inside. 'Lady Jeanne. How pleasant to see you again. I am just preparing for the evening's . . .'

He was silenced as the figure lurched in after her. Wide-eyed, fearful, he pushed past Jeanne and fell to his knees in front of the priest. 'Sanctuary! Sanctuary!'

Jeanne gasped at the sight of his shirt. It was dripping with blood, which in the candlelight looked almost black. The colour had seeped into the thin linen material making it appear bright and clotting! 'Who did this to you?'

Matthew frowned as Nicholas le Poter bowed his head and began to weep. 'I am innocent! Sir Geoffrey seeks to accuse me of murder. He says I killed Lady Lucy, but I had nothing to do with her death! I never saw her until they pulled her body out of the mire. It was nothing to do with me. I accuse Sir Geoffrey of killing her. He wanted to take her lands!'

'Man, be silent. Before anything else, we must wash your back,' Matthew said soothingly. He looked up at Jeanne, who nodded.

'I shall fetch some help from the inn. They must have water and cloths there. I'll bring some men, too.'

'I'm not sure we need . . .'

She curtly shook her head, then bent to the sobbing man. 'Who is after you now?'

'Sir Geoffrey. He has all his men with him and they mean to kill me.'

'No one will harm you here,' she said.

Nicholas looked up at her. His eyes were raw, and filled with the pain of his run all the way from the chapel to this church; his feet felt as though they were beaten to raw meat with the pace of his flight, and his lungs were sacks of loosened flesh. It was all he could do to take in air.

'No harm? No harm? After the way he burned out and murdered the poor man in the cottage here? I'm dead. It's just a matter of how long it takes him to pull me from the altar.'

Matthew stiffened. He lifted Nicholas and pulled his arm about his own shoulders, grabbing Nicholas's wrist in one hand, and putting his left arm about Nicholas's waist to support him. 'No one will pull you from my altar, man,' he declared sharply. 'This is God's house, and any damned heretic who seeks to pollute my sanctuary will find God's vengeance is swift!'

So saying, he led Nicholas up to the altar and set him at the side, pressing a fold of the altar cloth into his hand. 'Lady Jeanne? A pot of wine, too, please. I have a feeling this poor fellow will need it before long.'

Chapter Twenty-Eight

Baldwin entered the chapel silently.

It was a small place, only the one room, perhaps twelve feet by twenty, with a door to the left which no doubt led to a small chamber where the priest would sit and sleep. For the rest, it was an empty space with some patterned tiles set into the floor, and a small, low table at the far end for an altar. The cross wasn't gold, but it was a good pewter, maybe, and had been polished until it gleamed like silver. Over the table was a good quality altar cloth, with gold threads stitched into it. All in all, it was a pleasant little chapel, and the pictures on all the walls livened the atmosphere.

Still, it was very quiet, and he began to be aware of a certain unease.

At the wall to his left was a large chest, and he walked to it and threw it open. Inside was all the paraphernalia of a priest, from his robe to his alb, with a book laid on top. He shut the lid again, glancing at the room anew. 'Hello?' he called, but there was no reply.

On hearing his shout, Simon opened the door and peered in. 'Where's the priest, then?'

'A good question, Simon. Out, perhaps, seeing a parishioner . . .' Baldwin stopped speaking suddenly. He strode to the altar, where he had noticed a parcel wrapped in a large square of cloth. Unwrapping it, he found a shirt, some bread and some dried meat. 'What is this? A pack made up for a journey?'

Simon was at the inner door and now he called to Baldwin. 'I think I've found the priest.'

Baldwin caught his tone of voice and crossed to his side. 'My God.'

The coroner arrived at the hall in a bad temper.

He had expected the lights to be on and a welcome from his host, since he had obeyed Sir Geoffrey's commands – or, rather, suggestions. They were of equal rank, after all.

But there was no knight, no men-at-arms, only a couple of old fools who seemed to know nothing. Their master was gone out, and all the others had gone with him. How thoughtful of Sir Geoffrey!

'Damn his eyes. I ought to have gone home and not buggered about here. What's the point?' he muttered to himself, and a good deal more besides. He demanded wine, and the servants fetched him some in a hurry, as though they feared him almost as much as their master. So be it! If they were so easily cowed, that was fine by him. He sank the first jugful; then, as the level of the second began to fall, he started to feel rather more optimistic.

He was here as the king's representative, and if Sir Geoffrey had some scheme afoot which would allow him to fleece the locals, so much the better. So long as he paid his friend the local coroner. And he would! Oh yes! If he'd been committing murder for his own advantage, he would soon come to appreciate that it was in his best interests to look after his friends. Especially if he wanted those friends to help protect him from the consequences of his actions.

And still more especially if he didn't want his friends to try to remove him from this lucrative little manor and take it for themselves.

Sir Geoffrey was soon inside the little chamber with them, Edgar ever present behind him.

'Who can have done this?' he gasped.

'A good question,' Baldwin commented. 'You have the coroner on his way already, I believe? It is good. He will need to speak to everyone in the area.'

'Who'd kill a priest like old Isaac?' Sir Geoffrey said with a shake of his head.

If he had not been so suspicious of the man, Baldwin might have been inclined to take his words at their face value. As matters stood, though, he was not of a mood to trust Sir Geoffrey. He moved about the corpse, gazing intently at the old man's body. 'There is no apparent wound. Perhaps . . .' He pulled open the dead mouth and stared in at the yellowed teeth and tongue.

'What are you doing?' Sir Geoffrey demanded with distaste. 'You defile the man's body!'

'I am seeking to learn how he could have died,' Baldwin said impatiently. 'It wasn't an obvious poison, Edgar. No marks on the flesh, and he has not bitten his tongue in agony. If anything, I'd say his ending was happy.'

'*Happy!*' Sir Geoffrey snorted disdainfully. 'How can a man's death be happy?'

'If he has lived many good years,' Baldwin said ruminatively, 'and he has enjoyed them, and he has known that at the completion of his time on earth the good Lord would take him to His bosom, then I think you could say his end was happy.'

'He's been murdered by that man le Poter. I expect this poor priest refused to offer sanctuary to a killer of widows. When the priest denied him, he turned on him.'

'And felt so remorseful that he set the dead man on his bed like this, with his arms crossed, I suppose?' Baldwin demanded contemptuously. 'If you have a brain, Sir Geoffrey, please begin to use it. Besides, where is the wound that ended his life? Simon, could you help me to turn him over?'

Reluctantly, Simon took hold of the frail old shoulder and pushed.

'See?' Baldwin said delightedly. 'No wound. Plainly this was no murder, but a simple death of old age. May all our deaths be as gentle.'

'What is that?' Sir Geoffrey asked, eyeing the pack which Simon and Baldwin had left on the floor by the doorway.

'That? Only a parcel I found near the altar.'

'It's Nicholas's shirt. He *has* been here. Perhaps he sought to rob the church as well as kill the priest. He is entirely evil!'

'He is a man like any other,' Baldwin remonstrated. 'He entered, he found the priest dead, and he fled.'

'Why should he bolt if he had nothing to hide?'

'A man may have nothing to hide and yet still be wary of allowing himself to be caught by a posse bent on his destruction,' Baldwin said dismissively.

'You suggest my posse was . . .'

Baldwin looked at him for a long moment, then turned on his heel and left the chapel.

Humphrey tried to yawn. It seemed the natural thing to do, after waking from sleep, but even as he opened his mouth the pain shot from his temple to his jaw, and he hiccuped in pain.

'Oh! Oh! God in Heaven, *ow*!'

'Think yourself lucky, friend. You could have been struck with a knife instead.'

Opening an eye cautiously, Humphrey found himself staring at a rock.

The voice continued conversationally. 'Of course, if you had been killed outright, it might have saved you a not inconsiderable amount of grief for the future.'

Humphrey winced. The voice was educated, and that could well bode badly for the future. 'Um. We are all here in this miserable existence for our allotted time. We can all expect sadness and pain.'

There was a chuckle. 'Ah, but a man who pretends to be a priest? He can be made to suffer dreadfully, can't he?'

Humphrey tried to move his arms and found that he was effectively bound. A thong or cord tied him at the elbows, and his ankles were similarly restrained. He lifted his head and turned to face his gaoler. 'I *am* a priest.'

'No, I don't think so. And nor do many others about here. Especially Matthew, who felt sure you were out to take advantage of poor Isaac. In fact he thought you were probably after the silver from the chapel. I'm surprised you didn't bother to take all the altar trappings. The cloth would be worth a few shillings, and the cross too.'

'I am no thief !' Humphrey declared, managing to affect a tone of righteous indignation that he scarcely felt. He was glad now that he hadn't tried to shove the chalice in his pack when he left. It had been tempting, God alone knew.

'Oddly enough, you apparently are not.' Friar John stood and walked to a small cauldron that sat over the fire. He stirred the pottage and sniffed at it appreciatively. 'And yet you are not a priest, either, are you? So my interest in you is greater than it would normally be.'

'Why do you say that? I can speak the Pater Noster as well as any, and I can . . .'

'Oh, yes – so I have heard.'

'Then there is no reason for you to keep me tied up like this, Brother. Release me and let me go on my way. If you're so attached to your supper that you won't share it with another poor sinner, then set me free so that I can pick up what I may from other people who are more gracious and charitable,' Humphrey said with a note of indignation. He felt he had pitched the tone just right, and even this daft old sermon-gabbler would see the justification in his demand. There was no point in keeping an innocent man here. 'Come, there is no harm done, apart from my broken head, and I won't demand compensation for that. Clearly you thought that there was a draw-latch trying to break into your . . .'

He remembered where he was all of a sudden, and peered about him in the gloom.

'Ah, you are perhaps wondering what a shod friar is doing down here?' John asked amiably. He looked over at his prisoner and smiled gently. 'That, you see, is the interesting point and the reason why you must remain here as my guest for a little while.'

'I will not!'

'Oh, you may shout all you want, Humphrey, but you won't be released. Apart from anything else, I want to know what you are doing out here, so far from your little chapel. Did Father Isaac see you putting your hand into a pot of money that you should not have?'

'Of course not! I told you, I am no thief!'

'So you did.' John turned his attention back to the pottage. 'I do hope you are not, my friend, because if you are, I shall see it as my duty to turn you over to the secular authorities. I understand that they can be a little unkind so far from the city.'

'Brother, no . . . please!'

'I will wait. There is no hurry.'

'But I cannot stay here like this, Brother! Please, set me loose so that I can continue on my way.'

'I should like to – but I fear that my companion would become most upset if I released you.'

'But why?'

'Because he wishes to remain hidden for a little while. He must be unseen.'

'I'll not tell anyone!' Humphrey gabbled quickly. He had suddenly realised who this friar must be: a member of an outlaw gang. This associate of his must be another outlaw, and perhaps the fellow would seek to silence anyone who saw his face, or who knew where they had their camp. Sweet Jesus! It was enough to make a man weep! He'd done nothing, and now his life was to be cast aside just because he had come here to a quiet building to seek shelter for a night.

'Oh, no!' John said affably. 'How could we permit you to go without experiencing our hospitality?'

The Keeper was thoughtful as he climbed back on to his mount. He glanced across at Simon, who was watching Sir Geoffrey with a cold, flickering suspicion in his eyes. 'Simon? Are you all right?'

'It's possible that he's the man who got Hugh killed,' Simon said.

He was calm enough, but Baldwin could feel the waves of rage. 'Simon, do nothing foolish. You have no evidence. If we can find it, I swear, I shall see him in court myself.'

'I don't want him in *court* – I want him dead, if he killed Hugh.'

Baldwin nodded. 'I can understand that. I swear to you, I shall help you if it is at all possible.'

Edgar joined them and sat easily on his horse with his customary half-grin. Simon shot a glance at him and looked away. He was aware that Edgar had been a close friend of Hugh's, so he knew he must miss him, but just now the man's expression was almost sardonic. Yes, there was a cold gleam in his eyes, and Simon was sure that he'd be the first to make Hugh's killer pay, but just now he scarcely seemed to care that Hugh was dead.

When he turned away, he caught a glimpse of the hound master. The man was scowling at a pair of his brutes, who were sniffing and nuzzling at the ground. Simon jerked with his chin in the direction of the hounds, and Baldwin nodded. 'They've got his scent.'

'Sir Geoffrey! Sir Geoffrey!'

The knight came from the chapel and stood glaring about him, seeking the source of the call.

'Sir, I think they have him again!'

Sir Geoffrey ran to his horse and climbed up as the first of the hounds began to bay. As the other beasts took up the call, Simon and Baldwin were soon caught up in a fresh chase. The mass of men and horses began to mill about the chapel's yard, and then, as the hounds set off northwards, they leaped the low fence and set off in pursuit.

Over the fields they pounded, and Simon ignored a growing soreness on his left inner thigh from all the riding he'd done recently as he gave himself up to the pleasure of pursuit. The wind caught at his hair and it whipped about like a short mane, while his cloak tugged at his throat, snapping and cracking. There was another field, and a taller hedge this time, and he leaned forward as he felt the rounsey gather himself and surge as he rose over it; Simon just had time to force himself back before the beast's legs struck the solid earth at the other side, slamming Simon back against the cantle. It caught him slightly askew, the top raking along his left buttock, and the pain flared for a moment, but then he was concentrating on the race again.

All was forgotten in the mad rush forward, because few if any of the men remembered what they were here for now – they were lost in the excitement of the gallop. Simon had a moment of sudden clarity: all the men here were the same felons and cut-throats whom Baldwin and he had been warned of by Malkin and Isabel. When they found the man they hunted he would stand no chance against them, even if Baldwin and Simon tried to stop them stringing him up forthwith.

Those who would have restrained the posse, the local villeins, were too few, and they would hardly dare to thwart Sir Geoffrey and his hirelings. Looking about him, Simon was aware of a quickening concern about what might shortly happen.

At a rough bellow, the horses left the straight path they had taken, and slipped right to the road again. A low fence and hedge, wait for the horse to bunch up his muscles . . . *now!* The rounsey soared up as lightly as a blackbird, and Simon felt a fleeting satisfaction before they came to earth again. This time he was better prepared and his backside didn't suffer. His thigh was giving him grief, though, and he had to resettle himself in the saddle as they sped along.

The noise was deafening. In his ears was the constant swish and *whoom* of the wind, but even over that there was the clamour of a cavalry charge, the squeaking and rasping of leather against leather, the clashing of metal, the ringing of chains, the dreadful, persistent roaring of the hooves. No one hoofbeat could be distinguished; all was merged in a single, continuous, mind-numbing thud that seemed to last for ever. The only thing that mattered was staying on his horse, not falling and being crushed by the men and beasts behind him. More men died in fast horse races than in murders, he had heard once, and he could easily believe it.

He could see the buildings of Iddesleigh now. The clump of irregular houses seemed to shine in the darkness, their limewash glowing like starlight, thatch gleaming softly grey. And then Simon saw where the hounds were leading.

Baldwin was still at his side, and Simon could see that he wore an expression of fixed determination.

The whole posse turned up before the inn, and their horses stood stamping and blowing as the hounds jumped the rotten old fence into the churchyard, whining and pawing at the door.

Simon dropped from his mount and strode to the gate, but Sir Geoffrey was there before him.

'You have no jurisdiction here, Bailiff,' Sir Geoffrey stated.

'But *I* do,' Baldwin declared coolly. 'I am not sure that you do.'

'Whatever you think, this is a matter for the local court,' Sir Geoffrey snapped. 'He's my man, and I'll have him tried in my court.'

'He may be guilty of murder, and I'll have him tried in the king's court,' Baldwin responded.

'With all my men here you try to dictate to me?' Sir Geoffrey asked. He set his head on one side as though contemplating Baldwin with interest. 'I think you don't realise how matters are arranged here in the country, Sir Baldwin.'

'I know well enough!'

Simon could see that Sir Geoffrey's men were starting to encircle Baldwin. One was about to stand behind him when there was a cracking sound, and he disappeared. In his place stood Edgar with a heavy branch in his hand, which he discarded with a happy smile fixed to his face. The smile remained even as he drew his sword from its sheath.

Baldwin had left his own blade in the scabbard, but he hooked his thumbs into his belt as Sir Geoffrey leaned forward.

'Out of my path, Sir Baldwin. This is my quarry. We thank you,' he added, 'for your help in running him to earth! But he is ours, not yours. Leave him to us.'

Baldwin looked at all the men before him. He did not move to draw his sword, but met the eyes of all those who stood facing him. 'I am the Keeper of the King's Peace. You all know that,' he said, and then added in his loudest voice: '*I call on all the villagers of Iddesleigh to protect their church from attack by men from another parish. I call upon you to support the king's Keeper of the Peace!*'

'You can't do that!' Sir Geoffrey rasped. His hand was on his sword hilt now. 'If you think a few pissy villeins can stop me, you're . . .'

The rest of his words were lost. As he spoke, there was the sound of hooves from the south and west. Suddenly, up the hill from Fishleigh, there appeared a force of men.

Simon eyed them doubtfully. If this fresh force was arriving to support their neighbours, even if all the villagers came out to support Baldwin they must be cowed by such an armed host. The men reined in as they reached the church, circling the group at the door.

At their head was an older man, slightly short, badly scarred on one side of his face, who stood in his saddle and gazed about him as though he was surprised to see so many men already there. 'Is this a fair? Is there a party? What can all these men be doing on my lands without asking permission, I wonder?'

Sir Geoffrey cursed under his breath, and Simon realised that this new group must be his enemies.

'Sir Odo. God's blessings on you. It is good to see you,' Sir Geoffrey said as though the words were poison in his mouth.

'Yes,' Sir Odo said indulgently. He had a mild manner and a happy smile on his face as he spoke. 'I am sure it is. So tell me, Sir Geoffrey. Is there something about my manor that I can help you with? I don't think I have heard of so many men on my lands since . . . oh, since you visited my bailiff last Saturday. He's back home now, you know. And will stay there.'

'This is a different matter entirely,' Sir Geoffrey said. 'The poor

Lady Lucy of Meeth. You know she has been found? Murdered and thrown into a mire?'

'On Sir Geoffrey's land,' Edgar added helpfully.

Sir Odo appeared to notice him for the first time. He gave a small frown as he took in his appearance, and then looked over Baldwin. 'I believe we have met, sir?'

'At Lord Hugh de Courtenay's castle in Tiverton,' Baldwin agreed, bowing.

'Of course. You are the Keeper from Crediton? And I saw you in Exeter at the last court of gaol delivery. You were a Justice then.'

'I was. And I am here to apprehend a man who was once in Sir Geoffrey's household, but appears to have run to the nearest place of sanctuary.'

'You think he killed the widow Lucy?'

'It is possible,' Baldwin admitted. 'Although we shall only learn the truth if we are permitted to question him fairly in a court, or if he confesses.'

'He will confess,' Sir Geoffrey grated.

'That is no concern of yours,' Baldwin said.

'He is my man!'

'But he is not in your jurisdiction now. He is on Sir Odo's lands. Also, he is in the church, which means he has the rights of sanctuary. Until there is a coroner here, he is the king's man, and I will not have him removed by you.'

'Please, Sir Baldwin,' Sir Geoffrey said graciously, bowing. 'Would you stand aside that I may at least speak to him first? Perhaps I can persuade him to come out.'

'No,' Baldwin said flatly. 'I shall speak to him alone.'

'I could make you move,' Sir Geoffrey growled.

'I could demand the support of Sir Odo.'

Sir Geoffrey glanced up at his neighbour, and hesitated. 'Very well,' he said with as much grace as he could muster. 'If you wish to speak to him, so be it. The coroner will be here before long, I expect. He was only a short way from here, I believe. Surely your prisoner will be taken off your hands as soon as possible.'

'Perhaps,' Baldwin said. 'And now, Simon, Edgar, let us speak to this unfortunate man.'

Chapter Twenty-Nine

Nicholas watched them walk in with the terror of a man who knew he was facing death. He couldn't stop his arms from shaking, and as he gripped the altar cloth with his fists, kneeling at the side of it, the golden cross reflecting the light from the candles and bathing him in a rich glow, he felt none of the calmness that the Church used to offer him.

He knew who was outside. There was no mistaking that rough, coarse voice. Anyone who knew Sir Geoffrey would recognise that mixture of bullying and swearing. The row made by the horses and men arriving had been one thing, but listening to his old master threatening the knight in the gateway, that was another. And finally he'd heard more horses, and that was when Nicholas knew he was dead. He was convinced that it was a second force of Sir Geoffrey's men. It never occurred to him that it could be Sir Odo – someone who might save him.

But the thought of saving him was far from anyone's mind in here, he saw as he took in the expressions on Baldwin's and Simon's faces. The two men walked in, Edgar waiting near the doorway, and even as Nicholas glanced at the priest nearby, he was already sure that these men would see him destroyed. Foreigners wouldn't trust his word. Why should they?

'Father,' Baldwin said quietly. 'I have kept those men all outside for now, but until there is more sensible protection, do you mind if I remain here myself?'

'Of course not.'

Jeanne was at the rear of the nave, and she walked down to the altar now, a jug of wine in one hand, four cups in the other. 'I hope a little wine will refresh you?'

'Jeanne! What are you doing here?'

'I saw this man arrive, husband. I was able to help him a little. Don't worry, Richalda is at the inn.'

'With Emma?'

Jeanne smiled. 'With Jankin's wife. She is good with children and Richalda is playing with someone her own age. For the first time in a while she isn't bored.'

Baldwin glanced at the priest as he took a cup from his wife. 'The coroner will be here before long, I hope, but for now, do you object to my questioning this man?'

Matthew shook his head and waved his hand as though to invite Baldwin to begin. Jeanne passed him a cup too, and soon the men were all drinking from their cups, except for Nicholas. He sat with his head hanging, eyes wide with fear.

Baldwin faced him. 'Your name?'

'I am called Nicholas le Poter.'

'You have come here to seek sanctuary?'

'They'd kill me else! You can see that.'

'They say that you murdered this Lady Lucy of Meeth.'

'It was nothing to do with me! I don't think I ever saw her, let alone harmed her! Sir, you must believe me! What would I do with a woman like her? I'm just a man who lives by his hands, nothing else. She wouldn't even look at a man like me.'

'She was taken on the road from her manor when she had a man with her. The person who killed her is responsible for two lives,' Baldwin said. 'I am Keeper of the King's Peace, and I must learn who did this. Also, we know that Ailward was murdered, and the family of Hugh Shepherd from near to this place. I would discover who might be responsible.'

'You want to know who was responsible? Ask Sir Geoffrey. He could have desired Lady Lucy. Perhaps he tried to make her wed him? And the man Hugh, he died on the night that Sir Geoffrey had led his men against Sir Odo's sergeant, Robert Crokers. Maybe he sent some other men up to this man Hugh's house and killed them?'

'Why would he do that?'

'Because he's terrified that he's going to be removed from the manor! A stronger man will soon take the notice of Lord Despenser. If someone was to replace him here, what would happen to Sir Geoffrey? There'd be nowhere for him to go. So all he can do is try to remove anyone who shows an ounce of initiative, and then take over their ideas to increase the wealth of the manor. He's done it before, and he'll do it again. I have no doubt.'

Simon rasped 'What of the man Hugh?'

'Him? He was up here on Sir Odo's lands, wasn't he? If Sir Geoffrey wanted the favour of the Lord Despenser, he'd increase the lands he controls. If he could, he'd take this man Hugh's lands in the name of his master. Just as he'd take Lady Lucy's.'

'A mere bully trying to increase his master's estates by theft?' Baldwin murmured.

'It has been known,' Edgar said.

Something in his tone made Baldwin and Simon turn. There, in the doorway, facing Edgar, was Sir Geoffrey. A short distance behind him stood Sir Odo.

At the sight, Nicholas felt he must choke. The expression on Sir Geoffrey's face was adequate proof of his mood: he was in the blackest temper imaginable. There was no escaping those small, keen, grey eyes. Nicholas tried to look away at Sir Baldwin, but he found the Keeper's eyes too intense too, as though he trusted no one, and that by merely looking at Nicholas he had seen through to the depths of his soul. The man with him, the bailiff, was hardly better, with his pale complexion and staring eyes. The only man in the church who looked on him kindly was the priest – and Sir Odo. Nicholas knew why, though. 'My enemy's enemy is my friend,' he had once heard Sir Odo say, and it made good sense. That was the sort of rule that he could understand. Now Sir Odo looked at him in a friendly manner, which was in sharp contrast to the expression he wore as he turned back to Sir Geoffrey.

'This is *outrageous*! I demand that you leave this man alone until the coroner is here!' Sir Geoffrey blustered.

'There is no need. I am only asking some questions,' Baldwin said.

'There is every need. The interrogation should take place in front of the jury.'

'In your back room?' Sir Odo asked with a cynical lift in his eyebrow.

Sir Geoffrey stared at him. 'There is nothing out there I need be ashamed of.'

'Of course not,' Sir Odo agreed suavely. 'No, no! It would be terrible to suggest such a thing.'

'I demand that you leave this man here now. I shall post men to guard him through the night to be sure he is held until the coroner comes. If he wishes to abjure the realm and save us all a lot of time, he can do so then. For now he should be kept quiet and secure.'

'I agree,' Baldwin said. 'I shall remain here with him.'

'That would be much better, Sir Baldwin,' Sir Odo said, adding simply, 'and this is my parish, my manor. I shall decide, Sir Geoffrey, who shall remain here to protect the man.'

'I didn't say "protect",' Sir Geoffrey snarled.

'No. But I did,' Odo said, this time a little more pointedly. 'I see it as my duty to keep him safe and alive until the coroner can question him. That is what I shall do. So, with your leave, Sir Baldwin, I shall go and seek some men who can guard this place. You will not object to more men to back you up?'

Baldwin smiled. 'Not at all.'

'Do you accuse me of something?' Sir Geoffrey asked.

'Not I,' Baldwin said mildly.

'What of you?' Sir Geoffrey said, staring straight at Nicholas.

'Sir! What do you want me to say? That I will rather go to the gallows than denounce you? Then I do accuse you! I accuse you of the murder of the Lady Lucy of Meeth, and of the murder of the little family here in Iddesleigh. And I will repeat this before the coroner. I swear, sirs, I am innocent of these murders, and that man is guilty.'

At the chapel, it took Perkin and Beorn some little while to tidy the corpse.

'What are we doing this for, anyway?' Beorn grumbled. 'Have we become the church's unpaid fossors? I ought to be home. Look! It's dark already, and it'll be light soon enough. I need to go and sleep.'

'Stop your grumbling and help,' Perkin said unsympathetically.

'We may as well get him ready. We'll have to get him to the church tomorrow, no matter what time you want to sleep.'

That was the trouble, of course. The chapel had no churchyard for the dead. Its open space was dedicated to the living, for it was where the vill's people would gather on May days and festivals. For a serious matter, like a burial, they had to carry the poor corpse up to Iddesleigh where the church could arrange for a funeral and interment.

Usually it was a rather tedious job, wrapping the dead body and hauling it all that way on a cart, but it was easier than others. A travelling man had once told Perkin that in Dartmoor one parish was so vast that the poor folk of the moors had to walk miles to the nearest church. It was easy to believe. The Church had no interest in where a man might live, nor who his lord was. For the Church the only issue that mattered was the location of the nearest legal church. Churches owned their own lands and protected them as greedily and passionately as any local magnate.

At least poor old Isaac had been so old and desiccated that he would weigh little to transport. And they'd be able to borrow a cart from someone. Nobody would grudge old Isaac his last journey in comfort.

'Where's that little runt who was with him, though?' Perkin asked as they finished. 'Surely Isaac must have died a while ago. But I haven't seen Humphrey since he viewed Lady Lucy's body. Have you?'

'I know my little Anna said she saw him going up the road after our supper tonight, but that can't be right.'

'Why?'

'He'd have seen old Isaac, wouldn't he? No churchman would leave another priest lying in a room like this, would he? Stands to reason.'

'Yes. You're right, of course,' Perkin said, but doubtfully. 'What reason could he have had for leaving Isaac like this? If he had any other business, he'd have to send his apologies and stay here with his old master, wouldn't he?'

'Difficult to mistake him, though,' Beorn said.

Perkin had a sudden memory of Humphrey's face when they went to the chapel to ask the priest to come and say the words over Lady

Lucy's corpse. He'd looked shocked then, and he stood in the chapel's doorway like a man trying to block the view inside . . .

But that was mad. What on earth would one priest want to conceal the death of his companion for? He must just have missed Isaac's body.

Perkin and Beorn finished their work, and carried the body to the altar. There they set him down on the floor to lie in front of the cross, and stood back a moment contemplating the little huddle of cheap linen.

'Seems unfair for him to just pass away like that.'

Beorn had a choke in his voice. Perkin nodded, unsure of his own.

'I mean . . .' Beorn coughed. 'He baptised me, and my brothers, and all my children. He married me, he buried my old man and my mother up at Iddesleigh. There's nothing he wouldn't do for any of us.'

'Even a priest has to die,' Perkin managed. He was in the same position as Beorn. There had never been a time before Isaac. All his life he had known the old priest. Every moment of importance, Isaac had been there in the background, his grim, penetrating eyes watching over them just as the Church said her shepherds watched over her flock of souls. Isaac was the living embodiment of the Church down here. The chapel itself may have been a strong building of moorstone, but the rock was a pale imitation of the strength of his conviction.

'I'll . . . I'll get home, then,' Beorn said hesitantly.

'Don't worry. I'll stay here with him,' Perkin said. 'Go on. Be off with you. I'll see you in the morning.'

'Thank you, Perkin. I'll come at dawn with a two-wheeled cart.'

And when it was all silent in that little room, Perkin sat next to Isaac's body and put a hand on the cold, firm shoulder. 'I'll miss you, old man.'

Hugh entered with a pair of coneys over his shoulder. He dropped them on the floor before John, who stared at them.

'Found them on the roadway. Can't have been anyone's,' Hugh said defensively.

'Clearly not!' John said. He tried to separate them, and saw that Hugh had cut along the upper rear part of each rabbit's left leg. He'd thrust the right leg through the gap between tendon and bone, making a loop, and tied the two together so that they might hang on his shoulder without falling. John unjoined them and began to skin both carcasses as Hugh settled down, staring at their captive.

Humphrey was less imposing now. When Hugh had seen him before, he had that sort of arrogance that a priest has. That kind of look that tells anyone else that he's a man of importance, and you aren't, so get out of the way quickly. He had that appearance last time Hugh had seen him, when he had been in the road asking about Constance. When he had told Hugh to look after her, because she deserved all the care Hugh could give her.

Not now. Now Humphrey lay back in the mess of the floor with his bound hands held before him like a supplicant. His robe was marked and stained, and his hair was almost as wild-looking as his eyes. 'What do you want with me?'

Hugh squatted near him and stared deep into those eyes.

'I want to know why I shouldn't kill you right now.'

It took some while to persuade Sir Geoffrey and his men to leave the church, and only when Baldwin and Sir Odo were sure that the party was truly riding back towards Monkleigh did Baldwin relax a little and invite Sir Odo to join him in a jug of wine.

'I should be delighted . . . but first, please let me demonstrate how little I trust my neighbour,' Sir Odo chuckled. He beckoned a farmer's boy who stood nearby watching the goings-on with fascination. 'You want a farthing? Good. Then run down the road there, until you come to a place where you can see those men riding away. If you see any of them turn off and return this way, come to me at the inn at once. Yes?'

The delighted boy grabbed the coin eagerly and scurried off down the road.

'I think that answers my first question,' Baldwin said.

'What was that?'

'How honourable is Sir Geoffrey?'

Sir Odo laughed aloud as he limped along the roadway to the inn. 'Ach, he's not so bad by his own lights. But his master is a dangerous man, now that he's the king's own adviser. A man with so much power is always a threat. And if Sir Geoffrey thought that he'd be more well-regarded if he took another man's land – well, from all we've heard, Lord Despenser is less scrupulous than many others.'

'You are candid, sir.'

'I am a knight of Sir John Sully, and he is a loyal vassal to Lord de Courtenay. I am loyal too. I dislike this new fashion for men to sell their service for money. In my day, we took our oath because we loved our lord, and we served him faithfully to death.'

'Still, it might be as well to moderate your language with strangers, sir.'

Sir Odo threw him a look in which the grin smothered the shrewdness. 'You think so? Sir Baldwin, since you're known for avoiding any discussion of politics, other than stating that you're the king's man because you owe him allegiance, I think I can speak openly in your presence.' He nodded towards Simon. 'And every servant of Lord Hugh de Courtenay knows of the Puttock family. If I can't trust Lord Hugh's father's favourite steward's son, whom can I trust?'

'Thank you, Sir Odo,' Simon muttered. He felt more than a little out of his depth in this discussion. Sir Odo was a plain-speaking man, and a bluff, honest character, but in Simon's experience so were almost all leaders of warriors. They tended to have that skill of speaking to a man as though he were an equal, no matter what the actual difference in position. It was that which led men to trust them and follow them into battle.

'You've been praised often enough by our lord,' Odo said. 'So you see, Sir Baldwin, I feel no concern when I speak openly in front of you, and I do want to see if there's anything we can do to resolve matters here.'

They were at the inn's door, and they walked inside. There was one table on the right that was inhabited by two young men discussing the attractions of a maid, but when the two knights stood before them, and Edgar jerked his thumb, they soon took the hint and vacated their seats.

'So, Sir Odo,' Baldwin said when they were all seated with great earthenware cups filled with wine before them. 'Tell me more.'

The most part of Sir Odo's story told them little that was new. Sir

Geoffrey was an acquisitive soul and sought to take over Sir Odo's lands 'on this side of the river – at first, anyway. No doubt he'll want the whole of Fishleigh as soon as he can get his hands on it.' If he could take Lady Lucy's lands as well, he would have a great swathe of land east and north of Sir Odo, which would make it all the easier to subdue any possible revolts, and incidentally make it easier to swallow up any other manors he desired . . . 'all in the name of his master, of course,' Sir Odo said drily, and tipped his head back to finish his wine.

Baldwin poured him more. 'So I can understand why he should have killed Lady Lucy, if you are right. She was a barrier to his advance.'

'There are stories that she was tortured?'

Baldwin nodded.

'I dare say he tried to make her hand him her lands. When he failed, he killed her. A savage, brutal man.'

'Clearly. What of the land between here and the river? Madam Isabel and Malkin feel it is theirs and yet you hold it.'

'I do.' Odo grimaced for some little while, then tilted his head and nodded. 'It was theirs, and when they lost it, Sir Geoffrey had it along with his other lands. I bought it from him. Ach! I'm not proud to take advantage of the situation, but I have a duty to Lord de Courtenay. That land creates a buffer between Monkleigh and Fishleigh. I thought it made sound sense to purchase it, and Sir Geoffrey was keen enough to take my money. Now I realise he put my money straight into his own purse. He intends to win back the land for his own master.'

'I can understand that,' Simon said, 'and I can see how he might have sought to remove Lady Lucy. I suppose Ailward could have possibly tried to win back his lands in the future, so Sir Geoffrey had him killed: but I can see no reason why he should have killed Hugh.'

'Hugh?' Sir Odo asked, perplexed.

'My friend's servant, who used to live a little way up here,' Baldwin said.

'Ah, yes. I heard of that. The fire?'

'That was what the coroner said,' Simon said without conviction.

'Sir Edward?' Sir Odo gave a humourless laugh. 'Oh, yes. He'd agree to whatever Sir Geoffrey suggested to him. They are close, those two. But then, both serve the same lord.'

'Despenser?' Baldwin confirmed.

'Yes. And the coroner knows where his loyalties lie.'

'Why would he seek to remove Hugh?' Baldwin asked with a frown.

'If I'm right and he wants all my lands this side of the river, the first thing he'd do would be to launch raids on the outlying farms and properties. Well, on the same night he attacked my man Robert Crokers, and then your man up here. Didn't kill Robert, but then he probably thought that a man who was so high in my household would be too much of a provocation to me. It would force me to react. So he took your man instead. He left a message for me at Robert's, and killed someone else to show he wasn't scared. Both parcels of land are close to his estates.'

'So it would be easy for him to get an armed force to them without being seen,' Baldwin noted.

'Of course. I've been on edge ever since,' Odo said, drinking more wine and wiping his mouth with the back of his hand. 'I've a chain of men with horses at different places between all the outlying farms, just in case of another attack.'

'That was how you arrived today?' Simon asked. 'I wondered where you had sprung from.'

'A messenger arrived to tell me that Sir Geoffrey set off from his hall earlier this evening. At first I was convinced he'd gone to ruin poor Robert's house again, but there was no sign of his men there. So I thought to myself that he must have been heading this way instead, and we lashed our brutes to get here as quickly as we could. Just in time, too, from the look of it!'

'It was in very good time,' Baldwin said, but there was no warmth in his tone.

Chapter Thirty

Hugh sat back on his heels. 'Want to know what you meant.'

'I can't even remember seeing you there.'

He didn't believe the man. 'I was hedging. You told me to look after her. That night, she died.'

Humphrey's face suddenly paled. '*Pater Noster, Domine . . .*'

'You can say one thing for him,' John said idly, lifting a rabbit leg and dropping it into the pot with the others. 'He's certainly had training. He knows all the right words.'

'Of course I do,' Humphrey spat. 'What do you think I am? An impostor?'

His bluster didn't upset John. 'Yes.'

Humphrey gaped. His work had been faultless, surely. It was impossible that anyone could have spotted his deceit.

'You see,' John said, 'your error was in assuming that all parish priests are dullards. They aren't. In particular, Matthew at Iddesleigh is a very good and conscientious priest. He knows his Latin, he serves his flock as well as he might, he works his lands alongside the peasants, and he knows the church and the politics of the bishop's court. Perhaps if you had known more about that, he wouldn't have noticed you. But you didn't, so he did.'

'What are you talking about?'

'You knew too much, but your Latin was very rusty. It still is, I think. You can recite it, but it's not your strength. Your congregation wouldn't notice the difference. Tell me, did Isaac?'

'This is nonsense!'

'Perhaps he did and didn't want to embarrass you. I have no doubt he would have prayed hard for your miserable, devious, lying soul. But there we are. It was as plain as the buckle on your belt there that you weren't trained for the priesthood. No, I agreed with Matthew as soon as I saw you.'

'Agreed with what?'

'That you were a friar or a monk. And you've run away.'

Simon watched Sir Odo mount his horse. 'Thank God we've met him,' he said. 'At least we know we have a strong ally.'

Baldwin nodded, but his mind was not entirely with Simon. The bailiff recognised the look in his eyes. It was that slight distraction that meant that Baldwin was already beginning to see through the immediate problems to the core of the matter.

'Well, Baldwin?' he asked.

Baldwin knew his friend well enough now not to mind when he broke in upon his thoughts. 'Sir Odo is clearly anxious about Sir Geoffrey, and from what we've seen, so should he be.'

'It was a stroke of good fortune for us that he is,' Edgar commented.

Simon glanced at him. 'Because his men were there in good time?'

Edgar nodded. His face was set to the south and west. 'That's the way he came, wasn't it? I wonder where the messenger was stationed. The lad must have been a fleet rider to be able to get to Sir Odo and rouse him in time for Odo to ride out to his man's lands before coming here. We were not so slow ourselves in riding here from the chapel, were we?'

'He probably knows all the short cuts,' Simon said. Then a thought struck him. 'That may be how the men who attacked Hugh got to him, too, by using some quieter paths that didn't pass near the road.'

Baldwin nodded. 'Except the horses did come from Iddesleigh itself. I saw that in their hoofprints. They must have gone to Hugh's house under cover of the party at the inn, and then come back here quietly and ridden home when all was dark.'

'An easy ride,' Edgar agreed. A fast ride in the dark over rough land was never appealing to a horseman. A good, solid roadway like this was safe.

'Sir Odo's men are all about the church,' Simon noted. 'Even if Sir Geoffrey returns, I don't think he'll be able to break in there without raising the vill.'

'It would be a foolish man who'd try that,' Baldwin said. But even as he spoke, his eyes went to the church.

Seeing his look, Edgar gave a contented smile. 'There is one sure and certain protection if you are fearful, Sir Baldwin. Send Madam Jeanne's maid to guard the man. Not only would you guarantee that Sir Geoffrey would never dare attack, you would also ensure that the man would speak to you of anything you wanted as soon as you returned to see him.'

'Thank you,' Baldwin said coldly. 'If I were to take your advice, our only witness would be dead by morning if he had to gnaw through his own wrists to manage it, so cruel is the punishment you suggest.'

It was already late when Adcock appeared in the chapel's doorway. As the door opened, all the candles began to dance and smoke. He shot a look around, and pushed the door quietly shut behind him.

This place was proving to be a hell on earth. All Adcock had ever wanted was to be left to arrange for the good management of the land and the animals on it, but instead here he was, installed in a manor which was a hotbed of thieving and banditry. The serfs avoided him, seeing him as a henchman of the Despenser. None of them pretended to be an expert of politics at anything higher than the most local level, but all of them knew of the reputation that the Lord Despenser was earning. They had heard how he extorted and tortured people in order to enrich himself.

Adcock walked painfully to the earthenware stoup at the wall and crossed himself, then slowly made his way up the nave to the altar.

'What is it, Sergeant? Couldn't sleep?'

'Perkin? What are you doing here?'

'Watching over old Isaac. He deserved a mourner, if only one.'

'He would have understood. There's a lot of work on at this time of year.'

Perkin yawned. 'When is that not true?'

Tentatively Adcock approached the body and Perkin, who squatted near the head. 'Do you mind if I join you?'

'Why would you want to? You hardly knew the man.'

'He was a good man, though. We both know that. He served this vill well in his time, and it seems wrong to me that there is no official party here to watch over him as he lies in his own chapel.'

'That young priest should be here with him,' Perkin said bitterly.

'This will be a terrible shock to him, I expect,' Adcock said.

'You think so?'

Shocked by his tone, Adcock looked up sharply. 'You mean the priest had something to do with this man's death?'

'He was old. He had nothing more to live for, I believe. He'd done all he could.'

Adcock grimaced and shifted uneasily. His cods still felt as though they'd been broken. 'What is happening here? I hoped for a period of quiet to get the land sown so that we could win the best harvest ever – and all I have found is death and despair.'

'It's a hard life, and this is a hard vill,' Perkin said. 'But you'll be all right.'

Adcock had a sudden vision of his Hilda, the sun was behind her so he could see her whole form, the smile on her face still brighter than the sun itself . . . and he knew that he would never dare to bring her here to this manor. Better that they should live apart than that she should come and be leered at by the men under Sir Geoffrey. They were little more than brutes, all of them.

'Nicholas le Poter was all but killed by Sir Geoffrey,' he said. 'Whipped just because he took the piss out of a messenger from Sir Odo.'

Perkin looked at him. 'He was no friend to us who live here. If Sir Geoffrey took the skin off his back, not many of us would care.'

'You didn't see what happened to him,' Adcock said, thinking again of that terrible kick that had all but emasculated Adcock himself. In reality that was a part of the reason for his being here: to be safe from any further attack from Sir Geoffrey. The other part was despair. He had sealed Nicholas le Poter's death warrant when he told Sir Geoffrey that le Poter had suggested the draining of the mire, and the knowledge was destroying him.

'I've seen what's happened to others often enough,' Perkin grunted.

'Where is the young priest? He should be here too.'

'He's run away.' Perkin looked at him and sighed. 'The damned fool. It's going to cost him his neck.'

*   *   *

Jeanne was already asleep when Baldwin walked into his room. Simon and Edgar were still in the inn's main hall, drinking without speaking for the most part, although now and again Edgar would murmur a word or two about life at Crediton.

Emma was, thankfully, nowhere to be seen. Baldwin gave a quick frown, wondering where she could have got to. He hadn't seen her since Sir Odo had left, when he was sure she had been at the bar, talking and joking with a small clique of drinkers. One man had stood glowering at Baldwin – oh yes, David, the man who had led them to the mire where Lady Lucy had been found. He had some reason for disliking Baldwin and Simon, he supposed.

Emma would probably annoy someone else through the night with her snoring or her moaning and complaining. Baldwin could hope so, anyway. Certainly he would sleep all the better without her in the room . . . urged on by the temptations of the devil, he began to move a chest across the doorway to prevent her entering. Only the sudden change in Jeanne's breathing stopped him. He realised that he might wake her now by dragging the chest, and if he didn't, the blasted maid certainly would when she found the door barred against her. She'd be likely to pound on it and wake the entire house. Finally, as he was removing his sword and tunic, Baldwin started to chuckle to himself. In his haste to ban Emma, he hadn't noticed that the door opened outwards. Pulling the chest before it would achieve nothing.

It was a sign of how tired he was, he told himself as he sank onto the bed as gently as possible so as not to waken Jeanne.

His wound was giving him some grief again. That damned bolt from behind had so nearly killed him, it seemed perverse now to complain about the pain, yet he could not help himself. It was a constant grumbling ache at the best of times. Now, with his whole body exhausted after the ride here and the efforts he had expended since arriving, it was more of a pernicious anguish.

The thought that they were likely never to bring a murderer to book for the crimes committed against Hugh was a sore grief. Yet Baldwin was not sure that there was any possibility of seeing justice brought to bear against the Despenser's man down here. And he was growing to agree with all those with whom he had spoken that surely it was Sir Geoffrey who had the urge to remove Hugh, who had the opportunity, and who had been about the place that day. As for his allegation that another could have killed Lady Lucy and dropped her body in the mire – Baldwin was in two minds. It was unlikely that a man would have dropped the body in the mire to throw suspicion on Sir Geoffrey unless he knew that the mire was soon to be drained. Who could have known that in advance? Clearly the sergeant of the manor would have known. Perhaps Baldwin should speak to him. Then again, would Sir Geoffrey have allowed the mire to be emptied if he knew that the lady's body lay within?

As he lay back, the questions circled in his mind, but he could get no nearer an answer. All he was growing convinced of was that Sir Geoffrey would be enormously difficult to bring to justice.

Baldwin wondered how Simon would cope with that. It was a dreadful conclusion to reach, but if the culprit was Sir Geoffrey, the man was practically unassailable. Lord Despenser would protect his own.

It was a deeply unsatisfying conclusion, but he could see no alternative. He only prayed that Simon would not be irrational. He would speak to Edgar in the morning. If it looked as though Simon was going to burst out into righteous indignation and assault Sir Geoffrey, Edgar and he would have to prevent him by force.

There was no point having Simon getting himself killed as well.

Humphrey eyed the glowing tip of the blackened stick in Hugh's hand. It approached him with the relentlessness of a viper slowly stalking a mouse, and Humphrey felt like a mouse as he sat absolutely still, the warmth from the glowing point beginning to make him sweat.

'I have no patience with liars,' Hugh said quietly. 'Speak.'

'I know nothing! Nothing. But I saw Matthew the priest at Iddesleigh, and he told me that your wife was once a nun, that she had taken her vows when she was too young, and had fled here.'

'So?' Hugh demanded.

'I am the same. I was a monk, from the little priory of Otterton.'

'I know it,' John said, nodding to himself as he stirred the pot. 'A pleasant little place, but draughty rooms for guests.'

'I was sent there when I was a lad. My father thought I was wayward and too clever for his household. My older brothers were to have the estate and the glory, and all I had was the Church. So I went to the priory and began my novitiate. I soon realised that it was a harsh, cruel life. I couldn't live under the rules there. It was too much. But when I spoke to the prior, who was generally a decent old soul, he told me that I'd taken the vows and that was an end to it. So I ran away.'

'And that was all?' John asked.

'It's all I will say.'

Hugh took the stick away, studied the point, and then began to blow on it. 'What of my wife? You warned me to look after her.'

'All I meant was that the priest knew of her, knew of her secret. Good God, man, don't you understand? I am a runaway too. If they drag me back, I'll *die*! I couldn't do that, not return. They'd humiliate me, make me lie on the threshold of the door to the church before each service, keep me locked in the gaol all the rest of the time, and only feed me on rank water and hard bread . . .' He was weeping now. 'Sweet Jesu, I saw one man they brought back. He looked as though he was near to death, and we were made to step on his poor body each time we entered and left the church. He lost his mind, man! Became no better than an animal!'

Hugh had blown the stick to a dull orange glow again. He nodded as though to himself, and approached Humphrey once more. 'And that same night my woman was killed. You expect me to believe you?'

'I know nothing more!'

'What were you doing at Isaac's chapel, then?' John called cheerfully. 'Was it a mere matter of good fortune that you happened upon his chapel?'

'Yes. I met him in Hatherleigh at the market, and thought that to persuade a deaf and blind old man that I was a coadjutor sent to help him in his cure of the souls of the vill would be no difficult task. I was right. I could help him, and I did. There was so much to do, and I think I helped some of the people of the parish to find their way to God . . .'

John's voice was light with amusement. 'So you thought that you'd help him? And now you've run away.'

'I've stolen nothing!'

'True. So why bolt?'

Humphrey closed his eyes and shook his head. His hands were as cold as stone now, with the tight thongs binding them, and his head felt heavy. 'I realised that the woman's body was going to make my life difficult.'

'Lady Lucy?' John asked quietly. 'The lady found in the mire?'

'Yes. I went there to give her the *viaticum*, say some prayers for her, but then, when I saw her, I knew that there was no life for me here. As soon as the coroner found her dead, he'd be bound to start to make inquiries, and I would be uncovered.'

'Isaac would protect you,' John said with a frown.

'Isaac is dead. I went out and when I went back he was still. Calm, tidy, but dead. He just stopped.'

'So! You had no sponsor, no patron, and you thought you would be best occupied in escaping again?'

'What else could I do? I know Matthew suspects me. I shouldn't be surprised if he's already sent to the bishop and demanded to know where I was sent from. He never trusted me.'

'And yet you didn't steal from the church. That speaks well of you,' John said.

'I'm no thief. I only ran because I had to.'

'Why should the lady's appearance lead to suspicion against you?' John wondered.

'Someone might remember me running from the convent.'

'Yes,' John agreed. 'So you said.'

Hugh had thrust the stick in the fire and now it glowed white when he blew out the flames.

'It's the truth,' Humphrey said more desperately, staring at it.

Hugh said nothing, but eyed his stick as he began to thrust it nearer Humphrey's face.

It was enough. He couldn't bear to look at it. Closing his eyes and averting his head, he screamed, 'All right! I confess!'

John snapped, 'What?'

'On the Gospels, this is true! I killed a man at the convent. A brother monk. I didn't mean to, but he was evil to me, he was foul and cruel, and I only meant to strike him . . . when he was on the ground I realised what I'd done. I had to run. If the coroner was to see me and understand that I had run away, news would soon get back to the bishop or the convent and I would be gaoled for my life. I couldn't bear that, so I took myself off before the coroner arrived. I swear it! It's the truth!'

Nothing happened. Neither of the other men said a word. Opening an eye Humphrey found himself looking up into Hugh's scowling face.

Hugh contemplated him for a long moment, then touched the orange-glowing ember to a rushlight hanging over Humphrey's head. It hissed and sparked as it took light, and every sound made Humphrey's flesh creep.

'Thought so,' Hugh said.

Chapter Thirty-One

The food was late, and when it arrived, the walk from the kitchen to the house had allowed much of it to grow stone cold. Sir Geoffrey picked up his trencher and studied the congealing mass without speaking for a moment before hurling it at the servant's head.

'Christ Jesus! Get me *hot* food!'

'This place appears to be falling apart. I don't think our lord would be impressed to hear what's been happening,' Sir Edward said languidly. He was sitting at Sir Geoffrey's left hand, and he wore a smile of such smugness that Sir Geoffrey longed to wipe it away with a mailed fist. He'd lost some of the initiative.

'It wasn't Odo,' he said. 'That self-satisfied old cretin couldn't see further than the end of his nose. He's been in too many mêlées since his youth, and the constant banging of weapons against his helm has addled his brains. But that new Keeper, he was a pest and a problem. Do you know of him?'

'I've heard tell, I think, but only the usual gossip. He's clever enough, and could make a good representative to the next parliament. If the good king sees the necessity of receiving more advice, of course,' the coroner said with amusement.

'You should always assume the worst.'

'I do just now,' Sir Edward said. 'I fear some prime land is being threatened. If you cannot evict this Sir Odo from his holding on this side of the river by negotiation, surely our master would expect you to do so by force. That is why you have all these men here, after all.'

Insolent puppy! This man was half his age and he thought he could talk to Sir Geoffrey like a young squire?

Curbing his anger, Sir Geoffrey spoke quietly. 'If I attack now, while the Keeper is in the vill, he could be a dangerous witness. It would only reflect badly on our lord were I to attempt such a foolish act. Better by far to try to be cunning. It is better to use your mind rather than other men's bodies.'

'Oh, quite. How many men are there in the place this side of the river, by the way? A sergeant and I suppose some guards? If you want, I could go and knock them off myself. Present you with some land so that you can give it to our lord. He would be most grateful.'

Sir Geoffrey eyed him coldly. What if the fool were killed or unhorsed by more competent men-at-arms from Sir Odo's forces, and brought back to the manor on the back of a cart? That would give Sir Odo a wonderful success. His master's liege lord, Hugh de Courtenay, would be able to screw a marvellous reward after such an unprovoked attack.

There was no point in such actions. Speed was of the essence, people always said, but when you grew older you began to realise that things would always come your way anyway. All you needed was to be sure of what you wanted, how you could get it, and then stick to your plan.

Just now Sir Geoffrey knew that he had achieved maximum disruption to Sir Odo's household. Especially after tonight. For all the anger he had felt, for all the sour rage he'd expended at the men who had stood in his path and prevented him from taking back the sanctuary-seeker, he had guaranteed that Sir Odo's men were spread about the whole countryside. They were at Robert Crokers's hall, at the church at Iddesleigh, at Fishleigh and other little farms, not to mention all the gallopers who would have been stationed at every junction and viewing point from here to Iddesleigh and down to Monk Oakhampton, in all likelihood.

And that was the point. He had managed to push Sir Odo into setting his men to patrol and guard, when they all wanted to be at home wrapped well against the chill air. It was freezing outside again, and the thought that men might stay out until dawn to watch for an attack that wouldn't happen was a joy to contemplate. He could keep them on tenterhooks for two or three days like this, occasionally making a showing as daylight gave way to darkness, guaranteeing that the men would have no sleep, no ease. Only constant patrols.

Later, perhaps at the end of the week, when men were beginning to desert their posts no matter what Sir Odo wanted, that would be the time to attack. He could send some men in to Crokers's and secure the crossing at the river, while a second party went to the church and dragged that dishonourable cur le Poter from sanctuary and all the way back here to be hanged. Just a little time and the fellow would fall into his hands. And then no one else would think of removing the master of the manor and taking his place for a long time.

'I think we'll leave my plans as they are,' he said icily.

Sir Edward smiled thinly. 'I should go to my rest, then. I have a long day tomorrow.'

'Vain, conceited coxcomb!' Sir Geoffrey muttered under his breath. Then: 'Where's my food?'

Baldwin woke to a morning that was crisp and clear, with the only clouds showing over Dartmoor in the distance. By some miracle, Emma had not entered to trouble them in the middle of the night, and Baldwin had enjoyed his best night's sleep in many a month.

Pulling on some clothes, he walked out into the main hall and squatted at the fire. The boy must have been in already, because there was a fresh faggot on the previous night's embers, and already a crackling and hissing spoke of warmth to come. Smoke was issuing from both ends of the faggot, and Baldwin prodded it hopefully.

'Oi, sir knight, leave the fire alone. I won't have people play with it. It's a bugger to light, and I don't want to have it go out as soon as I leave it alone!'

Baldwin grinned and left it, instead walking to Jankin and asking where his well was, or his spring.

'We have a well at the back. Wait a moment and I'll send a boy for a bucket for you,' the innkeeper promised.

'Of course,' Baldwin said and cast his eye over the little room. Simon was snoring on a bench in a corner, his cloak over him, a hat obscuring his face. Edgar was nowhere to be seen, but there was nothing new in that. Baldwin knew his man would often be awake an hour or more before dawn. Some of the restlessness of their life in that twilight period between the collapse of the Knights Templar and their arrival back safe in England had never entirely left him. He liked to rise before the sun and walk for a little even in the coldest weather.

There were a few others dotted about the hall, but one face was conspicuously absent. 'Jankin, where is my wife's maid?'

At once Jankin grew shifty. He smiled, but his eyes avoided Baldwin's face. 'The maid?'

'Don't be daft, man! The ugly bitch with a breast like a mountain. When she beetles her eyebrows you could crack a nut in them. Where is she?'

'I couldn't say for sure, sir.'

Baldwin was inclined to feel alarmed. The woman was a miserable drain on his emotions, it was true, and she had caused more arguments and rages in the house than any servant before or since, but he didn't like to think that she could have come to harm. 'She was insulting your men at the bar last afternoon and evening.'

'Oh, that wasn't insulting. They've heard worse, Sir Baldwin. No, that would all have been taken in good part. Ah – here she is!'

Baldwin spun on his heel to see her walk in. She wore her customary glower again, her features slightly flushed, and Baldwin wondered if she was severely hungover. She stared at Baldwin as though daring him to make a comment. 'This place is miserable. Not even a decent pit to crap in,' she said, and shouldered her way past Jankin.

He looked at Sir Baldwin for a long moment. 'Was she already your wife's maid when you married?'

Baldwin said, 'What makes you ask that?'

'I thought so.'

It was past the third hour of the morning by the time the men began to gather in the yard near the church. Sir Geoffrey had sent a party of six of his men on horseback, and Sir Odo three of his own. However, Sir Odo also had the menfolk of Iddesleigh on his side should there be trouble. He had no cause to fear any action by Sir Geoffrey.

Coroner Edward was the man whom Baldwin wanted to study. As soon as he saw the man, he knew he had met him before. 'He was at the tournament at Okehampton,' he said, pointing him out to his wife.

Jeanne peered. 'Good-looking for a fair man,' she said musingly. 'It is fortunate that I prefer my men dark, husband.'

'That may be a problem soon,' Baldwin grunted. He ran a hand through his greying thatch. 'Even my beard's more white than dark now.'

'Not to me, husband.' Jeanne smiled, and kissed his chin.

'Come! I must accompany them. Will you stay with us or go back to look after Richalda?'

Jeanne pulled a face. 'I'll go back. Emma looks as though she had a night of debauchery and no sleep. I wouldn't trust her with our daughter for long.'

'Good! And now I must go from the look of things,' Baldwin said as the party began to move in the direction of the church. 'Simon?'

The bailiff nodded and dropped the stick he had been whittling, crossing the grass to join them. He looked as though he had rested, but not enough. His eyes had dark sacks beneath them, and he appeared to have aged by ten years in the last couple of days.

'Old friend, are you . . .?'

'I'll be fine. Let's get this over with.'

The men at arms all dropped from their horses and tied them to any available ring, post or sapling, while the crowd of villeins, some children, and a pair of low, skulking dogs, walked over the yard to the door.

By shoving unmercifully, Baldwin was soon at the front of the press of people. He entered the church a short distance behind the short, square figure of Sir Odo, and as he walked in caught sight of Edgar, smiling widely, leaning against the farther wall. The reason for Edgar's delight was unclear to Baldwin. It looked irreverent, given the present circumstances, and he was tempted to give a signal to register his disgust – but then he was pushed forward until he was at the side of the coroner. 'Sir Edward.'

'Yes?'

The man gave him a supercilious look that started at Baldwin's faded boots and gradually rose over the stained and marked old tunic to his face. In Coroner Edward's eyes there was amused contempt – until he met Baldwin's gaze.

There had been times when Baldwin had been interrogating witnesses or felons when all means of persuasion had failed and the men had stood resolutely silent. At times like that Baldwin would lower his head a little and fix his victim with an unblinking stare. He could do it by considering the man's offences, assessing his worth as a witness, or even, on one notable occasion, by trying to remember what it had been that his wife had told him not to forget to buy that day, but it always succeeded.

Today it served to cow the coroner.

'I am Sir Baldwin de Furnshill, the Keeper of the King's Peace. I am here to assist in the capture of the murderers of the family of Hugh of Drewsteignton, Ailward the bailiff of Sir Geoffrey, and Lady Lucy of Meeth.'

'Glad to hear it,' Coroner Edward said. He essayed a smile. 'Perhaps we can talk later? I have a sanctuary-seeking fellow in here to talk to.'

'You will wish to interrogate the man, of course.' Baldwin stood aside, but he walked to the altar and stood there in clear view of the coroner. He folded his arms and contemplated the proceedings as Sir Edward surveyed the scruffy and injured man-at-arms.

'You are Nicholas le Poter?'

'Yes.' Nicholas had both hands clutching at the altar cloth. If he were to let go, his sanctuary could be rendered null and void.

'And you are guilty of the murder of Lady Lucy of Meeth?'

'No! I've killed no one.'

'Really? Then you would like to surrender yourself to my authority so that we can evaluate your evidence.'

'I can't stay in the hall under him,' Nicholas declared, pointing with his chin at Sir Geoffrey. 'He'll kill me the first chance he has!'

'You have no choice,' the coroner said softly. He motioned to two men at his side. 'Take him. He's asked to have his case . . .'

Baldwin was about to step forward when he felt a movement behind him. Before the coroner could complete his sentence, Matthew was at Nicholas's side, a great staff in his hands.

'This man still claims sanctuary.'

'He wants to prove his innocence, Father. Let us take him away for you.'

Matthew shook his head. 'You can offer him the opportunity to abjure the realm, if you wish, and you can come here and speak to him for thirty days, but you will not take a man from the sanctuary offered to him by this most holy house. You will not, sir!'

Sir Edward set his head to one side a little. 'So be it,' he sighed after a short reflection. 'Which will it be, man? Abjure and live, or submit to the court?'

'I need time to think about it! I want more time!'

'You can wait until God's kingdom comes, as far as I'm concerned,' the coroner said. He bent down to one knee, his elbow on the other, and peered up into Nicholas's face. 'Why, he is crying! Is this guilt?'

It was delicious. This strong, hardy man-at-arms was actually weeping! Well, there was little more to do for now. Especially with the Keeper and the priest refusing to allow a sensible resolution to the problem. No, the Coroner was content to let matters ride for a while. All he need do was wait. It would take only one more failing to demonstrate that Sir Geoffrey had lost his grip of the manor, and then Sir Edward would be able to take control, after a few words in the right ears.

Coroner Edward smiled to himself, stood and walked from the church, dismissively thrusting the local villeins from his path as he went.

Outside he studied the land more closely. Always important to know the lie of the neighbouring lands when you ran a good-sized manor like Sir Geoffrey's.

Baldwin and Matthew stood before Nicholas as the people gradually left the church. Matthew held up his hand and roared quickly before they could all depart that he was about to begin a Mass, and a few men and women from the vill shrugged and turned back, but all the men-at-arms were gone before Matthew could even go to robe himself for the service.

As he was preparing to leave to fetch what he needed, eyeing the crowd with a certain satisfaction, Baldwin muttered, 'You will have to have someone guard this place, Father. They may come back.'

'Yes, of course. Um.' His mind was more on the prayers and service to come than on the felon sitting miserably at the end of his altar, and Baldwin doubted that he would remember Baldwin's words for the time it took a leaf to fall to the ground.

'No matter,' he murmured to himself as he went to join Simon and Edgar. But just before he had reached them, a thought struck him. He turned away and out into the crisp air. Long plumes of steam rose from the horses and men who remained in the churchyard, but the coroner was nowhere to be seen.

'Where is Coroner Edward?' he demanded of a peasant pushing a small two-wheeled cart.

'Him? Back to the hall, I reckon.'

'What of the inquest?'

'Oh, he held that before we came out here.'

Baldwin looked at him, at first appalled, then furious. 'That prickle held the inquest without us? Without me? When I'd told Sir Geoffrey that I wanted to be present? Who was there?'

Perkin drew the corners of his mouth down. 'Some of the vill's freemen, and others from the manor itself.'

'You were there?'

'Yes. I was there.'

'I shall want to speak to you.' Baldwin glanced at his burden. On the cart was a linen-wrapped body. 'You are here to bury someone?'

'Our priest,' Perkin said. 'He died yesterday. I was bringing him for burial.'

'Take him on to the church. I shall await you here.'

Chapter Thirty-Two

Humphrey woke with his head a screaming agony. For a long moment he remained with his eyes screwed tightly shut, petrified by the thought of what he might see when he opened them. Visions of Hugh with a sharp knife already smeared with blood – his blood! – sprang into his mind, and he whimpered at the thought of imminent death. 'Don't, please don't . . .'

'Don't what?' Hugh demanded.

Opening his eyes cautiously, Humphrey saw that Hugh was at the far side of the room. The pain in his head came from his having banged his bruised skull against a rock lying on the ground. He gazed at the rock reproachfully, then pushed himself up and sat with his back to the wall. His head still hurt abominably, and he felt dizzy, but he would recover. 'What will you do with me?'

Hugh glanced at him. He was like a man who had a single focus to all his thoughts and nothing else could intrude on them for long. 'What?'

'Will you kill me?'

'I don't know. I can't have you letting people know where I am, though,' Hugh said distractedly.

'Where is the friar?'

'He's outside making sure we're safe and no one's trying to find us.'

'Oh.'

'What would you have done? Were you thinking you could stay here for ever?'

'Hmm? What, there at the chapel? No, I suppose not. I think I did mean to rob Isaac and the church when I went to him in the first place. But then I grew to like him, and the people down here. It's a good little vill, Monkleigh. There are some arseholes, but most of the peasants are as good as any. I started to think that if I robbed the church, all I'd be doing would be taking money from them. The Church would demand compensation for any thefts from the place, and those fines would fall on all the poorest people in the vill. Fines always do.'

Hugh grunted agreement.

'What will you do?' Humphrey asked at last.

Hugh looked up at him, then out through the door, and lastly up at the sky overhead.

'I . . . I don't know,' he admitted brokenly. 'Someone killed my woman, and I want revenge – but how can I learn who killed her?'

'You were lucky to remain alive,' Humphrey said without thinking.

'Lucky?' Hugh spat. He jumped to his feet and strode to Humphrey. 'I saw her die, and her son, and they knocked me down and left me for dead.'

'I didn't mean to insult you, friend,' Humphrey said desperately.

The raised voice had alerted John. He stood in the doorway, his gaze going from one to the other. When he spoke, his voice was calm. 'Hugh, there's no need to lose your temper with him.'

'I know!' Hugh said, spinning on his heel and leaving the cowering priest lying at the foot of the wall. 'It's just . . . why *did* they leave me alive?'

'As a symbol? You were a living message to others that they should be fearful. Some men have minds that work in that way.'

Hugh tested his leg. It was all but mended now, and he grunted with satisfaction. 'They'll regret it.'

'Now Hugh,' John said, entering the room and sitting near the fire. 'What do you plan to do?'

'I want to find the man who had Constance killed.'

'And I want the man who killed Lucy of Meeth. Perhaps they are the same?'

'Perhaps.'

'Then we can work together to find him.'

Sir Geoffrey slammed the door and walked out into the open area before the hall when he heard the riders thundering down the lane towards him. At first all he could see was the steam rising as a form of heat-haze in the lane, beyond his old hedge. Then there were the two leather caps of his bodyguards, whom he had sent in order to make sure that none of the men tried to desert, then the horses breasted the entrance, and he could see them all. There in the middle was Sir Edward with his hair moving from side to side as the wind caught the short strands. A vain man, Sir Geoffrey thought, and vain men always had their weaknesses.

'And?'

'I almost had him,' Sir Edward said with a bitter shake of his head. 'I had him in the palm of my hand, and the priest defended him. The damned knight from Furnshill stood up to me as well and it seemed sensible not to force the issue. Especially with Sir Odo's men all around.'

'I understand,' Sir Geoffrey said, and turned on his heel.

'Wait! What do you mean by that?' Coroner Edward demanded. He had dropped from his horse, and now he stepped up to Sir Geoffrey in a hurry. 'Are you suggesting something?'

'I dare say many would be scared to think that they could be bested in a church,' Sir Geoffrey said harshly. 'All you had to do was bring him back here so that we could judge him here, on our land. And if we found he was guilty, we could have hanged him here.'

'You don't have the right!'

'I can impose a death sentence if the coroner is present to hear it, and I can hang a man if the coroner is there to witness it. Don't tell me my rights, Sir Edward! I have been here longer than you! I know the ancient rights of this manor, and I know your job too. I was a coroner before you were born!'

Sir Edward blinked. He had not anticipated such a storm of rage over losing the man. 'He is in the church. He will be permitted to abjure, if he wishes.'

'Abjure *my arse*! I want him here to answer our questions. I want to know why that girl was in the mire in the first place.'

'Really?' Sir Edward said, and he cocked an eyebrow. So far as he could see, Sir Geoffrey was building up an alibi and creating an environment in which his own determination to discover the culprit could not be in doubt. It was clever, the coroner thought, but hardly clever enough. 'You know that Keeper? He has the reputation of a man who sees the truth no matter how well hidden. He is supposed to be honourable.'

'All men are honourable until they need money,' Sir Geoffrey snapped.

'What will you do now?'

'Cause that poor soul to be returned to her manor to be buried, and then I shall do what I should have done yesterday.'

'What is that?'

'Attack Sir Odo's places this side of the river with all my men. I've had enough of this flouncing about in case someone is offended.'

'You cannot mean that? You'll start a war on Sir Odo's lands?'

'You've realised nothing, have you?' Sir Geoffrey spat. He turned, thumbs stuck in his belt, and stared at the coroner. 'You think I'm devious and manipulative, and I've set up all this machinery just so that I can take the spoils . . . but what if it's shown that I am little better than a felon and a cutpurse? Oh, I will win the king's pardon, no doubt, but that will be some while away. And in the meantime I'll be an outlaw. You think I want that? Someone has been acting with great skill and determination to make me look like a murderer. The death of the woman from Meeth, the murder of the family in Iddesleigh, the murder of my own damned sergeant – all done to point to my guilt. Can't you even understand that?'

Sir Edward nodded slowly. 'And you think that this was all Sir Odo's doing?'

'I'll spring a surprise on him that he will never forget. He wanted to make me outlaw? I'll return the gift with compliments. He will regret the day he sought to put the blame for these deaths on me!'

'So you are Perkin?' Baldwin said.

The body had been deposited in the church with Matthew, and now they were at the inn with quarts of ale before them all. Simon was glaring balefully at the fire, and for some reason Edgar was looking amused. Baldwin had hissed at him to wipe the grin off his face, but to no avail.

Perkin sat uneasily in this company. 'Yes . . .'

'Stop fidgeting, man!' Baldwin growled. 'I'm not going to hurt you, but I want to hear from you all about the death of Ailward, and of Lady Lucy, too.'

Simon leaned forward. 'But first, what can you tell us about the murder of the man up the way from here? Hugh Shepherd, his wife and their boy were all killed. Do you know anything about that?'

Shaking his head, Perkin said, 'If I knew anything, I would tell you, on my oath. It was one of those nights when I was . . . tired. I had been working hard all the day, and when I finished I went to my friend Beorn's house and drank with him. He had some ale that had to be finished so he could put another brew on. There was rather more than I'd expected, or it was stronger than I was used to, and I slept well that night. It was last Saturday, I think?'

Baldwin looked up at Jankin, who nodded.

Perkin continued: 'We all saw the men riding off in the late afternoon, and we wondered where they were going, but they set off down towards the river. Of course we know now where they were heading: to Robert Crokers's house. Sir Geoffrey and Sir Odo have been bickering about that bit of land for some while. Sir Geoffrey claims that it's part of the old estate and should have been passed to him when the lands were taken.'

'Taken from Ailward's family?' Simon confirmed.

'Yes. Poor Malkin and Lady Isabel have nothing left, really. They lost house, lands, livestock, the lot. Sir Geoffrey argues that the plot where Sir Odo installed Robert Crokers was actually part of the confiscated estate and should be passed to him, but Sir Odo claims that the land was held in fief from his lord, Lord de Courtenay. Both rattle their swords, but neither wants a war.'

'Did you hear the men come back?'

'No. As I say, I was at Beorn's house.'

'Did you know of any man who could have sought to harm Hugh?' Simon pressed.

'No. He was a miserable cur, though – never smiled, except when he looked at his wife or the boy. That was no surprise – she was a woman to be proud of. But apart from the normal ribaldry, no one made any comments. I don't know of any arguments with him. Both of them kept themselves to themselves, I think. He wasn't sociable.'

That was true enough, Baldwin told himself. 'What of Sir Geoffrey? He had his men at Robert's place earlier that same day – could he have gone from there up to Hugh's and attacked in the evening?'

'Yes, but I can't understand why he'd attack just the man Hugh. There are others up here whom he hates more.'

'Very well, then,' Baldwin said, after glancing at Simon. 'What can you tell us about the other dead man? Ailward?'

'That really rattled me,' Perkin admitted, and as he spoke his frame shook like a nettle in the wind. 'I'd seen him only a little while earlier, and suddenly there he was, stretched on the grass, dead.'

'Someone said that there had been a camp ball match that day?'

'Yes. It's an annual game we hold here between Monkleigh and Iddesleigh. Been going on for donkey's years. Everyone joins in; we play from one end of Furze Down to the other. First to get the bladder in the enemy's goal is the winner. And we'd have won this year, if it wasn't for bloody Walter. He was up there on the hillside when I got above the stream, and he just knocked me down and grabbed the thing.'

Baldwin could easily imagine the sight: twenty or thirty men haring along, one gripping the ball, and another thirty-odd hoping to take it from him. Camp ball was so dangerous, had caused so many brawls and arguments in his own manor, that he had been tempted to ban it from his lands, but there too the sport was ancient, and although he had seen the most appalling injuries, men and girls still wanted to play. 'Was that when you found the body?'

'No,' Perkin said. He looked away uncomfortably. 'I don't want to speak ill of the dead, you understand?'

'Of course,' Baldwin said. He allowed a little steel to enter his voice as he added, 'But I must have the truth about the whole circumstance.'

'There was something about it. When I was knocked down, I saw Ailward standing a little way distant. He was a Monkleigh man, but he made no effort to save me. He just stood and watched as Walter knocked me down and threw the bladder away. It troubled me.'

'And?'

'When Walter stopped me,' Perkin said more slowly, 'he grabbed me about the waist and legs, and threw me bodily to the ground. I was flying, and while I flew, I thought I saw some signs that looked odd – like blood on the heather. It was just a fleeting glimpse, though, nothing definite.'

'Where was this?'

'Near to where Ailward was standing.'

'Take us there,' Baldwin said.

It was about noon when John returned at, for him, a fast amble. Since staying here to look after Hugh, he had found his own feet were improving no end. Being able to rest with them warming by a fire at first made his chilblains protest, but later made them subside. The old cracks from too much walking that stabbed so cruelly were binding again, and soon he thought he might be able to move with less of the crabbed, sailor's gait that had grown so habitual since he left Exeter.

The house was quiet, and for a moment he was aware of a fear that Hugh might have executed their captive, but as soon as he entered, he saw Hugh scowling ferociously at the man as he ate voraciously from a bowl of the soup left over from the night before. John saw that Hugh had untied his arms and legs, and was relieved. He had been concerned that the man could lose all feeling in them if they were bound tightly for too long.

Humphrey glanced up as he entered, and in his eyes there was a little fear, but then his attention went to the doorway behind John, and as it became apparent that there was no one outside his brow cleared and he met John's eye with gratitude.

'So you sought to torture the poor fellow with your cooking?' John tried jovially.

Hugh set his head to one side. '*You* made it. *I* just heated it.'

'I think I have good news for you. There is a Keeper of the King's Peace here, and a Bailiff Puttock. They say that they were called here to seek your murderer.'

Hugh gazed up at him with hope filling his soul. 'Sir Baldwin and my master? They're here?'

'And actively hunting down the murderer, yes.'

It made Hugh glad, but it was also an anticlimax. He felt as though the responsibility for finding Constance's murderer was taken from him, and that was a relief . . . and a curse as well. She was *his* wife, her murderer was *his* enemy. It would be easy to rest now, to allow Sir Baldwin and Simon to find the killer, but Hugh had to do it. It was a matter of honour.

'Are you well?' John asked.

'I'm fine. Be all right in a while. Leave me.'

John nodded, understanding his confusion, and went to Humphrey. He glanced at the man's wrists, where the thongs had cut into the flesh. It was fortunate that Hugh had removed them when they had, or else this man could have lost his hands.

There was no longer any point in keeping him captive. He had admitted to his crime, and although it was shocking, it was not so rare. When so many men worked for the Church, occasionally anger would flare and a man would die. Jealousy or rage could consume an entire community. Yes, John could sympathise with this man.

'What would you do, Humphrey?' he asked. 'Stay here, or move on to another place where you'll have to scrape a living again?'

'I don't know. I can't remain at the chapel now, so I suppose I'll have to wander again,' Humphrey said mournfully.

'You can keep moving, I suppose, but it would make for no life,' John guessed.

Humphrey shook at the memory. The nights he had spent on the run . . . Once he had been lying under a hedge, mournfully reminding himself of his miserable fall, when he had noticed a shrew or a mouse in the stubble of the field not far from him. He watched, entranced, while the little figure scraped and muzzled about the ground searching for gleanings. Every so often it would rise to its hind legs and sniff the air as though convinced that there was someone watching it, but not sure who or where.

And then Humphrey all but leapt from his skin as a silent, pale, wraithlike figure swooped down and took it. He could have died in that moment, the way his heart thundered in his breast. It was so sudden, so terrifying!

The barn owl took off again, effortlessly rising through the cool night's air, and he watched it go with genuine terror, expecting a similar shape to appear at any moment and haul him away to hell.

There were very few nights when he had managed to make use of a rick, hayloft or barn. After a month he was rancid and exhausted. His bones ached, his feet were worn, and he was close to collapse. That was when he had arrived in Hatherleigh and seen Isaac for the first time.

'There may be a better way,' John said. 'Perhaps we could persuade the bishop to give you a trial at the chapel?'

'He will give me a trial,' Humphrey said bitterly.

'It is possible with the support of a local magnate and other priests in the area that you may receive a happier hearing than you might expect,' John said. 'It is worth trying, I should think. Better than living as a felon for the rest of your days.'

'Perhaps.'

John turned his attention back to Hugh. The morose figure was cross-legged on the floor near the fire. 'Have you eaten yet?'

'I'm not hungry.'

John crouched at his feet and fixed him with a firm eye. 'If you want revenge and justice, my friend, you will need to keep your strength up. Now eat, while I tell you what I saw and heard in Iddesleigh this day!'

Chapter Thirty-Three

It was a long, scrubby plain, with furze bushes sticking up here and there, a stunted tree, and rocks all about as always. The soil was good, but here on the moor there was only pasture. 'No plough would cut into this without breaking in the first yard,' Baldwin muttered, looking about him.

Perkin had taken them along the track past Hugh's house, and out the other side to the moor, and then led them across the rough ground to the top of the ridge from where they could look down into the stream.

'This is the way I came, you see. They expected us all on the plain there, because then we could have rushed them in a solid mass. But if we'd done that, they could have encircled us and done us great damage. So instead we sent a number of our men up that way, while Beorn and I came up here. It was out of the way, but we thought that the change of direction would confuse them. It looked as if it was going to work, too.'

'What happened?'

Perkin walked a little way along the ridge until he found a mess of mud. 'That's where we came up. Our feet churned the soil. Then I came over here, and I was running at my fastest to reach their goal over there.' He pointed. 'That's when I saw Walter and Ailward. Both of them were down here. Walter jumped up and went for me, and that was that.'

'So you were knocked to the ground where?' Baldwin asked.

Perkin shrugged, but then he slowly grinned. 'There, on that blasted rock. See this scrape on my arm?' he asked, pulling up his sleeve. 'That rock there gave me that. Christ, but it hurt! Felt as if a rat had nibbled all down my forearm.'

'Where was Ailward?'

Perkin closed his eyes and turned his head a little, as though orientating his mind with the reality of the landscape. 'Over here,' he said. 'And when I came back here, this was where he lay, too.'

'It's only a half mile from Hugh's house, if that,' Simon muttered.

'Yes. And I think that this could be giving us a stronger clue about his death than we have had so far,' Baldwin said. 'What do you think the two men were doing up here, Perkin?'

He looked away, over the rolling lands to his home. It was there, over at Monkleigh, a low, thatched house like all the others. It was not much, but it was all that he had ever known, and suddenly he found himself wondering whether he would be able to remain there for much longer. The only witness to murder was not in a strong position.

'I thought that there was a body here. Where Ailward stood. I only caught a glimpse, and that while I was in the air, but I could swear that there was colour at his feet, like a body wearing a tunic. And I thought that I saw redness, a deep redness, like blood.'

'Did you not tell anyone?' Baldwin asked disbelievingly.

'What, at the time? No – my brain was partly addled, my arm was in great pain, and the only memory I have is of stumbling back down that hillside there to get to the tavern and try to forget the pain in my head. But all through that afternoon, my conviction grew that I was right, and there was a body at Ailward's feet.'

'You said you wouldn't speak ill of the dead,' Baldwin reminded him.

'That's right. Ailward tried to be a friend and companion, but his frustration and despair gnawed at him. He should have been a great knight with a destrier and all that, but instead he was a serf here. The best serf Sir Geoffrey could have hoped for, it's true, but still a serf to his mind, and a serf is only a pale reminder of a real man, sir. Isn't that what knights say?'

Baldwin flashed his teeth in a smile. 'Perhaps some do. Since I cannot grow a stalk of wheat to feed myself, I find I appreciate those men who can.'

'I wish you were my master, then,' Perkin said sadly. 'Here we are not respected.'

'Ailward was a serf, and he let his jealous nature get the better of him on occasion?'

'Too often.'

'This man Walter,' Simon said. 'What was he doing with Ailward? Is he also from your manor?'

'No. He is one of Sir Odo's mercenaries.'

'Yet the two were together up here? What did you think of that? Two enemies together?'

Perkin had the decency to be embarrassed. 'I thought . . . well, I wondered, really, whether Ailward might have caught a woman and killed her in a rage when she turned down his advances.'

'You mean Lady Lucy?'

'She was in all our minds at that time, Sir Baldwin. There was a great deal of concern for her since she had disappeared. I don't know exactly what I thought, but I reckoned that Ailward being up there meant he was up to no good. And then Walter hit me, and my thoughts went back to the game.'

'And later you returned because you thought you'd seen something?' Simon asked.

'Well, yes. I just thought, if I could find some blood, then that'd prove that Ailward had killed someone.'

'And as you say, everyone was thinking of this Lady Lucy.' Baldwin nodded.

'But when I got back, all there was was Ailward himself, and his gore smearing the furze.'

'Was he in the vill after the camp ball match?' Simon frowned, kicking at the soil.

'No. He never appeared. We all thought he was gone home.'

'So Walter and he were up here, and they had a body with them. Why? Where were they going to go with it?' Baldwin said. He looked carefully all about them. 'That, north, that is where Hugh's house lies. What of those houses east of us?'

Perkin followed the direction of his pointing finger. 'That's where Pagan lives. It was his father's old smithy. He was an armourer, you know.'

'An armourer?' Baldwin said. 'And the house next door?'

'That is Guy's.'

'Perkin, you have been most helpful, and I have one last task to ask of you. Could you tell us the way to the farm where Crokers lives?'

'Of course. Now?'

'No – in a moment.' Baldwin paused and studied the land before them. 'It looks as though Sir Geoffrey is off hunting. I wonder what quarry he'll seek today? So long as he avoids the church at Iddesleigh, I'll be content.'

He peered about in all directions, but there were three that kept attracting his eye: southwards to the hall of Sir Geoffrey, east to Pagan's house, and north towards Hugh's ruined cottage.

'But what were they doing with a body on the day of the camp ball match?' he said at last. 'They must have known it was going to happen.'

'Yes,' Perkin said. 'Everyone in all the vills knew about it. They came from two or three miles away to watch it.'

'So they must have known that they would be seen up here,' Baldwin said. 'Why would they run the risk of discovery by carrying a corpse over here after executing the poor woman?'

Simon looked over at the houses east. 'They had tortured her, hadn't they?'

'They wouldn't do that in the open air,' Baldwin agreed.

'You say that the man Pagan's father was an armourer?' Simon said.

'Yes.'

'So there is a forge up there?'

'Always used to be, yes.'

'Let's go and take a look, Baldwin. It won't take long.'

It was good always to feel the wind in your hair. Sir Geoffrey expected a token resistance at best; urgently fleeing peasants would be more likely. There was no point in their trying to protect this chunk of land from him. All the men down there would know full well that he was more or less their legitimate master, so they'd not dare raise even a thumb to bite at him.

He had disposed his host adequately. The two sergeants, his bodyguards, would take their little forces to the mill down by the chapel and to the ford further up. Meanwhile, Sir Geoffrey would lead the main force down the main road to Crokers's house. If all went well, without bloodshed they would win the whole of the old lands on this side of the river. Then they could start to move northwards and begin to loosen Sir Odo's stranglehold on Iddesleigh itself. That would be a sweet cherry to pluck, with the inn in the middle. On this road it would not make so much money as, say, a tavern on the Oxford to London road, but it would bring in a small fortune compared to Ailward's inheritance.

The fool. Sir Geoffrey wasn't sure what had happened, but he was fully aware that he was being set up as the clear and obvious suspect in a series of murders. He would not submit to any man, not even the suave and polite Sir Baldwin, to be tried for murder. That would mark him for life, even if he received a pardon in due course.

But it hurt unbearably to think that Sir Odo could have been so cunning as to think up this scheme when all the time Sir Geoffrey had thought he had the upper hand.

The houses were little more than sheds: simple cruck-built frames with cob used to fill the spaces. Perkin took them to Guy's house first. It was empty, because Guy himself would be in the coppice with his children. He lived the outdoor life of a charcoal-burner, and even now he had a great pile smoking away. Perkin told them that his wife was off helping Beorn's wife brew ale. It was often a collaborative task.

Baldwin glanced at Simon as they moved towards the farther of the two properties. For his own part, his hand kept straying to the hilt of his sword, as though seeking comfort from it. But there could be no comfort in a place like this. Baldwin was aware of a heaviness in his soul at the thought that this was a place where a young woman could have been dragged, perhaps screaming and desperate, only to be bound and tortured to death.

'This Pagan,' he said. 'Tell me, Perkin: does he work for Sir Geoffrey?'

'No, never. He was always devoted to Sir William and Sir Robert.'

'Lady Isabel's husband and his father?'

'Yes. Pagan would spit on money offered to him by Sir Geoffr he still thinks that the family should return to their own house. As do most of us.'

'A bold comment, friend,' Baldwin noted.

'Our new master is a leader of thieves and felons. How can we be loyal to him?' Perkin snapped.

'If I am right you will not have to compromise your loyalty for long,' Baldwin said. 'If he has a part in this murder, I shall see him taken to Exeter, I swear.'

'You think he does?' Perkin asked hopefully.

Baldwin shook his head ruminatively. 'All I can say for certain is that Pagan appears to have some explaining to do, as does this Walter. This is the house?'

They had reached a ramshackle building with green walls and a roof composed of chestnut shingles – a rare sight in Devonshire. Baldwin put his hand to the door and opened the latch. He pushed. There was a squeak and a scraping noise as the timbers moved over the rough flooring.

It was a small chamber, perhaps only twelve feet by ten. A hearth lay in the middle of the floor, a cauldron nearby. There was a stench of rancid ale about the room, and on the single low table there was a hunk of dry bread and some ancient cheese, on which the flies were eagerly prancing. A palliasse was rolled neatly and rested on a shelf, while in a hollow dug out of the wall there stood all the man's most prized possessions: a small crucifix, a shell and lead pilgrim's badge. There was also a malformed horseshoe.

Baldwin picked it up. 'This is a terrible piece of work.'

'What of it? It's not for sale.'

'Ah! Pagan, I was wondering whether you would join us here,' Baldwin said, eyeing the old but well-polished sword in his hand.

'So what are you doing in my house?' Pagan demanded.

'Looking for evidence that you are a murderer,' Baldwin said.

'Me?' Pagan's face seemed to fall, but then he held his head at an angle and pointed the sword more aggressively. 'You dare to accuse me?'

'Man, I would put that sword down,' Baldwin said firmly, and waited until he had. 'We know that your father was an armourer, and that you are living up here. When Lady Lucy was killed she was tortured to death. Her body was taken all the way down to the camp ball game, and then over to the mire at the back of Sir Geoffrey's house – a mire you would know all too well since you used to live there with your master – and thrown in.'

'Why should I do all that?' Pagan blustered. 'She was no enemy of mine!'

'It is just possible that you decided to throw her in there to place suspicion on to Sir Geoffrey so that he would be removed from the manor. Perhaps you thought you might be able to win it back for your lady, if you first had him evicted from it.'

'I had nothing to do with her death. I only heard of her murder after she was found,' Pagan said.

'Show us your father's forge.'

Pagan wavered, then rammed his sword back into its sheath, and led the way back out through the front door, round the building to a small lean-to shed that stood at the rear. A square chimney of steel projected from the roof, and the ground here was all darkened with black dust. Lumps of clinker lay about; deformed, sharpened pieces of hardened stone or metal. They had been trodden into the ground all about here as a means of keeping the mud at bay.

Pagan opened the door and shoved it wide. 'Go on, take a look.'

Baldwin glanced at Edgar, who stood near the door with his eyes fixed on Pagan while Baldwin and Simon walked inside.

It was dark, but when Baldwin had released the two shutters and allowed the light to enter, he found himself in a room that was perhaps six feet by ten. There were racks of metal, mostly rough pigs of steel, and a sturdy little anvil that stood on a large oak block made from a single log. Staples had been hammered into it, and a series of tools hung from them: pincers, pliers, shaped devices to grip and twist hot metal. Baldwin looked about him and felt his flesh cringe. It was so like the rooms he had heard of in France during the torture of the Templars.

'Nothing here, see?' Pagan said.

Baldwin did not hear him, and it was only when Pagan touched his arm to repeat his comment that Baldwin reacted.

He spun, his hand reaching out and taking Pagan's shirt in his fist, while his other hand flew to his dagger and pulled it free. While he wrenched at Pagan's shirt, forcing him back against the wall, his dagger's point was under Pagan's chin.

'Did you do it to her? If you did, tell me now and I'll end your life quickly right here.'

Pagan's head was at the wall, but there was no fear in his eyes as he shook his head. Surprise, yes, but no fear. 'I am used to the idea of death, Sir Knight. Your blade doesn't scare me. I swear I had nothing to do with the death of that child. I couldn't have hurt a hair on her. Not a woman.'

Baldwin felt a thrill of revulsion run through his soul. He had a sudden vision of Pagan lying at his feet, the blood pumping from a slash in his throat, and the thought made him feel physically sick. Yet it was this room. It had all the atmosphere of a place of torture, and such places reminded him only too clearly of the hideous injustice committed against his companions in the Order.

'It's just a workshop,' Simon said.

Baldwin released the man and sheathed his dagger. 'I am sorry, Pagan. I should not have done that. It was . . . just a feeling I had. I am sorry.'

Simon was quite right, too. It was a smithy, nothing more. There was the forge. There was the anvil, the tools, the foot bellows to pump air to the fire, now well rotten. 'It is only rarely used now?'

Pagan shrugged. 'I don't think anyone has used the place in ten years or more. When was Kells? I forget. I have never used it myself. I once made a horseshoe, the one you saw. I would not have made a good smith.'

Simon grunted. He could understand that. While Baldwin and the smith's son talked, he wandered around the place. There was a fine black dust all about, and he ran his fingers in it, rubbing it between thumb and forefinger. It was rough to the touch, and smelled metallic. At one point there was a tall, straight tree-limb supporting the roof with another series of staples set into it, some hung with more tools like the ones on the anvil. All were rusty and darkened with the iron filings and dust. He moved on, and saw a little rag on the floor.

It was nothing, just a shred of bright green material, but it made him pause in wonder for a moment, and then he realised why: it was relatively free of the dust that lay all over everything else. He stooped to pick it up, and found that there was a crust of black stuff on the underside. Immediately he knew what it was, and even as he called Baldwin, his eyes were on the supporting timber in front of him.

This was farther from the anvil, and had no tools hanging from it, but there was one staple, set up high. It had one face that was bright and uncrusted.

'She was here,' he said.

Chapter Thirty-Four

Robert Crokers set the bowl at the bitch's head and she looked up at him appreciatively.

By some miracle, bearing in mind the barbaric wound inflicted on her, only two pups had been stillborn. She herself had lost some blood, and he wondered whether there would be a fresh gush, as he'd sometimes seen in other animals giving birth. When that happened, it meant that the mother was sure to die, and he only prayed that she would be safe.

And so she was. After giving birth to four healthy little squirming, mewling blind and bald lumps, she set to cleaning herself and them while he stood by watching them with delight. In that moment he had felt his heart swell with pride, as though these were his own creation. It must be how a father felt, he thought, on seeing a child for the first time. An awe and awareness of how unimportant he was; his only purpose was to serve these little scraps of flesh.

The pups looked much like rats, they were so small, pink and blind. It was impossible to look at them and see that they would one day grow to be like her. For now all he could do was hope that they'd show even a small portion of the intelligence she had. She'd always been a good worker, and the fact that she'd been so badly hurt spoke volumes of the way that she'd tried to protect her master and his land. He reached down cautiously to touch one, and stopped when he heard the low rumbling snarl.

'You're right, little girl. They're yours, not mine. I've no place here.' He smiled and backed away from her. She watched him for a moment, then appeared to give a mental shrug and set to cleaning them again.

That was when he heard the hooves.

*   *   *

'You still say you had nothing to do with the woman's death?' Baldwin rasped. He grabbed Pagan's arm.

'What are you talking about?'

Simon held the cloth to him. 'Whose dress did this come from?'

'I don't know.'

'Lady Lucy of Meeth. She wore a dress like this. And this has her blood on it.'

'I should think it was used as a gag,' Baldwin said. He was tempted to punch Pagan, to beat the truth from him. 'And the staple.'

Pagan shook his head. 'What of it?'

'It's been hammered in only recently,' Simon said. 'So when you said no one's been in here for ten years or so, that was a lie.'

'I don't know who could have been here. I haven't been inside in ten or more years. I lived at the manor until we were thrown from there, and then I lived with my master Ailward and his family, until Ailward's death. Then I came back up here to sleep, but only to my room. Not here to the smithy. Why should I?'

Simon grunted. 'Baldwin, that's one thing Isabel and Malkin told us, you remember? That Pagan used to live with them until Ailward died. And Lucy died before him, if we believe what Perkin has said.'

Baldwin slowly released Pagan. 'True. But who else could have come up here?'

'Ailward could have,' Simon said. 'He knew of this place because he knew his grandfather's armourer. And he knew that no one was living here now. So it would be secure.'

'Perkin,' Baldwin said. 'You say that the man Guy just near here is a charcoal burner? Was he burning coals when Ailward died? Charcoal burners often take their families with them. Does this Guy?'

'Yes his family was with him in the week before that.'

'So if Lady Lucy was here, no one would hear her screams?' Baldwin said.

'I suppose not,' Perkin said nervously. The sudden burst of anger from these two men had shocked him. It shouldn't, but he hadn't expected such raw ferocity.

'Ailward and Walter,' Simon breathed.

'I want to speak to this Walter,' Baldwin said. He took one last look about the room and swept out.

Hugh heard them first. It was a part of him, this wariness. In the past it had been so that he could protect his flock from wolves or foxes, keep the lambs safe from buzzards or crows or magpies; now it was the in-built defence against predators on two legs that sent him scurrying towards the door when he heard hooves.

There were two men on horseback cantering down the track, and he peered round the door frame as they pelted towards the bridge over the river that led to Iddesleigh.

'Who was it?' Friar John asked in a whisper.

'I don't know,' Hugh admitted. 'Men hurrying down that way . . .'

'They came from up there?' John asked, pointing.

'Yes.'

'I was there not long ago. It would be a good place to watch Fishleigh, Sir Odo's house.'

'Why would someone watch there?' Hugh said.

Humphrey cleared his throat. 'It was said in Monkleigh that Sir Geoffrey sought to take over the whole of the lands east of the river. If he was launching an attack, he might set men up here to see when Sir Odo's men were marshalled . . .'

Hugh nodded. 'True enough.' But now he was feeling a strange sensation. The noise of horses pounding past had set off a series of connections. It wasn't anything to do with horses, though, he felt. No, rather it was a set of noises at night. People . . . The priest, Matthew! That was it! Constance had seen the priest outside in the lane, and he had thought there could be no harm in it because he was a priest, and had slammed the door shut. 'The priest . . .' he murmured.

'What?' Friar John asked.

'Nothing. I have to go. See what's happening there,' Hugh said.

It was well past noon when Baldwin re-entered the inn.

'Jeanne, I am sorry to have been so long. I think that we are making some progress,' he explained as he walked into their little chamber.

His wife was sitting on their bed, breastfeeding Richalda. 'I am glad to hear that. I don't want to stay here alone too long. Emma is driving me mad.'

'What's she up to now?'

'She would try a saint. She keeps walking out, inventing errands. I have no need of her running to the farm to ask for milk for me to drink, but she feels the need to go. Earlier she went to seek a biscuit for me, and then it was a blanket for Richalda. I don't know what's got into her.'

'Nothing,' Baldwin said. 'It's just because she's hungover, I think. She is leaving here to go and vomit.'

'Possibly,' Jeanne said, wiping her breast as Richalda sat up and smiled at Baldwin. 'What are you going to do now?'

'We are off to question the man who was with Ailward on the day he died . . . the man who was carrying the body of Lady Lucy with him,' Baldwin said, and explained briefly what they had learned. 'I do not know how this man Walter will respond when I speak to him. He may be entirely blameless, although if he is not guilty of murdering that poor woman, I fail to understand what he was doing up there on the moor with a man from the other manor. He must have known that his master Sir Odo and Sir Geoffrey were at daggers drawn.'

'You will be careful?' she asked quickly.

'Against one man? When I have Simon and Edgar at my side? I have little to fear,' Baldwin said. He kissed her. 'Why is Emma taking so long? I don't want you alone. You should have her with you.'

'At least she was good enough not to disturb our sleep last night,' Jeanne pointed out.

'True enough.' Baldwin hesitated, wondering again where she might have been, but dismissed the thought as he hurried out to re-join Simon and Edgar. He busied himself making sure that his horse was ready again, and when he glanced up he saw again that curious expression of amusement on his servant's face.

It troubled him as he tested the girth of his saddle before swinging himself up into the seat. Edgar was not usually given to levity.

It was quick, it was easy.

Surprise was the most important element in a good battle. Don't give them time to think or plan, just get in and take what you need. Sir

Geoffrey led his men along the road from the rear of the house, up from the river, the line that that idiot sergeant would least expect, and by the time the force had come into view and the sergeant and his man-at-arms had realised that these were not men from Sir Odo, it was too late; the Monkleigh men were in among them. One rode up to the door and dropped from his horse to go inside and seek spoils, while others herded the two men from the place, forcing them out of the way.

Walter was petrified, Sir Geoffrey saw. Well, good! He knew what a raiding party like this could be capable of, and he had every right to be fearful. The other man, what was his name, that sergeant? Crokers? He had no spirit at all. He stood with his body downcast, and as the men circled and stamped about the place he simply looked up with a sort of pleading expression. Pleading, indeed. He was caught up in the theft of Lord Despenser's property, and Sir Geoffrey was here to recover it.

'You two are not to come back here,' he commanded from his horse. 'This land belongs to my Lord Despenser, and if you return as trespassers I will have you captured and gaoled. My gaol can be an unpleasant place. So go! Leave this place and don't return.'

Walter nodded quickly. He started to move, but only made a few steps when he realised that the sergeant wasn't with him.

'This land belongs to Sir John Sully,' Robert declared, 'and in his name I deny your right to appropriate it!'

'Go home, boy! This is not your land, it's not your fight, and it's none of your concern. This land was taken from Ailward's family long ago. It is time to return it to the proper owners.'

'It is theft!'

'Don't try my patience!' Sir Geoffrey roared. His sword was out, and he spurred his destrier forward. 'See this? This sword was made for me by my lord. I will not have you nor any other man denying his authority here. Understand?'

Robert looked up sulkily. He opened his mouth, felt the tip of the sword's blade tickle under his chin and swallowed hurriedly. Then he closed his eyes. 'This land is owned by Sir John Sully, vassal to Lord Hugh de Courtenay, and this act is theft!'

'Oh, just get him out of my sight,' Sir Geoffrey snarled. 'He makes me want to puke!'

Walter relaxed. He saw that they'd be able to escape now, and he wanted to get back to Fishleigh and safety. 'Come on, Robert. We'll soon be back.'

It was at that moment that there was a hideous shriek from the house. A man swore, and there was the sound of growling, a squeal, a series of hacking sounds, and then nothing.

As Walter watched uncomprehendingly, a man appeared in the doorway with a sack in one hand, a bloody corpse in the other. 'Does he want his dog, too? I saved the puppies,' he laughed, a high, lunatic giggle, and swung the sack against the house's wall.

Robert gave an incoherent gasp, and lurched forward. Then he pulled out his dagger and ran at the man – but Robert was no killer. He was too calm and gentle to have learned how to stab, slash and kill.

Sir Geoffrey lifted his sword high over his head and brought it down on Robert's head.

Nicholas le Poter ached all over. Sitting here at the side of the altar, his backside was sore, his arms had a loose, heavy sensation as though they were slowly being pulled from their sockets, and his neck was a mass of tense, corded muscles that felt as though they were going to snap at any time from the terrible weight of his head. On top of that, his back still seemed to be on fire, and now he had a headache from his dismal thoughts.

He hadn't dared sleep. Not even here, not while the priest was here to protect him. No, he couldn't, it was too dangerous. While Sir Geoffrey's men were after him, he could be cut down or dragged from this place at any time. He had no false illusions about their abilities.

The first thing Matthew had done was take away his dagger. 'I'll not have you causing bloodshed in here,' he had said.

'What if they come to kill me?'

'It's a risk you'll have to take. But you will not remain here with that knife about you.'

At least with the guards from Sir Odo's here he was probably safe. They were all rough, powerful men. Plainly Sir Odo had himself thought that he was in danger and wanted to protect him – if only to irritate Sir Geoffrey.

Last night he had nodded for a few moments at a time, but never long enough to become refreshed. He was dog-tired now, like a man who'd been training for too long in one session. Before, when he'd felt like this, he'd been able to take a hot bath, but there was nowhere for him to go if he wanted to be safe. If he was found outside this place, he'd be killed in a moment.

He could abjure: tell the coroner that he would swear to leave the realm by whatever route the coroner dictated, and then head for the sea to find a ship to take him away. All his property was forfeit, of course, but at least he would live. The only alternative was to remain here until his time ran out and the coroner could legally remove him to be held ready for the justices of gaol delivery. And then he'd be hanged. There was little doubt of that.

There were some he could count on, perhaps. Some of the men in Sir Geoffrey's camp were his mates. They wouldn't want to see one of their own get topped just because of politics. Sweet Jesus, even if he had killed the girl, there was no need for him to be thrown to the likes of Sir Edward. And most of Sir Geoffrey's men must realise that Sir Geoffrey was the man who'd done it. Not him; not Nicholas. If Sir Geoffrey could throw *him* to the wolves, who would be next?

No, there were some who would help him, like Adcock. Adcock had helped him up, had sent him on his way when Sir Geoffrey had told him he was going to be killed. There were others there like Adcock. They had told him that they'd support him if he tried to oust Sir Geoffrey, after all. Their loyalty must be worth something . . .

With a terrifying vision of the truth, he felt his bones freeze. His teeth chattered together, and his left arm gave a nervous twitch that made the cross shake.

Not one of them had done anything more than give him verbal support. Any of them could deny speaking to him. To cover their arses, they'd all act like his chief prosecutors, just to make sure that they were safe themselves.

He was so torn between rage and the sense of deep frustration that he had failed utterly at all he had attempted, that he felt he must burst.

And then he felt the sobs welling up with the tears, and he abandoned himself to the numbing terror. He had no idea what he should do, to whom he could turn, or where he might run to. All he could think of was the marginal safety of this church, and the fact of the altar cloth in his hands. They were real, they were substantial. With the tears falling from his cheeks, he bent to the cloth to sniff it, and took in the clean odour of the fresh air from when it had been left to hang in the open to dry. It smelled like freedom to him, sitting uncomfortably there on the cold church floor.

A freedom he might never know again. He screwed the thin material in his hands with his returning grief, and to his horror heard a slight ripping sound. There was a moment of agonised suspense, and then he looked at the cloth.

He had torn it. He felt as though he had savaged his hopes of safety.

Baldwin rode into Fishleigh's court with Simon and Edgar at either side.

The place was rather like a castle without the curtain wall. Set on top of a good-sized hillock, it had a ditch dug round it to make attack more difficult, and the entrance was reached by a small drawbridge. Once over it they were in among the bustle of the great house.

Servants were everywhere, fetching and carrying stores from one outer building to a large undercroft beneath what Baldwin took to be the great hall. A number of men-at-arms were present, all of them apparently set upon readying their weapons. Rasping could be heard from all sides as blades were whetted and honed, axes had their heads run over the great stones, and bills were taken from their short hedging handles and thrust upon long staves so that they could be used to slash at horses or their riders.

'This is an encampment readying itself for war,' Simon breathed.

'I fear so,' Baldwin said. He glanced about him with some anxiety. 'I can see no sign of the master. Where is Sir Odo?' he asked a man nearby.

A boy was sent scurrying to the stables, and after a few minutes the genial figure of Sir Odo was hobbling towards them, his scarred face twisted into a grin.

'Sir Keeper, and Bailiff Simon as well? We are glad to see you, gentles. Would you take some wine with me?'

Once in the hall with him, Baldwin was able to tell him what they had learned up on the moor.

'So you think that one of my men could have had something to do with this?'

'We know that a man called Walter was up there with Ailward. A witness says he saw what looked like blood on the ground near the two, and later the same day when he went up there, he found Ailward's body. This man Walter may know something of what was happening. It may be that there was a strip of red cloth on the ground, nothing more than that. But if it was the woman from Meeth . . .'

'I quite understand. I shall have him called to me here and you shall question him.'

'So you are his master?'

'Yes.'

Baldwin walked towards the door and peered out at the compound. 'You are expecting Sir Geoffrey to attack you and your lands?'

'He knows he has to. If he wants to iron out matters with his lord, he'll have to mollify the man somehow. One way to do that would be to take some extra lands. From anyone.'

'The land on which his manor stands once belonged to Ailward's family?' Baldwin asked, returning to the seat where a cup of wine waited for him.

'That's right. Until Ailward's grandfather died, his was a moderately wealthy family. The Irish campaign put paid to that – and then his father's headstrong rush to join Mortimer again . . . he was killed up in the north, you know?'

'We had heard. Some skirmish at Bridgnorth.'

'That is right. A great waste. He was a good man.' Sir Odo shook his head reflectively. 'You know, I think that Ailward could have made a good, competent squire. He had the physique for it. Strong torso, heavily built, with good arms and legs. He could ride like a knight, and had the grace with a lance to charm a princess.'

'His wife is a lovely woman,' Simon commented.

'Yes. He liked the better things in life. He was very badly affected by the loss of his manor. Very morose and dejected . . . and then to be forced to become a menial . . . it was a hard fate for a man who had hoped for so much.'

Simon said, 'Did he resent you too?'

'Why would he do that?' Odo asked with frank surprise.

'Because you had a part of his inheritance.'

Sir Odo laughed. 'On the contrary, that was all he was able to salvage. I made an arrangement with Sir Geoffrey that we would share that part of the manor. It is fruitful, that area within the river, and half the money went to Ailward. I kept nothing. But Geoffrey thought that we were sharing the profits.'

'Why did Geoffrey agree to that?' Baldwin demanded. 'Surely he could have simply added it to his existing lands and pleased his master . . .'

'But not to his own profit,' Odo said slyly, tapping his nose. 'I appealed to his greed. So no, Ailward liked me and trusted me. As he should have. I always helped him.'

'Do you think that he could have been capable of killing Lady Lucy and throwing her into the mire on his land just to lay the blame for the murder on Sir Geoffrey?' Baldwin asked thoughtfully.

'He would have been capable, I suppose. If he wanted to do that, though, wouldn't he have picked a place where she would have been easier to discover? Why choose a bog? She might have stayed there for ever, just as so many sheep and horses do each year. And who would have killed him?'

'Walter and he were there together. Could they have argued about the course of action they were about to take, perhaps come to blows, and Walter killed him?'

Simon took up the idea. 'So Walter took her body on his own shoulder and walked along the waste lands, round the back of Sir Geoffrey's lands, and then dropped her into the mire?'

'It is scarcely likely, is it?' Baldwin said reluctantly.

'No. Not unless they had an ally in Sir Geoffrey's camp,' Simon mused. 'Someone who would know the best way to avoid being seen so near to the house.'

'Any of the peasants would know all the less frequented routes, surely?' Sir Odo said.

'Perhaps,' Baldwin said. 'Could you have Walter brought here so that I may question him, please?'

With a good grace Sir Odo nodded and left them, adjuring them to be comfortable while they waited.

'You have had an idea?' Simon asked.

Baldwin nodded. 'The assumption we made originally was that Sir Geoffrey had intended to torture Lady Lucy to make her pass over her lands to him – but it now appears that Sir Geoffrey never pushed his master's claim to the whole of Ailward's inheritance too strenuously – Sir Odo still keeps a hand on some parts. I just wonder: if Sir Odo could have taken over Lady Lucy's lands, it would have been as beneficial to him as it would have been for Sir Geoffrey, surely?'

'I suppose so,' Simon said. 'What of the other men? Ailward could have allied himself with anyone, I reckon. He was bitter and vengeful after losing his entire estate. Walter was probably involved, since he was there on the moor with Ailward and, perhaps, Lady Lucy's body, if Perkin was right. Nicholas le Poter could have been connected to them as well. Three men: Ailward, Walter and Nicholas, all of them working together.'

'A fair hypothesis.' Baldwin nodded.

They were no nearer the truth, he thought, and walked to the door, his mind whirling with possibilities. But even as he began to see another possible explanation – only dimly, but there, like a path that was glimpsed through the fog only to be concealed again in a moment – his attention was caught by the shouting from outside the manor.

Chapter Thirty-Five

Sir Odo stood at the gate and stared at the body. 'When was this?' he demanded, all geniality flown.

'Sir, I did all I could to protect him. It was impossible, though. He just went for them, and Sir Geoffrey cut him down.'

Sir Odo had seen the injuries which a sword could make often enough, and this was clearly a blow intended to kill. It had sliced through the skull. He looked about him, estimating. 'How many men were there with him?'

'Six and twenty that I saw.'

'Where are the others, then? All my men are scattered about the place – I can't hope to throw him off the land with so few. It would be impossible . . .'

Baldwin and Simon were in time to hear his last words as they joined Sir Odo in the yard, Edgar standing nearby and gazing down at the body with interest. It was a fierce blow from a heavy sword; that much was clear. 'What happened here?' Baldwin demanded.

'This man was my sergeant over the river,' Sir Odo said heavily. 'This man, Walter, whom you wanted to meet, saw him cut down by Sir Geoffrey himself, and carried the body all the way back here.'

'You saw him killed?'

'We were there this morning, him just quietly pottering about the place trying to make it liveable after their last attack, me sitting and enjoying the sun, when we heard the horses.'

'You had warning? Why didn't the messenger come to me in time?' Sir Odo growled.

'They came up the river, and then charged up the main trackway from the ford, Sir Odo. I expect the lad was scared off and won't be found for some time,' Walter said. 'I was taken unawares because I expected the bastards to come from the east. We'd started a palisade facing that way to protect us, but they just came pelting up the track and overwhelmed us. There were too many for the two of us to achieve anything.'

'And what then?' Baldwin enquired, still staring at the man on the ground.

'A man went inside the house, and he killed Robert's bitch and her pups. That made him mad, and he just ran at the man with his dagger. Sir Geoffrey was still on his horse, and as Robert passed him, he took a chop with his sword. Then he told me to take the carcass away and never return.'

'You look about done in,' Sir Odo said. 'How are you feeling?'

'I can hold a sword, sir.'

'Good. Go and find a mount.'

'Sir Odo, I protest.' Baldwin stood and stared at the older knight with serious eyes. 'Attacking Sir Geoffrey can benefit no one. Least of all Lord de Courtenay.'

'Those murdering swines have killed my sergeant, Sir Baldwin! Look at him! Dead because of that arse-wipe from Monkleigh. All he seeks is the expansion of his lands at all times, nothing else. I will not have him taking over all the de Courtenay lands without a fight!'

'Good. But I should recommend that you consolidate the position you presently have, and that you pull some men back from other areas.'

'Why? So he can invade any stretch without a battle? That hardly makes sense . . .'

'As it stands, you have too few men, and they are dotted about in small packets. Any of them can be easily overwhelmed, just as these two were,' Baldwin said bluntly. 'If you wish to waste your men's lives, that is your responsibility, but I'd prefer to save as many as possible.'

'So would I!' Sir Odo protested angrily. 'But if I don't respond to this provocation, what will he try next? He'll slip a dagger between me and my lands at Iddesleigh, and take them too, or . . .'

Baldwin irritably held up a hand. 'You say that he would try to shave away your holdings?'

'It has happened elsewhere. The barons are too scared to control the king or his *adviser* now that they see the bodies rotting on the gibbets up and down the land. What is the point of fighting to save your lands if it loses you your life?'

'But you would do that?'

Sir Odo set his jaw and looked away.

'You had a pact with him over that last stretch of land. You say he agreed for his personal profit, but what would have happened to him if his lord had learned of the deal? He would have been at risk of his life. Why would he agree to that for short-term treasure?'

'To calm local fears,' Sir Odo said. 'With Lady Lucy so worried about her position, and my master Sir John Sully nervous of further encroachment on his territories, it was clearly a good policy to calm any anxiety. I persuaded Sir Geoffrey that it would be to his master's advantage too, if he kept a sizeable portion separate.'

'What made the situation change?' Baldwin wondered. 'Now he threatens war.'

'All was well until Ailward died. His death seems to have precipitated action. Or maybe it was Lady Lucy – she was taken not long before.'

'Why should they have made Sir Geoffrey discard what had been a beneficial arrangement?'

'I don't know. Unless he thought that I was responsible for Ailward's murder . . . and I swear I was not! I know nothing at all about his death.'

Baldwin nodded. The man's confusion was evident. 'I still say that an attack now would be unproductive, Sir Odo.'

'What else can I do, except leave the land to Sir Geoffrey and his men until a lawyer can fight my cause for me? That would take time and treasure, Sir Baldwin. Better to resolve the question now.'

'You must do as you see fit. But better to hold your hand a little while. Let them grow complacent, believing you will do nothing, while you marshal your forces. And don't use that man Walter.'

'He's the one with the most cause to desire revenge!'

'He is also the man most likely to lose all reason. If you don't want a feud on your hands, I should send him elsewhere.'

* * *

Hugh found the pain returning before they had travelled any distance. He walked with John and the reluctant Humphrey down to the river ford on the way to Iddesleigh, where Humphrey stood staring at the waters dejectedly.

Leaning on his staff, Hugh grunted, 'You don't have to come with us.'

John shot him a look, and Hugh returned it belligerently. 'I don't care what he did in some convent ages ago. I just want the man who killed Constance, and bringing Humphrey along won't help me, will it?'

'Shouldn't he be handed over to the Church?'

'Why? What good would that do us?' Hugh demanded. 'He's just a wanderer. Let him go.'

'What do you think?' John asked Humphrey. 'What does your heart tell you?'

'You're asking me?' Humphrey asked. 'I want to go away. I never meant to hurt anyone, and I didn't want to leave my convent, but now? I just want to go and find peace. I was happy here, but I can't stay, so I have to run.'

John pulled a face and looked from one to the other. 'It's my duty to report him, Hugh. If I don't, I'll be in trouble later. Yet I think he won't err again. He's a good enough fellow.'

'Please!' Humphrey said.

'Go on! Just go, before I change my mind,' John said. He clapped Humphrey on the shoulder. 'Godspeed, Brother. May peace find you, and may you come to rest in a safe and happy home at last when your wanderings are done.'

'I . . . Godspeed, Brother. I don't know what to . . . Thank you.'

Hugh watched him from narrowed eyes. When Humphrey slapped him on the upper arm, he nodded, but said no more. His mind was bent on the man he knew he must speak to: Father Matthew, the man who had been in the lane outside his house a short while before the place was fired.

Sir Odo reluctantly agreed to wait until he heard from Baldwin before he launched any counter-blow to the forces currently occupying what he still called 'his' lands, but he was determined to prepare his men. Baldwin offered to speak to Sir Geoffrey, and Sir Odo agreed to send Walter off to Iddesleigh.

'That is a bargain. There are eight men at the church. If I send Walter there to hold the place against any attack, I can bring two back. There's no need for eight men there. Seven should be plenty, and the other two can come here and help . . . I wonder if seven are needed. There's hardly likely to be an attempt on the place while all this is going on . . .' and he had stalked off, muttering to himself about men and numbers.

'There will be a lot of blood shed if we can't stop this nonsense,' Simon said. He sighed and put a hand to his brow.

Baldwin looked at him sympathetically. 'And it hardly helps us to learn what happened to Hugh, does it? Still, perhaps there may be a clue in among all this tangle.'

'Sir Geoffrey, you think?'

Baldwin was quiet a moment. 'I wish I thought so. No. I think that he is as unwitting as Sir Odo. Both seem to have been content to live their lives quietly enough until this trouble came to them. All appears to have started with the death of Lady Lucy, or at least her abduction. There was no dispute between the two manors until then . . .'

'You have a thought, Sir Baldwin?' Edgar enquired.

'Only this: is all this dispute over the increase of the manors? Lady Lucy was taken and killed for her lands. In the meantime, if Lord Despenser had heard that the property he had taken from Ailward was less than it should have been, he would have been sure to tell Sir Geoffrey to acquire the rest. Ailward would have had a good motive to kill Lady Lucy and leave the evidence with Sir Geoffrey to make it appear that he was guilty.'

Edgar interrupted, saying, 'Aha, but so would Sir Geoffrey. If Despenser had learned of his arrangement with Sir Odo over Ailward's lands, he would have removed Geoffrey for incompetence and installed another in his place.'

'That is true,' Baldwin reflected. 'If a dog bites you, you will be more cautious in future, and if a man shows he cannot even read the evidence of the land's records, would you trust his judgement a second time?'

'Not unless he had some excellent excuse to offer.'

'What do you say, Simon?'

'Me? I should say that the pair of them deserve everything that is coming to them. Sir Geoffrey for his theft from his lord, and for, I think, his attacks on the innocent. And Sir Odo for concealing what he had been doing from Lord Hugh de Courtenay.'

'Why?'

'It is clear enough what the two of them were doing: stealing a patch of land. Sir Geoffrey took the larger piece for Despenser, and left the smaller part in the hands of Sir Odo. But I will bet that Sir Odo never told Sir John Sully or Lord de Courtenay. No, I would think that he held that as a secret for himself, and from the moment that the two men took the land, they have been sharing its profits, never mind Sir Odo's story about passing his share to Ailward.'

'So why fall out now?' Baldwin wondered.

'Perhaps one grew greedy. Thieves often fall out,' Simon said dismissively.

'Lady Lucy,' Edgar said.

Baldwin shot a look at him. 'What do you mean?'

'If one of the knights decided that this arrangement was too profitable not to duplicate, might not one of the two decide to capture her, steal her lands and set himself up as a minor lord in his own right?'

'It is possible,' Baldwin admitted with a frown. 'But how to do that? Offer a kindly opportunity, and provide her with his hand in marriage?'

'And when that was rejected, resort to the first plan: torture until she agreed to give up her territories, and then death,' Edgar said.

Simon scowled. 'Why now? That is what I cannot understand. Hugh is dead, and I think it must be because the men who killed Ailward thought he might have seen them. I can understand that. But why do all this just now?'

'Yes,' Baldwin agreed. 'Just as every fire needs a spark to start it, so too there must have been something that initiated this chain of events. Once we know what that was, perhaps we'll be closer to learning the full details.'

Hugh and John made their way along the roadway and then climbed the hill up to Iddesleigh. All the while they had a view of the steeple in front of them, and Hugh was aware of a growing feeling of nervousness as he approached it.

He did not fear killing a man, or being killed. That was of no concern to him. Someone had murdered his wife, and deserved punishment. Even if he died in the attempt, he wouldn't care. The man who ended Constance's life had gone a long way to ending Hugh's own. Hugh would find him and kill him.

But he was scared. He was scared of not finding the man; of failing to kill before he was himself killed; even of finding the wrong man and executing an innocent who'd had nothing to do with his wife's murder. All were dreadful thoughts, the last possibly the worst of all, and he found himself struck with a strange feeling, for him, of irresolution and doubt.

His bruises and wounds were giving him more pain now as he climbed the hill to the church, but his gradual slowing was not caused by them; it was the feelings of misgiving and uncertainty that seemed to sap at his strength as he went. By the time he had reached the top of the hill, he had little confidence.

'Hugh?' John murmured. 'Is there something wrong?'

'I don't know what I can do. What if I'm wrong?' Hugh explained what he had remembered about Constance's seeing Matthew outside his house all those days ago.

'You don't have to kill the priest, Hugh. Just make sure you understand what he was doing there. And who was with him,' John added thoughtfully.

'You won't stop me if I find the murderer and kill him?' Hugh asked suddenly.

John looked at him, then glanced westwards towards his sister's manor of Meeth. 'I swear I won't. If you fail, I shall strike for you, Hugh.'

Chapter Thirty-Six

They had made their way along the road back into Iddesleigh, and now took the southern road to Monkleigh. Baldwin had been reluctant to take the direct route straight to the sergeant's house in case their horses led Sir Geoffrey's men to expect an attack. Easier and safer to avoid the place entirely and make their way to Sir Geoffrey's seat of power.

The hall's grounds were very quiet. Servants walked about nervously, throwing anxious looks at the three bulky men on their horses as they rode up the pathway to the hall.

'We're here to see Sir Geoffrey,' Baldwin said as a servant came through the door.

'He's not here, master. He's . . .'

'Over at Robert Crokers's house. Very well. We'll go and speak to him there.'

Baldwin was about to wheel away when he saw the other face in the doorway. 'Ah, Sir Coroner! You weren't with him to see him execute his justice, then?'

'I don't understand what you mean,' Sir Edward said silkily. 'He has gone to one of his outlying farms to handle some little local argument, I believe.'

'He has killed one man already, Sir Coroner, and I shall have great pleasure in reporting your part in that murder.'

'You speak too loudly, Sir Baldwin. This is none of your affair!'

'Murder and felony are both my affair, sir!' Baldwin said forcefully. 'Do not presume to tell me where my duty or responsibility lies!'

'Although you feel justified in telling me off? What have I done?'

'I am not sure yet. But you come from Barnstaple, do you not?'

'What of it?'

'Was it not most convenient that you were so near when Sir Geoffrey had need of a coroner when the woman's body was discovered? His *favourite* coroner, the one man from his lord's household, the one man upon whom he could count, and you just happened to be less than a half-day's ride away?'

'It was fortunate. I had decided to stay there after another death.'

'And then rode here urgently to hold your inquest. So urgently, indeed, that there was no time even to invite the local Keeper of the King's Peace.'

'If I had known you would like to . . .'

Baldwin's horse lurched beneath him as he roared, '*Do not take me for a fool, man!* You know the rules under which we serve as well as I do. I should have been there to see if I could do more to find the murderer. And I shall discover him, believe me!'

His evident anger spurred Sir Edward to step outside. 'Sir Baldwin, do you really think it would be in your interests to learn the truth? It could be that you would be plunged into the midst of disputes you would prefer to know nothing about.'

'I want to know the truth when a man has been killed. I want to know why and how and who did it,' Baldwin spat. 'And when I have a coroner who has seen two women, a child and now three men dead, and who yet does nothing to seek the guilty, I have to wonder why he is so reluctant.'

'You're mad! Look, you know who my master is. Do you really want him as an enemy? You think your post as Keeper would protect you?'

Baldwin smiled and leaned down towards Sir Edward. In a quiet voice he hissed, 'And do you really want him to learn that you are helping protect his steward here, even though Sir Geoffrey has been systematically robbing him?'

'You are joking!'

'This land that he has invaded today? It was a part of the whole which he acquired for the Despenser. He merely left aside the most profitable lump. That he was keeping for himself, sharing all the profits with Sir Odo.'

'That's nonsense!' Sir Edward scoffed. 'He couldn't have. He and Sir Odo never got on.'

'Not in public, no. But they have known each other for longer than you have yet lived,' Baldwin said. 'Still, if you won't help but instead are set on obstructing us, there is nothing more to be said.'

'Wait!' Sir Edward snapped as Baldwin began to pull the reins to turn his beast.

'What? Be quick, man. We have to get there before your incompetence leads to still more deaths.'

'What do you want to know?'

'Why were you so close when Sir Geoffrey sent for you to view Lady Lucy's body?'

'Sir Geoffrey had told me that he expected a fight soon over this extra piece of land. He said that it might become a cruel one.'

'And this fight was over the land where he is now?'

'I believe so. I cannot be sure. When I had a call from a messenger to come here to view the body of Lady Lucy, I assumed he'd actually decided to take over another manor. I was shocked. It never occurred to me that I'd be called back here to a woman's body. It made me think I should be seeking some sort of bribe from him.'

'What of the man Hugh and his family at Iddesleigh?'

'Them? They were only peasants.'

Baldwin saw a movement from the corner of his eye, but when he flicked a glance at Simon, Edgar had already snatched his reins, and was pulling Simon away from the discussion. 'Were you told to speed the inquest and find that it was an unknown killer?'

'Yes. Sir Geoffrey didn't want any dispute about that. He felt sure that the jury must decide that it had been one of his men who was responsible, and he wanted to ensure that any such speculation was nipped in the bud.'

'What of today's action? Did he not ask you to join him? That would have been normal in an entirely legal reoccupation of stolen lands, wouldn't it?'

'Perhaps – but I didn't feel that it lay fully within my responsibilities. Come, Sir Baldwin, I have to ensure that my master is happy with me and my work, but going to behave as an observer . . .'

'Especially when you were not aware that there was a fully

legitimate excuse for the invasion,' Baldwin noted coldly. 'I wonder why he never explained that to you.'

'I do not know. He is a very secretive man.'

'Murderers often are!' Simon burst out, and he snatched his reins back and whipped his rounsey away, down the path to the road.

There was shouting. Blearily Nicholas le Poter looked up through eyes misted with tears. He had dozed for a while, and now, peering up at the door, he saw men bringing in another body.

The first, that of Isaac, was already set out on trestles in front of the altar, and now the shape of a woman was set alongside his on a fresh pair of stands. 'Who is that?' Nicholas asked.

'Lady Lucy. You killed her, you can rest here with her until it's time for both of you to be buried,' came the reply from a hulking peasant with a rough laugh that made Nicholas shake.

The candles at the altar were snuffed, but there was a bright ray of sunshine that lanced in through the open window at the south, and sparkled from the clean cross and all the metalwork in the church.

'You slept a long time, my son,' Matthew said.

'I could sleep much longer.'

'But if you do, you will be escaping your problems for only a short while. Better to plan what you wish to achieve.'

Nicholas wiped a grubby sleeve over his brow. Realizing he had let the altar cloth slip from his hand, he snatched at it eagerly, like an insecure horseman grabbing at a dropped rein. Only when he had it in his hand again could he breathe more easily.

'I have brought you some wine and water, a pair of good apples, and some meats. They will keep you going for a little,' Matthew said gently.

'Father, you are so kind . . .'

'I behave as a father must to his flock. No more.'

'And I behave as a coward. If I had any courage, I would go out and declare Sir Geoffrey's guilt to all and demand to be put to the justices. But I can't, because he owns all the serfs here, and if I try to accuse him, he'll pay all in the jury to find against me and I'll hang!'

'If you think that is the right action,' Matthew murmured, 'then you should pray to God for courage.'

Nicholas looked up at the priest gratefully. 'I know you try to help,' he said, 'but it's so hard . . . if I abjure, I may at least live.'

'In a state of shame, though. While if you do your duty and accuse him, you will be more attractive to God.'

And *dead*, Nicholas added for him. There was no benefit to him in being dead. If he succeeded in having a knight condemned for his crimes, the man would probably be pardoned as soon as he wrote to the king. Especially if he offered a good enough bribe. That was how justice was dealt – if you had money, you could do no wrong; if you had none, you were guilty.

'What should I do, Father?'

Matthew smiled down at him. Then he motioned to Nicholas to move up. Grimacing a little, he bent down to kneel at the altar next to the suspect. 'First, we pray, you and I, and then you ask God to help you to decide.'

Accommodatingly Nicholas bent his head, and as Matthew began to speak, Nick heard the door open, squeaking on its hinges.

'Ah, I always loved that sound, you know, Father,' John said cheerfully as he and Hugh walked in.

Sir Geoffrey was almost finished at Robert's house. He had engaged all the men in cutting saplings and dragging them to the road just after a sharp bend. With any luck, Sir Odo's riders would be surprised to find such a barrier to their passage. Some might be thrown from their mounts, while the others would be a bunched, confused mass of men and beasts, easily picked off one by one by Sir Geoffrey's archers, or even simply dragged from their saddles and knocked on the head.

He had completed the initial build when he heard that there were visitors to see him. Cursing mildly under his breath, for he was never best pleased to learn that others wanted his time, he issued orders for the rest of the work to be completed, then stomped back to the house.

Baldwin was crouched at the doorway, where there was a sack filled with dead puppies. Nearby was the body of their mother.

In a life which had seen so many deaths, Baldwin had grown largely immune to the sadness of most murders and accidental deaths. There had always been deaths and always would be. That was all a man needed to know. But wanton slaughter was something he always deprecated. And to kill young creatures for no purpose was deplorable. He put out a hand to touch one of the short-nosed little bundles. It was cold already.

'You have started a fire today that will engulf you,' he said coldly.

Sir Geoffrey pursed his lips. 'I had expected someone from Sir Odo, but not you. What's your relationship to him? Are you merely his paid attendant or has he offered you a part of the profits?'

'You think I am in the same league as your friend the coroner? I wonder how much you expected to pay him. He will require more, now, I think. You had hoped to get away with very little, I expect. It can't have been easy, especially when you realised that you must get Sir Odo off the land you and he had planned to keep.'

'You know of . . .'

'I rather think that he believes you broke any pact with him when you invaded this place today.'

Sir Geoffrey shrugged. 'What could Odo expect? He's been making my life hard enough. Putting that poor child's body on my land and then I assume conspiring with my men to get the mire drained . . . That was a provocation I could hardly ignore.'

'You say you did not kill her or have her killed?'

'Of course not! I couldn't behave in such an unchivalrous manner. The poor woman was so young – who would do such a thing? Only an avaricious man bent on his own profit!'

'And that is how Sir Odo strikes you?'

Sir Geoffrey was still a moment. 'You know men better than I, or so it is rumoured. What would you say?'

'I should say that he, like you, would take any prize that was offered to him if it promised few risks and easy benefits. I should think either of you would be pleased to take a woman like her to be your wife, and that you'd neither of you have any compunction about taking all her manor and treasure to yourselves in the process, but to actually slaughter her in cold blood, that I find hard to believe,' Baldwin said. His eyes flickered away from Sir Geoffrey and down to the sack at the doorway.

'I would have said the same myself,' Sir Geoffrey agreed. 'But who else could have benefited from putting him and me at loggerheads?'

'Perhaps I can learn that,' Baldwin said. 'In the meantime, these puppies. Who killed them?'

'What?' Sir Geoffrey asked with a blank expression. He looked over to the doorway and shrugged. 'I think it was . . .'

'No! Don't tell me,' Baldwin said quickly. 'But whoever he is, you should discard him. Any man who can do that to puppies is as dangerous as a viper. He has caused the death of the man who lived here, only because of his motiveless slaughter of a litter.'

Sir Geoffrey shrugged. 'Crokers took a dagger to one of my men.'

'Because of your attack on his animals. He would have done nothing, were it not for this wanton destruction.'

'I do not know that,' Sir Geoffrey said. 'He tried to attack one of my men, and I stopped him.'

'Just as you would remove any other obstacle to your ambitions. A stone in your horse's hoof, a man protecting his lands, either can be removed and destroyed, can't they? Perhaps other barriers can also be heaved aside.'

'I don't know what you're talking about.'

'Lady Lucy – she was a barrier, wasn't she? You wanted more land, either for yourself or for your lord. Either way, she owned it, and you wanted it. So you decided to capture her and take her in marriage, forcibly, or kill her and steal what you wanted.'

'That is a foul untruth!'

'Is it? I think that perhaps it is a truth in the eyes of many,' Baldwin said.

'If you try to tell others that, I shall destroy you!'

'I am a knight, Sir Geoffrey. I am not so easily destroyed.'

'All men can die, Sir Baldwin.'

'That is true,' Baldwin replied. He crouched down at the sack of puppies again, touching the little bodies. One squeaked and kicked feebly, and Baldwin reached down to pick it up. Somehow this one had not been hurt when the others had been smashed against the wall. Baldwin stroked it, and it started to squeak again, mouth wide, searching for a nipple.

'Did I miss one?' A skinny man with a leering face suddenly appeared in the doorway.

Baldwin eyed him a moment, the puppy in his arm. He was about to pass it to Simon when Edgar stepped up to the skinny man and punched him with full force in the belly. The man's eyes bulged, his mouth formed a perfect 'O', and he collapsed to his knees, gasping desperately for breath.

At the blow all the men in the area stopped their work, and a few picked up swords and daggers. Baldwin shifted the puppy to his left hand and drew his sword. 'Keep back! Sir Geoffrey, if you value your honour, tell them to keep away.'

Sir Geoffrey raised a hand, and his men returned to their labours. Meanwhile Baldwin went to the choking man on the ground, and put the point of his sword on his throat. He hissed, 'You should be grateful. If I'd reached you first, I'd have killed you for what you did to that bitch and her litter. If I hear of you again, I shall seek you out and throw you into the gaol at Rougement Castle.'

Chapter Thirty-Seven

Baldwin was quiet on their return. Only when they were almost at Fishleigh did he turn to Simon and mutter, 'I could imagine that band of felons doing anything.'

Simon said nothing. His friend was still cradling the mewling puppy, and every so often his serious dark eyes would move to the little creature. Simon knew full well how fond Baldwin was of dogs, and seeing them abused was merely proof to Baldwin of the bestial nature of the men Sir Geoffrey led.

At the manor, they called to the doorman for Sir Odo.

'He's not here, sir. He's ridden off.'

'Where to?' Simon demanded.

'I think he's gone to Lady Isabel, sir.'

'Do you know why?' Baldwin asked. 'Doesn't he have enough to cope with up here?'

'He forgot to tell me, sir,' the gatekeeper said snidely. 'No doubt he will when he gets back.'

They rode on towards Iddesleigh as dusk was falling, and now Simon saw that his companion was meditating more on the murders than on the actions of one brutal felon towards a litter of pups.

'What would he be doing with the lady?' Baldwin said as they began the climb up to Iddesleigh. 'I have a suspicion I have missed a crucial point, Simon.'

'What could we have missed?'

'Why a man like Odo, used to warfare and the spoils of war, is here in a quiet rural backwater without any of the benefits a man like him would expect. Just like Sir Geoffrey.'

Friar John gave a groan when he saw the bodies at the altar. His light mood left him, and he walked slowly across the nave to Lucy, sinking slowly to his knees and bowing his head in prayer.

Hugh had scarcely noticed him. In his mind there was only one thing here that mattered, and that was the figure of the priest as he clambered to his feet.

'What is the meaning of this?' Matthew demanded, not angrily, but in surprise. And then he recognised Hugh, and his eyes widened. His hand went to his breast, and he tottered slightly. '*You!* But you were dead!'

'Don't think so,' Hugh said. He took his billhook from his belt and hefted it in his hand. 'My wife is, though, and the lad.'

'What are you doing? This is a church, man. You mustn't threaten people in here!' Matthew swallowed hard. Then a flare of resentment came over him, and he stepped forward between Hugh and Nicholas, who remained sitting at the altar, gripping the cloth with a despairing determination. 'You won't hurt him, man! He is safe here; he has claimed sanctuary.'

Hugh glanced at the man. 'It's not him I want. It's you.'

Matthew felt as though the tiled floor had moved suddenly. 'Me? Why?'

'You were there. In the lane outside my house, weren't you? Who were you with?'

'I don't know what you . . . in the lane?'

'The day of the camp ball game. You were out there in the dusk, arguing with a man. Who was he? What were you arguing about?'

'That night? That was just old Pagan, the steward to Lady Isabel and Madam Malkin. I remonstrated with him because he was drunk, that was all.'

'He was drunk?' Hugh scowled. He twitched the billhook in his hand and let his gaze fall away from the priest. When he came here, he had hoped to learn something that would make sense of Constance's and Hugh's deaths, but there was nothing to be learned from what Matthew said. Hugh had pinned all his hopes on being told that the man out there in the lane had some reason to harm Hugh or his wife, but it was just a drunk wandering in the night. Nothing.

Friar John wiped his face free from tears. There was important business here for him, and he must try to contain his grief. First he had to learn who might have been responsible for his sister's death; second he must help Hugh – whether that meant protecting him or preventing him from killing another man. He sniffed, wiped his face briskly with a hand, and walked over to join the others.

'So Pagan was drunk that night? What was he doing so far from his home? If he lives down with those women, shouldn't he have been there with them instead of wandering the lanes in the dark?'

Matthew looked at him in surprise, not expecting a friar to take a part in this inquisition. 'It is not my place to ask such things – but I think he sleeps away from them. He has his house up east of here.'

'Near Guy the charcoal burner's place?' Hugh asked.

'Yes. I assumed he was making his way home from there. He used to live with the family while Ailward was alive. After that, of course, Lady Isabel rightly considered it more fitting that he should sleep at his home again.'

'That was the night Ailward died,' Hugh muttered.

'Yes. Bless his soul!'

'My wife saw him earlier that day. Said so to me,' Hugh muttered, straining with the effort of recollection. 'She said he was there with . . . with a man-at-arms from Fishleigh. Together.'

'That is preposterous,' Matthew said easily. 'No one from Monkleigh gets on with anyone from Fishleigh.'

Friar John smiled calmly. 'Do you really believe that a man who was born here as a squire's son would not be able to get on with men from the lowliest peasant to the lord of the manor next to his own?'

'It's different here,' Matthew said. 'If Sir Geoffrey knew that Ailward was fraternising with men from Fishleigh, he would be so furious he'd . . .'

'Yes?'

'He'd kill them,' Matthew said slowly, with dawning shock. 'But you can't think that!'

'Why on earth not?' John said.

'Sir Geoffrey is no low felon. He's a knight!'

John said nothing, but glanced at Nicholas. 'What are you doing here? Claiming sanctuary for what?'

'Sir Geoffrey attacked me with a whip, and then he accused me of murdering that woman there.'

John's eyes glittered, and he had to stop himself from stepping nearer. 'And did you? On your oath, mind. Father Matthew, do you have the Gospels?'

Only when Nicholas had set a hand upon the holy book and sworn that he had not harmed Lucy did John feel his blood begin to cool.

'That is good. So why should he seek to accuse you?'

'He wants a scapegoat. I'm easiest for him because I am known to our master, and Lord Despenser could install me in his place. He sees me as a threat to his position, so he seeks to discredit me.'

'Do you know who could have killed the girl?'

Nicholas shook his head with certainty. 'No. It was nothing to do with me, that's all I know.'

'Were you involved in the attack on the sergeant of Fishleigh?'

Hugh looked at John when he asked that, then shrugged and turned back to Nicholas.

'Yes. I was there.'

'And later at this man's house just east of here?'

'No. There were no men from Sir Geoffrey's hall involved in that.'

'How can you know?' Hugh grated.

'I was one of the men first back from Fishleigh, and all the rest came back later in one group. If there'd been another attack, I'd have heard. I made sure I heard everything in the household.'

Emma was sitting in the bar with Richalda when the door opened. She threw a look behind her and saw Baldwin, Edgar and Simon walk in, grim-faced. They glanced at her, Baldwin with a glowering mien which softened as soon as he took in the sight of his daughter playing with Emma, and then they all went to a separate table and sat, Baldwin calling Jankin's wife over and passing her a tiny bundle, asking that she keep it warm and feed it milk. No one told Emma what it was or why it should be cosseted, and she refused to demean herself by asking.

It was that sort of behaviour that Emma found so intolerable about these people. She was human, wasn't she? Didn't she have feelings too?

Yes, she did, and there was no reason for her to be ignored by these high-and-mighty men just because they seemed to think that they were so superior to her. They weren't. As her old mother had told her, all men and women were the same: all had to crouch to defecate in the morning. 'If there is any man who seems arrogant, my girl, just you imagine what he'd look like when he's doing that,' she had chuckled.

Not that her mother had said 'defecate'. She was more . . . earthy than that.

Emma saw Deadly Dave walk up to the door. He glanced at the bar, then saw Baldwin, and his face stiffened. When he saw Emma he was red of face, like a man flushed with embarrassment. He licked his lips as she averted her face, and she heard his steps going to the bar, and his voice asking quietly for an ale.

Baldwin and Simon were talking in low tones, and she idly tried to overhear what they were saying, but she could make nothing of their words. In the end she gave up trying. Instead she concentrated on Richalda. A fresh ale appeared at her side, and she nodded and gruffly muttered her thanks, wondering where Jeanne was. Probably asleep again. She was always sleepy when she was pregnant.

As she had that thought, she heard the door open again, and she looked over her shoulder, expecting to see her lady.

'*God's tarse!*' she shrieked, leaping up. Her bench went over, spilling her ale across the floor, and she grabbed Richalda to her enormous bosom, cuddling the child and backing away.

Baldwin sighed, 'Woman, sit down. He's no ghost. He never died.'

There was a sudden change in the weather after Humphrey left Hugh and John at the ford on the way to Iddesleigh. As he trudged up the hill westwards before turning east towards Meeth, a colder wind struck his face, stinging at his cheeks. Then he found that there were fine pinpricks pricks of rain on the wind, making him blink and shiver. His eyes kept fogging as tiny drops caught on his eyelashes, and he pulled his robes closer about him in the vain hope that they might keep him warm.

He could not help but glance behind him, reflecting on all that had happened to him since he first saw the easy target, as he had thought.

Isaac. The old man had been as innocent and gullible as he had hoped, and yet . . .

There were some odd comments, some quiet ways he had of looking at a man that made him seem more aware than Humphrey would have guessed. Perhaps it was only that he had a certain stillness, his eyes focusing somewhere else while he listened to a man talking . . . but that wasn't because he was clever, it was because he had to concentrate. His eyes were bad, and so was his hearing. He was easy enough to fool into taking Humphrey's word that he had been sent from Exeter, after all. Others had been more suspicious, like Matthew.

Matthew had been the sort of man who might have written to the bishop to demand whether an assistant had been sent to help Isaac or not. He wasn't the sort of fellow to take a man's word if he mistrusted him. No, he must have written . . . and yet there had been no summons to Exeter.

He can't have written, and Humphrey reckoned he knew why. Isaac had talked him out of it. The old man must have realised that he had a good thing going. All the while Humphrey was there, he had food ready at the right times, he had his rooms swept, he had the vegetables and grain looked after. It was a comfortable existence, and Humphrey himself was undemanding. It wouldn't have occurred to Isaac that Humphrey could have lied.

Except that wasn't entirely true. Isaac was no fool. He usually spotted irregularities and curious behaviour. He did in the case of Hugh's family, guessing that Hugh's wife was a nun before anyone told him. He was sharp enough in that sort of way; he had a peasant's wits. But he hadn't figured out Humphrey; hadn't guessed that Humphrey was a threat and could rob the chapel in a moment.

That he hadn't was only because – well, it was just *because*, that was all. There was no point in robbing the place. And it didn't feel right, not while Isaac was lying in there like a guard.

'He knew all along,' Humphrey breathed. Dejectedly, he gave up trying to convince himself otherwise. The priest had known what sort of man he was. He had not been reported to Exeter, because Isaac had stopped Matthew writing; he had been given free access to the chapel and all its riches because Isaac knew he could trust him. In a few short months Humphrey had been given his soul back. After the killing he'd thought he'd never know peace again, but Isaac had showed him how to live. He had saved him.

The rain started to fall more seriously, and he glared upwards. 'All right. I'll stop,' he declared, and instead of continuing to Meeth, he stopped at the ruined house. The roof wasn't entire by any means, but there was enough to protect him from the worst of the weather, and at least there was the remains of the little family's fire. He could rekindle it and have a warm place to rest the night. And while there he could muse over his life. He had a great deal of thinking to do.

He was almost at the place when he glanced over towards Fishleigh. There were many torches in the hall's yard, he saw. And then he saw them begin to move. It was too far away to be certain, but he thought that they were taking the road towards the ford that led to Iddesleigh.

It was a large force, he saw, and he wondered why they would all be riding that way at this time of night.

Hugh walked in and sat with his head lowered. He knew that Simon was at his side, and he heard voices speaking, but somehow they made little sense. Suddenly he felt as though there was a great dizziness washing over him, and he must fall, but he managed to keep himself upright with an effort.

There was an arm about him, and he looked down to see that it was his master's. Simon was holding him. Hugh wanted to speak, but Simon's eyes were brimming, and Hugh didn't know why. He sniffed. There was a heaviness in the middle of his breast, and he found that he couldn't speak, or at least, not without his voice quaking with sobs.

'Hugh, I thought you were dead,' Simon said. He closed his eyes and squeezed Hugh's shoulder. 'I am so glad, Hugh, so glad to see you're well. And so sorry to know that Constance and little Hugh . . . that they were killed.'

'Is there anything you can tell us about that night?' Baldwin asked.

Hugh could only shake his head, incapable. It was just as if he'd been storing up the misery and loneliness for the last days and now all his grief was overwhelming him. Surely his heart must burst!

'Hugh? Look at me. Look into my eyes.' Baldwin's tone was

insistent. 'You have to speak to me. We are seeking the murderous bastard who killed Constance, but we need your help.'

Looking up, Hugh saw the depth of compassion in Baldwin's face. He sniffed, and saw that Edgar was at Baldwin's side. Edgar nodded gently, and for once Hugh saw Edgar without a smile on his face. This was a lean, sympathetic warrior, not the arrogant servant of a knight. He leaned forward and touched Hugh's knee, nodded, and then signalled to the pot boy for an ale.

'I have been looking after him,' Brother John said hesitantly.

'Brother, I am glad,' Baldwin said. He grinned. 'I didn't expect to meet you again so soon after you left Exeter.'

'Nor did I. Especially in such circumstances,' John said.

'What brought you here?' Simon asked.

John sighed. 'Oh, I was looking to see my sister one last time. I hoped . . .' He found he had a catch in his throat now. Seeing Hugh failing to cope with his emotions had brought to the fore all his own feelings of loneliness and despair. 'I hoped to meet my sister. But she is dead.'

Baldwin stood. 'Brother, be seated. I shall fetch you wine. Your sister, was she Lady Lucy?'

'Yes,' John said, and sat himself down carefully. Suddenly he felt as though he was among friends, and for no reason he could discern, he burst into tears.

Chapter Thirty-Eight

Later, when the two men had recovered somewhat, their story came out, and Baldwin and Simon told them all that they too had learned.

'What would Pagan have been doing in your lane, though, Hugh?' Simon asked.

'Come to that, what was Matthew doing there?' Baldwin wondered. 'Are there any other houses than yours nearby?'

'There are – farther up the hill,' Hugh said. That's as far as his parish goes.'

'So he was either walking up there or over to Pagan's house,' Baldwin said.

'We're as sure as we can be that Pagan's house is where the torture was conducted,' Simon said. 'But we don't know who was responsible, nor who killed the girl.'

'Where's this man Walter?' Baldwin wondered. 'He's the only man we know was there with whom we have not yet spoken. Sir Odo said he was coming here. Jankin? Do you know if a man-at-arms called Walter is guarding the church?'

'There is a man called that up there, I think. Davie, could you fetch him? Tell him there's a quart here for him.'

Baldwin nodded his thanks, and the men waited a few minutes. When Deadly reappeared, Walter was behind him. He glanced about the room, then walked in, shifting his sword to rest more comfortably on his hip as he came.

'Friend,' Baldwin called. 'We would like to speak to you. There is an ale here for you.'

Walter looked him up and down. The man was plainly a knight, and Walter had seen him at Fishleigh when he returned from the sergeant's house over the river. 'I am tired, and I'm supposed to be guarding the sanctuary-seeker. I don't have time, friend.'

'Then, as Keeper of the King's Peace, I tell you to come here and answer our questions,' Baldwin said, his smile broadening. 'I want to know all about you and Ailward and Lady Lucy of Meeth.'

'I don't know anything about that,' Walter declared quickly. 'It was nothing to do with me.'

'What was nothing to do with you?' Simon demanded.

'The death of that woman. Or Ailward. I had nothing to do with them.'

'But you were involved in carrying the woman away, weren't you?' Baldwin said. 'You were seen.'

'One man's word is . . .'

'Whoever told you only one man saw you?' Baldwin said with frank, if counterfeit, amazement. 'I've spoken to three this night already.'

'It was Ailward's fault. I know nothing about it. He took me to her body, and then had me help him carry it away, that's all I know.'

'Where was she?'

'Bound to a post.'

'*Where?*'

He sighed. 'In Pagan's forge. Someone had stabbed her to death with a red-hot poker. Left it in her. Poor thing.'

'And you told no one of this discovery, but instead took her away?' Baldwin said mildly.

'She was only a young woman. I wasn't going to risk my neck for her,' Walter said reasonably. 'What else would you expect me to do?'

Baldwin had a hand on John's shoulder to restrain him. He left it there, not gripping tightly, but not allowing John to forget it was there. 'I would expect you to tell the local officers. Where did you take the body?'

'We took her over to the mire . . . but that damned camp ball game came towards us! We thought that was one day we'd be safe moving her, because the players don't usually attack up towards the edge there. But Perkin and Beorn came straight at us, and I had to do something. As Sir Odo's man I was their natural opponent anyway, so

I clobbered Perkin and took the ball from him, throwing it as far as I could down the slope. I suppose it was him who saw her?'

'You can suppose what you like!' Baldwin said with more force. 'What then?'

'We took her to the mire. Ailward set stones on her, and we carried her into the middle and set her down.'

'Why?'

'Eh?'

'Why put her there in the middle of another man's land?'

'Ailward wanted to put the guilt firmly where it was earned. He told me that Sir Geoffrey had been going to Pagan's forge and torturing the girl up there for days. He killed her, and I didn't mind putting her there so people could see who'd done it to her.'

'What if Ailward lied to you?' Simon demanded roughly. 'Are you really so stupid?'

Baldwin said, 'What was going to happen then? If she was hidden, weighted down with rocks, how was she to be discovered?'

Walter eyed Simon warily before answering. 'He was going to get someone to suggest that the mire could be drained. That would lead to her being found. Seems he did that.'

'Who was he going to tell?'

'That arrogant prickle, Nicholas le Poter. He was as keen as Ailward to have his master removed. Both wanted the same thing, like my . . .'

Baldwin's eyes hardened. 'Like your what?'

'Nothing.'

'Were you going to say your master?'

'I don't know what he'd want. It's nothing to do with me.'

'You know full well that he would have liked to have had Sir Geoffrey away from here, don't you?'

'I don't know what . . .'

'And he could have wanted Lady Lucy's lands. He is not married, so he could even have asked her to marry him,' Simon breathed. 'He could have tried to win her lands legally, if by force.'

'Is that what you suspect, Walter?' Baldwin pressed him. 'If you know something which you are keeping from us, think again.'

'I don't know anything else.'

'Not even about the attack on the house just up from here?'

Walter frowned. 'What attack? On the miserable . . .' He caught sight of Hugh. 'Oh!'

'Yes. He didn't die,' Baldwin said quietly. 'Who did that to him? Who killed his family?'

'How should I know?'

'You are sweating, man. What would cause that? Who was it?'

It was at that moment that Humphrey burst in through the door.

'Sir Baldwin! You have to go at once! They'll kill each other otherwise!'

Baldwin glanced at Walter. 'Jankin! I want two men of yours to hold this man here until I return. He is not to be allowed a weapon, and he is not to leave this inn until I get back. Is that clear?'

Sir Odo rode along at a steady pace. He wasn't bothering with a flaming torch. No, there was little point in it. He'd prefer to have his hands free for a sword and a dagger.

There were risks in taking direct action, but since Sir Geoffrey had already begun to escalate the pressure, Sir Odo had little choice. He had to reassert his authority, and one means of doing so was to avenge his man's murder. That was what it was, clearly enough.

What was ridiculous was, there was no need for things to have come to such a pass. The two stewards had always managed to iron out any petty little problems that had popped up between them in the past. Sir Odo couldn't understand why Sir Geoffrey had allowed himself to be bullied into this sudden over-reaction.

Their venture could have proved quite fruitful. Why Sir Geoffrey had to ruin everything just now, Sir Odo couldn't comprehend. It seemed insane, unless it was something to do with Lady Lucy's body appearing on his land. Sir Odo didn't see why that should affect their relationship, though.

They were trotting up the track to Iddesleigh. Sir Odo and this group would ride down from Iddesleigh to Monkleigh, and hopefully surprise Sir Geoffrey's men there, while a second party was cantering along without torches, taking the road almost due east to distract the Monkleigh men. They would ride to the sergeant's house – what was left of it. Since Crokers was dead, Sir Odo assumed that Sir Geoffrey's men would have done as much damage to the place as they could. He didn't like to think what sort of condition the house would be in by now.

They were past Iddesleigh now, and Sir Odo led them down the Monkleigh road for a few hundreds of yards, and then up the trail that led to Pagan's house. Sir Odo would lead the men along the top here, and they'd come at Monkleigh's hall from behind. Sir Geoffrey wouldn't expect that, with luck. At the trail, Sir Odo passed the order, and all the torches were handed over to the grooms who had accompanied them, with a couple of men-at-arms in charge. These all set off down the main road as Sir Odo led his main force up the shallow incline.

In war, it was always best to surprise the enemy.

Adcock had returned home after the chase of Nicholas le Poter feeling as though his ballocks were ruined. He would never father a child now, he told himself that night as he sat on his bed and gently cupped them, too anxious to actually look at them, for fear of what he might see.

This morning he had slowly, cautiously, lifted his blanket to look at them, filled with trepidation. They still felt double their normal size, and he was confronted with a colourful landscape when he eventually faced them. There were dark purples, but also interesting salmon pinks and yellowish browns, rather like a sunset on a summer's day. Not that he put it like that at the time – that was the description he gave Hilda much later.

They were still bruised, that much was clear, and as he swung his legs over the side of the bed he was rewarded with an appalling ache that reached from the pit of his stomach to the top of his thighs. It was enough to make the breath stop in his throat, but not quite enough to make him cry out.

After a day's careful walking about the estate, generally keeping well away from Sir Geoffrey, he felt somewhat better. He completed the work on the small mire, and as dusk fell he was still there, unwilling to return to the hall even for his supper.

'How are you now?'

He looked up to see that Perkin and Beorn had joined him. They stood behind him, eyeing the new ground where the mire had lain. Some way behind them he saw Pagan. He too was staring at the mire, but with an expression that stilled the blood in Adcock's veins. It was a look of pure loathing, as though he detested the place with every fibre of his body.

'What are you doing here?'

'Nothing. We're going up to our friend Guy's house. He's got a few gallons of ale left from his last brewing, and we wondered whether you'd like to come with us?' Perkin said. 'I've heard it said the ale his wife brews is the best in the parish.'

Adcock looked up at the sky. It was past dusk now, and nearer full night time. There was a pale glow on the horizon to the west, but apart from that the sky was turning from blue to black, and all the stars had begun to glimmer: a silver frost on the dark velvet background. 'I would like to,' he said.

Perkin looked like a man who had used up his last words. He nodded and turned away towards the north. Adcock stood slowly and stretched. He felt drained and uncomfortable, but at least now he was apparently accepted by the people among whom he must live. That to him was more important than anything. Even if his life here was to be troubled and full of fears, the fact that he had the support and companionship of the peasants on the manor would be some consolation.

'Are you all right, Pagan?' he asked as he passed him.

'Me? Yes. Not too bad.'

Adcock followed his gaze to the mire. 'It's pretty foul.'

'Yes. That's where the young woman was found, isn't it? Lady Lucy?'

'In the middle. Horrible sight.'

Pagan shook his head. 'I can imagine,' he said, turning away and walking to where the other two men stood patiently waiting.

Adcock walked slowly and carefully, and saw Perkin and Beorn exchange a glance. 'I'm fine. It's just . . .'

'We know what happened. He's done it to others before now,' Perkin said. 'We can walk more slowly.'

'There's no need,' Adcock said gratefully. 'Once I start moving, the pain abates somewhat.'

'Good, then let's be going,' Beorn said.

Adcock looked at the two men in front of him. 'Why? What's the hurry?' Now he could see them, he saw that they were worried themselves. There was some anxiety in their features that he couldn't understand. 'What is it?'

'We reckon it'd be a good idea to be away from here, that's all,' Perkin said.

Adcock stood still. 'Why?'

It was Beorn who growled deeply, 'If you want to be caught up in a fight, stay here. If you want to live without more pain, you'd best come with us. We have heard that Sir Odo is going to attack this place tonight.'

'I should be back at the hall, then! So should you!' Adcock said.

Perkin walked back to him. 'Look, if Sir Odo and Sir Geoffrey want to battle things out, that's fine – but don't expect any of the demesne's peasants to join in. We're going up to Guy's house, and you can join us if you want. If you want to remain here or at the hall, that's good too. But you'd be much safer with us.'

Adcock licked lips that were suddenly dry. 'What will they do?'

'Sir Odo will attack with a small force and he'll kill a number of Sir Geoffrey's men. Then he'll leave. If you're there, he'll probably kill you too. So hurry up and come with us, man!'

Adcock nodded and made an effort to keep up as Perkin and Beorn set the pace up the hillside, away from the house.

'Are you sure of this?' he asked at the top when he stopped to catch his breath.

Pagan nodded grimly. 'Aye. Sir Odo told me.'

It was only a few minutes later that Adcock heard the hooves approaching down the lane.

'Down!' Pagan shouted.

Chapter Thirty-Nine

Sir Geoffrey was in his hall when the shout came: 'Torches in the road! A lot of them!'

He ran to the door and pushed a man out of the way, peering in the darkness. The guard stationed there pointed, and Sir Geoffrey swore quietly under his breath, then: 'Get your weapons!'

The men in the lane looked as though they were moving only very slowly. Either they were walking their horses to keep the noise of the attack down, or they were moving at the speed of men-at-arms without horses. Either way, they would soon be here, as far as he could see. They were only a matter of half a mile away.

Thank God his guards had seen them.

Men had begun to tumble from the doorway into the yard, some buckling on their belts or pulling leather baldrics over their heads, others grabbing at polearms. Soon there was a sizeable gathering outside the door. More men were fetching bows and arrows, but in this light they'd be little use until the enemy was much nearer.

If only he hadn't left so many men down at the sergeant's house. It would have been much easier to protect the hall. Still, if he hadn't taken the place back, there probably wouldn't have been an attack here either. And whining about 'if only' wouldn't serve to help just now. He could worry about that later.

He barged his way past more men as he went back into the hall. 'You still there?'

Coroner Edward smiled and lifted a mazer of wine in salute. 'This is none of my affair.'

'You think so? Then you'd better start planning how to explain to my Lord Despenser why it was that you rested while his estates were under attack. I shall tell him exactly how you sought to defend his manor, with the greatest of pleasure.'

He hurried to his table, grabbed the jug of wine, and poured a good measure into his mouth. This was the way to fight a battle. At night, with a full belly and plenty of wine. Ideal!

Already he was feeling a distinct optimism. He'd fought and won worse fights than this. Sir Odo didn't have that many men, and there'd been no time for reinforcements from Sir John Sully to turn up, even if he'd sent for support. No, Sir Geoffrey could beat him off. He nodded to himself, spat in the direction of the languid coroner, and rushed out again.

His men had already started to deploy themselves. They knew their business, and while some shouted for horses, more were stringing ropes between trees on the approach to the hall, at a little above a man's head height, in the hope that they might unhorse a number of their attackers. Others had set the archers at either side of the main body of men, so that as the horses pounded up the hill they would be at the mercy of the bowmen on either side before running into the shields of the men in front of the house.

Hearing another shout for a horse, Sir Geoffrey went to the stables and yelled at the top of his voice that no one was riding off in cowardice tonight. All horses were to be put back in the stables and no one was to mount.

'Damn fools imagine I don't know how they think,' he grunted to himself as he returned to the front of the house.

The torches were hardly any closer, and he suddenly came to a halt, staring. They must have seen his men, heard the shouting, and yet they hadn't come on to attack. And now he looked down at the road, he noticed that the immense number of torches seemed to be closely bunched together, as though for mutual support – or because *a small party of men was carrying a large number of torches!*

And then he heard the rumble of hooves and the screams, and he felt his scalp crawl to think how he had been duped.

Sir Odo drew his sword and waved it above his head. Without a word, he clapped spurs to his mount, and the beast fairly flew down the hill into the rear yard of the house.

A man was standing by a water butt, a yoke over his shoulders and two full buckets of water dangling, and Sir Odo gave a shrill shriek as his sword ran him through, and then there was another man, screaming in terror and running, and Sir Odo pushed the point of his sword through the man's back, the force of his charge ripping the blade up through two ribs and then out as the man fell.

His men were with him, about him, as he charged onwards.

At last there was some resistance as he curved round the wall and saw the line of men waiting. Archers at the end swung round, their faces pasty as they realised their danger, men-at-arms struggling to turn and bring their shields to bear on this unexpected attack from behind them. And then Sir Odo and his men crashed into, over, and through the line, leaving a tangled mass of injured and wounded men.

'Back!' he bellowed, and turned his beast back to the line. His destrier was a good brute, expensive as hell, but superb. He would kick, stamp and bite at anyone in his way, and he started now, an enraged animal dealing death with his hooves. Sir Odo saw a man in front of him, and before he could think of raising his sword the horse had flailed with a hoof and the man's face had disappeared, simply disappeared, pummelled into nothing by the force of a hoof with all the power of that immense foreleg behind it.

Seeing a figure running, Sir Odo thought it looked familiar. He slapped the horse with the flat of his blade, and set it off in pursuit.

There was no means of pulling back the initiative tonight. The battle was lost already. Perhaps it had been as soon as Sir Geoffrey set off to attack Robert Crokers's house earlier. Whatever the truth, Sir Geoffrey intended escaping, and now he hurried to reach the farther side of his manor and escape behind it.

But even as he conceived the idea, he heard the ferocious roar of his enemy, and he knew he'd been seen. Instead, he changed his direction, and pelted down the track towards the road. He had only one possible defence against a knight on horseback, and he took it, running for his life, down the way where he and his men had expected to trap Sir Odo's men only a few minutes before.

Faster, faster, until his heart felt as though it must burst in his breast, until his lungs were on fire, until his legs were all but ruined, and then, blessed relief, he saw the rope and ran at full tilt underneath it.

The ground was trembling with the destrier's hoofbeats, and he thought he could feel its breath on his neck, and then there was a loud cough, and the horse lost his concentration as Sir Odo was caught by the rope and flung backwards like a straw doll to land on his back, while his horse continued a short distance, then seemed to notice that all was not well.

Sir Geoffrey did not hesitate. He left the horse – trained destriers were all too often trained to serve only one man – and went back the way he had come, past the house and up the hill, his sword still in his hand, racing for his life up the hill and away from the slaughter.

Sir Odo was badly winded, and he lay for some little while, his vision black and his senses dulled. It was only when he began to hear the shouting and clamour of battle that he realised where he was, and he rolled over to climb to all fours, wondering what could have hit him. Then, kneeling, he saw the rope between two trees and swore. The simplest trick in the world, and he'd fallen for it.

Sir Geoffrey made it to the top of the hill with his sword still in his hands. Once there, he turned, panting, to gaze behind him.

The house was lighted by a yellow, unnatural glow. As he looked, he thought he could see a shower of sparks rising, and he frowned with incomprehension until he saw the first flames licking at the thatch. Then he understood: someone had thrown torches up into the roof. When he glanced back at the road, he saw that the men gathered there were all gone. Clearly they had taken the opportunity of the attack to charge the place and hurl their flaming torches into the building or up at the straw. Now the flames were taking hold.

He could have wept. Sitting, he put his face in his hands and covered the scene from himself. Shaking his head, he was drained of all emotion. He was desolate. This would be an incalculable loss to him. His master would be sure to remove him and replace him with some arrogant prickle like Nicholas, while Odo would grow in smugness at having beaten him.

Soon men could be coming up here to find him. He had to get as far away as possible. He thrust his sword home in its scabbard, and started.

This path was so well-known to him that he could almost find his way in the dark. There on his right was the drained mire, where the fool of a sergeant had found that woman's body. He set off up the hill and, panting, reached a tree. From here he could see the house and several miles about. The moon was shining down silver on the whole countryside, and now he could make out the fires at his hall more clearly. There was more, too. He saw the moon glinting off steel. Men were running away along the road to Monk Oakhampton; two were over the hedge and hastening down towards the chapel. And there were no men in the road any more. They'd brought their torches to his hall, and that was that.

It was enough to make a man weep.

Pagan and the others stood at the top of the hill, gazing down in the direction the horses had taken when they galloped past them. The battle was invisible to them, at the other side of the house, but they could hear the screams and roars of the men battling for their lives down there, and then they saw the flames begin to rise in the dark night's sky.

'Is this the end of the manor?' Adcock wondered.

'There's never an end,' Perkin said. 'Nope. Tomorrow we'll all be called back to start to rebuild it, just as Sir Odo told his men to go and rebuild the sergeant's house. They destroy, we build up again. It's always our efforts that keep the demesne working. Come on, tonight we can still enjoy ale. The work won't start until morning.'

He turned his face to the north and set off again. Pagan saw that Adcock was in pain still and offered his hand, but the fellow refused it, saying that he had no need of help. It somewhat added to Pagan's sense that the lad was not cast from the same mould as the rest of the men at Monkleigh Hall.

He could feel the guilt falling on his shoulders that his actions could have led to this man's being brought here and made to suffer so much. But if not him, then it would only have been another. It was hardly Pagan's fault that a man must follow his destiny. That was just God's way. A mere human had no control over events – all he could do was react to them. That was what Isaac had once said to him when he asked how God could let so much harm and ill-fortune affect his master. It was so cruel of God to allow his Squire William to be so cruelly torn from his family in a foreign land, and then to kill his son too. Poor Ailward perhaps had not had a chance. Born dispossessed and poor, he had done the best he could with the means at his disposal.

But this Adcock, he had done nothing. He had been a pleasant man, a young fellow with ambition and hope in his breast when he came here. Pagan had a weight of guilt to support, and that weight seemed to grow each time he looked on the fellow.

He had done what he thought was best. That was his only excuse. He only hoped it would be enough.

'There's someone coming behind us!' Adcock hissed.

Pagan hesitated, torn by the desire to flee and leave Adcock as a tempting target for whoever might be chasing after them, but then his better nature took over. He grabbed Adcock and bodily hauled him off the path. The other two had already melted into the bushes and trees at the side of the road, and now Pagan pulled Adcock down into the security of the grasses and bushes. Both were soon hidden, and as Pagan listened, he heard the rough, strained breathing of a man pushed beyond his endurance.

He looked up and down the path, but there was no sign of further pursuit. This man appeared to be all on his own, and as he passed by them, Pagan suddenly recognised Sir Geoffrey, and felt a wild joy kiss at his heart.

Here was the man who was responsible for the woes of his lady's family, the man who was the architect of his own shame, delivered up to him. It was the work of a moment to mutter 'He's mine!', to draw his dagger, and to leap up after him.

Sir Geoffrey for his part had no idea that he was now being pursued. He hurried on his way, stumbling occasionally, tripping over a large tree limb that had broken off and lay on the ground in his path. All that was in his mind was the desire to reach a place of safety, ideally some distance from Monkleigh. The nearest and safest he could think of was Dolton, and that was several miles north. It would take him ages to get there if he walked through the night. Better to find somewhere to rest for the night – perhaps a barn or outbuilding away from other people. There were some sheds up near Pagan's father's smithy. That would do.

And then he would be able to start to plan his revenge on Sir Odo. The mad bastard must have thought he could get away with this – well, he'd soon learn how mistaken he had been! Sir Geoffrey would not rest until he'd taken revenge. He'd come back here with the Despenser host, and he'd take apart Sir Odo's property stone by stone. Sir Odo himself would be declared a felon and outlawed throughout the land. If he could, let him make his way to the continent and seek a new life there, because Sir Geoffrey would be damned before he saw him return to Fishleigh. That manor would become forfeit, and damn Sir John Sully if he wanted to argue. No one could argue with the Despensers, not now. He would . . .

His foot caught on something and he tumbled headlong. Eyes closed, he lay on his belly cursing his fortune before even thinking about rising. It was typical of his luck that he should fall. What next, a twisted or broken ankle? Perhaps he would manage to break his neck and end his misfortunes in style.

He tried to get up, and realised that the hand gripping his sword was stuck. It was the sword. It wouldn't move. Opening his eyes, he peered at it, and saw that there was a man's boot resting on it. Following the leg upwards, he found himself staring at Pagan's grim features. 'Get off my sword, you motherless son of a cretin!' he snarled.

To his astonishment, Pagan appeared to ignore him. Instead he reached down and took hold of Sir Geoffrey's short hair, pulling his head up. 'Shut up! You've done enough already.'

'What?' As the cold metal of the blade touched his throat, Sir Geoffrey was suddenly still.

'Leave him, Pagan. Let me kill him!'

'Adcock?' Sir Geoffrey said, trying to look over his shoulder while not moving his head. He was pulled up so far that his fingers could hardly touch the ground, and the pressure on his scalp was terrible, but he daren't move his legs in case Pagan thought he was readying himself to attack.

'Leave him, Pagan. He nearly killed me, and all because I was doing our lord's work, clearing unusable land. I say I kill him now and we throw *him* into the mire.'

'Adcock, don't be foolish!' Sir ·Geoffrey said. 'You can't kill me, I'm your master here. Steward to the . . .'

'You are nothing now, Sir Geoffrey. You're a fool who's lost a manor, that's all. And wandering about at this time of night you are a suspected fugitive. Come, Pagan, let me kill him. God knows I have enough reason, the bastard!'

'No.' Pagan sighed deeply. 'I can't, Adcock.'

The fellow was brimming with enthusiasm, the blade gripped so tightly in his hand fairly shaking with desire. He wanted to kill this man more than anything he'd ever wanted. And it was all Pagan's fault.

'I can't let you, Adcock. We'll take the knight back down to Iddesleigh, and hand him over to that Keeper and his friend. They'll know what to do.'

No, Pagan couldn't let this fellow commit murder. When Adcock had arrived here, he'd been a cheerful enough lad, from the look of him, and now he was ruined. He had been subjected to Sir Geoffrey's cruelty, insulted, demeaned, and changed into a brutal facsimile of the man he had been such a short time before. And all because of Pagan's crime. It was all his fault that Adcock was here in the first place.

Adcock protested, 'I want to kill him, though. Look, it'll take one stab and we throw him into that mire there. No one will ever find him if we don't clear it, and after being beaten for clearing the other one, I'm not going to do that in a hurry.'

'Don't think you can kill me with impunity, boy!' Sir Geoffrey grated.

'Who,' Pagan asked quietly, 'is there up here who would stop us?'

And suddenly Sir Geoffrey felt panic. He tried to pull his sword free and then grabbed for the dagger at his belt, but there were too many men, and he could only scream his defiance and abuse as they roughly turned him over, binding his wrists.

Chapter Forty

Baldwin and Simon watched the flames roar skywards. Edgar was helping a few others to keep the two sides apart, while men ran about the place fetching and carrying buckets of water from the well to try to douse the flames. Hugh was standing morosely staring at the blaze, remembering the fire at his own house.

'There is little chance of putting that out,' Baldwin said.

'Old thatch that's had a good chance to dry is never easy to put out,' Simon said.

The clouds of smoke, thick, greasy, and greyish green even in the darkness, roiled about the area. Invariably when it sank down and engulfed all the men, it made them choke and splutter, it was so thick and foul.

They had seen the fires as they hurried down the road, hoping to prevent bloodshed, and both had known that they were too late before they had caught sight of the house. 'At least there are few dead,' Baldwin said.

'So far,' Simon replied. 'There are some bad wounds in among that lot.'

They had brought all the men from the bar at Iddesleigh with them, in the hope that they might compose a force to thrust between the warring factions, but by the time they reached the hall most of the men were already separated. The fighting took second place to watching the manor burn for those who had no direct investment in the building. When Baldwin and Simon arrived, Sir Odo's men had more or less taken the place, and he and a few others were impounding their prisoners against a fence, having taken their weapons from them.

'Sir Odo, this is an outrageous abuse,' Baldwin said as he met the knight.

'It was an outrageous abuse when that man decided to invade my lands,' Sir Odo said. 'This was just an attempt to persuade him to leave me alone. He sowed, and he has reaped the harvest. It's the behaviour of the Despensers that makes the country so dangerous today. If more men stood up to their bullying, the realm would be safer.'

'You think this is safer?' Baldwin demanded, waving at the fires and the bodies on the ground.

'It's better than giving up everything, every time the Despensers or their men decide they want to grab another piece of territory,' Sir Odo said.

'Is that all this was? An attempt to stop him taking your lands? Or was it to stop Despenser – or, for that matter, Lord Hugh de Courtenay – ever learning that you'd kept back parts of the lands he had taken from the widow of Squire Robert?' Simon asked.

'That is an unworthy thought,' Sir Odo said.

'It would be a deeply dishonourable act,' Baldwin said.

Sir Odo glanced at him, then shrugged. 'Well, I cannot help what you two think to yourselves, but bear this in mind, lordings. My action here has protected Lord Hugh de Courtenay's lands. While he is thought to be a bold and courageous defender of his property, he is more likely to be safe from the Despensers' attempts to rob him as they have so many others.'

'Don't seek to threaten me into supporting you,' Sir Baldwin hissed. He stepped nearer Sir Odo. 'I shall tell the truth about this night, Sir Odo, and you will be named as guilty in this.'

'Guilty of what, Sir Baldwin? Is there any proof that I have done something wrong? There is no one here who is likely to accuse me, is there? Do you have any evidence that I am guilty of taking lands or anything else? No! So I should forget your sourness. You have done what you came here to do: you have found the murderer of your man's family. You have found the murderer of Ailward, too, I expect, and of Lady Lucy. At the same time, you have helped me to thwart an attempt by a lackey of the Despensers to steal lands from our lord. I should stick to that story. It's believable, after all. Who knows? It might be true.'

'Sir Baldwin? Get this oaf off me!'

Baldwin turned in time to see Sir Geoffrey being walked up the track towards him, gripped by Pagan.

'Sir Baldwin, I found this man scurrying away up behind the hall. Thought I ought to bring him home again.'

'Thank you, Pagan,' Baldwin said, and as Sir Odo moved imperceptibly towards Sir Geoffrey, Baldwin drew his sword and put it between Sir Odo and his prey. 'There will be no more bloodshed, Sir Odo, unless you want to challenge me?'

Sir Odo shrugged, smiling broadly. 'If you say so.'

Pagan was not finished, though. 'Sir Baldwin, I brought this man to you because I want him to hear the truth. I murdered Ailward on the day of the camp ball match. I confess my crime, but I also denounce Sir Odo and accuse him of the murder of Lady Lucy of Meeth and the murderous attack on Hugh's family.'

It was not practical to try to hold a court in the middle of the night, and Baldwin demanded that all returned with him and Simon to the church. There, in the nave, in full view of as much of the Iddesleigh congregation as could be mustered at short notice, Sir Odo swore that he would return to be tried the next day. He gripped the Gospels with a firm hand, and he stared at Baldwin as he spoke, loudly and clearly, and then he passed the book back to Matthew with a small bow and spun on his heel.

The people parted as though miraculously. None remained barring his path, which was normal, and showed the correct reverence for his position, he thought, but there was something in the air that grated on his nerves. It was less as though this was a mark of respect for his status, than as though they loathed to share the same space with him. They would not touch him in case he polluted them.

Idiots! They couldn't understand. How could they? He'd been in the service of other men all his life, and he had wanted fortune. If he'd been luckier, he could have won it, but as things were, it was impossible. He was always in the pay of his masters. The first, the very first chance he'd had of winning his own rewards had been when he'd met Lady Lucy. And he would have been honourable with her, if she'd let him. He would have married her, and allowed his son to take all the money when he died – but she'd have none of it. That look of terror and horror had never left her face, not from the moment when he killed her steward to the last moments when he'd left her in the smithy. She had loathed him.

Outside he stood a few seconds and stared about him at the men standing silently. Then he gave a dry chuckle and walked to his horse. Peasants couldn't understand because how can property comprehend how another piece of property might be fought over? If you have never owned or desired, you cannot see how a man might be pushed to extraordinary lengths to protect his possessions, or to acquire more.

He sprang on to his horse, whirled the beast's head about, and rode off along the lane to his hall. There was not much time. He had to collect all his movables, pack them, and clear off urgently. Probably best to head for Tiverton. He seemed to remember someone saying that Lord de Courtenay was up there.

'Can I tell you what happened?' Pagan asked as Baldwin and Simon led the way back to the inn.

Baldwin glanced at Simon and Hugh. 'I suppose so. You will have to explain yourself tomorrow anyway,' he said.

Pagan walked into the inn and sat at the table with the others. Baldwin and Simon sat opposite him, Hugh and Edgar stood behind him, and Sir Geoffrey perched himself on an upturned barrel nearby, arms folded while he glared at Pagan with loathing. Villagers from Monkleigh and Iddesleigh filled the room, while Perkin and Beorn were up at the bar with a pale and shaken Adcock.

Poor lad. He'd hardly got over the shock of being savagely attacked and injured by that idiot Sir Geoffrey when he'd been overwhelmed by the desire to kill. He'd lusted for Sir Geoffrey's blood as a youth might lust for a wench. And now the reaction was upon him. He was himself again, and the idea of what he had so nearly become was a terrible burden.

'I killed Ailward, sir, because I saw what he had done. He and Sir Odo had captured Lady Lucy, and they took her up to my father's smithy, because they knew that no one ever went there any more. They could do all they wanted to her without fear of discovery. Her screams would go unheeded.

'I didn't realise at first, of course. I only found out on the day of the camp ball game, when I saw Ailward. He was smothered in black mud, up to his groin. I had no idea what had happened, and when I asked, he told me! He had murdered the child and taken her to the mire and thrown her in. She was guilty of refusing to marry Sir Odo. For that they killed her.

'I was disgusted by what I heard. I went to my father's old smithy, and found it reeking still of burned flesh. They had slaughtered her in the most revolting way so that when her body was found, people would assume the Despenser family had committed this evil act. I came across Ailward on my way back to the house where I lived with Lady Isabel, and my rage knew no bounds. I knocked him down and left him for dead. I would do it again. He murdered that poor child, and he did it in my father's chamber. Yes, I would do it again.'

'But he was your master's son!' Sir Geoffrey exclaimed. 'I thought you were so loyal to him and his seed!'

'I was. I am. I would lay down my life for his child.'

Baldwin nodded. 'Tell me, Pagan, was it your mistress's choice that you should move back to your old home when Ailward died, or was it yours?'

Pagan allowed a half-smile to curl his lips. 'How did you guess that?'

'I was very slow,' Baldwin admitted. 'But then I started to think. It seemed curious that you should move back to your home just when the women would ideally require a man in their house to guard them. Unless you thought that they would be safe enough on their own. And then I heard Sir Odo had visited the women.'

'He went there often enough after dark,' Pagan said. 'It was much as it had been before, when Squire William was fighting. He often took his son with him when he was fighting, so he could teach him the way of war. As soon as they went, Sir Odo began to pay court to Lady Isabel, and she was so lonely and scared, it's no surprise she succumbed to his wit and perseverance. But then, when Squire Robert was dead, I think she repented and felt guilt. It was eight and twenty years ago that Robert first went north with his father William, and the two won renown and some fame, under good King Edward, the Hammer of the Scots, although they were not lucky with the spoils of war. The Scottish never seemed to have much to steal. Although he didn't know it, Robert lost more than his money in fighting for the king. It cost him dearly, and he wore a cuckold's horns from then on.'

'So Ailward was Sir Odo's son?' Simon asked.

'Aye. Ailward was Sir Odo's. He was always aware of it. Sir Odo would ever make conversation with him if he saw the lad out and about, and I think that after Squire Robert died, my lady Isabel must have told him the truth, because his manner changed after that. He grew more arrogant, more froward. It was hard to contain myself sometimes, with the way he spoke to me. And then he told me what he had done with his father to Lady Lucy.'

'What did he do?' Baldwin asked.

'It was his father who captured her. He had known this lady for some years, and I suppose he always desired her. He was a bachelor, she was a young and beautiful woman . . . It is not hard to see what thoughts began to fill his mind. Lady Isabel was still feeling the guilt that her behaviour had produced. She feels it every day, or used to until Ailward's death. Now she only hopes for Odo to visit her again.'

'He did yesterday,' Baldwin grunted.

'I know. Now that one avenue is closed, he is prepared to consider the other again.'

'So he desired Lady Lucy,' Simon pressed.

'Aye. And she did not reciprocate. She spat in his face once, I heard, because he pressed his suit too strongly. She was a spirited woman. Then came a time when Sir Odo decided he would have her. He drew his sword, killed her guard, and captured her, expecting her to wither in his arms and accept his hand, but she wouldn't. She rejected him entirely, and I think that was when his love turned to loathing. He knocked her cold, and carried her body to my house, tying her there and keeping her out of the way of all others. It was easy enough. He knew what he would do with her, because the news of the Despensers' treatment of Lady Baret was being bruited abroad at the time, and he knew that Sir Geoffrey would take the blame for any act of cruelty towards a widow. So he killed her.'

'What then?' Baldwin asked gently.

'Then, he told his son and a man-at-arms, Walter, to go and take the body to Sir Geoffrey's land. Ailward told me all this. He thought it was a splendid idea: to put the blame firmly on to the Despenser's man, and to quietly take over Lady Lucy's manor while everyone was disputing Sir Geoffrey's role in her death.'

'How would he take the land?'

'There was no heir, and her husband was a knight of Lord de Courtenay. It would take a little persuasion, but Sir Odo planned to have Lord Hugh de Courtenay take over the lands and make him the master of them. Lord Hugh may well have agreed. In the meantime, the disputed land where Crokers died would be made over to Ailward, because Lord Hugh and Despenser did not know of it. Ailward would have an inheritance, and if Sir Geoffrey was accused, he might somehow regain his old territories.

'That was what he told me, his old servant, knowing that I was devoted to his father and his grandsire, but he didn't realise how I would feel about him using a young widow and killing her in order to win so much. He told me gleefully how he and Walter had carried her body to the mire, weighted her down, and thrown her into the foul waters. Later, he said, a man at Sir Geoffrey's manor would suggest that the mires were drained, hoping for advancement, and the body would be found. It could hardly be kept secret; from that moment Sir Geoffrey would be in difficult waters.'

Baldwin felt sickened. This behaviour was anathema to a man raised to the concept of chivalry. That a knight could consider such treatment of a widow was almost inconceivable, but there was no doubting Pagan's words. 'So you killed him?'

'He was telling me all about how he had thrown her in, and he wanted me to go and help him clean my house. My home. The place where my father brought me up. I grew so angry to hear of how he had defiled my home that I lashed out at him. There was a rock, and while he spoke, I picked it up and hammered and hammered at him. He died.'

Simon and Baldwin exchanged a look.

'For my part,' Simon said, 'I think you have done well to execute a murderer's accomplice. If a man were to kill my daughter like that, I would like to think that a man like you would be there to do the same.'

Baldwin nodded, thinking of his own little daughter. If his wife was widowed, a recurring fear of his, then what would happen to them? A man such as Ailward deserved his end. As did Odo. Tomorrow he . . . 'Where is Hugh?'

Hugh hurried down the road, limping slightly with the effort. He had taken a staff from beside the inn's doorway, and it helped him as he made his way along the road towards Fishleigh.

'Friend Hugh, I do hope you aren't thinking of attacking a knight in his hall?'

Hugh turned and scowled at the friar. 'Leave me.'

'I can't, Hugh. If you attack him, it'd harm your immortal soul,' John said sadly. 'How could I, a friar, live with myself if I were to let you do that to yourself ?'

Hugh gritted his teeth and set off again.

'Hugh? Look, there's no point in going and killing him. He'll be in court in the morning, and there he'll be convicted.'

'And released when he pays amercement. He'll be free for ages. When the justices get here, they'll take his money and make him innocent.'

'Perhaps. Perhaps others will prevail and he'll be hanged.'

'That's if he's here.'

'Hmm?'

Hugh stopped and turned to face him. 'You don't think he'll be there. Do you? He'll be on his horse tonight. You know that too.'

'I fear it,' John confessed.

'I won't let him. I want him dead.'

John said no more. The two men trotted on side by side, and it was only when they were in clear view of the hall that they began to slow their pace. 'What now?' John said.

'He won't come north. Means going through Iddesleigh; that'd be dangerous. He'll go to Hatherleigh, and on from there.'

'You are sure?' John smiled. So was he.

*   *   *

Sir Odo had everything he could pack quickly in two saddle-sacks tied behind the saddle. The sacks clanked and rattled, for he had taken all his best plate. It would be easy to pawn when he needed ready cash. Hopefully his master's lord would take his case to heart and protect him, but only if he reached Lord Hugh before news of this little matter could reach his ears from an unfriendly source.

He clapped spurs to his beast, and was off in an instant, pelting through the open gateway, out into the night, and immediately turned south on the road to Hatherleigh. That road would take him down to the main road to Crediton and up following the river to Tiverton and the castle where he hoped to find de Courtenay.

When he was out of sight of the hall, he whipped his mount again. Speed now was crucial. He had to get out of this damned area as quickly as he could. He had to . . .

His horse staggered and rose, neighing wildly. At that speed there was little Odo could do to stop the animal slipping sideways, the hindquarters sliding underneath, and suddenly his own leg was under the brute, the flesh being raked by the stones in the trail, and the horse was down, thrashing madly. Sir Odo kicked himself free and looking down felt the first glimmerings of panic and fear set in. The damned creature had broken a leg!

Swearing to himself, he drew his sword and swept it swiftly over the throat, jerking himself away as the blood fountained. Only then, wiping some of the blood from his tunic, did he have time to study the damage to himself, and as he peered at the blood seeping from the long graze all along his upper thigh, he cursed again.

Hugh smiled to himself. He cut the rope they had set across the road, and he licked his lips with a fierce excitement. Stepping forward, he stood in front of Sir Odo. 'Remember me?'

Sir Odo glanced up with a feeling of disbelief. He had thought himself alone and ruined, but here was a man. He squinted up at Hugh. 'Do I know you? Do you have a horse I can buy? I have money here, and I need a beast urgently.'

'I didn't bring you down to sell you a horse,' Hugh said.

'Didn't . . . you mean *you* brought my horse down?' Sir Odo exclaimed, reaching for his sword.

Immediately the staff in Hugh's hands whipped out and cracked against Sir Odo's knuckles. The metal-shod tip broke two bones in his hand. Sir Odo felt them crack, and a terrible numbness overcame his hand. Then the pain began, and he clutched at the ruined limb. 'Who are you?'

'I'm Hugh Drewsteignton, or Hugh Shepherd. I used to have a little house up in Iddesleigh.'

Sir Odo felt his stomach lurch, but he tried to keep his voice calm. 'So? I recall – your poor wife and child were killed, weren't they? That was terrible. Wasn't it a fire?'

'You and your men were there, weren't they? You killed my woman so you could blame Sir Geoffrey for starting a war between Fishleigh and Monkleigh. You didn't want to hurt any of your own peasants, so you had my house burned, you killed my woman and son, and left me alive to accuse Sir Geoffrey.'

'Why should I do that? It would hardly help me, would it?'

It was John who answered now. The friar stepped forward from behind Hugh. 'You would use anything to remove Sir Geoffrey, wouldn't you? You might as well confess, Sir Odo, because this man intends to kill you anyway. At least if you admit your crimes, I can hear your confession first.'

Sir Odo's eyes narrowed. 'You would help a murderer kill me?'

'Only because of your many crimes,' John agreed sadly. 'Your offences have convinced me that you deserve death. There is nothing I can do to stop this fellow, clearly. Come! It is true, isn't it?'

Sir Odo stared at him, then up at Hugh, and nodded. He spoke with a fierce rage. 'I wanted him out, yes. He was in my way.'

'And you had killed Lady Lucy and this man's family?'

'He wasn't one of my serfs. I wasn't going to hurt the men who generate the manor's income when he and his woman were there instead. They didn't matter.'

Hugh gave a groan, and covered his eyes with a forearm. 'Didn't matter? *Didn't matter?*'

Sir Odo sneered at him. 'She was a good wench, too. Wriggled like a stoat when my man had her,' he said. His hand was slipping to his dagger.

'Stop!' Hugh said brokenly. 'I'll . . .'

There was a loud, dull thud, and Hugh's eyes rolled up into his head as he collapsed like a pole-axed ox. Friar John pursed his lips and stared down at him, shaking his head. 'Sorry, Hugh, but I couldn't let you do it.'

'Thank you, Friar! You were getting a little close to too late, though,' Sir Odo said with a weak smile. He shoved the dagger back in the sheath. 'Could you help me up, please? My ankle is . . .'

Friar John closed his eyes, shook his head a little, and then smiled at Sir Odo. 'What of the confession? Did you kill Lady Lucy too?'

'Yes. The little whore wouldn't accept me when I wanted her to marry me, and I lost my temper. I must have asked her a dozen times, but she wouldn't listen. I killed her, I admit it.'

'Then may God damn your soul!' John said, and brought the rock crashing down on Sir Odo's head. He heaved it up and dropped it five times, until the skull was broken and bloody, and only then did he throw the rock aside and sit down, weeping.

Chapter Forty-One

Simon wanted to go to search for his man as soon as the crowds had left. 'I only found him again this afternoon!'

Sir Geoffrey heard his anguished tone. 'With any luck your man will have found Sir Odo and killed him already. The devious, lying, duplicitous bastard deserves death after all the grief he's caused.'

'And you are a saint?' Baldwin sneered. 'I suppose when you tried to chase Robert Crokers off his land, that was a kindly gesture to the poor man?'

'That was different. That bastard Odo had told me that we could run the manor there to our mutual advantage, and it seemed a good enough . . .'

'So you were prepared to steal from your master,' Baldwin noted. 'You knew it was a part of the estate he had taken, yet you retained it.'

'I expected rewards, and I would naturally have shared them with my master,' Sir Geoffrey said loftily.

'It will be interesting to see whether he agrees with you when your little investment comes to his ear.'

Sir Geoffrey looked less happy at that thought. Bad enough to have to explain the ruin of his manor without Lord Despenser learning about the disputed parcel of land.

'And there is still the matter of the murder of Robert Crokers,' Baldwin reminded himself.

Simon put his hand on Baldwin's shoulder. 'I have to go. You know why.'

Baldwin nodded. 'Take Edgar. He knows these lanes quite well already.'

Edgar was first at the stables, and he grabbed his horse and saddled and bridled him while Simon was still looking for his saddle. It was often the way, Edgar had noticed, that men who were otherwise entirely sensible would all too often lose track of where their horses had gone in a stable. For him it was entirely natural to see to his horse first. A warrior would always see to his mount's comfort before his own, because he would depend on the beast for his life. He had also spent too many years avoiding capture, while he and his master wandered about the continent as renegade Templars, not to know exactly where all his equipment was at all times.

When his own horse was prepared, he hurried to help Simon, and soon both were ready. They mounted, and Edgar took the lead, cantering up past the church, then taking the left turn down towards the river. They crossed it, and were soon on their way to the old hall at Fishleigh. As they approached it, Edgar slowed his mount, patting the horse's neck and studying the hall closely.

'They aren't alarmed,' he said.

'Why should they be?'

'If a crazed peasant had run in demanding the head of the master, I'd expect either a lot of noisy fighting, or hilarious celebrations,' Edgar mused, and nodded to himself. 'I think Hugh must have found Sir Odo as he fled.'

'Where will he be, then?' Simon said despairingly.

'On this road. We didn't see any sign of them up towards Iddesleigh, so they must have gone south instead,' Edgar said imperturbably. He urged his horse into a trot.

'What's that?' Simon demanded when they had covered perhaps another quarter mile. 'There's something in the lane – a horse!'

Edgar said nothing. He had seen the little bundle just beyond the horse, and he clicked his tongue. His mount hurried onwards and Edgar slipped from his saddle as Simon joined him. 'Here he is!'

'Oh God! He's not . . .'

'He's breathing too loud for a corpse,' Edgar said shortly. His hands were at Hugh's head. 'Yes, there's a lump the size of a goose's egg here.'

'What could have happened?' Simon wondered, leaving Edgar. A short way beyond he found another body. 'Sir Odo, too!'

Edgar left Hugh for a moment, and reached down to Sir Odo's

body. 'He's dead. It's clear enough what happened, Bailiff. Sir Odo was riding along here at full tilt, and Hugh was in his path. His horse tried to avoid Hugh, stumbled, and fell, hitting Hugh as he went. Sir Odo also fell and broke his head.'

Simon looked at him for a long moment. 'You think so?'

'I will do by morning,' Edgar assured him. 'Would you gather up Hugh? We shall need to carry him back.'

'Of course,' Simon said, and marched back to Hugh's body.

Edgar watched him go, and as Simon bent to pick up Hugh, Edgar took the rock from beside Sir Odo's corpse, and hurled it as far as he could into the furze that lined the road.

'What was that?' Simon snapped.

'Just a fox or something,' Edgar said calmly.

It was another three days before Hugh could hope to be mounted on a horse, and Simon did not, for the first time in his life, grudge him all the rest he needed. Jeanne helped him nurse his servant back to health, and when Hugh was at last able to stand and hobble about with a staff, Simon felt as pleased and rewarded as a man watching his son take his first steps.

Emma was not pleased by the recovery, apparently. Jeanne confided in Simon that she thought her maid had rather liked Hugh when she thought him dead, but now that he was on the path to health, she was happier remembering all the disputes and quarrels she had had with him.

'She can't even bear to be near him now,' she said.

It was Edgar who explained the truth. 'I don't think Emma will return with you, if you give her permission, my lady.'

They were all sitting in the inn's hall. It was smokier than usual, because of a green log that was too fresh, but as Jankin had explained, they had used almost all the stores of firewood this year, it had been so cold.

'Why would she want to leave me?' Jeanne asked, bemused. 'She has always been happy with me. We've been together for ages.'

'I think you may find she's discovered a new interest.'

'You are talking in riddles, man!' Baldwin snapped. 'You are as confusing as when you kept laughing to yourself while we . . .' His face hardened. 'You don't mean she's . . .'

Edgar grinned broadly. 'If I told you, you wouldn't believe me!'

'Who?' Baldwin demanded.

'It's Deadly,' Edgar said, and then he couldn't restrain himself, but burst into laughter. 'You remember how flushed she was, how tired-looking? I found her in the arms of Deadly in the hayloft that night. Snoring fit to wake the dead, and as naked as the day they were born . . . it was a terrifying sight!'

Baldwin winced. 'I can live without the details, thank you.'

'Am I not to be allowed love?' Emma said. She stood in the doorway, her face scowling and flushed as red as St George's cross.

Baldwin was suddenly very still.

'Emma, of course you are. I wouldn't dream of stopping you from finding love – I am as happy as I could be with my husband, and if you have found a man whom you love, that would make me more than happy. But are you sure?'

'He asked me to marry him, and we exchanged our vows,' Emma said firmly.

Baldwin licked his lips anxiously and gazed at his wife.

'That is wonderful,' Jeanne said, although her tone betrayed a certain doubt. 'But you have not known him for long.'

Edgar sniggered. 'But you have known him very well in a short time.'

Baldwin glared at him furiously.

'Madam, would you release me? I once knew love, and left him because you were coming here to marry. I don't want to lose another.'

Baldwin held his breath. Jeanne looked at him and he tried to keep the hope from his eyes.

'I shall miss you, Emma,' Jeanne said.

And Baldwin felt as though the sun had suddenly burst through the ceiling and lighted the whole room with a roseate glow.

Perkin grunted as he pulled at a beam. It wouldn't move, and he shook his head in disgust. 'Hoi! Beorn! Get off your arse and help with this thing, will you?'

Already black with the soot that lay all about, Beorn wiped a hand over his forehead and snorted, hawking and spitting as he rose and walked through the fine ash to his friend. 'Why you want to move that one?'

'Don't start, Beorn. Just help me with it, will you?'

'It looks the wrong one to start with. I'd go for one of those on top.'

'This is the one I want to move, all right? Just help me pull it out of the way.'

'If you're sure.'

'Christ's balls, just pull!'

Beorn smiled accommodatingly, and bent his knees. He gripped the section of wood and grunted that he was ready. Perkin took the end again, and the two strained. There was a creak, and the beam shifted slightly.

'That's it! Come on, a little more!' Perkin gasped.

'I really don't . . .'

'Just bloody pull!'

Beorn shrugged, pulled, and the beam squeaked, then moved, and Perkin found himself falling backwards as it came out.

'I told you!' he said, and smiled. His smile grew glassy as there came a slight rumbling noise.

Beorn was already moving backwards. 'And I told *you* so.'

'Oh, bugger!'

The farther wall of the house suddenly sprang a crack. Where the beam had lain, a second had fallen on to the old cob wall, and where it had struck, the wall was slowly but surely collapsing.

Perkin took some quick steps backwards. 'I didn't think that would . . .'

The roar of falling stones and timbers drowned his words. He stood, staring dumbfounded, his mouth gaping as a hole appeared in the wall before him.

Beorn walked to him and clapped a hand on his shoulder. A small cloud of ash burst upwards, and he narrowed his eyes against it. When it was somewhat dissipated, he sniffed with an air of satisfaction. 'I reckon they'll soon see the advantage of it, Perkin. Takes a genius to see that a house needs a new door. I wouldn't have seen that myself.'

'What's all the noise? I heard a . . . Christ in a wine barrel, what's happened here?'

'Now, Emma, don't you worry,' Perkin said quickly. 'Look, there was this bit of an accident, and the wall . . .'

'She's stepping towards you,' Beorn said warningly.

Perkin held his hands before him. 'Emma, please, it was just one of those . . . Emma!'

'Just one of those things, eh?' Emma asked. She bent and picked up a small lump of blackened timber. 'I'll show you one of those things, I will . . .'

Perkin took a look at the lump of timber in her hands and gave up any ideas of diplomacy. He darted back, and dived through the new hole in the wall.

Beorn looked at her. 'Could you ask Davie to get his arse in here and help me?'

Emma nodded. She scowled at the hole Perkin had created, and tossed the timber through it, pretending not to hear the thump and cry of anguish. She wouldn't let them know how happy she was here. They didn't need to know that. She glowered at the men outside, before smiling at her Davie.

This place was perfect for her. Hugh's old home was no good to him, but she would change this into a marvellous little house. When the new roof was up, she'd clean all the soot and grime from it, and Davie could start to fence in the pasture, and then they could spend a little of the money which Jeanne had given them on purchasing some good animals, an ox, some pigs, maybe some lambs too. They'd soon have this little place thriving.

Or she'd know the reason why.

Lady Isabel watched him all the time with suspicious eyes, but he didn't care. He knew what she was feeling, because he knew perfectly well what it was like to love and to lose a love. She had lost her man; she wasn't the only person in the world to have lost.

Although she sat still and her eyes were still regularly brimming with tears, he could give her his sympathy, but not his compassion. Why should he? He served her with her food, and she and Malkin took their meagre shares and began to eat.

It was an unspoken rule now that he would not speak to them. Nor would Isabel knowingly make any comment while he was within earshot, but he didn't care. Her words would have been barbed, and he was happier to live in this silence.

She had been hoping that Sir Odo would return to her, apparently. When she heard from others that Sir Odo was dead, she had been disbelieving at first, then furious and almost lunatic, but that all changed when she heard the actual details of his death. She had flatly refused to entertain the concept that he might have been fleeing from Fishleigh without her. That, she asserted, was impossible. And since that was, the whole manner of his death was also impossible. Someone had made it up to fool her, and she wouldn't swallow it. No, he had been going to come and fetch her at last. They would share their misery at losing their son, and could comfort each other.

Malkin knew the truth, of course. No one in their right mind could doubt the truth behind Sir Odo. He was the man behind all the violence, and the cause of the deaths, including his own son's.

She'd never been happy about Odo coming to visit her mother-in-law, Pagan knew. It was a question that Pagan's mind would turn to every so often, whether or not Ailward had told Malkin that he was Odo's son, not Squire Robert's, but he doubted whether he would ever learn the answer. And in fact the speculation was enough. He didn't need to know, and he didn't want to know.

No, he had only ever loved the once, and it was enough for him. When Squire Robert died, he had felt the pain more than anything else he had ever known, and the only thing that kept him sane for many years was the knowledge that he was doing his duty by guarding Robert's son Ailward. Except Ailward was not his son.

But Robert had *thought* he was, and that in some way was as good as Pagan could have hoped for. If Ailward was good enough for Robert to treat as his own son, Malkin's son would be enough for Pagan too. He would serve the child as he had served Ailward.

For love.

Chapter Forty-Two

Coroner Edward knew that he would not remain in his post for very long. Not when the full details of the matter were aired. And they would be. He had Sir Baldwin de Furnshill's personal assurance of that.

He had tried his best to explain how important it was that he was kept out of the story – after all, the matter was little to do with him. He had been an unwilling accomplice at best. He had accepted a small retainer to be in the area when he was called, but that was all, really. The errors of his inquests over the body of Constance and the others were just that: mistakes. He was new to the post of coroner, and these were very difficult times, what with so many people being involved, and Sir Geoffrey trying to demand favours.

Lord Despenser was keen to see that his men worked together well, too. He would hardly expect a hard-working man like Sir Edward to ignore requests for help from a man so senior as Sir Geoffrey, would he? No, of course not.

It had looked for some while as though Sir Baldwin was being swayed by his arguments, but then he'd made the little slip of offering a sweetener to him. At once the shutters had fallen behind his eyes. It was just as though Edward had become invisible to him all of a sudden. Baldwin was looking at him, focused, and then he was looking through him unheeding. All because he had asked that justice be allowed to be *flexible* on this one occasion.

'Are you ready yet?'

'I have been ready for some while now,' Sir Edward lied. He disliked Sir Geoffrey more and more each time he saw the man. Now, with the remnants of the men who had served the steward, they were to leave Monkleigh Hall. And a good thing too! Sir Edward could hardly wait to be well shot of this place. It held only foul memories.

Sir Geoffrey, to his surprise, seemed to be sad to be going. Well, probably not a surprise. Once the Despenser heard of the mess that this manor was in now, he'd not be best pleased.

That was important, too. Sir Edward had to have his story planned so that when he was asked for his version, he had it ready. The truth would work – in places . . . but there were plenty of aspects which he had to hone.

After all, he didn't want to be sunk with Sir Geoffrey. Perhaps he might even be able to rescue something from it all. Maybe even a small manor of his own, if he was credible enough and managed to put all the blame on Sir Geoffrey.

Yes. That was the way forward. He would have to see how he could deny all knowledge and responsibility. Then, even if Sir Baldwin told some different story later, he could deny it, saying that these were the words of a man who was a natural enemy of Lord Despenser, and who would be delighted to slander and malign Lord Despenser's loyal supporters. With any luck, Sir Baldwin would be too busy to do anything for quite a while, and by the time he did, Sir Edward's story would already have been commonly accepted.

What story could he tell? That he was asked to come down here, naturally, and wanting to help another vassal of Lord Despenser, had hurried down to protect Lord Despenser's interests, but then, when he arrived, had learned that the deaths could have been caused by Sir Geoffrey's dreadful relations with his neighbours. Being suspicious, he didn't return home, but stayed nearby so that he could fly back quickly if there was more trouble, and when a fresh body was found . . . Yes, that would do it. With luck, soon he would be Lord Despenser's hero, and would have a larger manor, or some other form of recognition. Yes, he told himself. Life was good. Sir Geoffrey could sulk and complain, but Sir Edward was going on to better things.

Hopefully he wouldn't have to carry on his duties as coroner, either.

He would have been much less happy if he had known of the messenger Baldwin had sent ahead of him with a sealed package that held a full explanation of all that had happened, including allegations that the coroner had offered him a bribe to conceal the details.

* * *

Walter was amerced before Baldwin left the vill, and forced to deposit a large sum to guarantee that he would turn up at the next court.

He had been to courts before, and just now he wasn't of a mind to expand his knowledge of the system. In the old days, it could be ten years before the Justices might arrive to try a case in a vill like this. That was how long it took them on their Grand Eyre, constantly on the move from one county to another, hearing all the felony cases put to them by the juries of every Hundred.

No longer, though. One of the changes which the old king had implemented was the change in the court system, and now the courts were held more regularly. That was not a result which appeared attractive to Walter.

Tonight there was a celebration to be held at the manor to celebrate the departure of Sir Geoffrey and his men from the ruin of their hall. While the peasants of Monkleigh were forced to clear up the mess and rebuild much of the place, the men of Fishleigh were intending to hold a big feast, sponsored in part by the treasure which some of the men had secreted after their attack on Sir Geoffrey's hall. Walter had been told he wouldn't be welcome there, and he had volunteered to help look after Nicholas while the normal guards went to drink.

He wasn't alone, but there were only two others, and he knew their routines. One was at the far side of the church, and by the middle hours, he would be snoring. The second was a little more reliable, but he liked his ale too, and he'd be at the inn for much of the early evening, so just now, Walter told himself, quietly opening the door, just now was the ideal time.

The figure at the altar stirred and blearily looked up. 'Who's that? What do you want?'

'Don't panic, Nick. It's me, Walter. Come on, let's get away from here. If you're here when the coroner arrives you'll be forced to surrender or abjure the realm. Do you want to swing, or leave the country for ever? No? Then get your backside off the floor there and come with me. I can't stay, because if I'm still here for the next court, I'll hang too. So I'm running, and if you want to, you'd best make the most of it.'

'Why should I come with you?'

'Well, Nick, if you come with me, you and I can watch over each other, and when we get to a town, we can separate if you want. But for now, while we are on the run, two minds and two pairs of eyes are better than one.'

Nicholas considered, but only for a moment. 'All right!'

And meanwhile, outside, Matthew grunted his approval. 'Godspeed, Nicholas!'

His companion grunted. 'You were right.'

'It was only a matter of time. I'm just glad that Walter took my hint,' Matthew said. 'It cost me a lot to donate a barrel of ale to Fishleigh. I wouldn't have been happy had it been drunk and the fool didn't take advantage!'

Humphrey nodded, then sipped from his jug again. There was some comfort in being here in a vill far from ecclesiastical courts. When the bishop's man had arrived a few days ago to speak to Matthew about the chapel and whether a man should be selected to fill the post left vacant by Isaac's death, Matthew had turned and looked at him, and Humphrey had been sure that he was about to be denounced in front of this cocky clerk; but Matthew had merely asked, 'What do you think, Humphrey?'

'Me? I don't know, Father.'

'And neither do I,' Matthew said to the clerk. 'You pick a man you feel most suitable. Anyone will find it hard to stand in Isaac's shoes. He was so kind and perspicacious. But we shall make any replacement most welcome. Humphrey here used to help Isaac. Perhaps he could do the same for a new man, too?'

'Do you think she will be safe?' Jeanne asked her husband as she played with her daughter.

'Is that a serious question?' Baldwin asked with frank astonishment. 'How is your belly?' he added nervously. He was not squeamish about the dead, but the reality of birth terrified him, and he was still anxious that Jeanne could have been hurt by such a long journey homewards to Furnshill.

'Don't be silly. I am fine. Now, come – poor Emma's not really all that bad,' Jeanne said.

'My lady, your maid was more venomous than a viper, more ferocious than a tiger, more cunning than any fox, more cruel than . . .'

'No. Not cruel. Loyal.'

'Noisome, harsh, loud, complaining . . .'

'Kindly, devoted and . . .'

'Entirely unrestful.'

'Did you really hate her?'

'No! Not in all truth. But she was no comfort to me. I am happy that she is also happy, and I am content that she lives with a man she loves now. Far better that than remaining here and ruining what little peace we have known.'

'Yet she stayed with me to see to my happiness even though it meant leaving her own lover behind. I never knew that.'

'Nor did I.' Baldwin admitted to himself that it put a different complexion on his view of her. 'It showed a great deal of generosity on her part.'

'Yes,' Jeanne said. But she could not help wondering if Deadly realised how his life must change with Emma as his wife. After a short while, she said, 'I wonder what happened to that friar?'

'John?' Baldwin said with a smile. 'I hope he lives long and happily. He stopped Hugh from killing a man, and that was a good act. Hopefully he'll be preaching somewhere.'

'He murdered Sir Odo, didn't he?'

'His sister was avenged. I saw no evidence that Sir Odo was murdered.'

'You told the coroner to go and view the body, but you didn't go with him,' Jeanne pointed out.

'There was no need,' Baldwin said. 'Sir Odo fell from his horse and his head was crushed.'

'You believe that?'

'It is what the records say, so surely it must be true,' Baldwin said, and smiled to himself. Sometimes, he reflected, justice was not perfect – yet the best result could be achieved by men who intended to achieve it.

*   *   *

It was early afternoon when Simon and Hugh arrived back at Simon's house at Lydford. For his part, Simon was sore and weary, and he felt as though he needed a week's rest before he would be recovered, but he forced himself to forget his own aches and pains as he glanced at Hugh on his pony.

Riding was one of those pursuits which Hugh had gradually come to accept as necessary, but it was not one in which he excelled. There was something about a horse that he found unnatural. A beast so large, so dangerous, was not the sort of creature he would want to sit upon. They were too powerful for him to control them, and he disliked intensely being so high from the ground on them. Still, there were times when a horse was necessary, and while travelling he must ride.

After the last few days, since Odo's death, he had found himself suddenly weeping for no apparent reason. The slightest reminder of his wife was enough to set him off. Once, in Iddesleigh, he had seen a young maid with her lover, and the way she had set her hand upon his forearm, and gazed into his eyes, was so entirely like Constance's way of looking up at him that the sight made his tears flow once more. Then, on the way here, Simon had suggested that they should pause for a while at Exbourne, but outside the tavern by the roadside Hugh had seen a girl gracefully swaying, her hips moving gently as she scattered grain for chickens, and the scene was again so reminiscent of Constance that it brought tears to his eyes.

'Don't worry, old friend,' Simon had said kindly. 'It's good to remember her. She loved you as you loved her. It's only right that memories of her should come to you. Better by far than that you should just forget her and the happiness she gave you.'

He was right, Hugh knew, but it didn't help.

Simon tried to offer consolation at first as they rode southwards towards Lydford, but after Oakhampton it seemed pointless and heartless. Hugh was happier with his own thoughts.

At last, when they drew up outside Simon's house and Meg appeared in the doorway with Edith, Simon was reassured. If anyone could effect a cure for Hugh's broken heart, it was Edith. He watched indulgently as his daughter went straight to Hugh and helped him from his pony.

'Simon, I'm afraid I have some terrible news,' Meg said.

He smiled down at her. 'Now I am home, I am sure that there is nothing that can spoil my day.'

'The Abbot, Simon – Abbot Robert. He's died.'

Simon closed his eyes. 'May God bless him,' he said.

It was sad, but he didn't realise yet just how much the death of his patron would affect him and his family.

In Barnstaple, the sun gleamed from the sea. The little port was warm today, and the clouds were few and high, so the sun shone almost uninterruptedly.

There was a festive atmosphere to the place, and as the scruffy, bedraggled man stood up in the churchyard, many cheered and applauded.

'My friends,' John began, 'some of you have families. You should never forget your families. It may be hard for you to realise, but even I had a family once. I loved my brothers, but most especially I loved my sister. And when she was taken from me, I learned what loneliness was. But from God's good grace, I have realised that I have a larger family now. And it is to you, my brothers and sisters, that I have come to speak today.'

Not his best start, he reckoned, but hopefully he'd get more fire in his belly later, and then he'd be back on form. There was a good little friary here, and he was sure that they could make use of his skills.

He hoped so.

And at the inn, Jankin threw open his door with a feeling that all was well with the world. His purse was full after the last few weeks, Deadly was spending less time at the bar, which meant that others were spending more time there, and he had a new delight.

'How is she?' he said as his wife came in.

'She's fine. I think she'll be a marvellous little thing.'

'I should hope so. The little monster's had a hard enough beginning,' Jankin said, and he picked up the little pup and peered into the dark blue eyes. 'You fight on, little one. You'll have plenty of work to keep you busy later in life. For now, you concentrate on being healthy, eh?'

The puppy gazed at him with a serious expression for a moment, and then bit his nose.

Author's Note

There are several strands to this story which gave me pause for thought when I first read them.

The first item was the matter of the murder of Nicholas Radford in about 1445. This poor fellow was a close friend of Lord Bonville, who was not by any means a friend of the Earl of Devon. Radford, who was a prominent lawyer and had been a Justice of the Peace, was surprised by a party of men on the night of 23 October. They went to his home at Upcot and set fire to his outbuildings. When he went to his door, he was told that he was safe, and no more damage would be done to him or his property. Reassured by this he allowed them inside. This was a serious mistake.

The thugs went through his house, stealing what they wanted, while their leader demanded that Radford should provide him with food and drink. He told Radford that he was there to take him to his father. Yes, this man was Sir Thomas de Courtenay, the Earl's son. A noble, chivalric knight in his own right.

'How can I get to your father now you've taken all my horses?' Radford is said to have pointed out.

'You'll ride easily enough,' Courtenay apparently responded, and left Radford with six of his men. They drew their weapons and hacked him to death. In a final, appalling twist, the Courtenays sent men back to Radford's house four days later, where they held a 'mock Coroner's Inquest on Radford' which concluded that he had committed suicide. When Radford's servants took the body to his grave, these men forced them to sing lewd songs on the way. A more despicable act is hard to imagine.[1]

[1] Andrew McCall, *The Medieval Underworld* (Sutton, 2004), page 108

Second came the terrible record of crimes committed by the Despensers. We know that all too often such allegations were made by people who were keen to gild the lily. Many medieval cases demonstrate this propensity. You only have to look at the ridiculous accusations levelled against the Knights Templar to realise that. But I refuse to climb on that soapbox here.

It was a chance reading of Ian Mortimer's excellent book *The Greatest Traitor* that made me consider this. He mentioned the execution of the younger Despenser at Hereford, at which there was a massive list of accusations read out against him. As Ian himself says, 'It would be tedious and depressing to list all of Despenser's misdealings.' However, one specific allegation that caught my attention was the case of Lady Baret.

I must express my gratitude to Ian Mortimer, who spent some time explaining his own researches to me. It would seem that Lady Baret was the widow of a minor knight, probably Stephen Baret of Swansea, who was killed fighting against the Despensers during the Boroughbridge campaigns.

So why was she mentioned in the case against Despenser? Because it was alleged that he had her kidnapped, and then tortured. All her limbs were broken and she lost her mind from the pain. This was not done because he had any hatred for her personally, but because she had land that he coveted.

It would seem that this was pretty much a standard means of acquiring territory for Despenser. He was so over-powerful, so aggressively acquisitive, that he would even capture and torture a poor widow in order to deprive her of the little she did possess. Lady Baret was not the only woman whom he robbed. There are countless other examples, including even his sister-in-law, the king's own niece, Elizabeth, Roger Damory's widow.

She was forced to sign away 'the lordship of Usk (worth £770 per year) in return for that of Gower (worth £300 per year).'[2]

Then he had the Gower taken from her too, to give it to a friend.

However, the main thing about Lady Baret's story was that she was

---

[2] Ian Mortimer, *The Greatest Traitor* (Cape, 2003), pages 127 and 161

treated so abominably that his actions seem to have appalled his peers (most of whom could have been equally ruthless).

And that was the point. When I read these two stories, I was forced to confront the fact of the violence that was so common through this period. It is hard – in fact almost impossible – to comprehend the power that a few men could have over the lives of others. In some cases the way that even the weakest in society were treated is a matter for astonishment almost, rather than simple shock. The younger Despenser was a truly dreadful person. He sought only his own benefit at all times, and yet he was by no means unique.

Such, then, were the two items of research which pointed me in the direction of this story. Naturally I have not felt the need to be constrained by truth or actual events in Iddesleigh, Monkleigh or Fishleigh, though. This is entirely a work of fiction.

As always, I can happily confirm that all errors are my own, while I have to acknowledge the marvellous help given to me by Ian Mortimer.

Michael Jecks
North Dartmoor
April 2005

Glossary

Abjuration   When a felon was found in a place of sanctuary, he could be given an opportunity to abjure the realm. This meant forfeiture of all possessions, and the man would have to dress in sackcloth like a pilgrim, and make his way by any route specified by the coroner to a port, there to take passage abroad. A hard option, but easier than the rope!

Amercement   A sum paid to ensure that witnesses or accused would turn up to their trials. The money was forfeit if no one appeared, rather like a bail payment today.

Cantle   The rear part of the saddle. On a knight's war saddle, this would be raised to about hip-height to stop the man being pushed out when struck with a lance.

Coadjutor   Assistant to a cleric.

Destrier   A war horse, or 'great' horse. Usually trained to fight, biting, kicking and stamping. They were larger than many other types of horse, but probably not so large as a Shire.

Hele   Hiding-place.

Rounsey   A more general purpose horse, the rounsey would be used as a travelling horse, sometimes as a packhorse, for the moderately well-to-do. In times of war, a man-at-arms would rely on his rounsey as his war horse too.